Conrad and Masculinity

Andrew Michael Roberts
Senior Lecturer in English
University of Dundee

palgrave

© Andrew Michael Roberts 2000

Published by PALGRAVE
Houndmills, Basingstoke, Hampshire RG21 6XS and
175 Fifth Avenue, New York, N.Y. 10010
Companies and representatives throughout the world

PALGRAVE is the new global academic imprint of
St. Martin's Press LLC Scholarly and Reference Division and
Palgrave Publishers Ltd (formerly Macmillan Press Ltd).

Outside North America
ISBN 0–333–66285–7   ·

In North America
ISBN 0–312–22782–5

This book is printed on paper suitable for recycling and
made from fully managed and sustained forest sources.

A catalogue record for this book is available from the British Library.

Library of Congress Catalog Card Number: 99–42654

10   9   8   7   6   5   4   3   2
09   08   07   06   05   04   03   02

Printed and bound in Great Britain by
Antony Rowe Ltd, Chippenham, Wiltshire

To the memory of my mother,
Judith Roberts

Contents

Acknowledgements

I would like to thank Jeremy Hawthorn for his knowledgeable and insightful comments on drafts of this book; Robert Hampson for learned advice on matters Conradian and Hugh Epstein for numerous little, nameless (but not unremembered) acts of kindness. Many fellow Conradians have provided inspiration and food for thought over the period when this book was developing, among whom I would particularly like to mention Padmini Mongia and Jakob Lothe. Special thanks to Jim Stewart for his work on the index. Some of the material in this book has appeared, in earlier form, in *The Conradian* (Journal of the Joseph Conrad Society, UK), *L'Époque Conradienne* (Journal of the *Société Conradienne Française*), *Kunapipi* (Special Edition, also appearing as *Imperialism and Gender*, ed. C.E. Gittings, Dangaroo Press, 1996) and *Joseph Conrad: Critical Assessments*, ed. Keith Carabine (Helm, 1992). I am grateful to the editors or publishers of these works for permission (where appropriate) to reprint material.

Abbreviations and Note on Texts

Conrad's works

AF	*Almayer's Folly: A Story of an Eastern River* (1895).
AG	*The Arrow of Gold: A Story between Two Notes* (1918–20; 1919).
C	*Chance: A Tale in Two Parts* (1912; 1913).
CL	*The Collected Letters of Joseph Conrad*, eds Frederick R. Karl and Laurence Davies, 5 vols (Cambridge: Cambridge University Press, 1983–96).
HOD	'Heart of Darkness', in *Youth, a Narrative, and Two Other Stories* (1899; 1902).
K	'Karain: A Memory', in *Tales of Unrest* (1897; 1898).
LE	*Last Essays* (1926).
LJ	*Lord Jim: A Tale* (1899–1900; 1900).
N	*Nostromo: A Tale of the Seaboard* (1904).
NN	*The Nigger of the 'Narcissus': A Tale of the Sea* (1897; 1898).
OI	*An Outcast of the Islands* (1896).
R	*The Rescue: A Romance of the Shallows* (1919; 1920).
SA	*The Secret Agent: A Simple Tale* (1906–7; 1907).
SL	*The Shadow-Line: A Confession* (1916–17; 1917).
T	'Typhoon', in *Typhoon and Other Stories* (1902).
UWE	*Under Western Eyes: A Novel* (1910–11; 1911).
V	*Victory: An Island Tale* (1915).

Note on texts and quotations

Where two dates are given above, the first indicates serial publication. The second (or, in some cases, only) date refers to the first appearance in book form of the particular text. The titles of collections are those of the Dent's Collected Edition, and all page references to Conrad's works are to this edition (London: J.M. Dent & Sons, 1923–8) and are given in the text. The plates of this edition are photographically reproduced, with some minor corrections, in the World's Classics (Oxford University Press) editions of Conrad's texts, which therefore in most cases share the same page numbers for the main text (though the roman numerals of the Author's Notes are not the same). Minor corrections made in the World's Classics editions have been silently incorporated in quotations.

The Dent edition, long regarded as standard, is gradually being superseded by the new Cambridge University Press edition, which establishes more accurate texts based on research in the original documents. However, at the time of writing, only *Almayer's Folly* and *The Secret Agent* have been published. I have checked all quotations against the Cambridge editions of these two works, and noted any amendments which significantly alter the sense of the quoted passage.

Conrad quite frequently made use of ellipses in his fiction. In quotations from Conrad's work, I have followed the convention established by other critics of Conrad, in which spaced dots indicate an ellipsis in the original text, while three unspaced dots indicate my own ellipsis.

Other texts

AT   Andrea White, *Joseph Conrad and the Adventure Tradition: Constructing and Deconstructing the Imperial Subject* (Cambridge: Cambridge University Press, 1993).

BM   Eve Kosofsky Sedgwick, *Between Men: English Literature and Male Homosocial Desire* (New York: Columbia University Press, 1985).

CG   Andrew Michael Roberts (ed.), *Conrad and Gender* (Amsterdam and Atlanta, GA: Rodopi, 1993).

DD   René Girard, *Deceit, Desire and the Novel: Self and Other in Literary Structure*, trans. Yvonne Freccero (Baltimore, MD and London: Johns Hopkins University Press, 1965).

EC   Eve Kosofsky Sedgwick, *Epistemology of the Closet* (1990; Hemel Hempstead: Harvester Wheatsheaf, 1991).

EI   Nina Pelikan Straus, 'The Exclusion of the Intended from Secret Sharing in Conrad's "Heart of Darkness"', *Novel*, 20 (1987), 123–37.

EM   Chris Bongie, *Exotic Memories: Literature, Colonialism and the Fin de Siècle* (Stanford, CA: Stanford University Press, 1991).

FP   Karen Klein, 'The Feminist Predicament in Conrad's *Nostromo*', in *Brandeis Essays in Literature*, ed. John Hazel Smith (Waltham, MA: Dept of English and American Literature, Brandeis University, 1983), pp. 101–16.

FS   Mark Wollaeger, *Joseph Conrad and the Fictions of Skepticism* (Stanford, CA: Stanford University Press, 1990).

MS   Kaja Silverman, *Male Subjectivity at the Margins* (New York and London: Routledge, 1992)

NT   Jeremy Hawthorn, *Joseph Conrad: Narrative Technique and Ideological Commitment* (London: Edward Arnold, 1990).

PPT   Peter Stallybrass and Allon White, *The Politics and Poetics of Transgression* (London: Methuen, 1986).

PU   Fredric Jameson, *The Political Unconscious: Narrative as a Socially Symbolic Act* (1981; London: Routledge, 1989).

S   Luce Irigaray, *Speculum of the Other Woman*, trans. Gillian C. Gill (Ithaca, NY: Cornell University Press, 1985).

SD   Steve Neale, 'Sexual Difference in Cinema – Issues of Fantasy, Narrative and the Look', *Oxford Literary Review*, 8.1/8.2 (1986), 123–32.

TS   Luce Irigaray, *This Sex Which is Not One*, trans. Catherine Porter (Ithaca, NY: Cornell University Press, 1985).

TW   Gayle Rubin, 'The Traffic in Women: Notes on the "Political Economy" of Sex', in *Toward an Anthropology of Women*, ed. Rayna R. Reiter (New York and London: Monthly Review Press, 1975), pp. 157–210.

Introduction

Conrad is still sometimes regarded as a 'man's author', and it has traditionally been the case that he is more popular with male than with female readers. Until relatively recently, consideration of gender in Conrad's work was mostly confined to debate about the merits of his women characters. Some critics saw these as largely unsuccessful, while others defended Conrad's women, but frequently in terms which were implicated with sexist stereotypes.[1] However, with the development of gender studies and attention to the issues surrounding masculinity there has been increasing interest in questions of gender in Conrad. During the 1980s certain pioneering studies of gender in Conrad were published, notably articles by Nina Pelikan Straus and Karen Klein.[2] These critics began to consider his work in terms of a sophisticated awareness of gender theory, going beyond the question of Conrad's overt ideas about women to analyse gendered structures in his fiction and to bring masculinity into question. During the 1990s, alongside increasingly sophisticated feminist critiques (and defences) of Conrad's portrayal of women,[3] a debate around masculinity in Conrad began to develop in works by Padmini Mongia, Jeremy Hawthorn, Andrew Michael Roberts, Scott McCracken, Rebecca Stott, Robert Hampson, Elaine Showalter, Joseph Bristow and others.[4] Critical attention to homoerotic undertones in Conrad's fiction goes back at least to the 1970s, in works by Jeffrey Meyers and Robert R. Hodges, but has intensified recently, with discussion by Robert J. G. Lange, Wayne Koestenbaum and Richard Ruppel.[5]

This book explores the importance of masculinity in Conrad's work in the light of feminist theory, and of theories of masculinity which take their lead from feminism. By this I mean theories of masculinity

1

that accept and work with the basic premises of feminism: the historical and continuing (though widely varying) oppression of women in many cultures, including Western culture; the distinction between biological sex and socially constructed gender; the acknowledgement that masculinity has been and continues to be constructed in a manner which has oppressive and destructive consequences (often for men themselves, but more so for women). There are, of course, diverse forms of feminism; my main point at this stage, however, is to distinguish theories of masculinity that seek to learn from and respond positively to feminism from those that react against it. I begin with the assumption that an adequate consideration of gender in Conrad's work requires a developed theoretical basis with respect to both femininity and masculinity, drawing on feminist, psychoanalytical and cultural theory.

Conrad's representation of gender needs to be understood in its historical context. Since the construction of masculinity at the present time is part of a social and discursive history, showing both continuity and change between Conrad's time and our own, a historicized reading of masculinity in Conrad has considerable contemporary relevance, as well as illuminating his fiction and his times. Among the many factors shaping representations of gender in late nineteenth-century and early twentieth-century British culture, two of undoubted importance were the continuing development of the British Empire and the debate over the economic situation and political rights of women. Each of these factors not only formed part of the general cultural context of literature, but also found expression in specific literary genres. Narratives of travel and exploration, and adventure stories, especially those intended for boys, expressed and developed the ideology of Empire.[6] The 'New Woman' novels and drama of the 1890s and 1900s contributed to the debate concerning women's rights in the period, leading up to the changes in gender roles associated with the First World War and the eventual achievement of votes for women in the United Kingdom in 1918 and 1928. Conrad was influenced by writers of adventure stories and his own work, up to and including 'Heart of Darkness', has important affinities with the genre even while seeking to transform it.[7] Conrad makes direct allusion to feminism in *Under Western Eyes*, in a satirical portrait of an exploitative male 'feminist', but comes closer to dealing with the idea of the 'New Woman' in *Chance*, which is oddly divided between a largely sympathetic account of the oppressed heroine, Flora de Barral, and a grotesque and hostile caricature of the 'feminist', Mrs Fyne. However, as Laurence Davies argues, it would be a mistake to take this caricature as demonstrating that Conrad was opposed to the women's movements of his time, given his support for women's voting rights.[8] The late nineteenth century, as numerous critics and social historians have observed, brought a crisis in the discourses of masculinity, gender and sexuality in Britain.[9] The following developments are often taken as indicative of a crisis in masculinity: the emergence of homosexuality as a concept and an identity during the 1880s; the Labouchère Amendment to the Criminal Law Amendment Act of 1885, which made all male homosexual acts illegal; the Cleveland Street affair of 1889–90 (a scandal resulting from the police discovery of a male brothel with some aristocratic clients); the trials of Oscar Wilde in 1895 (a *cause célèbre* which raised public awareness of homosexuality while also creating an atmosphere of moral panic and repression).[10] The work of such writers as Edward Carpenter (who had an overtly homosexual lifestyle and also campaigned for women's rights) and Henry Havelock Ellis (a pioneer of sexology) contributed to a sense of the possibility of radical changes in gender roles and the understanding of sexuality.

Conrad's own unusual life, especially his complex cultural background and his career in the male world of the merchant navy, gave specific inflections to his ideas of masculinity and femininity. His early life as the son of a Polish nationalist father who was imprisoned and then sent into internal exile with his family, included traumatic experience of political oppression and led him into exile in the British merchant navy and then in Britain where, despite his eventual literary success, he remained in some senses a cultural outsider. This fuelled his powerful awareness of alienation, isolation and powerlessness, an awareness on which he draws for his depiction of strong but isolated women characters, such as Mrs Gould in *Nostromo* and Winnie Verloc in *The Secret Agent*. Conrad's experience of displacement and cultural marginality may go some way to explain his scepticism about identity, certainty and effective action. This scepticism leads to a highly problematic sense of masculinity as fractured, insecure and repeatedly failing in its attempts to master the world, in particular the world of modernity. Since this is not a biographical study, I do not seek to draw conclusions about Conrad's own gender identity and sexuality, nor to consider in any detail his personal relationships, feelings and opinions except as these are brought into the sphere of the fiction. One place where this does happen is in the 'Author's Notes', written by Conrad for the Collected Editions of his works which began to appear in 1920.[11] These often relate his life to his work in suggestive though enigmatic ways, showing a certain playfulness around the borders of fictionality and treating Conrad's characters as figures in his inner life.

In 1990, Todd K. Bender stated that 'the two most hotly argued issues in current criticism of Conrad can be summed up in the question: "Is Conrad fundamentally racist and sexist?"'.[12] Although the issue of Conrad's attitude to gender is potentially illuminating with regard to his work, the question 'Is Conrad fundamentally sexist?' seems to me unhelpful. First, it doesn't allow adequately for the distinction between the values prevalent in Conrad's time (many of which are obviously sexist by today's standards) and Conrad's own attitude to women.[13] Second, it blurs the distinctions between Conrad's personality, his work and our reading of his work. A far more interesting question, I would suggest, would be 'Is our *reading* (or a particular reading) of Conrad's work fundamentally sexist?' We can read Conrad's novels, some one hundred years on, recognize their different values and learn from that difference, without compromising our own values. Where that process become problematic is if we start to claim that those novels embody universal and transhistorical values. If we argue that 'Heart of Darkness' reveals a timeless truth about man's soul then we do indeed risk producing a racist and sexist interpretation.[14] It is not the intention of this book simply to defend Conrad's treatment of masculinity, nor simply to attack it, but rather to chart the ways in which masculinity interacts with the themes and techniques of Conrad's fiction. This is not to deny, of course, that I am engaged in making value judgements about masculinity, and ones which reflect my own values. This will emerge most specifically in my use of the terms 'ideological' and 'utopian'.

Masculinity as a socially constructed identity needs to be distinguished from biological maleness which has a genetic basis. The relationship between the two remains a subject of research and debate within various disciplines, including genetics, philosophy, psychology, literary criticism and cultural studies. The dominant assumption of Conrad's time was that masculinity was innate, an essential and 'natural' quality of the male. Yet masculinity was also employed as a moral or social ideal, as in the common injunction, 'be a man!' (which is somewhat ironically addressed by Belfast to Wait's corpse (*NN*, 160)). As a result the dominant idea of masculinity was always internally incoherent. How can masculinity be both an innate, biologically given quality and a moral status to which men should aspire?

Conrad's own (infrequent) use of the word 'masculine' tends to reflect this tension by referring to inherent 'masculine' qualities, but in a tone or context which draws the reader's attention to the possibility of variation, conflict or paradox within the 'masculine'. Sometimes this involves irony of tone, as when the narrator of *Nostromo* refers to 'the heroic Garibaldino' and his 'masculine penetration of the true state of the case' (*N*, 542), when Viola is in fact deceived as to the motives of Nostromo. Masculinity is presented as paradoxical in *The Secret Agent*: 'On account of that shrinking delicacy, which exists side by side with aggressive brutality in masculine nature, the inquiries into her circumstances had not been pushed very far' (*SA*, 160). In *Under Western Eyes* Sophia Antonovna describes men as 'squeamish' (*UWE*, 249) and speaks of 'masculine cowardice and prudishness' (250) and 'masculine nature' as 'ridiculously pitiful in [its] aptitude to cherish childish illusions' (246). Again in *Nostromo*, the possibility of innate gender distinctions failing to operate is mentioned: 'It must not be supposed that Mrs. Gould's mind was masculine. A woman with a masculine mind is not a being of superior efficiency; she is simply a phenomenon of imperfect differentiation — interestingly barren and without importance' (*N*, 66–7). This combined assertion and unsettling of inherent gender qualities reached its apogee in *Chance*, in Marlow's ruminations, which will be discussed in Chapter 6. The tendency of recent work in cultural and literary studies has been to stress the historical and social basis of masculinity, whereas many in the natural sciences (in particular geneticists) seem to want to base it entirely in biology. Cross-disciplinary debates on the subject are often marked by mutual distrust and incomprehension. It seems likely that masculinity is constructed out of elements, some of which are biologically given, but that such construction takes place through social and discursive means, producing a wide diversity of masculinities, actual and potential, and allowing the historical development of these many forms of masculinity. Any attempt to reduce masculinity to a mere function of maleness seems to me as implausible as the contrary endeavour to deny any connection between the two. Masculinity, then, might be regarded as a psychic structure, as a fantasy, as a code of behaviour, or as a set of social practices and constraints.[15] To describe it as an ideology brings all of these together, while raising the question of whether masculinity is a form of false consciousness (since there is disagreement as to whether an 'ideology' is necessarily false in this way).[16] The most general and 'neutral' definition of 'ideology' ('a collectively held system of ideas') could be applied to the shared assumptions about gender of a given society at a particular time. A more coloured definition of ideology ('ideas and beliefs which help to legitimate the interests of a ruling group or class specifically by distortion and dissimulation') is appropriate to the role of men as a dominant group in society of Conrad's time, maintaining that dominance partly through the agency of a set of prejudicial ideas about the capabilities of men and women.[17] The concept of ideology also applies to masculinity as psychic structure or fantasy, if we bear in mind Althusser's definition of ideology as 'a "representation" of the imaginary relationship of individuals to their real conditions of existence'.[18] Juliet Mitchell explicates the link between ideology and the unconscious: 'The patriarchal law speaks to and through each person in his unconscious ... The unconscious that Freud analysed could thus be described as the domain of the reproduction of culture or ideology.'[19]

I shall therefore apply the term 'ideological' to the ways in which Conrad's fiction reproduces and re-enacts oppressive aspects of the masculinity of his time. I also want to borrow Fredric Jameson's pairing of the terms 'ideological' and 'Utopian' for the 'twin negative and positive features of a given phenomenon – what in the realm of political forces Marxism traditionally terms reactionary and progressive' (*PU*, 235). This does not indicate that I am adopting Jameson's Marxist framework, but only that I am indebted to his sense that a literary text, and even a broader cultural phenomenon such as modernism, can be read both for its ideological expression of certain values of the culture within which it was produced, and for its more utopian possibilities. Jameson focuses on class repression and tends to ignore gender, but some forms of feminism have also found a value in the utopian. Margaret Whitford points out that a conception of the individual as the product of the existing social forms tends to close off the possibility of new social and ethical forms and new ways of being. Hence 'we *need* utopian visions ... imagining how things could be different is part of the process of transforming the present in the direction of a different future'.[20] I shall apply the term 'utopian' to those moments and structures in Conrad's fiction which offer a potential transformation, ironizing or destabilizing of its own ideological formations of masculinity.

This book does not have a single model of masculinity. Such a model would tend to be 'phallic' in two senses: it would involve the imposition of a single master discourse, and would also be likely to be based around the idea of the phallus, given the dominance of that idea in most accounts of masculinity. I do make some use of the concept of the phallus, which is more or less inescapable in discussions of masculinity. As Stephen Heath writes:

> The truth about men and their bodies *for the moment* is merely repetitive ... the régime of the same, the eternal problem of the phallus, etc. (with its celebrants from Lawrence on, through Miller and Mailer on into the present day) ... for today, telling the truth about the male body as freeing subject is utopia, about the female body *actuality*.[21]

Heath describes his argument as leaving him 'between a male writing as oppression and a male writing as utopia'.[22] This dichotomy resembles that between ideological and utopian versions of masculinity, except that I am seeking to give a more positive connotation to the idea of utopia, reflecting the way in which social change and critical writing (particularly the new prominence given to gay men's experience) has, since Heath wrote, opened up more possibilities for imagining an other sort of masculinity.[23] This seems to me an instance of precisely the need for the utopian that Whitford describes. Masculinity as an ideology has always misrepresented the complexity of experience, has always been a 'legitimation' through 'distortion and dissimulation'. Part of the effect of an ideology is to obscure the contradictions on which it is based. Conrad's fiction, through its complexity and ambiguity, provides rich ground for what Edward Said terms a 'contrapuntal reading', which opens a text out 'both to what went into it and to what its author excluded'.[24] By reading both with and against the grain, by reading both exegetically (what the text seems to want to say) and deconstructively (what it seems to repress, deny or omit), it should be possible to learn from both Conrad's insights and his illusions, and to learn more about our own insights and illusions.

I want to suggest, then, that Conrad's texts are of special interest for the study of masculinity, partly because of the particular social contexts which he depicts, but also for reasons connected with those literary and aesthetic qualities for which he has long been valued. Among these qualities narrative self-consciousness is especially significant. The most distinctively modernist feature of Conrad's technique is the way in which his works foreground the acts of narrating and listening or reading. This self-consciousness is associated with scepticism about the possibility of truth and understanding, a doubt as to whether one can ever know definitively what is true (even subjectively true of one's own experience), whether one could ever express such truth if one attained it, and whether it would be understood were it expressed. Not only does this generate scepticism about the 'truth' of masculinity, but it also means that his novels attend closely to processes of communication and exchange. Conrad's fondness for setting up chains or groups of male tellers and listeners creates structures which, by implication, can extend beyond the bounds of the fiction to include both author and readers. Such a process raises crucial questions of gender-specific reading, placed on the agenda by Nina Pelikan Straus when she describes her experience, as a woman reader of 'Heart of Darkness', as one of exclusion. Straus argues that 'Marlow's relation to Kurtz as his commentator is a paradigm of the ... male critic's relation to the Strong Poet' (EI, 134) and that 'Marlow's cowardice consists of his inability to face the dangerous self that is the form of his own masculinist vulnerability: his own complicity in the racist, sexist, imperialist, and finally libidinally satisfying world he has inhabited with Kurtz' (EI, 135).[25] As much feminist work has pointed out, patriarchy involves social, economic and psychic structures in which men exchange women. In such structures, men are assigned the role of subjects, those who do the exchanging, while woman are objectified and possessed as that which is circulated or exchanged. Precisely because Conrad's novels are mostly about men, and are highly self-conscious about the processes of exchange between men (exchange of stories and thus of fantasies), they reveal with particular force the functioning of such patriarchal structures.

My account of masculinity in Conrad is, therefore, particularly indebted to those critics who have elaborated the idea of a gendered economy (involving both social practices and psychic structures) and the related concept of the 'homosocial'. René Girard's *Deceit, Desire and the Novel*, though it neglected the asymmetries of gender, laid important groundwork in its idea of mediated desire, in which the (usually male) subject's desire for the object (typically a woman), is prompted by imitation of the desire of another (also usually a male, and termed 'the mediator' by Girard) (DD, 2). Girard's crucial insight, that 'the impulse toward the object is ultimately an impulse toward the mediator' (DD, 10), offers rich potential for the understanding of bonds of rivalry between men, based on a shared female object of desire and competition. This potential has been developed by Eve Sedgwick in her conception of 'male homosocial desire', a continuum of sexual and non-sexual forms of bond between men. She argues that this continuum is implicated with the mechanisms of patriarchy, but that its continuity has been concealed by homophobia, which insists on the radical separation of homosexual desire from other sorts of male bonds (*BM*, 1–4). This provides one of the most illuminating models for Conrad's treatment of masculinity. I would agree with Richard Ruppel that Conrad investigates a wide range of relations within the male homosocial continuum, although it is an exaggeration to claim that he encompasses 'the most taboo homosexual orientation and behaviour'.[26] However, Sedgwick sounds an important note of caution when she writes that the 'hypothesis of the unbrokenness of this [male homosocial] continuum is not a *genetic* one – I do not mean to discuss genital homosexual desire as "at the root of" other forms of male homosociality' (*BM*, 2). Ruppel discusses whether various Conrad characters, such as Heyst, Jim, the language teacher and Marlow, are or are not homosexual, reaching varying conclusions.[27] Such speculations add to the richness of the texts and are a salutary correction to the invisibility of same-sex desire in much traditional criticism. Indeed, I will suggest a possible reading of 'Heart of Darkness' in terms of such desire, though such a reading strikes me as possible rather than in any way inevitable. However, the question of whether, say, Marlow 'is homosexual' seems to me ultimately imponderable. Sedgwick's point is precisely that the continuum was obscured and fractured, that homophobia exerted a pressure on the structure of all sorts of masculine bonds, a pressure which might result in the concealment of sexual bonds but equally might result in a rhetoric of anxiety and secrecy being thrown around non-sexual bonds. To put it another way, there is no reason to *assume* that all male intimacy is sexual, any more than there is any reason to assume that it is *not*. Nor, in the absence of definite sexual activity, can the line between the sexual and non-sexual be sharply drawn. Ruppel's own comment that to read 'The Secret Sharer' as a 'veiled coming-out story' (as Robert Hodges does) 'seems oxymoronic' is apposite.[28] In general, homosexuality is neither definitely present nor definitely absent in Conrad's work, but figures as an occluded part of a homosocial structure, not as the key which undoes that structure. That structure, as I have already suggested, resonates with the narrative structures of the fiction. It resonates also with social and economic structures. Sedgwick quotes Heidi Hartmann's definition of patriarchy as 'relations between men, which have a material base, and which, though hierarchical, establish or create interdependence and solidarity among men that enable them to dominate women'.[29] Sedgwick notes that this definition both makes 'the power relationships between men and women appear to be dependent on the power relationships between men and men' and implies that 'large-scale social structures are congruent with the male–male–female erotic triangles described most forcefully by Girard'. (*BM*, 25). This congruence between narrative structures, articulated by desire and knowledge, and social power structures is a major source of meaning, and especially of irony, in Conrad's fiction. Of the other sources cited by Sedgwick, Gayle Rubin and Luce Irigaray are of particular relevance to the present book. Gayle Rubin, in her influential 1975 article 'The Traffic in Women: Notes on the "Political Economy" of Sex', develops a feminist elaboration and critique of Lévi-Strauss's anthropology of kinship structures, seeking 'an alternate explanation' of 'the nature and genesis of women's oppression and social subordination' (TW, 158, 157). She notes that the incest taboo orders a network of relations through the exchange or giving of women, and quotes Lévi-Strauss:

> The total relationship of exchange which constitutes marriage is not established between a man and a woman, but between two groups of men, and the woman figures only as one of the objects in the exchange, not as one of the partners.
>
> (TW, 174)

She claims that in 'civilized' as well as in 'primitive' societies, men are 'trafficked – but as slaves, hustlers, athletics stars, serfs, or as some other catastrophic social status, rather than as men', while 'women are transacted as slaves, serfs, and prostitutes, but also simply as women' (TW, 175–6). Luce Irigaray has developed most fully this economic analysis of gender relations, to argue that 'the economy ... that is in place in our societies thus requires that women lend themselves to alienation in consumption, and to exchanges in which they do not participate' (*TS*, 172).

There are of course significant divergences and problems here. In particular, Sedgwick makes some telling criticisms of Irigaray's direct linking of male homosexuality to male supremacy, as well as of her lack of a historical dimension.[30] Nevertheless, these various thinkers provide the basis for an interpretation of the relations between men portrayed in Conrad's fiction, and the relations between men produced by the reading of that fiction. In writing, as a male critic, about gender structures in Conrad's fiction, I must acknowledge that complicity is inescapable; at the same time, by attempting to face rather than deny the issues about masculinity which that fiction raises in acute form, I try to stage a critique, not a repetition, of the process of identification with the male and exclusion of the female.

The arrangement into chapters is thematic rather than chronological, with pairs of chapters examining a particular theme in relation to masculinity: thus Chapters 1 and 2 focus on Imperialism, Chapters 3 and 4 on the Body, Chapters 5 and 6 on Truth and Knowledge, and Chapters 7 and 8 on Vision. The first two chapters deal with early work, and the final two chapters with late work, so that the overall sequence is roughly chronological. However, it may be worth noting in particular that 'Heart of Darkness', which is chronologically prior to *Typhoon*, *The Secret Agent* and *Nostromo*, comes after those texts in the sequence of the book, while the final two chapters reverse the chronological order of *The Arrow of Gold* and *Victory*. In the case of 'Heart of Darkness', this arrangement serves to place it at the start of a discussion of truth and knowledge, since it provides a template and point of comparison for the gendering of knowledge in *The Secret Agent* and *Under Western Eyes*. In the case of the concluding chapters, I felt (without accepting the 'achievement and decline' view of Conrad's work in its pure form) that *Victory* was a more satisfactory text than *The Arrow of Gold* with which to end.[31] This was both because of the somewhat greater intrinsic interest of *Victory*, and because it brings together Conrad's long-term interest in cultural difference with one of his most sceptical and exploratory examinations of masculinity.

1
Masculinity, 'Race' and Empire: *Almayer's Folly, An Outcast of the Islands*

Work and imperialism were two crucial contexts for the definition of masculine identity in late nineteenth- and early twentieth-century British society. The two were closely related, since one of the functions of Empire was to provide work for males of the British ruling classes, and to provide markets and materials for the products of the labour of the British working classes. At the same time, imperialism allowed some classes of society not to work, but to live on the proceeds of the labour of others. A striking feature of Conrad's fiction is that he writes a lot about work, certainly more than Woolf or James and arguably more than Lawrence or Joyce. Work is also a central source of moral value for Conrad. Furthermore, the work he writes about is above all the work of Empire: of the sailors who carried its trade, the adventurers who opened up new territories for conquest or exploitation, and the myriad other professions which followed, from hotel-keepers to accountants. This is particularly so of his early fiction up to and including *Lord Jim*, which will be the focus of this chapter and the next.

If Conrad's fiction has much to say about work and empire, it is also much concerned with 'race'. Work and empire can be seen as political and economic structures and as social institutions. As such they helped to determine the forms of masculine identity. 'Race' is better regarded as a discursive construction which interacted with the discourses around masculinity. The scare quotes around 'race' in this context mark the fact that, arguably, 'race' is a term best used under erasure, since it is at best problematic and at worst positively dangerous, yet cannot be simply avoided because of its history and currency. Paul Gilroy suggests that '"race" is an especially pernicious illusion which we need to purge from our thinking'.[1] Kwame Anthony Appiah argues that we have inherited from the nineteenth century a spurious 'racialism': a belief 'that we could divide human beings into a small number of groups, called "races," in such a way that all the members of these races shared certain fundamental, biologically heritable, moral and intellectual characteristics with each other that they did not share with members of any other race.'[2] The term 'race' will, then, be used in this book (without repetition of scare quotes) to refer to a discursive and ideological construct, but with no implication that it has any biological or genetic basis.[3] It may nonetheless make sense to speak of racial identity in certain contexts, given the power of such constructions in the discourses through which many individuals have understood their own identity.[4]

There are, then, good reasons why a discussion of Conrad and masculinity begins appropriately with a discussion of imperialism and race. As well as the general features of his work and his times already mentioned, his fiction begins in a way which foregrounds these questions. His first protagonists are European males in imperial settings: *Almayer's Folly* and *An Outcast of the Islands* introduce us to Almayer, unsuccessful Borneo trader, and Willems, disgraced clerk in a Dutch imperial trading concern. In Conrad's work, gender, racial identity and national or cultural identity are, from the first, always already interlocking and reciprocally determining: what it means to 'be a man' begins with 'what it means to be a white man'. Not only that, but a white man in the realm of the Other. In these Malay novels 'white' women are on the whole conspicuously absent. European, Malay and Arab men are engaged in various forms of competition, bonding and hostility around the commercial and politics rivalries of late nineteenth-century imperialism, while women, characteristically presented as of mixed race, figure as temptation, danger, affliction and objects of desire or hope for the European males. Thus in Conrad's first two novels, the emphasis is on rivalry, competition and aggression between men. There are some significant male bonds, but these turn out to be insecurely based, and generally lead to betrayal and punishment. The most powerful bonds in these novels are those between men and women, either as fathers and daughters or as the result of sexual passion. My discussion of these two novels in the present chapter will therefore focus primarily on the articulation of masculinity through sexual relations with women. However, as his writing develops, Conrad seems to more become progressively more interested in the possibility of masculinity transcending race and culture, and seeks to identify some way in which being a man might

unite, say, a European and a Malay. Chapter 2 will focus on certain of
the works which followed the first two Malay novels, including the
story 'Karain', Conrad's next (short) novel, *The Nigger of the 'Narcissus'*,
and *Lord Jim*, often seen as Conrad's first 'major' work.[5] These fictions
continue to engage with ideas of race and Otherness, but there is a
new emphasis on the potential power of male bonds. Chapter 2 will
explore the significance of these bonds for the conception of
masculinity and for the wider import of the texts.

My discussion of Conrad's first two novels will focus primarily on
one key relationship within each: in *An Outcast of the Islands*, the
doomed passion of Willems for Aïssa, the daughter of the old, blind
former warrior Omar; and, in *Almayer's Folly*, the successful courtship
of Nina, Almayer's daughter, by Dain, a heroic and glamorous young
trader from Bali. In each of these sexual relationships gender identity
and racial or cultural identity are jointly negotiated under the pressures of desire and fear, and within the constraints of petty imperial
political manoeuvrings by Dutch, Malays and Arabs. In each miscegenation and associated anxieties about the stability of cultural
identity also implicate questions about the stability of masculinity.
However, whereas in *An Outcast of the Islands* the relationship threatens a dissolution of masculinity through interracial passion, in
Almayer's Folly Nina's mixed parentage, presented as offering her a
choice between European and Malay heritages, is resolved by her
departure with a Malay man who embodies ideals of exotic pre-
modern masculinity unavailable to her doomed father. *An Outcast of
the Islands* is miscegenation threatened and punished through
tragedy, whereas *Almayer's Folly* is miscegenation resolved through
exoticist fantasy. In these broad terms, each novel is trapped within
the ideological binaries of the imperial encounter, where miscegenation can be understood only as a mixing of racial elements and the
assumption is that these elements need to be resolved out, if a destructive collapse of boundaries is to be averted. Within the interstices of
the narratives, however, a contrapuntal reading can detect signs of
what Homi Bhabha terms 'hybridity', in which subjectivity, no longer
imagined as a unified essence, can 'elude the politics of polarity'.[6]

Such a reading requires a model of the interaction of gender and
race, or more specifically, of the ideologies of masculinity and of
imperialism. Andrea White, in her book *Joseph Conrad and the
Adventure Tradition*, places Conrad's early work in the context of the
tradition of travel writing and adventure fiction, arguing that this pro-
imperialist tradition is subverted in Conrad's fiction. However, apart

from a few interesting historical observations on late nineteenth-century debates about manliness, White tends to ignore gender issues (*AT*, 83). Furthermore, in praising Conrad for representing sympathetically the point of view of non-European characters, she fails to consider whether the point of view represented may be a projection of the hankering of the European male for a violent heroism which seems no longer available to him. So she argues that in *An Outcast of the Islands* the 'heroic discourse of the white man in the tropics is absent', while we are asked to 'take a sympathetic view' of the heroism of the Malay adventurers Babalatchi and Omar (*AT*, 148). But what exactly is at stake in sympathizing with their 'manly pursuits of throat-cutting, kidnapping, slave-dealing, and fire-raising, that were the only possible occupation for a true man of the sea' (*OI*, 52)? Might not a male European longing for 'heroic' aggression express itself through the representation of the supposedly untrammelled masculinity of the male Other? While White sees Conrad as increasingly subverting the adventure genre, Joseph Bristow argues that 'Heart of Darkness' 'remains within the generic frame of popular adventure writing', so that it 'exposes, but never the less maintains, the presuppositions – of race and gender – of the genre it is ostensibly contesting'.[7] Bristow's sensitivity to issues of masculinity renders him more sceptical than White about Conrad's degree of resistance to the ideology of the genre (White also assumes too readily that to subvert the genre is politically subversive). Bristow argues that the celebration of male bonds blunts the potential radical edge of 'Heart of Darkness':

> To come to terms with Kurtz ... is, for Marlow, to know what manhood means. Heroism has not so much been eradicated but [*sic*] raised to a metaphysical power. The glamour of adventure has been exposed, and in its place there is [the] altogether more resonant 'glamour' of the 'idea'.[8]

In a later chapter I shall suggest ways of reading 'Heart of Darkness' which might reinstate some radicality. At this point I merely want to note that Bristow's account highlights the way in which the ideological contents of such a fiction is overdetermined by the discourses of race and gender, since he regards the critique of imperialism in 'Heart of Darkness' as weakened by its allegiance to heroic masculinity. Both race and gender involve ideas of sameness and otherness, and when both are in play these ideas can reinforce, undermine or complicate each other in a variety of ways. Feminist theory and postcolonial theory have developed a network of ideas around the concept of the Other and the Same, and it is in terms of these two concepts that I will seek to articulate a model of masculinity and imperialism.[9]

White argues that to show the imperial subject as changed by the encounter with the Other, or as (like Kurtz) desiring to return to the 'wilderness', is 'subversive' and challenges 'the assumptions of imperialism' (*AT*, 24). In this she underestimates the complexity of imperial desire and the paradoxical nature of ideology (its ability to embrace, and seemingly reconcile, contradictions). Chris Bongie's *Exotic Memories: Literature, Colonialism, and the Fin de Siècle* is a study of exoticism as a literary and cultural phenomenon, with Conrad as one of the principal examples. For Bongie exoticism represents an impossible desire to escape from the modern world to a fantasy other realm of authentic experience. He uses the term 'exoticizing exoticism' for 'an erotic attachment to both the Other "creature" and his / her world' which figures them as 'a possible refuge from an overbearing modernity'. Such exoticizing exoticism, though it is likely to include some criticism of the effects of imperialism, can nevertheless be just as powerful a motor of destructive imperialism as 'imperial exoticism', which overtly espouses 'the hegemony of modern civilization'. As Bongie points out, both forms allow the fantasy of an 'heroic subjectivity denied him [the imperial subject] in post-revolutionary Europe' (*EM*, 17). Thus both involve the appropriation of other cultures for the psychic or social needs of the imperial power, and so run readily in parallel with economic exploitation. Indeed the very idea of the 'wilderness' or 'jungle' as constructed in imperial fictions, including those of Conrad, represents the projection of the fears and fantasies of the imperial subject onto an imagined Other space of horror, or challenge, or adventure, effacing the culture of the Other by rendering it as contained by a 'primitive' 'nature'.[10]

White also assumes that an 'insistence upon distinctions between them and us is at the heart of the imperial subject' (*AT*, 80), so that for her, Conrad was unconventional and subversive because he stressed 'the similarities between "us" and "them" rather than those differences that privilege "us"' (*AT*, 119). This ignores the complementarity between 'otherness' and 'sameness' as constructions. To recognize and denigrate someone as my Other, my opposite, that which I am not (and which therefore defines what I am) is to place him or her within what Hélène Cixous calls 'the Empire of the Selfsame', that is, within the sphere of my own construction of identity:

What is the 'Other'? If it is truly the 'other', there is nothing to say; it cannot be theorized. The 'other' escapes me. It is elsewhere, outside: absolutely other. It doesn't settle down. But in History, of course, what is called 'other' is an alterity that does settle down, that falls into the dialectical circle. It is the other in a hierarchically organized relationship in which the same is what rules, names, defines, and assigns 'its' other.[11]

Homi Bhabha writes of 'that "otherness" which is at once an object of desire and derision, an articulation of difference contained within the fantasy of origin and identity'.[12] The supposedly 'primitive' Other is used by the imperial subject to define both what he is not, and what he once was, what he desires and what he fears, what he seeks and what he denies. Such a discourse of the Other implies that progress can only be towards sameness on his terms, or a discovery of (his idea of) universal human nature. Such tendencies are obvious enough in the practices of imperialism, from early missionary endeavour (the attempt to impose the same culture) to contemporary pressure to globalization and standardization of economic and cultural practices.

This is not to imply that the differences White identifies between Conrad and the adventure tradition are insignificant, nor to claim that the act of imagined identity with the Other has no moral or political value. However, the concept of 'subversion' (with its assumption of a monolithic imperialism which is being undermined) seems inadequate. Bongie makes a significant historical distinction between the 'initial optimism of the exoticist project' and 'a pessimistic vision in which the exotic comes to seem less a space of possibility than one of impossibility'. The latter emerges in the last decades of the nineteenth century, along with 'the New Imperialism', a 'phase of acute geopolitical expansion initiated by the European nation-states'. As modernity becomes a global phenomenon it 'inevitably, and irreparably, puts into question the Other's autonomy, absorbing this Other into the body of the Same and thereby effacing the very ground of exoticism' (*EM*, 17–18). Thus the change which White describes in terms of a progressive subversion by novelists (starting with Haggard and developing in Conrad's work), a change from the Other as other (contrasting them and us) to the Other as same (them as like us), might rather be described in terms of the historical development of imperialism. The question remains what space (if any) opens up within the fiction for a structure resistant to imperialism. Such a structure might be named in various ways: in terms of 'the Other of the other' (as opposed to the Other of the same) or in terms of plurality or polymorphic identity.[13] The most useful formulation here is Homi Bhabha's concept of cultural hybridity, which 'entertains difference without an assumed or imposed hierarchy', neither castigating the Other for a difference assumed to be inferiority, nor assimilating it to a sameness which assumes the superiority of the colonizer.[14]

An attempt to relate masculinity and imperialism in Conrad's work requires some model of how the Same, the Other and the hybrid operate in terms of gender and in terms of race. However, it is important to avoid imposing too rigid a model on the complexity of the individual instance and to avoid assuming a neat homology between the discourses of gender and race, which are so different in structure and history. What is in common, however, is a binary structure of Same and Other which tends to subdue the multiplicity of differences.[15] Jonathan Dollimore, citing Derrida's claim that the binary opposition is a violent hierarchy, suggests that 'the opposition masculine/homosexual, a conflation of two classic binaries (masculine/feminine; hetero/homosexual) has been one of the most violent of all'.[16] While this specific conflation of binaries is highly relevant to imperial masculinity, what is significant for the present argument is the notion of a violent discursive conflation of binaries, linked to material violence. There is a pressure to such a conflation operating in imperial fiction where gender and race interact. The two oppositions of masculine/feminine and European/non-European are in play, but because both are hierarchical, there is pressure to resolve them into a single opposition. One reason for suspecting a violent conflation of binaries in imperial fiction is the strength of the impulse to exclude, or at the least rigorously marginalize, 'white' or European women, as if their presence on the scene of the imperial encounter would conflict with its dominant dynamics. On one level it is a matter of experience and realism, since in Conrad's life as a merchant seaman in the Far East he would have encountered relatively few European women. Yet it is also a matter of choice of subject matter and presentation. A novel which Conrad began in 1896 as *The Rescuer* was to admit a white woman to centre stage on the imperial scene, but only as an implausibly romanticized agent for the destruction of the male adventurer, Lingard. Furthermore Conrad did not succeed in completing the novel until 1919 (when it appeared as *The Rescue*). European women could be neither the subject of the imperial encounter (because of their gender), nor its object (because of their racial identity). This exclusion is very explicitly stated in the fiction of Rider Haggard, which tends to present in cruder form aspects of imperial ideology which are rendered more problematic in Conrad's fiction.[17] Haggard's narrator, Allan Quatermain, assures the reader early on in *King Solomon's Mines* that:

> I am going to tell the strangest story that I know of. It may seem a queer thing to say, especially considering that there is no woman in it – except Foulata. Stop, though! there is Gagoola, if she was a woman and not a fiend. But she was a hundred at least, and therefore not marriageable, so I don't count her. At any rate, I can safely say that there is not a *petticoat* in the whole history.[18]

Quatermain only 'counts' women who (like Foulata) are potential objects of sexual desire, while what is excluded here is less women as such than the social and moral space attributed by Victorian society to (respectable) white women: the domestic sphere of the 'petticoat'.[19] Foulata, whose relationship with Good introduces the threat of miscegenation, dies with a convenience that she herself recognizes in her last words: 'I am glad to die because I know that he cannot cumber his life with such as I am, for the sun may not mate with the darkness, nor the white with the black.'[20] Quatermain later reflects that 'her removal was a fortunate occurrence', despite her 'great ... beauty, and ... considerable refinement of mind'.[21]

Although European women were by no means absent from the Dutch East Indies at this time (and are indeed briefly mentioned in Conrad – for example Mrs Vinck in *An Outcast of the Islands* is presumably Dutch), they play no significant role in either of Conrad's first two novels.[22] It is as if Conrad, in his early work, can only approach the otherness of women by heightening that otherness through ideas of racial or cultural difference. The dual binaries of race and gender are conflated into a single imperial binary between the white male and the Other female, whose dangerously 'mixed' racial identity is part of her Otherness and threat. A certain amount of discursive energy is expended in presenting Aïssa, in *An Outcast of the Islands*, as of mixed race. Aïssa's father is described as an 'Arab' (*OI*, 59) and her mother as 'a Baghdadi woman with veiled face' (47), while Lakamba describes her as 'a she-dog with white teeth, like a woman of the Orang Putih' [i.e. the white people] (47).[23] As critics have noted, in *Almayer's Folly* Conrad makes Almayer European where his real-life model Olmeijer was of Eurasian descent. This makes the choice faced by Almayer's daughter Nina, between her father and Dain, into a choice between two races and two parts of herself.[24] The threat posed by the female other is crudely disposed of in Haggard's novel with the death of Foulata, but the eroticized figures of the female other in Conrad (Nina in *Almayer's Folly* and Aïssa in *An Outcast of the Islands*) are more ambivalently treated. Nina rejects the interest of the Dutch naval officer, who thinks that she was 'very beautiful and imposing ... but after all a half-caste girl' (*AF*, 126), and leaves her father to go with Dain. She is thereby restored to the realm of the exoticized Other, perhaps to produce a son whose birth, as Bongie points out, would signal 'an extension of the Other's line into the indefinite future' (*EM*, 153). Aïssa, presented as threatening both in her sexuality and her racial otherness, is transformed into a figure who, like the evil Gagool in *King Solomon's Mines*, is 'not marriageable'. By the end of the novel she has become a 'doubled-up crone' (*OI*, 366). Like Zola's Nana, Aïssa turns rapidly from an object of desire into an object of disgust, as if no other role were available. Such, indeed, is the common fate of glamorous Malay or Arab women in Conrad's fiction: in *The Rescue* Jörgenson's 'girl' has acquired wrinkles, grey hair and black stumps of teeth (*R*, 104–5).

Many attempts to relate gender and imperialism have done so in terms of sexuality, an approach encouraged by the obsessive concern with sexuality in imperial discourse itself.[25] Some critics and historians, such as Ronald Hyam, have adopted a Freudian hydraulic model of sexuality (as a drive or flow of energy which can be channelled in different directions) and have seen imperial expansion as an outlet for excess male sexual energy or as a sublimation of sexuality.[26] Criticizing such approaches, which tend to present sexuality as cause and empire as effect, Ann Laura Stoler poses a series of questions:

> Was the strident misogyny of imperial thinkers and colonial agents a by-product of received metropolitan values ('they just brought it with them'), a reaction to contemporary feminist demands in Europe ('women need to be put back in their breeding place'), or a novel and pragmatic response to the conditions of conquest?[27]

Stoler herself sees imperial sexuality in Foucaldian terms, as part of a mechanism for the regulation of social identity.[28] Sander Gilman argues that sexuality, as the most salient marker of otherness, is likely to figure in any racist ideology. He demonstrates that, in the iconography of the nineteenth century, 'the "white *man's* burden" ... becomes his sexuality and its control, and it is this which is transferred into the need to control the sexuality of the Other, the Other as sexualized female'.[29] Christopher Lane develops a sophisticated theoretical model of colonialism and sexuality, rejecting approaches such as Hyam's, which 'conceive of sexuality in a functional relation to colonialism'. Instead Lane offers a vision of Britain's empire lying 'in the midst of a complicated and indeterminate field of "unamenable" desires', a 'picture of colonial rule shrouded by doubt, ambivalence, and antagonism'. He focuses on

> the failure of self-mastery, the insufficiency and overabundance of drives to colonial sublimation, the relation between imperialism and the death drive, the service that colonialism performed in the realm of sexual fantasy, and the influence that all of these factors brought to bear on the symbolization of masculinity and homosexuality.[30]

The linking of imperialism to the death drive (rather than to the assertion of the power of the ego) suggests ways of reading Conrad's self-destructive anti-heroes without taking their failure as automatically a subversion of a coherent imperial project. Lane's whole vision of Empire in terms of 'doubt, ambivalence and antagonism' is a useful corrective to a homogenizing idea of the imperial project which (as in White's account), can make it rather too easy to categorize anything that does not fit the idea as 'subversive'. The idea of 'the service that colonialism performed in the realm of sexual fantasy', inverting the more common tendency to see sexuality as recruited in the service of Empire, suggests a mutuality between the discourses of masculinity and of imperialism which avoids hypostatizing one as essence or cause.

Faced with this profusion of competing and interrelating models, it is important to bear in mind that they are only models. That is to say, they are heuristic and interpretative devices with which we can analyse and perhaps explain imperial practice and discourse (and, in the present instance, Conrad's fiction). Different models may be more appropriate in different instances, and any model must be liable to modification in the light of the specific instance, since neither imperial practice nor imperial discourse was unified and homogeneous. For example, Sander Gilman observes that

> Miscegenation was a fear (and a word) from the late nineteenth-century vocabulary of sexuality. It was a fear not merely of

interracial sexuality but of its results, the decline of the population. Interracial marriages were seen as exactly parallel to the barrenness of the prostitute; if they produced children at all, these children were weak and doomed.[31]

However, Stoler, while agreeing that *métissage* ('racial mixing') was a focal point of debate by the mid-nineteenth century and was seen as a source of degeneration and decay, also notes that in the Dutch East Indies of the 1880s 'concubinage' (informal but stable liaisons between European men and Asian women) was encouraged by the Dutch East Indies Company on pragmatic grounds which included a theory that the children of mixed marriages were stronger and healthier.[32] Conrad's Malay fiction both symbolizes miscegenation as danger and corruption and represents marriages between European men and Asian women as fairly unremarkable. The point here is to note both the variability of practice and the ability of imperial ideology to embrace contradictions, contradictions which nevertheless were liable to impose a strain. Thus Stoler suggests that concubinage both reinforced racial hierarchies *and* rendered them problematic.[33]

While drawing on various of the models which I have outlined, I shall also borrow Fredric Jameson's terms 'ideological' and 'Utopian', as discussed in the Introduction. Identifying the 'twin negative and positive features of a given phenomenon' (*PU*, 235), they assist a reading of the ways in which desire and fantasy generate structures exceeding the binaries of ideology. Bhabha's concept of hybridity is similarly helpful for such a reading because it involves a sense of subjectivity itself as fractured. On the basis of the distinction between the 'I' that speaks and the 'I' that is spoken about, he posits the existence of a 'Third Space', which renders meaning and reference ambivalent, destroys the 'mirror of representation in which cultural knowledge is customarily revealed' and so 'challenges our sense of the historical identity of culture as a homogenizing, unifying force, authenticated by the originary Past, kept alive in the national tradition of the People'.[34] Part of his argument is that, because our subjectivity or identity always operates in language, which is neither transparent nor fully under our control, cultural identity is never fixed or unified. This is particularly useful for reading masculinity in relation to cultural identity and its phantasmagoric shadow, race, because it is an argument based on the structure of identity in general, applicable to gender identity as well as cultural identity. It leads Bhabha to a vision of 'an *inter*national culture, based not on the exoticism of multiculturalism or the *diversity* of cultures, but on the inscription and articulation of culture's *hybridity'*. He suggests that

> it is the 'inter' – the cutting edge of translation and negotiation, the *in-between* space – that carries the burden of the meaning of culture. It makes it possible to begin envisaging national, anti-nationalist histories of the 'people'. And by exploring this Third Space, we may elude the politics of polarity and emerge as the others of our selves.[35]

While my own concern in this book is primarily with the possibility of eluding polarities of gender, issues of gender and cultural identity are closely interwoven. Whether Conrad's fiction has anything to offer to a quest for hybridity such as Bhabha specifies is the question to which I now turn. Rather than treat imperialism as a unified set of practices and discourses, which a literary text either endorses or subverts, I prefer to follow Lane and Bhabha in taking imperialism to be complex, ambivalent and divided within itself. A similar sense of complexity is implied by Bongie's view that exoticism takes exoticizing and imperial forms. The relationship to the Other involves desire and fear. As well as desire for the Other, it can include a suppressed identification with the Other, a desire to be in the place of the Other which is then repressed and denied with a violence of disgust which produces fear and loathing.

Reversing the order of composition and publication (though following that of fictional chronology) I shall begin with Conrad's second novel, *An Outcast of the Islands*, in which the relationship of Willems and Aïssa presents the imperial encounter in its most polarized terms. The rhetoric of *An Outcast of the Islands* – generated by its symbolism, its irony, its metaphors and similes – is not subtle, though it is effective in its way. It draws heavily on the standard discourses of race and gender in imperial Britain, in which the Other, racial or sexual, to the white male colonizer is represented as debased and debasing, alluring, threatening, dirty, unstable, moist, fecund. There are of course inconsistencies within these sets of associations, but such inconsistencies (the Other as beautiful yet repulsive, as listless yet full of life) are characteristic of an ideology expressing itself through a set of images. What is subtle in Conrad's deployment of these discourses is the reader's uncertainty as to the moral and political stance of the implied author, so that we are unsure how far the ironies extend.

It is in the description of the courtship of Willems and Aïssa that we can observe most clearly the ideological and utopian strains in Conrad's representation of masculinity. The depiction of this sexual relationship is ideological in so far as it draws on a misogynistic and imperialist discourse, made more explicit in Haggard, according to which women, their beauty, their sexual desire and desirability, are fatal to the white male hero of the adventure narrative.[36] It is, however, susceptible of a more utopian reading in part because, as many critics have pointed out, Conrad's white male heroes (unlike the stereotyped boy's adventure heroes of Haggard) are always, in fact, white male anti-heroes. Conrad's intense scepticism about 'human nature' necessarily infects his representation of masculinity. As Willems's infatuation with Aïssa develops, he feels that his masculinity is threatened:

> he ... realized at last that his very individuality was snatched from within himself by the hand of a woman ... All that had been a man within him was gone.
>
> (*OI*, 77)

Were a Haggard hero to experience such a threat, he would be likely to be saved by the gruff warning voice of a fellow English gentleman, or the threatening non-white female would conveniently die. (When the adventurers in *King Solomon's Mines* realize they are buried alive, Quatermain does note that 'All the manhood seemed to have gone out of us', but this is only a temporary phenomenon.)[37] But in the fiction of Conrad (who allegedly 'stigmatized' Haggard's work as 'too horrible for words'), the masculinity that is under threat is itself a tissue of vanity, illusion and self-deception:[38]

> Where was the assurance and pride of his cleverness; the belief in success, the anger of failure, the wish to retrieve his fortune, the certitude of his ability to accomplish it yet? Gone.
>
> (*OI*, 77)

Although Willems's 'anger of failure' may be real enough, the reader is already well aware, at this point in the novel, that his pride is conceit, his cleverness largely illusory, his certitude of success a precursor of defeat. In Willems's mind, his individuality, his manliness, and his success as an ambitious servant of imperialism are all interlocked, and are all lost together through his desire for Aïssa. Yet the reader knows that that 'manliness' was always a sham. Here

Conrad's psychological portrait inhabits that paradoxical structure of masculinity which involves anxiety and instability alongside power and persistence. One is required by the ideology of masculinity both to be a man and to become one, to be in assured possession of a masculinity which is always at risk because it constantly needs proving and could at any time be lost.

Conrad's radicalism goes beyond a sceptical view of human nature and human motives, to embrace ideas of the instability and potential dissolution of the self. Robert Young has pointed out the connection between the structuralist and poststructuralist decentring of the self and the postcolonial critique of imperialism:

> Structuralism's so-called 'decentring of the subject' was in many respects itself an ethical activity, derived from a suspicion that the ontological category of 'the human' and 'human nature' had been inextricably associated with the violence of Western history ... [the] inscription of alterity within the self ... can allow for a new relation to ethics: the self has to come to terms with the fact that it is also a second and a third person.[39]

Young links this to the recognition that the First World is 'no longer always positioned in the first person with regard to the Second or Third Worlds'.[40] Willems, in the face of his overwhelming desire for the Other, experiences an existential fragmentation and undermining of self:

> He was keeping a tight hand on himself ... He had a vivid illusion —as vivid as reality almost—of being in charge of a slippery prisoner. He sat opposite Almayer ... with a perfectly calm face and within him a growing terror of escape from his own self.
>
> (*OI*, 78)

The image that follows, of Willems 'slipping helplessly to inevitable destruction' (78) is echoed shortly afterwards by his symbolic letting slip of his boat, a means by which he makes it inevitable that he will go and see Aïssa (79). This conceit, of the escape from his own self, is developed (with the unsettling reversal that now the self is doing the escaping), when he is with Aïssa, in an extended vision which Willems has of his self as 'a well-known figure ... diminishing in a long perspective' (145).

As we shall see in relation to *Almayer's Folly*, Conrad's use of narrative point of view also unsettles the centrality of the white male self, though not decisively so. The presentation of Aïssa remains within the racist and misogynist stereotypes of imperialist discourse, as when she feels 'with the unerring intuition of a primitive woman confronted by a simple impulse' (*OI*, 75) and when she is repeatedly linked to nature and to darkness, appearing to Willems as 'the very spirit of that land of mysterious forests' (70), and as part of 'that exuberant life which, born in gloom, struggles forever towards the sunshine' (76). This linking is akin to that in Haggard, in whose work, as Gail Ching-Liang Low notes, 'the deliberate gendering of the natural world as female, and all human agency as male, means that women who possess agency ... are inevitably punished for it.'[41] Yet while this ideological construction of the female Other remains in place, the 'self' pole of the imperial binary is shaky. Jeremy Hawthorn has shown that 'a study of the role of FID [free indirect discourse] in Conrad's fiction leads us straight into the moral complexities of these works' (*NT*, 4). The sustained use of irony and free indirect discourse in order to reveal Willems's faults and weaknesses risks, at times, implicating the narrative voice with certain of his attitudes. From the first sentence of Chapter 1 there is a strong sense of proleptic irony, as we observe a character whose false sense of security proceeds from self-deception. This irony pervades the chapter, with its account of Willems's complacent fantasies of security and future success. As soon as we read the first sentence we know that Willems is heading for trouble: 'When he stepped off the straight and narrow path of his peculiar honesty, it was with an inward assertion of unflinching resolve to fall back again into the monotonous but safe stride of virtue as soon as his little excursion into the wayside quagmires had produced the desired effect' (*OI*, 3). Indeed, by the end of the chapter the irony has become somewhat heavy-handed: 'He saw him[self] quite safe; solid as the hills; deep – deep as an abyss; discreet as the grave' (11). When, later in the novel, we are told that Willems 'had a sudden moment of lucidity – of that cruel lucidity that comes once in life to the most benighted' and 'seemed to see what went on within him, and was horrified at the strange sight' (80), we may momentarily imagine that the anti-hero is being afforded a brief glimpse of his own true nature. Yet the next sentence tells us that this is still a complacent delusion: 'He, a white man whose worst fault till then had been a little want of judgement and too much confidence in the rectitude of his kind!' (80). This passage hovers between interior monologue (which is simply the thoughts of the character), free indirect discourse (which renders the character's thoughts but partakes of the authority of the narrator), and narratorial comment (carrying the full authority of the narrator).[42] Presumably it is Willems who thinks that he had 'a sudden moment of lucidity', a moment which, as the narrator makes clear to us by ironic means, is in fact one of yet more profound self-deception. It seems unlikely, even in this moment of crisis, that Willems thinks of himself as one of 'the most benighted [of men]'; this view seems to belong to the narrator. If Willems (but not the narrator) thinks it is a 'sudden moment of lucidity', while the narrator (but not Willems) thinks that Willems is 'benighted', the questions then are whether the remainder of the passage represents Willems's deluded thoughts or the narrator's observations, and how clearly and consistently Conrad distinguishes between these two. Ruth Nadelhaft cites this passage, and argues that the negative and stereotypical views of Aïssa, for which many critics have attacked Conrad, are wholly attributable to Willems. While I would agree with her statement that 'the opposition of civilisation and savagery, so important to this book, is always subject to the irony of attribution', I feel she understates the complicity of the narrative voice with the some of the attitudes which it ironizes:[43]

> That woman was a complete savage, and . . . He tried to tell himself that the thing was of no consequence. It was vain effort. The novelty of the sensations he had never experienced before in the slightest degree, yet had despised on hearsay from his safe position of a civilized man, destroyed his courage. He was disappointed with himself. He seemed to be surrendering to a wild creature the unstained purity of his life, of his race, of his civilization. He had a notion of being lost amongst shapeless things that were dangerous and ghastly. He struggled with the sense of certain defeat—lost his footing—fell back into the darkness. With a faint cry and an upward throw of his arms he gave up as a tired swimmer gives up: because the swamped craft is gone from under his feet; because the night is dark and the shore is far—because death is better than strife.
>
> (*OI*, 80–1)

Masculinity and racial identity both seemed threatened here. The rhetoric of the Other (female and racial) as shapeless, dark and threatening (like Haggard's Gagool), and of miscegenation as death is in full flow. At first this rhetoric is implicitly ironized as the deluded thoughts of a morally bankrupt man. Yet the final sentence reads as the comments of the narrator, rather than Willems's thoughts, or at least implies a rapprochement between the two. The passage evokes the dissolution of imperial masculinity. But the radicalism of this should not be exaggerated: to offer it as a defence of Conrad's representation of race would be vulnerable to the critique made by Terry Eagleton in relation to 'Heart of Darkness'. The novella, he suggests, shows Western civilization to be 'at base as barbarous as African society – a viewpoint which disturbs imperialist assumptions to the precise degree that it reinforces them'.[44] Willems's self-image as proud white male is destroyed, but only by representing the female Other as shapeless death-bringer. Nevertheless, the ideologies of masculinity and imperialism are identified with moral corruption.

Lane's suggestion of a connection between imperialism and the death drive accords well with *An Outcast of the Islands*. Freud saw the death drive in terms of a fundamental desire to return to an earlier, inorganic state. Death offers a final discharge of excitation, and 'desire culminates in the extinction of the subject'.[45] However, the death drive can be dealt with, though not disposed of, by the individual, through sexuality and aggression. In *The Ego and the Id*, Freud argues that the 'death instincts' can be

in part ... rendered harmless by being fused with erotic components, in part ... diverted towards the external world in the form of aggression, while to a large extent they undoubtedly continue their internal work unhindered.[46]

An account of imperialism in terms of the death drive might seem, then, to risk being merely a more complex version of the hydraulic model criticized by Lane and Stoler. In place of a flow of sexual energy diverted towards imperial expansion, we would have an innately self-destructive instinct, channelled into both sexuality and aggression. More usefully, however, we might see the death drive as a fantasy. That is, without accepting Freud's postulation of a basic instinct or drive, and therefore explaining imperialism in a reductively psychologistic manner, we could take Freud's model as an articulation of fantasies of annihilation, repetition, regression and return. Such an articulation, as Linda Ruth Williams points out, 'locked into a wider cultural concern with repetition and return emerging from modernist aesthetics and Nietzschean philosophy'.[47] Freud's concept of the death drive emerged in 1920, partly in response to the First World

War. Nevertheless, the concept may help us to explore ideas and fantasies of regression and self-destruction in the discourse of late nineteenth-century imperialism. Particularly appropriate is Freud's linking of regression and self-destructiveness to mastery, sadism and aggression in a fantasy structure where one set of terms can be converted into the other. So, for example, a certain repressed desire to be in the place of the Other (to 'regress', according to the racist construction of the Other) is not a subversive corrective to imperial mastery and control but its hidden complement. Furthermore, Freud's highly gendered theory illuminates the gendered nature of imperial fantasy, as conquest of the (mother) earth and return to the 'primitive' mother, a fantasy in which self-assertion and self-destruction shadow each other in a specifically masculine configuration.

In a striking if portentous peroration by the narrative voice, *An Outcast of the Islands* anticipates, over twenty years earlier, Freud's claim that 'the aim of all life is death'.[48] Chapter 4 begins, 'Consciously or unconsciously, men are proud of their firmness, steadfastness of purpose, directness of aim'. The paragraph evokes with heavy irony the resolute path through life of the 'man of purpose', to conclude:

> Travelling on, he achieves great length without any breadth, and battered, besmirched, and weary, he touches the goal at last; he grasps the reward of his perseverance, of his virtue, of his healthy optimism: an untruthful tombstone over a dark and soon forgotten grave.
>
> (*OI*, 197)

It is Lingard's deluded optimism and approaching decline that is foreshadowed here, but the trope of the path is likely to remind the reader of the first sentence of the novel, referring ironically to Willems's 'straight and narrow path of ... peculiar honesty' (3). The descriptions of Willems with Aïssa are highly suggestive of the death drive in their symbolic overtones and representation of his conscious and unconscious processes. Regaining the mother, excitation leading to extinction of the self and orgasm as the 'little death' are all aspects of the fantasy of the death drive, and all are suggested by the scenes of love and conflict between Willems and Aïssa. Willems's repeated fantasy of the disappearance or dissolution of his self has already been discussed. Aïssa's gaze induces in him an almost literal ecstasy (or standing outside of the self), in which reason gives way to an extreme excitement which is nevertheless passive and infantile:

With that look she drew the man's soul away from him through his immobile pupils, and from Willems' features the spark of reason vanished under her gaze and was replaced by an appearance of physical well-being, an ecstasy of the senses which had taken possession of his rigid body ... [producing] an appalling aspect of idiotic beatitude.

(140)

A range of discourses are evidently in play here, including ironic use of a clichéd 'primitive' superstition (the stealing of a soul) and of the discourse of degeneracy (facial features marking the absence of reason). Shortly afterwards Willems lies with his head in her lap, and expresses the romantic desire for death: 'I wish I could die like this – now!' (141).

The fear of, and desire for, 'regression' and the 'primitive' in imperial discourse can easily join forces with the fantasy of a return to a pre-rational, pre-human, even pre-organic self, given the tendency of imperial discourse to construct the Other in terms which involve darkness and death. The discourse of gender shows a similar compatibility. As Elisabeth Bronfen points out, Freud selected three objects of choice for man: the mother, the beloved (woman) and Mother Earth. Moreover, there is a

cultural convention that the mother's gift of birth is also the gift of death, and that the embrace of the beloved also signifies a dissolution of the self. Woman functions as privileged trope for the uncanniness of unity and loss, of independent identity and self-dissolution, of the pleasure of the body and its decay ... Given that woman is culturally constructed as the object of a plethora of contradictory drives, the death drive and the drive for femininity are readily aligned.[49]

In Haggard's fiction the death drive is projected outwards in celebratory visions of mass slaughter (of both humans and animals) and demonized portrayals of monstrous women. Conrad's writing is more able to explore the idea of an internalized self-destructiveness, and so his vision of imperial masculinity is a far more troubled and sceptical one. *An Outcast of the Islands*, then, reveals the fault lines in imperial masculinity, representing powerfully the destructive and self-destructive aspects of male imperial desire. What Conrad's text seems unable to do is to represent the desire of the Other in non-ideological terms.[50]

Conrad had already attempted to represent the desire of a non-European woman in *Almayer's Folly*, with mixed results. The woman in question in this, Conrad's first novel, is Nina, whose father is the Dutch Almayer, and whose mother was captured as a child (by Lingard) from Sulu pirates. Nina is possessed of a sexual and desiring look, which is evoked in striking if clichéd terms, and is presented as dangerous to masculinity:

> She drew back her head and fastened her eyes on his in one of those long looks that are a woman's most terrible weapon; a look that is more stirring than the closest touch, and more dangerous than the thrust of a dagger, because it also whips the soul out of the body, but leaves the body alive and helpless, to be swayed here and there by the capricious tempests of passion and desire ... bringing terrible defeat in the delirious uplifting of accomplished conquest.
>
> (*AF*, 171)

However, the object of this look is not a degenerate white man who will be destroyed by it, but a heroic Malay 'Rajah' who will become a 'god' (172) through the firm binary logic of romance gender stereotypes:

> She would be his light and his wisdom; she would be his greatness and his strength; yet hidden from the eyes of all men she would be, above all, his only and lasting weakness. A very woman! In the sublime vanity of her kind she was thinking already of moulding a god from the clay at her feet. A god for others to worship.
>
> (172)

Robert Hampson, who quotes the description of Nina's 'look', hears in the novel a misogynistic voice expressing 'a male fear of "passion and desire" [in which] sexual feelings are feared as loss of control', generating 'a discourse of sexuality that is marked by the woman's will-to-power, intimations of male sexual anxiety, and the association of love with death and decay'.[51] He argues that this discourse, and the associated imagery of the competing jungle vegetation, show the influence of Schopenhauer's belief in woman as the agent of the 'Will'. However, the woman's conquest is at best an ambivalent one, since the paragraph describing Nina's look ends: 'It is the look of woman's surrender' (*AF*, 172). Underlying this apparent contradiction is a rather conventional idea, that women achieve power indirectly through their sexual influence over powerful men, though Conrad mystifies this idea somewhat by attributing such power to Malay women in particular, as 'that great but occult influence which is one of the few rights of half-savage womankind' (22).

The description of Nina's powerful look is only one of many references in the novel to eyes, and to looking. Feminist film theory has identified a failure to represent female desire in mainstream cinema and such analysis of a more obviously visual medium may help us to understand the rhetoric of the visual in Conrad. One form which the effacement of female desire takes is the directing of the female desiring look at nothing (nothing that the spectator/reader can see), whereas the woman herself is voyeuristically presented as the object of male desire, inviting the spectator/reader to join in the desiring look of male characters. Focalization is the nearest equivalent in fiction to the camera in film, and in the opening chapters of the novel Almayer is the predominant focal character, although there is some non-focalized narration. We are occasionally told Nina's sense perceptions (external focalization on Nina) but very little of her thoughts and feelings.[52] Thus there is no sense of the narrative reaching towards what Teresa de Lauretis terms 'another (object of) vision and the conditions of visibility for a different social subject', one that would be less male-oriented.[53] The object of Nina's desire is invisible and her own visibility is within a masculine economy that objectifies her as passive object to be seen and penetrated. In the earlier chapters, Nina is often described with eyes averted from her father, with a veiled gaze of half-closed eyes, or looking out at the natural environment in a way which suggest contemplation of a transcendent dream:

> Her face turned towards the outer darkness, through which her dreamy eyes seemed to see some entrancing picture.
>
> (16)

> Nina had listened to her father, unmoved, with her half-closed eyes still gazing into the night.
>
> (18–19)

> ... leaning back with half-closed eyes, her long hair shading her face.
>
> (46)

This presentation of her culminates in the scene when she and Dain first meet. Yet since this is also the scene in which her desire is given an object, it involves a significant play of desiring looks. Furthermore, the passage leading up to this scene includes, for the first time, a narration focalized on Nina, thus opening up the possibility of the representation of her desire.

The scene stages a contest of male and female desire and partially unsettles the identification of masculinity with power and the right to look, only decisively to reassert it. It begins by emphasizing a male body as spectacle of power and wealth, as an excited Ali tells Nina of a Malay visitor: 'And his dress is very brave. I have seen his dress. It shines! What jewels!' (*AF*, 51).[54] Nina and her mother compete for the position of voyeur at a rent in a hanging curtain, and Nina is described in a clichéd sexualized manner:

> Nina ... had lifted the conquered curtain and now stood in full light, framed in the dark background of the passage, her lips slightly parted, her hair in disorder after the exertion, the angry gleam not yet faded out of her glorious and sparkling eyes.
>
> (54)

Resisting her mother's demand to veil her face (53), and matching her father's dismissive comment to Dain ('It is nothing. Some women') with her own dismissal ('It's only a trader') (54), she claims the right to appear and to look: 'She took in at a glance the group of white-clad lançeman ... and her gaze rested curiously on the chief of that imposing cortège' (54). This is a description of Nina in the act of looking, yet it reads as a description of her being seen: the rather weak epithets 'glorious and sparkling' present her eyes as object of desire and reflectors of light, not as the means of expression of her own desire. Indeed, the description is prefaced by a 'reaction shot': as Dain sees Nina emerge Almayer is 'struck by an unexpected change in the expression of his guest's countenance' (54). Following the description of Nina, there is a description of Dain as she sees him:

> The crude light of the lamp shone on the gold embroidery of his black silk jacket, broke in a thousand sparkling rays on the jewelled hilt of his kriss protruding from under the many folds of the red sarong gathered into a sash round his waist, and played on the precious stones of the many rings on his dark fingers. He straightened himself up quickly after the low bow, putting his hand with a graceful ease on the hilt of his heavy short sword ornamented with brilliantly dyed fringes of horsehair.
>
> (54–5)

This description anticipates those of the Malay chief, the eponymous hero of the story 'Karain', which will be discussed in the next chapter. In particular, the rather insistent allusions to the sword suggest fetishization, a need to reassert the phallic. Masculinity is then overtly stressed: 'Nina, hesitating on the threshold, saw an erect lithe figure of medium height with a breadth of shoulder suggesting great power' (*AF*, 55). When it comes to Dain's face the idea of the feminine is explicitly introduced as a supposed racial feature, but only after having been equally explicitly 'corrected' in advance:

> a face full of determination and expressing a reckless good-humour, not devoid, however, of some dignity. The squareness of lower jaw, the full red lips, the mobile nostrils, and the proud carriage of the head gave the impression of a being half-savage, untamed, perhaps cruel, and corrected the liquid softness of the almost feminine eye, that general characteristic of the race.
>
> (55)

Here femininity is safely distanced by projection onto a racial Other. Nevertheless, if it is the impression of the 'savage' that protects Dain's masculinity, that protection is partial: is 'half-savage' equivalent to half-masculine? Steve Neale notes that 'within the image ... the male body can signify castration and lack, can hence function as the object of voyeuristic looking, insofar as it is marked as such', one sort of marking occurring when the male body is 'specified as racially or culturally other'. On the other hand, 'the male body can be fetishised inasmuch as it figures within a fetishistic image or inasmuch as it signifies masculinity, and, hence, possession of the phallus, the absence of lack' (SD, 130). The Lacanian concept of Symbolic castration (the self as constituted by lack) has affinities with Bhabha's sense of otherness and hybridity within the self. Objections to Lacan's gender-specific terminology will be considered in a later chapter, but for the present I want to allow Neale's Lacanian assumption that both men and women are subject to 'Symbolic castration'. His argument, then, is that since 'Symbolic castration is distinct from and irreducible to the Symbolic specification of sexual difference', there is a considerable degree of mobility and variety in the symbolic meaning of images of the male body (SD, 130). His suggestion that a male body marked as 'racially or culturally other' can thereby 'signify castration' is highly suggestive in relation to the presentation of Dain, but needs refining. As Bongie observes, Dain belongs to the traditional world of nineteenth-century exoticism, being one of those 'sovereign figures who conjure up the image of what Conrad would much later refer to ... as those "real chieftain[s] in the books of a hundred years ago"' (*EM*, 151). Dain represents the nostalgic (European) fantasy of a heroic masculinity untrammelled by bureaucratic modernity. He signifies both the possession of the phallus (that is, a fantasy of male power) and its absence (the Other within the self). His racial otherness allows both sides of this polarity to be rhetorically indulged.

Up to the point where Dain is described in these ambivalent terms, the scene has employed a mobility of viewpoint. We see Almayer observing Dain looking at Nina, then we see Nina looking at Dain and see her as she is perceived by him and then we see Dain as perceived by Nina. The effect might be understood on analogy with the concept of 'suture' in film theory, or 'the constant reconstruction of the spectator/subject through each successive image of the film'.[55] In cinema, this is often effected though the 'shot-reverse shot structure, which establishes the optical point-of-view of characters within the fictional space of the film at moments ... when they are looking at one another'.[56] The concentration on the visual appearance of the characters, combined with the shifting point of view, might be seen as effecting a suture: constructing the reader via a series of identifications with the looks of different characters. The mobility of the focalization would thus draw on the fluidity of fantasy identification claimed by Neale, who cites Constance Penley's argument that in fantasy 'all the possible roles in the narrative are available to the subject'.[57] However, it is precisely the instability of the location of the look in this scene which distributes identification according to gender, staging an effacement of the woman's desire even as it evokes it. The description of Nina hesitates between evoking the inception of her desire and fetishizing her as desired object. Her active assertion of her right to look in defiance of her mother's attempt to restrain her paradoxically serves only to heighten a conventional eroticization, since the struggle leaves her with 'lips slightly parted' and 'hair in disorder'. This creates for a male reader a potential identification with the desire produced in Dain, while inviting the female reader to identify with Nina on the terms described by Mary Ann Doane:

> For the female spectator there is a certain over-presence of the image – she *is* the image. Given the closeness of this relationship, the female spectator's desire can be described only in terms of a kind of narcissism – the female look demands a becoming.[58]

So Nina's desiring look invites identification with her desire (an identification which need not, of course, be limited to women readers), but invites it on condition that a female subjectivity thus sutured into the narrative accepts a narcissistic self-imagining as sexual object. This is confirmed by the outcome of the exchange of looks:

> Nina saw those [Dain's] eyes fixed upon her with such an uncontrolled expression of admiration and desire that she felt a hitherto unknown feeling of shyness, mixed with alarm and some delight, enter and penetrate her whole being. Confused by these unusual sensations she stopped in the doorway and instinctively drew the lower part of the curtain across her face, leaving only half a rounded cheek, a stray tress, and one eye exposed, wherewith to contemplate the gorgeous and bold being.
>
> (*AF*, 55)

Just as her mouth, opened to breathe hard in the struggle with her mother, becomes less an expression of her self-assertion than an invitation, so her newly aroused sexual desire, in this passage, becomes something which penetrates her, becomes the occasion of Dain's desire, as she 'instinctively' reverts to a traditional half-veiled feminine modesty. One process going on in this scene is, then, the sustaining of a falsely unified masculinity for Dain, for Almayer and perhaps for the male reader. Following the staging of the threat of active female desire, combined with the threat of a femininity within Dain (his eyes, his 'gorgeous' appearance'), these threats are firmly repressed by subsuming Nina's look into an economy of male looks (her father's, Dain's) and a gender-specific suture of reader-identification is organized. Gender, race and class are all in play here: Nina's initial confidence is based on Dain being 'only a trader' (*AF*, 54), but afterwards she confesses that her mother was right to call him 'some Rajah' (56). In a Lacanian argument which will be further elaborated in Chapter 8, Kaja Silverman distinguishes between 'gaze' as the social power of constructing the identity of another and 'look' as a function of one's own desire. Dain's social position and his gender position allow his desiring look to appropriate the gaze. The scene illustrates the process which Silverman describes in mainstream cinema: 'the male look both transfers its own lack to the female subject, and attempts to pass itself off as the gaze' (*MS*, 144). Nina's look is given a certain power, as Hampson notes, but that power depends on the adoption of a stereotypically 'female' role. Dain, on the other hand,

possesses the social and gender power that enables him to masquerade
as the owner of the gaze so as to construct Nina as a traditional Malay
woman and finally to carry her off as the possession of his look:
'Come, delight of my eyes' (*AF*, 193). A comparable process occurs, in
much more compact form, in *An Outcast of the Islands*, in one of those
intensely rhetorical and symbolic passages describing Aïssa and
Willems:

> She stepped back, keeping her distance, her eyes on his face, watch-
> ing on it the play of his doubts and of his hopes with a piercing
> gaze, that seemed to search out the innermost recesses of his
> thought; and it was as if she had drawn slowly the darkness round
> her, wrapping herself in its undulating folds that made her indis-
> tinct and vague.
>
> (*OI*, 154)

Aïssa's vagueness here helps her to appropriate the role of impersonal
gaze which, in a reversal of the more usual gender relations, penetrates
and fixes the male. Yet the allusions to darkness, veiling and 'undu-
lating folds' reinscribes her vagueness in the familiar symbolism of
dark otherness, so that 'lack' rebounds upon her. Her identity
dissolves into cliché even as her fierceness further undermines the
identity of Willems.

Conrad's first two novels, then, raise questions as to how we should
read texts which are in many ways in the grip of a stereotyped imperial and misogynistic discourse, and yet deploy irony and ambiguous
narrative technique so as to fracture the coherence of that discourse,
offering moral and political insight of far greater interest than mere
restatements of cliché. The complexity of this situation is in part a
result of the complexity of Conrad's texts, and in part arises from the
historical situation of reading a century later, when critiques of race
and gender have acquired prominence. The tendency for discussion of
these issues to resolve into pro-Conrad and anti-Conrad polemics is
unhelpful. White's 'subversion' model – essentially an attempt to
present Conrad as relatively in tune with late twentieth-century political values – remains somewhat one-dimensional. Bhabha's concept of
ambivalence as integral to colonial discourse seems to me more
convincing than postulating a monolithic colonial discourse which
Conrad (partly) subverts. However, ambivalence can easily become
too bland a concept, too lacking in the force that would enable us to
distinguish between, say, Haggard and Conrad. Hence my suggestion

of reading ideological and utopian elements together, as interlocking aspects of the same discourse.

This approach involves an element of what Said terms 'contrapuntal reading', as regards both masculinity and empire. Reading wholly with the grain of the text can produce a critical discourse which replicates or repeats ideological aspects of the text. The following comments, from an introduction to the novel, seem to me to exemplify such an effect:

> The Willems-Aïssa relationship also powerfully enacts late-Victorian fears about degeneracy and atavism, the potential for 'falling back' into the pre-conscious and pre-historic, and vivifies the split between 'culture' and 'barbarism' that so obsessed a colonial power forcing its technologies and moralities on conquered peoples.

> Insistently associated with trance, dream, and sleep, she [Aïssa] represents at the very outset what she does at the conclusion – immobility and the loss of individuality and of consciousness – in a word, death.

> Once a man of defined social and economic status, Willems is transformed by her [Aïssa] into a creature alone and adrift, and his loss of consciousness signals not only a reversion to animal existence but the reassertion of the feared Other lurking, like Robert Louis Stevenson's Mr Hyde, within the post-Darwinian self.[59]

The author of these comments, J.H. Stape is, of course, not endorsing the nineteenth-century racist theories which would associate the Malays with 'degeneracy and atavism', but illuminating them for the reader. His use of scare quotes around 'culture' and 'barbarism' as well as his comment on colonial power make this obvious. Nor, presumably, does he share the gynophobia which connects women with death and the unconscious. Rather, he is offering these as the text's own terms, and proposing that it is in these terms that we should read it. Nevertheless, he also wishes to argue that 'Conrad's allegorical gestures and symbolism in *An Outcast* repudiate colonialism'. The basis on which he does so is a claim of universalism: 'Betrayal and greed recognize no national boundaries ... Cultural and individual particulars dissolve (and re-form) before the varieties of desire.'[60] Having made this claim of cultural universalism himself, Stape also quotes Conrad, asserting a universal similarity of humanity, inflected by a universal difference of gender: 'They [Willems and Aïssa] both long to have a significance in the order of nature or of society. To me they are typical of mankind where every individual wishes to assert his power, woman by sentiment, man by achievement of some sort – mostly base.'[61] Conrad is obviously using gender stereotyping here. But the conclusion Stape wishes to draw is that, because Conrad sees all races and peoples as equally subject to greed and ambition, he is repudiating colonialism. Are we not back here with the 'Empire of the Selfsame', in which the Other takes its place 'in a hierarchically organized relationship in which the same is what rules, names, defines and assigns "its" other'?[62] Again the forced interaction of binaries is part of the process, since Conrad is able to assert the unity of races by subsuming them in a strongly marked gender binary (an effect which we shall observe in his fiction in the next chapter). Stape has earlier argued that the exoticism in the novel is 'largely a matter of setting', since 'the cultures and peoples of the Malay Archipelago serve mainly as a backdrop for quintessentially Western crises of identity'.[63] The Empire of the Selfsame: Westerners have identity and quintessentially Western crises, whereas the Malays are at best the same as, or no better than, the Europeans. Our identity is distinct and theirs is merely part of (our) 'universal'. While overtly critical of colonialism, Stape's argument comes close to justifying it on the grounds that everyone does it, or would if they could. To illustrate how Conrad transcends any 'claims to cultural or racial superiority', Stape point out that the Arab trader Abdulla is 'as much a colonizer as Lingard', and that Babalatchi is 'another outsider' who only ushers in a more ruthless 'system of exploitation'.[64] He is making a valid point here, in that Conrad is portraying a society of competing adventurers and traders from various parts of the world, all in search of wealth and power, while the indigenous population of Sambir play very little part in the story. But is it not a little too convenient for a Western critic to defend a Western author as anti-colonial, because that author supposedly sees imperialism as 'only another manifestation of a fundamentally human rapaciousness, limited neither by time nor by place'?[65] Just as the combination of gender and racial otherness produces Conrad's darkest rhetoric (and bearing in mind that Cixous describes the Empire of the Selfsame as a system which supports both patriarchy and colonialism), so it is gender and racial otherness (in the character of Aïssa) which rouses Stape to a defensive attack on feminism and on Aïssa herself.[66] He cites her statement that all evil come from the outside, from 'that

people that steals every land, masters every sea, that knows no mercy
and no truth' (*OI*, 153). Commenting that this is 'comically inadequate as an interpretation of the nexus of political and social forces
that govern human action', Stape argues that 'her reading of the colonial situation is a characteristic splitting-off and projection of the
negative upon the Other, with the outsider as a convenient scapegoat
for one's own moral inadequacies and failures.'[67] But Aïssa's comment
is not an interpretation of a 'nexus of political and social forces', but
a subjective and heartfelt comment on her own life, which has been
traumatically marked by a colonial conflict in which the Dutch are
increasingly dominant. Aïssa is indeed simplifying matters, but it is
hardly just to describe the European colonial exploitation of the
Malay Archipelago as equivalent to one of her 'own moral inadequacies'. It is the idea that Aïssa might represent some positive feminist
value that prompts Stape's particular scorn:

> Aïssa's total misunderstanding of him [Willems], combined with
> her desire for his conquest, makes her relation to him yet another
> colonizing project pointedly resembling those that form the
> novel's larger historical and political backdrop ... she symbolizes a
> poisoned blossom bringing perfumed death, and any sentimental-
> izing of their relationship – whether articulated as a meditation on
> the nature of love or as an attempt to see her as an alternative to
> male power systems, confronting and undermining patriarchal
> hegemony – necessarily ends in an egregious misreading of the
> novel ... [Willems] never clearly sees that he has merely been a
> means by which she hopes to achieve her self-serving ends, ends
> that differ not a whit from those of the 'colonizers' who figure
> among Conrad's main targets.[68]

Stape's argument here, like his earlier use of the ideas of projection
and the Other, is characteristic of male backlash criticism, in appropriating the language of political criticism while misrepresenting the
politics of the situation. The point of a feminist or postcolonial
critique is not (or at least should not be) to idealize the disempowered,
but to point out the mechanisms of their disempowerment.

The critic to whom Stape is probably responding here (though he
does not name her) is Ruth Nadelhaft, who celebrates Aïssa's 'mental
and emotional power of analysis and speech' as carrying a 'critique of
patriarchal Western values'.[69] Nadelhaft's reading is strongly argued,
but it does indeed tend to idealize Aïssa, prompting I would suspect

Stape's dissent. Although a contrapuntal or utopian reading of Aïssa's character, such as Nadelhaft offers, is possible, the presence of a misogynist and imperial ideology in the novel is not confined to the discourse of characters such as Willems and Lingard, but also inhabits the discourse of the narrator (for example in the descriptions of the jungle). However, in response to Stape I would suggest that the difference between the colonial project and Aïssa's relationship to Willems is that whereas the Dutch (and, to a lesser extent, the Arab and Malay traders) possess social and military power, Aïssa has no power apart from her supposed erotic power, which is a projection of a white male fantasy. Artfully bracketing a politicized feminist reading of the novel with an apolitical reading of it as a meditation of love, Stape argues that Aïssa cannot represent an alternative to male power systems because her motives are not pure, as if a woman is only allowed to have idealistic motives. She is only after power, Stape objects. Yet that is, after all, what the disempowered usually are after.

The significance of my disagreements with Stape for the wider aims of the present book is not merely.to contrast my own reading with his, but to highlight the role of masculinity in the processes of critical reception and debate. Stape's introduction is that of a scholarly and intelligent Conradian critic, and has much to offer the reader in terms of both information and critical judgement. Yet it also strikes me as distorted by a sort of possessive and defensive rage against feminist criticism intruding its critiques onto the imaginative bond between male author and male reader/critic. Here Nadelhaft's suggestion that 'along with Willems, it is the Conradian critics who have been threatened by the characterisation of Aïssa' seems apposite.[70] Somehow, in Stape's argument, it is a non-European woman, treated as a possession by her father, as a tool by Babalatchi and as an object of desire and disgust by Willems, a woman who ends up a prematurely aged servant, who becomes the epitome of oppressive power.

I am aware that my own criticisms of Stape reveal my own emotional investment in both Conrad and certain critical values and positionings, an investment vulnerable to Stephen Heath's question: 'To what extent do men use feminism for the assurance of an identity, now asking to belong as a way of at least ensuring their rightness, a position that gets her with me once more?'[71] The response has, I think, to proceed from the comment which Heath quotes from Claire Pajaczkowska: 'I am tired of men arguing amongst themselves as to who is the most feminist, frustrated by an object feminism becoming the stakes in a displaced rivalry between men because of a refusal by men to examine the structure of the relations between themselves.'[72] This is not quite the situation here, since Stape is not, I take it, making any claim to be a feminist. Nevertheless, it is rivalry between men that is at issue at some level of the critical process, and a rivalry that repeats outside the text something of the structure of rivalry inside the text: a structure in which the Other (here, particularly, Aïssa) becomes the stakes. In the next chapter I shall examine how Conrad's fiction moves to a more explicit examination of male bonds, and of how this might affect us as readers, male or female.

2
Imperialism and Male Bonds: 'Karain', *The Nigger of the 'Narcissus'*, *Lord Jim*

In *Almayer's Folly* and *An Outcast of the Islands* male loyalties and friendships, such as those between Lingard and Willems, and between Dain and Almayer, are fractured by tensions surrounding the binaries of race and gender. Sexual passion in the context of the imperial encounter generates a mixture of fear and desire, evoking the death drive and forcing resolutions which re-establish fantasies of racial security, as Willems goes down to self-destruction and Nina is despatched into the imaginary future of a purely exotic world. Aïssa, whose racial and sexual otherness threatens to engulf the male imperial self, is transformed from object of desire to object of pity and disgust. Miscegenation or *métissage*, with its exciting and threatening potentialities, is held at bay, while elements of otherness, even of hybridity, within the male imperial self are evoked only to be suppressed.

In the works which follow, Conrad seeks to re-establish the strength of male bonds. In his next long work, *The Nigger of the 'Narcissus'*, this involves the total exclusion of women characters (unless one counts the Captain's wife, who appears briefly when the ship reaches dock, 'as strange as if she had fallen there from the sky' (*NN*, 165)). In other texts women are firmly inscribed in a homosocial structure which reaffirms male power through the exchange of women, although male weakness is also much in evidence: this applies to 'Karain', 'Heart of Darkness' and *Lord Jim*. Imperialism and ideas of race play a major part in all of these works, though in varying ways. This chapter will explore the ways in which this reassertion of male bonds is haunted by the anxiety of *fin de siècle* masculinity, leading Conrad towards the creation of a masculine textual economy based around the act of narration.[1]

Conrad's early works, with their Far Eastern or nautical settings and
their links to adventure fiction and to the imperial novel as practised
by Kipling, Stevenson and others, are often seen in isolation from
their British social context, in particular the crisis of masculinity
outlined in the Introduction.[2] However, as Daniel Bivona has argued,
the maintenance of a wall between the 'imperial novel' and the
'domestic novel' can obscure the discursive and material interdependence of British society with British colonial activity; an
interdependence which Bivona conceptualizes by seeing imperialism
as the unconscious of nineteenth-century Britain.[3] In considering
Conrad's imperial and sea fiction, one might invert this formulation,
and ask whether the crisis of masculinity at home operates as the
unconscious of Conrad's texts. Such a view gains much support from
the role of Britain as 'home' in *Lord Jim*, from its role as epistemological frame in 'Karain', and from the parallel and contrast in *The Nigger
of the 'Narcissus'* between shipboard society and land society, as well
as the mood of the ending in London. We also find at the boundaries
of Conrad's fiction, in his 'Author's Notes', and in associated texts
such as letters and memoirs, images of Conrad himself which chime
suggestively with some of the characteristic images and concerns of *fin
de siècle* and decadent masculinity, and it is with these intertexts of
the fiction that I shall begin.

The year in which Conrad completed his first novel, 1894, was also
marked by two major events in his personal relations with other men.
In that year his uncle, Tadeusz Bobrowski, who had served as effective
guardian and as mentor to Conrad since his father's death when he
was eleven, died. This event, Conrad recorded, made him feel 'as if
everything has died in me'.[4] In the same year he met Edward Garnett,
senior reader for the publisher Unwin's, who was to become Conrad's
friend and literary mentor. In the 'Author's Note' to *An Outcast of the
Islands*, Conrad gives a somewhat mythologized account of this
meeting, making Garnett responsible for the inception of his second
novel, and implicitly for Conrad's decisive shift to a literary career.
The note begins by invoking that state of 'immobility' and 'indolence'
which recurs in his accounts of himself and is so much at odds with
the dominant Victorian ideals of masculinity, and so much a part of
their decadent mirror-image. He describes himself as a 'victim of
contrary stresses', adding that 'since it was impossible for me to face
both ways I had elected to face nothing' (*OI*, vii). Elsewhere Conrad
famously described himself as 'homo duplex' or double man, as if
facing both ways was not unknown to him.[5] Here, however, he claims

to have been stuck facing nothing, a nothing which may be read in one sense as himself in a state of unmasculine indolence, without work, that great bolster of Victorian masculinity.[6] The Victorian sense of work as both constitutive and protective of manliness is concisely conveyed in lines written by Ford Madox Brown to accompany his own painting of 1852–65, *Work*:

> Work! which beads the brow and tans the flesh
> Of lusty manhood, casting out its devils!
> By whose weird art transmuting poor men's evils,
> Their bed seems down, their one dish ever fresh.[7]

It is indeed work that is at issue in Conrad's 'Author's Note', since the 'contrary stresses' represent Conrad's impulses towards the life of the sea and the literary life. Amid the jostling and confusion of discovering new values, Conrad tells us, he experienced 'a momentary feeling of darkness' and 'let my spirit float supine over that chaos' (*OI*, vii). He presents himself as rescued from this state by the intervention of Garnett, who suggests that he should 'write another [novel]' (viii), though in fact Conrad had already begun the story which was to become *An Outcast of the Islands*.[8] In a version of the trope of the work of fiction as the offspring of male friendship (examined in detail by Wayne Koestenbaum, who discusses Conrad's collaboration with Ford Madox Ford), Conrad's novel becomes a product of Garnett's 'desire' and 'gentle' manner:[9]

> A phrase of Edward Garnett's is ... responsible for this book. The first of the friends I made for myself by my pen it was but natural that he should be the recipient ... of my confidences ... I believe that as far as one man may wish to influence another man's life Edward Garnett had a great desire that I should go on writing. At that time, and I may say, ever afterwards, he was always very patient and gentle with me.
>
> .(vii–viii)

Garnett himself invoked the language of gender roles to describe his early impressions of Conrad, writing that 'I had never seen before a man so masculinely keen yet so femininely sensitive', that 'there was a blend of caressing, almost feminine intimacy in his talk' and that 'Conrad's moods of gay tenderness could be quite seductive'.[10] The evening ends, in Conrad's account, with the two new friends walking the 'interminable streets' of London 'talking of many things', before Conrad goes home and writes half a page of the new novel before going to sleep (viii).

Herbert Sussman, in his study of *Victorian Masculinities*, considers the uneasy relationship of 'the bourgeois model of manhood as active engagement in the commercial and technological world' with 'the romantic ideal of the male writer as detached observer'.[11] Citing Brown's picture *Work* and the lines quoted above, he also quotes a comment on the picture from Brown's grandson, another of those friends Conrad made by his pen, Ford Madox Ford: 'At the further corner of the picture, are two men who appear as having nothing to do. These are the brain workers [Carlyle and F. D. Maurice], who, seeming to be idle, work, and are the cause of well-ordained work and happiness in others – sages.'[12] Brown's picture dates from an earlier phase of the Victorian era, and the contrast it depicts is not symmetrical to that within Conrad's career, since the men obviously working are specifically working-class manual labourers. Nevertheless, a version of the same anxiety is evident in Conrad's reflections on his own transition from the evidently 'manly' role of merchant officer (unusual in that it allowed gentlemen to engage in physical labour without loss of class status) to the more inward and reflective role of writer. Conrad undertook this transition at a time when the idea of the writer as sage, as a sort of intellectual Captain of Industry and cause of work in other men, was less easily sustained.[13] Indeed, by 1911 Ford was complaining that, in England of 'today', 'a man of letters is regarded as something less than a man, whereas any sort of individual returning from the colonies is regarded inevitably as something rather more than two supermen rolled into one'.[14] For Conrad, then, the relationship between imperial setting and metropolitan centre is shadowed by a pairing of the manliness of physical and productive labour in the service of imperial trade with a more problematic and passive intellectual and artistic masculinity, as he writes about the former role while beginning to occupy the latter.[15] In the Preface to *The Nigger of the 'Narcissus'* Conrad writes of the artist as one who 'descends within himself, and in that lonely region of stress and strife ... finds the terms of his appeal' (viii). This manages to make introspection sound a little like a sea voyage. Later, and more surprisingly, he links the artist with a manual labourer in a passage which expresses some of the same anxieties as Brown's picture. It begins from the perspective of the idle gentleman: 'Sometimes, stretched at ease in the shade of a road-side tree, we watch the motions of a labourer in a distant field, and after a time, begin to wonder languidly as to what the fellow may be at.' But shortly the workman's labour, and his possible failure, are used to figure those of the artist: 'And so it is with the workman of art. Art is long and life is short, and success is very far off' (xi). While expressing the fear of failure, this lays claim to at least the status of honest workman.

The anxiety surrounding Conrad's transition to a literary career is both mitigated by, and articulated through, male literary friendships. Koestenbaum observes of the collaboration between Conrad and Ford that it 'may have alleviated their hysteria, but it also inspired new anxieties. Writing with another man meant entering his prose's body.'[16] In Conrad's account of another literary friendship, with Stephen Crane, the setting is again the phantasmal city, the dark heart of empire of 'Heart of Darkness' and *The Secret Agent*:

> In the history of our essentially undemonstrative friendship (which is nearly as difficult to recapture as a dream) that first long afternoon is the most care-free instant, and the only one that had a character of enchantment about it. It was spread out over a large portion of central London ... after a long tramp amongst an orderly multitude of grimy brick houses—from which the only things I carried off were the impressions of the coloured rocks of Mexico ... —there came suddenly Oxford Street ... I don't remember seeing any people in the streets except for a figure, now and then, unreal, flitting by, obviously negligible.[17]

In the background, pointing up Conrad's absorption in his new friendship, yet also standing in for it since that friendship is dream-like and difficult to recapture, is the dream-like city of modernity with its ghostly figures, the *Fourmillante cité, cité plein de rêves* that Eliot inherited from Baudelaire.[18] These are also the streets of Dorian Gray's secret life, of *Dr Jekyll and Mr Hyde*, of Eliot's Prufrock and of Conrad's own Verloc, with his parodic respectability. They are streets infused with the anxiety of modernity, and its uneasy sexuality. Conrad and Crane 'resumed our tramping—east and north and south again, steering through uncharted mazes the streets [sic]' (*LE*, 105) and later 'the Monstrous Shade' (*LE*, 106) of Balzac makes an ironic appearance (as Crane asks for a description of his work).

Close male friendship was both part of conventional Victorian masculinity, and, at least potentially, part of its repressed underside, an underside which came to the fore at the end of the century. Eve

Sedgwick's work on the structure and history of nineteenth-century homosociality provides the crucial framework for understanding here. In her examination of 'the *structure* of men's relations with other men', she postulates 'the potential unbrokenness of a continuum between homosocial and homosexual', without any implication that 'genital homosexual desire is "at the root of" other forms of male homosociality' (*BM*, 1–2). In other words, sexual and non-sexual bonds between men shared certain structural features, even while the ideology of the time held them apart and contrasted them. This would explain why male friendships might be both reassuring and a focus of anxiety for Conrad in his new literary life. They offered companionship, support and models for a new (to Conrad) way of being a man – through writing – but at the same time drew him into the structures of a modern, urban, British, middle-class masculinity in a condition of crisis, or at the very least transition. In his literary works, Conrad imagines male bonds established far from the corrupting streets of the metropolitan centre, but these narratives obsessively return to that metropolis as repressed origin and final destination.

Those London streets which Conrad paced with Garnett and with Crane also provide a crucial point of reference in 'Karain', *The Nigger of the 'Narcissus'* and *Lord Jim*, functioning in each fiction as the image of a powerful but occluded scene to which the imperial adventure is in some way referred back for its significance, with a sense of irony, nostalgia or loss:

> A watery gleam of sunshine flashed from the west and went out between two long lines of walls; and then the broken confusion of roofs ... The big wheels of hansoms turned slowly along the edge of side-walks; a pale-faced youth strolled, overcome by weariness, by the side of his stick ... a line of yellow boards with blue letters on them approached us slowly, tossing on high behind one another like some queer wreckage adrift upon a river of hats.
>
> (K, 54–5)

> The roar of the town resembled the roar of topping breakers, merciless and strong, with a loud voice and cruel purpose; but overhead the clouds broke; a flood of sunshine streamed down the walls of grimy houses. The dark knot of seamen drifted in sunshine. To the left of them the trees in Tower Gardens sighed, the stones of the Tower gleaming, seemed to stir in the play of light, as if remembering suddenly all the great joys and sorrows of the past, the

fighting prototypes of these men; press-gangs; mutinous cries; the wailing of women by the riverside, and the shouts of men welcoming victories. The sunshine of heaven fell like a gift of grace on the mud of the earth, on the remembering and mute stones, on greed, selfishness; on the anxious faces of forgetful men. And to the right of the dark group the stained front of the Mint, cleansed by the flood of light, stood out for a moment dazzling and white like a marble palace in a fairy tale. The crew of the *Narcissus* drifted out of sight.

(NN, 172)

His rooms were in the highest flat of a lofty building, and his glance could travel afar beyond the clear panes of glass, as though he were looking out of the lantern of a lighthouse. The slopes of the roofs glistened, the dark broken ridges succeeded each other without end like sombre, uncrested waves, and from the depths of the town under his feet ascended a confused and unceasing mutter. The spires of churches, numerous, scattered haphazard, uprose like beacons on a maze of shoals without a channel.

(LJ, 337)

The precise significance of these passages is different in each case, but each has certain features in common. London streets are associated with the noise and chaos of modernity, and are metaphorically compared with a natural world of sea or river with which they are also implicitly contrasted. London is the point from which an imperial narrative is recalled, or to which it returns. In 'Karain' this passage occurs near the end, when two of the European characters, meeting by chance in London some years after the events in the Malay archipelago which the story describes, recall their friend Karain and one of them (Jackson) asks the other (the narrator) whether he believes that the Malay chief's story of ghostly haunting 'really happened' (54). The narrator appeals to the sight of the London streets as evidence against any belief in such supernatural stories, to which Jackson responds, 'Yes; I see it ... It is there; it pants, it runs, it rolls; it is strong and alive; it would smash you if you didn't look out; but I'll be hanged if it is yet as real to me as ... as the other thing ... say, Karain's story' (55). This is followed by an ironic comment from the narrator – 'I think that, decidedly, he had been too long away from home' (55) – with which the story ends. The passage from *The Nigger of the 'Narcissus'* is again near the end, and presents the dispersal of the crew, whose bonds, forged in struggle at sea, acquire an almost mystical value here, transcending, yet about to be dissolved by, the harsh mercantile world of urban modernity. And in *Lord Jim*, the scene is viewed from the room of the 'privileged man' among Marlow's original Eastern narratees (that is, his after-dinner listeners), who alone learns the end of Jim's story, when Marlow sends him a 'thick packet' (337) with documents and narrative.

The inner story of 'Karain: A Memory' (narrated by the warlike Malay chief to the three European men who come to his kingdom to sell him arms) is a story of male bonds betrayed because of a woman, and more specifically because of the erotic power of her appearance. But the act of narration becomes an affirmation of male bonds which partially transcend the (visually emphasized) differences of race. The story Karain tells his European friends begins with a vision of a woman as object of shared male obsession, as Karain and his friend Pata Matara pursue the latter's sister (who has eloped with a Dutchman). Karain recalls that

> He [Matara] spoke of her with fury in the daytime, with sorrow in the dark; he remembered her in health, in sickness. I said nothing; but I saw her every day—always! ... I saw her! I looked at her! She had tender eyes and a ravishing face.
>
> (K, 34)

Karain is baffled by his own feelings, though certain of their strength and their close connection to his male friend:

> Thrice Matara, standing by my side, called aloud her name with grief and imprecations. He stirred my heart. It leaped three times; and three times with the eye of the mind I saw in the gloom within the enclosed space of the prau a woman with streaming hair going away from her land and her people. I was angry—and sorry. Why?
>
> (30)

Karain's evidently sexual obsession is provoked by the desire of other men: although he has himself seen her face, he stresses that he has heard 'all men say' that her beauty is 'extreme' (29). His anger and sorrow are initiated by Matara's cry, while his obsessional 'seeing' of visions of her beauty is provoked by Matara's obsessional speaking of her. A homosocial structure seems to determine the story of Karain, Matara and his sister. The idea of honour which leads Matara to try to kill his sister is evidently an assertion of the commodity status of a marriageable woman: he feels disgraced partly because 'she had been promised to another man' (30). Matara's obsessional pursuit of her suggests the operation of unacknowledged sexual desires within this patriarchal system of control. Karain's desire for Matara's sister might seem to produce a disruption of this attempt violently to enforce patriarchal rights, since it leads him to save her life. However, his action might also be seen as the expression of his desire for his male friend, displaced onto the sister, since the spirit or vision of the sister, which haunts Karain up until the killing of Matara, is then replaced by the ghost of Matara. Perhaps Karain saves Matara's sister because her death would have removed the woman who functioned as object of shared desire, displacing and denying the desire between him and Matara.

The subsequent male bonding between Karain and the three Englishmen, presented as potentially transcending cultural difference, culminates in the scene of narration. This bond is reaffirmed by Hollis as he is about to present Karain with a sixpence, as a magical charm to protect him from the ghost of his murdered friend:

> 'Every one of us,' he said, with pauses that somehow were more offensive than his words—'every one of us, you'll admit, has been haunted by some woman . . . And . . . as to friends . . . dropped by the way . . . Well! . . . ask yourselves . . .'
>
> (47)

This remark oddly shifts what is presented as 'literal' in Karain's story into the metaphorical, so that the supernatural (or neurotic) haunting of Karain by the image of Matara's sister (succeeded by a haunting by Matara's ghost) becomes the colloquial 'haunting' of romantic desire, while Karain's 'dropping' (killing) of his friend becomes a social dropping. This naturalizes obsession and aggression as part of a shared universal masculinity.

The descriptions of Karain during the course of the story are, to borrow a phrase from Richard Dyer's description of a photograph of Humphrey Bogart, 'hysterically phallic'.[19] He is constantly associated with guns, swords, knives, spikes, columns and erect male figures:

> His followers thronged round him; above his head the broad blades of their spears made a spiked halo of iron points, and they hedged him from humanity by the shimmer of silks, the gleam of weapons, the excited and respectful hum of eager voices.
>
> (10)

He snatched the sword from the old man, whizzed it out of the scabbard, and thrust the point into the earth. Upon the thin, upright blade the silver hilt, released, swayed before him like something alive. (18)

Yet this excess of conventional masculinity is also presented as an act or pose, as implied in the following passage:

It was the stage where, dressed splendidly for his part, he strutted, incomparably dignified, made important by the power he had to awaken an absurd expectation of something heroic going to take place—a burst of action or song—upon the vibrating tone of a wonderful sunshine. He was ornate and disturbing, for one could not imagine what depth of horrible void such an elaborate front could be worthy to hide. (6)

This idea of the 'horrible void', combined with Karain's fear of a space behind him, would suggest castration anxiety. This anxiety is partially relieved by the presence of his sword bearer, and also when he enters the privileged world of homosocial exchange on the schooner. Here, as Karain himself puts it, 'he was only a private gentleman coming to see other gentlemen whom he supposed as well born as himself' (12). It is as if Karain is aware of the phallic role which racial difference enables the Englishmen to project onto him. Their patronizing attitude to him as a naive, faintly ridiculous native allows them to indulge vicariously their admiration for his egregiously phallic qualities. In the narration by the unnamed third European who is the first-level narrator of the story, Karain is fetishized as the embodiment of the phallus, yet the suggestions of a masquerade concealing a void suggest simultaneously that his body is marked as castrated. This paradoxical combination can be understood in terms of Steve Neale's argument, quoted in Chapter 1, that the male body 'specified as racially or culturally other' can signify castration and lack, while it can also be fetishized 'inasmuch as it signifies masculinity, and, hence, possession of the phallus, the absence of lack' (SD, 130). As the attitude of the Europeans hesitates between the affirmation of a male bond with Karain and the maintenance of a racial and cultural difference, so his role in their narrative hesitates between fetishization as the phallus and stigmatization as lack. It is in terms of the phallic that the cross-cultural bonding takes place:

We remember the faces, the eyes, the voices ... and we seem to feel the touch of friendly brown hands that, after one short grasp, return to rest on a chased hilt.

(4)

In terms of the phallic, but also in terms of women. Gayle Rubin proposes the complementarity of circulating women and circulating the phallus:

In the cycle of exchange manifested by the Oedipal complex, the phallus passes through the medium of women from one man to another ... women go one way, the phallus the other.

(TW, 192)

Matara's sister facilitates both the homosocial exchange between Karain and Matara and its extension via the act of narration to the Englishmen, in that the story of her beauty becomes a token of exchange between Karain and them. He says that she was 'ravishingly' beautiful, but does not describe that beauty, whereas male bodies are extensively described. In the token-exchange scene, where, in exchange for the story of a beautiful woman Karain receives the image of a powerful woman (Queen Victoria) in the form of a coin, the male body is eroticized and aestheticized through this same tension between shared maleness and cultural or racial difference:

One must have seen his innate splendour, one must have known him before—looked at him then .... His dark head and bronze torso appeared above the tarnished slab of wood, gleaming and still as if cast in metal.

(26–7)

They looked close into one another's eyes. Those of Karain stared in a lost glance, but Hollis's seemed to grow darker and looked out masterful and compelling. They were in violent contrast together— one motionless and the colour of bronze, the other dazzling white and lifting his arms, where the powerful muscles rolled slightly under a skin that gleamed like satin. Jackson moved near with the air of a man closing up to a chum in a tight place.

(50)

We have earlier been told that Karain was obsessed with Queen

Victoria and it is suggested that he associated her with his own mother, a powerful Malay ruler. Victoria is specifically described by Hollis as commanding the spirit of British imperialism.

Karain, like Dain in *Almayer's Folly*, appears as a figure of heightened or 'pure' masculinity, a masculinity to which he has access by reason of his 'primitive' or 'half-savage' freedom from the trammels of modernity. Yet the hollowness of this exoticist fantasy, which, according to Chris Bongie, Conrad comes to recognize (*EM*, 20), is foreshadowed in the ominous sense of vacancy, lack, void and masquerade haunting such figures of ideal masculinity. Like the ending which returns to the London streets, the beginning of 'Karain', which presents the whole story as a memory, suggests that modernity haunts even this fantasy of the exotic. The opening paragraph contains a filmic 'dissolve' from the physical eye to the eye of the mind (of memory):[20]

> I am sure that the few who survive are not yet so dim-eyed as to miss in the befogged respectability of their newspapers the intelligence of various native risings in the Eastern Archipelago. Sunshine gleams between the lines of those short paragraphs—sunshine and the glitter of the sea. A strange name wakes up memories; the printed words scent the smoky atmosphere of today faintly, with the subtle and penetrating perfume as of land breezes breathing through the starlight of bygone nights.
>
> (3)

This retrospective aspect of 'Karain', identified in its subtitle ('A Memory'), indicates that it is written and narrated from the position of a modern, urban, 'civilized' masculinity, which no longer has access to such a heroic destiny as that of Karain. Furthermore, the mention of the lines of print introduces an element of self-conscious (and self-referential) textuality. The dual nature of the symbolic representation of Karain (as pure untrammelled masculinity and void masquerade) is no more than a projection back and away into an imagined past and an imagined exotic scene, of the dilemmas and uncertainties of the imperial subject. For this reason I would want to add a caution to Cedric Watts's claim (in an essay which usefully explores the mythic role of London in Conrad's work) that at the end of 'Karain', 'the predominantly pejorative notion of the "monstrous town" can be deployed in a way that usefully complicates a familiar Victorian colonialist view of exotic races'.[21] It does indeed complicate the most simple and crude colonialist view (one which merely valorizes the 'civilized' over the 'primitive'), but does so only by employing the imagined exotic Other as mirror for the complications of Western masculinity.

In *The Nigger of the 'Narcissus'*, the gender binary is largely excluded by the shipboard setting (though it appears in the form of supposedly feminine or masculine qualities within men). At the same time binaries of race and of class are exaggerated, the former in the interests of a symbolic deployment of Wait's 'blackness' as part of an incoherent existential and psychological parable, the latter in the service of a reactionary depiction of the future labour organizer, Donkin, as motivated by base *ressentiment*. As Jim Reilly observes, Donkin is treated with an 'absurd, spluttering invective' which Conrad reserves for characters with socialist ideas.[22] These manoeuvres produce a text which, for all its fineness of description and evocation, is marred at times by a sense of the author's ideological thumb pressing on the scales. As Fredric Jameson puts it, 'these two strategies – *ressentiment* and existentializing metaphysics – allow Conrad to recontain his narrative and to rework it in melodramatic terms, in a subsystem of good and evil which now once again has villains and heroes' (*PU*, 216). Elements of the treatment of masculinity are of interest, such as the curious passion of Belfast. Belfast's devotion to the dying black sailor Jimmy renders the former 'as gentle as a woman, as tenderly gay as an old philanthropist, as sentimentally careful of his nigger as a model slave-owner' (140), a series of comparisons which begins with what might be admiration but ends in what must surely be irony. This devotion also includes obsessive aggression towards others, 'a blow for any one who did not seem to take a scrupulously orthodox view of Jimmy's case' (140). Conrad's depiction of Belfast's behaviour seems a satire on that form of sentimental male protectiveness (usually directed towards women) which serves to justify violence and aggression. This is all too familiar from postwar cinema, where the vulnerability of women or children routinely provides a moral screen for the celebration of 'heroic' violence. One might gloss it by the psychoanalytical observation that sentimentality is a denial or repression of aggression and therefore complementary to it.

By and large, however, the commitment of *The Nigger of the 'Narcissus'* to a parable of the value of a hierarchical society contains and limits the interest of its treatment of masculinity. Geoffrey Galt Harpham reads the story, along with many other Conrad texts, in terms of homoerotic suggestion, finding it full of words with slang

sexual meanings. He persuasively relates this effect to Conrad's relationship to English: 'Conrad makes "mistakes" by failing to perform
the kind of "screening" that is performed more or less effortlessly by
native speakers.'[23] Thus for Harpham the absence of women in the
story enables rather than removes the representation of sexuality. He
argues that 'in a monosexual and presumptively ascetic environment, Conrad's sexual imagination becomes extravagant, complex,
and rich; he becomes capable of conceiving of satisfactions unthink-
able with a women in the vicinity.'[24] In his reading of the story
Harpham rightly corrects Tony Tanner's naive suggestion that 'no
women' means 'no desire' in sea stories.[25] However, Harpham seems
content to accept an existential reading of Wait as 'a universal mirror
in whom everyone sees himself' and as 'a human instance or form of
the sea', echoing Conrad's own claim that Wait 'is nothing; he is
merely the centre of the ship's collective psychology and the pivot
of the action'.[26] As Scott McCracken accurately observes, Conrad's
comment

> Is an example of how Conrad effectively writes out a presence
> which is central to the text ... This writing an absence dehistoricizes
> the relationship between black sailors and white. The text
> constructs a white discourse in which being is expressed in exis-
> tential terms and not as part of a historical narrative, and that
> being is the subjectivity of a white masculinity.[27]

Harpham deals interestingly with sexuality but neglects the interaction of race and gender, and especially the politics of representing a
black man as merely a 'pivot' or 'mirror'. In *The Nigger of the
'Narcissus'*, Conrad is feeling his way towards the use of mediating
narrators, a device which emerges fully in *Lord Jim*. In the former work
the narrator's role is uncertain and inconsistent. As Jeremy Hawthorn
argues, the book exhibits 'a narrative indecision that stems from ideological contradictions and uncertainties' (*NT*, 102):

> From the earliest reviews of the novella mention has been made of
> the fact that the work appears to have a single narrator who mainly
> adopts the viewpoint and perspective of an ordinary crew-member
> ... but who sometimes sounds more like an officer and who even
> becomes omniscient on a number of occasions [giving us access to
> private thoughts and conversations] ... There are, too, regular shifts
> between the narrative use of 'we' and 'they' to refer to the crew ...

and in the final four pages of the work the narrator becomes, for
the first time, 'I'.

(*NT*, 104–5)

The technique in which the act of narrating itself figures and prob-
lematizes male bonds has not yet clearly emerged.

In *Lord Jim* the principal male bond evoked is explicitly a professional
code in an idealized form, identified by Marlow when he claims Jim as
'one of us' (78). This bond implicates gender and race in that the code is
associated exclusively with European males (officers in the merchant
marine), an 'insignificant multitude' in the 'ranks' of which Marlow is
'keeping [his] place' while Jim is a 'straggler' (334). This bond is sancti-
fied by moments of male intimacy which transcend professionalism and
reach uneasily for the metaphysical: 'There was a moment of real and
profound intimacy, unexpected and short-lived like a glimpse of some
everlasting, of some saving truth' (241). In *Lord Jim* racial otherness is
less foregrounded than in the early Malay fiction because of the intensity of the focus on Marlow and Jim, though Jim's relationship with
Jewel brings it to the fore in the later part of the novel. Implicitly, it is
important throughout, as in the exoticizing and aestheticizing description of the pilgrims on the *Patna*: 'in the blurred circles of light thrown
down and trembling slightly to the unceasing vibration of the ship
appeared a chin upturned, two closed eyelids, a dark hand with silver
rings, a meagre limb draped in a torn covering' (18). Most crucially there
is an emphasis on Jim's literal and symbolic 'whiteness'. This reaches
greatest intensity in Marlow's two partings with him, each of which sets
his whiteness against a contrasting racial other, creating overtones of
imagined racial purity. When Jim first sets off for Patusan, Jim's whiteness is set off against a routinely derogatory portrait of a 'half-caste':

My eyes were too dazzled by the glitter of the sea below his feet to
see him clearly; I am fated never to see him clearly; but I can assure
you no man could have appeared less 'in the similitude of a corpse,'
as that half-caste croaker had put it. I could see the little wretch's
face, the shape and colour of a ripe pumpkin, poked out somewhere
under Jim's elbow.

(241)

Later, Marlow's last sight of him on leaving Patusan, as 'only a speck,
a tiny white speck, that seemed to catch all the light left in a darkened
world', is similarly provided with a foil in the form of 'two half-naked

fishermen ... pouring the plaint of their trifling, miserable, oppressed lives into the ears of the white lord':

> Their dark-skinned bodies vanished on the dark background long before I had lost sight of their protector. He was white from head to foot, and remained persistently visible with the stronghold of the night at his back.
>
> (336)

These partings are both moments of emotional intensity for Marlow, moments when the bond between him and Jim is intensified by the poignancy of separation, giving rise to the sense of 'profound intimacy' cited above.

Jim's life is the product of the imperial export of masculinity. Inspired by the popular literature of imperial exoticism, it is made possible by the existence of imperial trade and commerce. The relationship to 'home', an England to which he will never return, is central to Jim's ego-ideal. This becomes apparent to Marlow when Jim invokes the need to 'keep in touch with ... those whom, perhaps, I shall never see any more' (including, as he says, Marlow himself, but also implicitly his family at home) (334). Marlow imagines the importance of this link as he reads a letter from Jim's father (342), and he also enacts it through his narration by letter to the 'privileged man' 'at home' (337). As in 'Karain' the story is framed from London, the heart of empire, except that here London figures not as the end of the text itself, but as the location of the intra-textual reading of its end. Only one man among Marlow's listeners in the East 'was ever to hear the last word of the story' (337), and he hears it (or rather, reads it) back home in London. This privileged narratee is also explicitly an advocate of white supremacy, and Marlow associates this belief with the 'ranks' which consecrate his bond with Jim. In the following passage Marlow addresses the unnamed reader of his letter:

> You said also—I call to mind—that 'giving your life up to them' (*them* meaning all of mankind with skins brown, yellow, or black in colour) 'was like selling your soul to a brute.' You contended that 'that kind of thing' was only endurable and enduring when based on a firm conviction in the truth of ideas racially our own, in whose name are established the order, the morality of an ethical progress. 'We want its strength at our backs,' you had said. 'We want a belief in its necessity and its justice, to make a worthy and

conscious sacrifice of our lives. Without it the sacrifice is only forgetfulness, the way of offering is no better than the way to perdition.' In other words, you maintained that we must fight in the ranks or our lives don't count.

(339)

This is clearly recognizable as a version of the redemptive 'idea' behind colonialism which Marlow evokes near the start of 'Heart of Darkness', only to break off when his own metaphor ('something you can set up, and bow down before, and offer a sacrifice to ....' (HOD, 51)) reminds him of Kurtz. The more explicitly racist views of the 'privileged man' are not ironized in this subtle way, though neither are they endorsed, either by Marlow or the implied author. Rather than pausing to reflect on the moral implications of this position, the Marlow of *Lord Jim* seeks to set Jim apart from such service in the 'ranks':

Possibly! ... The point, however, is that of all mankind Jim had no dealings but with himself, and the question is whether at the last he had not confessed to a faith mightier than the laws of order and progress.

(339)

This view of Jim is at odds with Marlow's sense of him as 'one of us', a point to which I shall return shortly. Whatever the hesitation in Marlow's account between a vision of Jim as a member, albeit a straggler, in the 'ranks' of imperial progress, and a vision of him as a transcendently individual tragic hero, the bond between Marlow and Jim is interwoven with the imperial project and with ideas of racial identification. Furthermore, this is emphasized in the extension of that bond, via the act of narration, to the 'privileged man', and hence to the implied reader. It is this strategy, of projecting and exploring male bonds via the processes of narration, that is central to Conrad's representation of masculinity in the Marlow fictions (*Lord Jim*, 'Heart of Darkness', *Youth*, *Chance*), as well as in *Under Western Eyes*.

In *Lord Jim*, then, there are two versions of 'home'. One is the quasi-idyllic, insular, rural world of Jim's father the 'good old parson', 'equably trusting Providence and the established order of the universe' (341), in a 'quiet corner of the world as free of danger or strife as a tomb' (342). Marlow's attitude to this world is a mixture of sentiment and irony, but the heterodiegetic narrator of the first four chapters is more unequivocally ironic about the parson's social role as part of the ideological state apparatus of religion:[28] 'Jim's father possessed such certain knowledge of the Unknowable as made for the righteousness of people in cottages without disturbing the ease of mind of those whom an unerring Providence enables to live in mansions' (5). The other vision of home in the novel is the London where the end of Jim's story is read, the slightly sinister, modern, urban world of the crowd.

I have suggested a structure in which the crisis of masculinity at home operates as the unconscious of the imperial novel. This might involve the newly problematic binaries of gender being replaced (via a turn to the imperial setting) with an alternative, and seemingly more secure binary between dangerous otherness abroad (confronted via adventure) and a seemingly safe, stable home of moral values. Another version, as in Haggard, involves a rediscovery of triumphant 'primitive' masculinity through exoticizing adventure, critiquing and rejecting a home which has lost its masculine vigour.[29] In Conrad the impulse to simplify 'home' as a place of secure identity and values is present, but his own cultural and personal history and his sense of epistemological relativism does not allow Conrad to sustain this fiction. The satirical treatment of the parson as an ideologist of class domination conflicts with Marlow's presentation of him as a locus of stable, if insular, values and infects it to the extent that, even for Marlow, these values are somewhat deathly ('as a tomb' (342)). Furthermore the visions of the chaos of London streets and the threatening crowd of modernity suggest the repressed unconscious of imperial discourse: the crises and transformations of class and gender relations in Britain.

In René Girard's model of mediated or triangular desire, desire is prompted by the imitation of another's desire (the mediator). He distinguishes between external mediation, as in *Don Quixote* and *Madame Bovary*, where the mediator is sufficiently distant not to be a rival, and internal mediation, as in *Le Rouge et le Noir*, where the mediator is close enough to be seen as a rival, and hence is both the model for desire and the obstacle to its fulfilment. Denial is essential to the structure of internal mediation:

> In the quarrel which puts him in opposition to his rival, the subject reverses the logical and chronological order of desires in order to hide his imitation. He asserts that his own desire is prior to that of his rival; according to him, it is the mediator who is responsible for the rivalry.
>
> (*DD*, 11)

When Marlow suggests to the 'privileged man' that Jim 'had no dealings but with himself', he represses the mediated nature of Jim's
desires. Though he correctly identifies Jim's egotism here, he forgets
the dependence of that egotism on imagined others. These include
both the others at home and in the merchant service to whose
approval Jim ultimately looks, and the Others of Patusan whose
destiny Jim seeks to shape. Marlow's forgetfulness of the former is all
the more surprising in that in his next paragraph he recounts Jim's
final, abortive, verbal message, 'Tell them! ...' (339) followed by 'No.
Nothing' (340). Jim's desire for 'that opportunity which, like an
Eastern bride, had come veiled to his side' (416) is thoroughly mediated, beginning, like that of Don Quixote and Madame Bovary, with
external mediation via literature. Jim shares the goal of Flaubert's
protagonists, to 'see themselves as they are not'.[30] Jim would seem to
fit well the category of the 'romantic *vaniteux*', who

> does not want to be anyone's disciple. He convinces himself that he
> is thoroughly *original*. In the nineteenth century spontaneity
> becomes a universal dogma, succeeding imitation. Stendhal warns
> us at every step that we must not be fooled by these individualisms
> professed with fanfares, for they merely hide a new form of imita-
> tion. Romantic revulsion, hatred of society, nostalgia for the desert,
> just as gregariousness, usually conceal a morbid concern for the
> Other.
>
> (*DD*,15)

This comment, as applicable to Kurtz and Nostromo as to Jim,
points up the limits of Conrad's understanding of his own protagonists. Unrivalled perhaps in his charting of the envy, hatred,
self-hatred and sense of impotence which accompany the almost
inevitable thwarting of mediated desire, Conrad often succumbs
nevertheless to the romantic myth of originality and transcendence
(in tragic, doomed form), as the endings of *Lord Jim*, 'Heart of
Darkness' and *Nostromo* show. As Girard suggests, it is modernity, with
its reduction of firm hierarchical differences, that causes internal
mediation to triumph (*DD*, 14). That same modernity, as Bongie
shows, generates exoticism.
   What is the relationship between Girard's Other, who mediates,
stimulates and frustrates the desire of the subject, and the racialized
Other of imperialism? Jim's initial model is the white imperial subject,
presented to him as external mediator through adventure literature,

'saving people from sinking ships, cutting away masts in a hurricane ... confront[ing] savages on tropical shores' (6). On the training ship, he acquires an internal mediator and rival, in the form of the boy who rescues two men from the sea. Jim denies this rivalry and his desire to emulate the boy, deluding himself that he feels contempt for the very quality of vanity which he is strengthening in himself:

> Jim thought it a pitiful display of vanity. The gale had ministered to a heroism as spurious as its own pretence of terror. He felt angry with the brutal tumult of earth and sky for taking him unawares and checking unfairly a generous readiness for narrow escapes. Otherwise he was rather glad he had not gone into the cutter, since a lower achievement had served the turn. He had enlarged his knowledge more than those who had done the work ... He could detect no trace of emotion in himself ... he exulted with fresh certitude in his avidity for adventure, and in a sense of many-sided courage.
>
> (9)

Following the devastating blow to his self-image dealt by Jim's jump from the *Patna*, Marlow and Stein become crucial figures for Jim; they become the mediators of his desire insofar as they offer role models. Yet the more dominant aspect of the bond between these men is rather the vicariousness identification which Marlow and Stein feel in respect of Jim's heroic ambitions.[31] Jim is at once the straggler and the leader, the failure in need of redemption and the ultimate embodiment of the adventure hero. The suppressed mediator of Jim's newly formed desires in Patusan is the racially other male leader, the (imagined) tribal chief with his prestige and almost magic power, whose role Jim seeks to fill, both politically as leader and sexually with Jewel. The other, marked or imagined as racial Other, provides a model/mediator of desire who is particularly exciting because of the transgression of boundaries which such imitation involves, and particularly denied and deniable *as* model because the ideology of racial difference offers a barrier, a way of disclaiming identification. For Jim, and via him for Marlow and Stein, the wish to be the Other can be indulged under the sign of racial difference, precisely because that sign disallows the identification as beyond the pale. This process is more obviously operative in 'Heart of Darkness', where the identification comes closer to being acknowledged, and as it does so generates a rhetoric of the unspeakable, the imperial sublime of horror. There is a moment in *Lord Jim* when the identification with the Other is glimpsed, in the very moment of the imagined return 'home':

> Here they all are, evoked by the mild gossip of the father, all these brothers and sisters ... gazing with clear unconscious eyes, while I seem to see him, returned at last, no longer a mere white speck at the heart of an immense mystery, but of full stature, standing disregarded amongst their untroubled shapes, with a stern and romantic aspect, but always mute, dark—under a cloud.
>
> (342)

No longer white but dark, Jim is able at last, in Marlow's fantasy, to return from the imperial scene to the domestic, in a microcosm of the process by which London becomes the heart of darkness in 'Heart of Darkness', and its streets the dark imperial centre in *The Secret Agent*. The return home is the return of the repressed. Revealing, as Bivona argues, that imperialism is the unconscious of 'domestic' England, Conrad simultaneously reveals the crisis of male identity at home as the unconscious of the myth of imperial adventure. Significantly, it is a written text (Jim's father's letter) which provokes Marlow's vision of a dark Jim returned home. Conrad finds a way of exploring the process of male rivalry, of denied identification with the Other, by setting up a sequence of mediating structures in the form of narrative technique. Marlow's desire is mediated by Jim (in 'Heart of Darkness' Kurtz mediates Marlow's desire, while in *Chance* both Captain Anthony and Powell play such a role in relation to Marlow). In turn the desire of narratees (the 'privileged man' in *Lord Jim*, and listeners on the boat in 'Heart of Darkness') is mediated by Marlow. The next step in this sequence is the implied reader. The gains of this technique in terms of subtlety and an embodying of the structure of male desire in the structures of narrative (and the processes of narrative desire) are accompanied by a limitation: a tendency to specify the implied reader as male.

Both of the theorists whose models I have employed here – Girard and Sedgwick, whose work took Girard as a starting-point – deploy economic models of desire, in the sense that they consider it in terms of structures of exchange and substitution. The idea of economies (that is, systems of exchange) is helpful in understanding some of the conflicts and aspirations in Conrad's fiction. Imperialism is, arguably, driven by economic forces. One might of course describe it in psychological terms, as driven by the will to power, in social terms, as determined by the desire for the Other, or in ideological terms, as fuelled by the ideologies of rational progress and religion. However, any account of nineteenth-century and early twentieth-century imperialism is likely to acknowledge the centrality of the exchange of money and goods, and the activities of manufacture and trade. Conrad's fiction inhabits this sphere but wishes to rise above it by discovering some existential or spiritual truth (however bleak) within the processes of empire. Since the spiritual, for Conrad, is always tentative and elusive, never a matter of firm religious faith, we can reasonably identify this aspiration as an aspiration to an existential revelation: to some condition of being, or of being human (perhaps of being a man) which exceeds the mundane and even degrading terms of economic exchange.

An essentialist view of masculinity becomes increasingly unsustainable for Conrad in the light of his own scepticism about identity and the human will. Thus in *Almayer's Folly* and *An Outcast of the Islands*, Conrad's demolition of human delusions of power, vanity and ambition generates, almost as a by-product, a seemingly fragile masculinity, inhabited by the death drive rather than a heroic will. Conrad attempts to discover a more valorized and powerful essential masculinity within the other realm of the exotic (in 'Karain') or the enclosed and retrospective shipboard world of the Narcissus. However, this collapses on contact with the urban modernity to which the narrative must return (and which is its repressed origin and motivation). Faced with the collapse of existential models of masculinity, Conrad seeks to rescue the economic model of masculinity from mere instrumentality in the project of empire by reinventing it as a literary and textual economy. Like Conrad's biographical relations with male literary friends, the textual exchange of knowledge, desire, language and above all stories in his fictional texts serves to affirm a set of male bonds that operate within the structures of modernity and empire while articulating the desire for a shared meaning before or beyond those structures. The figure of Marlow plays a crucial role in the establishment of these bonds in *Lord Jim*, while the bonds receive a more definitive delineation in the (contemporaneously written) 'Heart of Darkness', where the association of male bonds with darkness and the exclusion of women is made more explicit.[32] Chapter 5 will explore those bonds and that exclusion as part of a consideration of the relationship of masculinity to truth and knowledge. First, however, Chapters 3 and 4 will address masculinity in more material terms, via the body.

3
Masculinity and the Body:
Typhoon, The Secret Agent

The first sentence of Conrad's story 'Typhoon' informs us that 'Captain MacWhirr, of the steamer *Nan-Shan*, had a physiognomy that, in the order of material appearances, was the exact counterpart of his mind' (T, 3). This description not only attributes meaning to the body, but seems to heal the mind–body split by making the body the exact correlate or transparent signifier for the mind. We are then given eight sentences of detailed physical description, as if MacWhirr's body were the key fact about the story to follow. However, this description immediately creates problems for the opening claim of transparent correspondence. For one thing, what his face accurately reveals about his mind is, specifically, nothing in particular, since it

> presented no marked characteristics of firmness or stupidity; it had no pronounced characteristics whatever; it was simply ordinary, irresponsive, and unruffled.
>
> (3)

Furthermore, the very details of Conrad's description seem a challenge to the reader's ingenuity. For example MacWhirr has hair on his face which 'resembled a growth of copper wire clipped short to the line of the lip ... no matter how close he shaved, fiery metallic gleams passed, when he moved his head, over the surface of his cheeks' (3). If his physiognomy is the exact counterpart of his mind, then what mental attribute corresponds to fiery gleams passing over the surface of his cheeks? Lively romantic imagination or fiery passions might come to mind, but these are precisely the qualities which MacWhirr lacks to an exaggerated and comic extent, since this is a portrait of a man whose strengths and weaknesses are the result of a total lack of imagination.

On the first page, then, Conrad explicitly evokes the meaningful, expressive body. At the same time he renders that expressivity problematic so as to suggest the idea of the body which exceeds or eludes meaning.

This paradox corresponds to tensions in recent theorizing of the body. These are tensions between an emphasis on the body as a privileged symbolic domain, a site where social meanings are inscribed, and an emphasis on the body as that which has been left out or repressed by the discourses of Western rationality. The body has been a significant area of investigation in recent literary and cultural theory, a tendency which can be traced primarily to feminist ideas of 'writing the body' or *écriture féminine*, and to the work of Michel Foucault. *Écriture féminine* implies a two-way link between body and writing, including as it does both the idea of the body as imprinting itself upon text or speech, and the idea of the expressive body itself as written upon, or imprinted with meaning. In Cixous's celebratory account of a woman speaking at a public gathering these two are interwoven and even indistinguishable: the woman is described as both speaking from her body and inscribing what she says upon it:

> She throws her trembling body forward ... all of her passes into her voice, and it's with her body that she vitally supports the 'logic' of her speech. Her flesh speaks true. She lays herself bare. In fact, she physically materializes what she's thinking; she signifies it with her body. In a certain way she *inscribes* what she's saying, because she doesn't deny her drives the intractable and impassioned part they have in speaking.[1]

But the antithetical idea of the body as eluding meaning is also present in the relationship of *écriture féminine* to 'the unnameable', as in Cixous's claim that 'it will always surpass the discourse that regulates the phallocentric system'.[2] The work of Foucault tends to emphasize the body as written upon by institutions and discourses, and as an object of power.[3] He does, however, regard the body as potentially resistant to power as well as subservient to it. He has commented that 'power, after investing itself in the body, finds itself exposed to a counter-attack in that same body'.[4] Jane Gallop argues that the body has been left out or repressed by Western rationalistic discourse, and comments that 'rather than treat the body as a site of knowledge, a medium for thought, the more classical [male European] philosophical project has tried to render it transparent and get beyond

it, to dominate it by reducing it to the mind's idealizing categories'.[5]
But Foucault emphatically denies the notion that it has been
repressed:

> First of all one must set aside the widely held thesis that power, in
> our bourgeois, capitalist, societies has denied the reality of the body
> in favour of the soul, consciousness, ideality. In fact nothing is
> more material, physical, corporal than the exercise of power.[6]

Stallybrass and White regard the body as particularly important to the
ordering of social meaning. They demonstrate that 'the high/low
opposition in each of our four symbolic domains – psychic forms, the
human body, geographical space and the social order – is a fundamental basis to mechanisms of ordering and sense-making in
European cultures' (*PPT*, 3) and that 'discourses about the body have
a privileged role, for transcodings between different levels and sectors
of social and psychic reality are effected through the intensifying grid
of the body' (*PPT*, 26). Any attempt at a generalized theoretical
synthesis or reconciliation of such theories may be of limited useful-
ness. To answer questions about meaning and the body one has to be
specific: about historical context, about which bodies, which
discourses. For example, anthropology, unlike sociology, has paid
great attention to the body ever since the nineteenth century, partly
because anthropology is generally concerned with other societies, and
the body of the Other is more readily given meaning.[7] A comparable
process can be detected in the discourses of Western literature, art,
medicine, science and law: the Other bodies of women, the working
class, the 'degenerate', the criminal, have been the subject of attention
but the bodily existence of the dominant middle-class and upper-class
white male has been elided in favour of an emphasis on the power of
his mind and will.

Thus the body tends to occupy a paradoxical situation in relation to
meaning. It seems that desire and power in various ways are always
trying to lay hold of the body, to place meaning upon it, or to extract
meaning from it, yet in philosophical terms the body in some way
seems to elude discursive meaning. There are two obvious reasons for
this. The first is that attempts to consider the relation of body and text
take place mostly within texts (for an alternative, one might need to
turn to performance art). The second is that the writer always has a
body, which is always doing things other than writing. One's own
body is too close to ignore but also too close to see clearly: as

Stallybrass and White observe, in thinking the body 'adequate conception founders upon the problematic familiarity, the enfolding intimacy, of its domain' (*PPT*, 28). Rosi Braidotti summarizes the conception of the body arising out of the dialogue of feminism, psychoanalysis and poststructuralist theory:

> The body ... cannot be reduced to the biological, nor can it be confined to social conditioning ... the body is seen as an inter-face, a threshold, a field of intersection of material and symbolic forces; it is a surface where multiple codes of power and knowledge are inscribed; it is a construction that transforms and capitalizes on energies of a heterogeneous and discontinuous nature. The body is not an essence ... it is one's primary location in the world.[8]

In considering the role of the body in Conrad's representation and construction of masculinity, I will refer to a number of these aspects: in particular, to the material and the symbolic, and to power, knowledge and inscription. In 'Typhoon' men's individual bodies, and bodies of men (the officers, the crew, the Chinese passengers) are engaged in strenuous physical struggles within the body of a ship. How does the materiality of body, ship and storm interact with symbolic meanings (the storm as symbol of life or of the unknowable) in endorsing or unsettling normative ideas of masculinity and the male body? In *The Secret Agent*, does the physical destruction of the marginally masculine body of Stevie inscribe or circumscribe male power in a bureaucratic, alienated modern urban society? Nostromo discovers that his physical prowess and macho heroism, which seem to give him power, only make him the passive victim of larger structures of economic and political power. How does this reflect on the place of the male body in structures of power?

The usage 'the body' is of course open to question on at least two grounds. By seeming to refer to an abstract essence, or at the very least announcing a 'concept', it risks dematerializing and homogenizing just at the moment when the issues of the materiality and variety of bodies are introduced.[9] Furthermore, in its implicit singularity and unity it may be thought to reproduce masculinist modes of thinking.[10] However, Pamela Banting argues that 'nominal pluralizing' (changing 'the body' to 'bodies', 'woman' to 'women', 'feminism' to 'feminisms', etc.), is merely essentialism 'spelled "differently"'.[11] To reject the use of 'the body' would, I believe, be limiting, but it should be used with an awareness of the risks of generalization. The problem of abstracting the physical can similarly only really be dealt with (within discourse) by a combination of overall awareness and tactical attempts to notice what might be being lost or left out of account.

A certain contradiction appears in accounts of the degree of visibility of the male body in modern Western discourses. Much theorizing about the construction of normative masculinity emphasizes an estrangement from the body. Cixous states that 'Men still have everything to say about their sexuality ... Conquering her [woman], they've made haste to depart from her borders, to get out of sight, out of body.'[12] Rosalind Coward argues that 'it is in reality men's bodies, men's sexuality, which is the true "dark continent" of this society'.[13] Jane Gallop suggests that 'men have their masculine identity to gain by being estranged from their bodies and dominating the bodies of others.'[14] Clearly such statements need historical inflection. Recent studies of masculinity in the Victorian period have found extensive use of bodily metaphor and representations of the male body used to construct, defend or vary ideas of maleness. Herbert Sussman finds in a number of literary, philosophical and aesthetic texts of the period, as well as in the visual arts, conceptions of male desire based on hydraulic metaphors of fluidity, flow and eruption, linked to ideas of the seminal but also of pollution, so that there is a perceived need for containment or channelling of such energy.[15] Christine Buci-Glucksmann argues (as summarized by Mary Ann Doane) that, in the late nineteenth century,

> the male seems to lose access to the body, which the woman then comes to *overrepresent*. The 'working body' is 'confiscated by the alienation of machines' and 'submitted to industrialization and urbanization'. At the same time, in a compensatory gesture, the woman is made to inhere even more closely to the body.[16]

Conrad's life placed him in an unusual relationship to such alienation. The role of officer in the merchant navy remained one in which physical labour was compatible with middle-class status, and in which it was possible to feel a certain distance from 'industrialization and urbanization'. This distance is thematized in *Lord Jim* in the description of Jim 'in the fore-top' (*LJ*, 6), looking down with the contempt of a romantic hero at the roofs and factory chimneys of urban modernity (6).[17] In an essay on 'Ocean Travel', Conrad mourns the impact of machine technology (in the form of steamships) as a loss of 'the vast solitude of the sea untroubled by the sound of the world's mechanical contrivances'.[18]

Partly in response to the alienation which Buci-Glucksmann describes, the male body became a focus of aesthetic and political programmes for many modernist writers, a point made by John Fletcher in a study of E. M. Forster's *Maurice*:

> The motif of the thinking body that bypasses a debilitating intel-
> lectuality is characteristic of radical literary theories of the period –
> Forster's own 'flesh educating the spirit'; Yeats's 'unity of being';
> T.S. Eliot's 'unified sensibility' that experiences an idea as immedi-
> ately as the odour of a rose; D.H. Lawrence's 'sympathetic solar
> plexus' opposed to mental consciousness.[19]

Many studies of masculinity concur in suggesting that the masculine body is, normatively, impermeable, hard, active, and that ideas of penetration into the male body, of the fluidity or the softness of its insides, are repressed or provoke anxiety. Cixous suggests that such anxiety cuts men off from the form of 'writing' which is open to otherness:

> 'Today, writing is woman's ... woman admits there is an other ... It
> is much harder for man to let the other come through him. Writing
> is the passageway, the entrance, the exit, the dwelling place of the
> other in me ... for men this permeability, this nonexclusion is a
> threat, something intolerable.[20]

The emphasis on borders, boundaries and control has wider social and political significance, as suggested by Carole Pateman's observation that women have often been perceived as 'potential disruptors of masculine boundary systems of all sorts', an idea developed by Elaine Showalter who sees the crisis of masculine identity at the end of the nineteenth century in terms of threats to established borders.[21] Showalter, in her study of the *fin de siècle*, notes that 'there were few overt cultural fantasies about the insides of *men's* bodies, and opening up the *man* was not a popular image', going on to argue that 'men do not think of themselves as cases to be opened up. Instead, they open up a woman as a substitute for self-knowledge.'[22] Tim Armstrong suggests that in modernist aesthetics, we see 'states of interiority coded as "feminine" succumbing to a "masculine" intervention seen as "surgical"'.[23] Both penetration of the male body and permeability to its own products seem threatening: Christine Battersby notes the idea that 'the repressed of masculine consciousness might be the sense of the "flowing out and away" of ejaculated bodily substances', so that 'the boundaries of normal male selves are secured against flowing out'.[24] Sussman's account of the dominance of metaphors of fluidity and flow would modify but on the whole support such a view, since the fear of pollution and need for control which he identifies might be seen as indicative of the work of repression. Such accounts of the male body imply that in the discourses and practices of modern Western culture, masculinity has been produced, reproduced and modified through the foregrounding of certain aspects of the male body and the repression of other aspects, and that the repressed aspects have often been those most stressed in relation to women's bodies, in a process of projective denial. I want to suggest that these repressed aspects – specifically abjection, hysteria and the grotesque – return to haunt and unsettle masculinity in 'Typhoon' and *The Secret Agent*. Each represents a model of the relationship of the body to meaning and the meaningless.

The fear of pollution and ejaculated substances suggested by Battersby would imply a special relationship to the Kristevan abject. The abject – literally that which is cast off, cast down, thrown away, rejected – is for Kristeva a product of the process of infantile self-formation, and is distinguished from the object, although both are opposed to 'I', to the emergent sense of identity. The object opposes the self, but as a correlative of the self, allowing the self to feel detached and autonomous by providing it with someone or something else to relate to. The object, through its opposition to the self 'settles me within the fragile texture of a desire for meaning'. The abject, on the other hand, provokes desire mixed with repulsion; it is 'radically excluded and draws me toward the place where meaning collapses'.[25] The abject is associated with defilement and death; Kristeva describes it as a 'border' and comments that 'refuse and corpses *show me* what I permanently thrust aside in order to live. These body fluids, this defilement, this shit are what life withstands.'[26] Kaja Silverman offers an account of the role of the abject in the construction of such a masculinity:

> Through a symmetrical gesture to that whereby the child 'finds' its 'own' voice by introjecting the mother's voice, the male subject subsequently 'refines' his 'own' voice by projecting onto the mother's voice all that is unassimilable to the paternal position ... the boundaries of male subjectivity must be constantly redrawn

through the externalizing displacement onto the female subject of what Kristeva would call the 'abject' ... whereas the mother's voice initially functions as the acoustic mirror in which the child discovers its identity and voice, it later functions as the acoustic mirror in which the male subject hears all the repudiated elements of his infantile babble.[27]

One might detect elements of such infantile babble in the hesitating, excited speech of Stevie (whose relationship to masculinity is problematic). Babble is also suggestive of hysteria, a concept with a highly gendered history, having a special place in nineteenth- and early twentieth-century conceptions of femininity.[28] While some feminists have criticized the use of the concept, others have sought to revalue it in terms of resistance to social constraint.[29] Pamela Banting seeks to account for the seeming paradox that the body is both highly subjected to discourse and seemingly resistant to it:

Although the body is discursively and socially constructed, its materiality allows it also to elude in some measure the totalizing effects of such meaning ... As material substance, that is, as non-name and nonsense, the body resists and displaces the official order which it acquires along with its native tongue ... As flesh, the body is both vulnerable and resistant to languages, discourses and social constructions. And in both its vulnerability and its resistance, the body writes back ... it is not only in its resistance but in its very susceptibility to inscription that the body preserves some measure of agency or signifying capabilities ... the body protests. The body goes on strike. The body has other agendas. This is perhaps most strikingly evident in hysteria.[30]

Banting here equates the body's resistance to social meaning, not with a resistance to signification as such, but rather with the preservation of 'some measure of agency or signifying capabilities': that is, with the body's ability to mean what it wants to mean, rather than to mean what society takes it to mean.

The idea of the grotesque body is drawn from Bakhtin and elaborated by Peter Stallybrass and Allon White in *The Politics and Poetics of Transgression*. They argue that there exists a 'cultural process whereby the human body, psychic forms, geographical space and the social formation are all constructed within interrelating and dependent hierarchies of high and low' (*PPT*, 2). They draw on Bakhtin for the distinction between the 'classical' and 'grotesque' bodies. The classical body, like classical statuary, is elevated, static, monumental and singular, 'the radiant centre of a transcendent individualism'. It 'structuréd ... the characteristically "high" discourses of philosophy, statecraft, theology and law, as well as literature, as they emerged from the Renaissance' (*PPT*, 21). The grotesque body, on the other hand, is multiple, teeming, mobile and split, part of a throng, manifests its bodily orifices, and represents 'a subject of pleasure in processes of exchange' (*PPT*, 22). As with hysteria, the grotesque body can be seen in terms of resistance to social norms. In the work of Mikhail Bakhtin the grotesque body is associated with carnival, and is seen as a site of popular resistance to official culture. However, many have suggested that 'the "licensed release" of carnival' may be 'simply a form of social control of the low by the high' which 'serves the interests of that very official culture which it apparently opposes' (*PPT*, 13). This 'subversion/containment debate', as Jonathan Dollimore terms it, is of considerable relevance to the representation of 'aberrant' bodies in Conrad.[31]

If we return, then, to the description of Captain MacWhirr with which I began this chapter, we can see that it postulates a one-to-one mapping of psychic forms onto the human body (two of the symbolic domains identified by Stallybrass and White). Conrad's first sentence – MacWhirr's face as the transparent window through which we see his character – would seem squarely within the tradition which Gallop describes and critiques, one which has 'tried to render [the body] transparent and get beyond it, to dominate it by reducing it to the mind's idealizing categories'.[32] Yet the implications of Conrad's description accord better with Gallop's own view of the body as enigmatic. She quotes Roland Barthes's listing of his own likes and dislikes, and his comment that 'thus out of this anarchic foam of tastes and distastes, gradually emerges the outline of a bodily enigma'.[33] Gallop asserts that, as 'bedrock given, a priori to any subjectivity, the body calls out for interpretation', but that

> Outside the theological model there is no possibility of verifying an interpretation ... if that word ['body'] means all that in the organism which exceeds and antedates consciousness or reason or interpretation ... perceivable givens that the human being knows as 'hers' without knowing their significance to her ... a taste for a certain food or a certain color, a distaste for another ... We can, a posteriori, form an esthetic, consistent series of values ... But the

theorizing is precisely endless, an eternal reading of the 'body' as authorless text, full of tempting, persuasive significance, but lacking a final guarantee of intended meaning.[34]

It is hard to imagine anyone less like Roland Barthes than Captain MacWhirr, yet MacWhirr's body too seems 'full of tempting, persuasive significance, but lacking a final guarantee of intended meaning'. My starting point in considering 'Typhoon' is a brief discussion of the story by Francis Mulhern, in an article about the criticism of F.R. Leavis. Leavis, in *The Great Tradition*, reads 'Typhoon' in accord with his own normalizing ideology of 'Englishness'. Leavis's account celebrates the triumph of the rational white male officer class over the chaotic bodily confusion of the Chinese:

And the qualities which, in a triumph of discipline – a triumph of the spirit – have enabled a handful of ordinary men to impose sanity on a frantic mob are seen unquestionably to be those which took Captain MacWhirr ... into the centre of the typhoon. Without any symbolic portentousness the Captain stands there the embodiment of a tradition. The crowning triumph of the spirit, in the guise of a matter-of-fact and practical sense of decency, is the redistribution ... of the gathered-up and counted dollars among the assembled Chinese.[35]

Mulhern opposes to this a very different interpretation of 'Typhoon':

The ship's captain, MacWhirr, is an obsessional. Locks and charts are the emblems of his life ... The ship has been transferred from the British to the Siamese flag ... Sailing under 'queer' colours, its crew outnumbered by their freight of alien bodies, the *Nan-Shan* heads into 'dirty' weather. The storm attacks every established social relationship of the vessel. Masculinity is abandoned for hysteria; linguistic order fails, as speech turns figural or obscene, is blocked by superstition or swept away by the gale ... *Homo Britannicus* is abandoned to a chaos of effeminacy, homoeroticism, and gibberish – the terrifying counter-order of the Chinese labourers below. The ship survives. But the restoration of order is understood as a furtive improvisation ... The chief officers of the *Nan-Shan*, ultimate guarantors of imperial order, bear the typhoon within themselves.[36]

The opposition between the classical and the grotesque body seems very evidently in play in 'Typhoon', notably in the scenes on the bridge and in the hold during the storm. These two locations within the 'body' of the ship are themselves hierarchically organized in terms of the geography of the ship, its class and power structure, and in terms of race. The captain and chief mate, despite the storm, manage to stand upright, clasped together for support, on the bridge which elevates them above the mass of the crew, the materiality of the cargo and the racial otherness of the 'coolie' passengers. When the boatswain appears on the bridge, to warn of trouble below stairs, we are given a physical description which marks out his association with the grotesque body:

> He was an ill-favoured, undersized, gruff sailor of fifty, coarsely hairy, short-legged, long-armed, resembling an elderly ape. His strength was immense; and in his great lumpy paws, bulging like brown boxing-gloves on the end of furry forearms, the heaviest objects were handled like playthings.
>
> (T, 49)

Moreover, the boatswain announces his arrival, through the symbolism of the body, in a form of parody of some ritual obeisance to a social superior, though tinged with the homoeroticism noted by Mulhern:

> [Jukes] felt himself pawed all over ... Jukes recognized those hands, so thick and enormous that they seemed to belong to some new species of man.
>   The boatswain had arrived on the bridge, crawling on all fours against the wind, and had found the chief mate's legs with the top of his head. Immediately he crouched and began to explore Jukes' person upwards with prudent, apologetic touches, as became an inferior.
>
> (49)

The first reaction of Jukes, the chief mate, is to be irritated by this irruption from below – 'What could that fraud of a bos'n want on the bridge?' (49) – and the news brought by the boatswain identifies the Chinese labourers as grotesque in Bakhtin's terms: 'All them Chinamen in the fore 'tween-deck have fetched away, sir ... In a lump ... seen them myself ... Awful sight, sir' (51). The Chinese labourers are indeed the crucial grotesque body in the story, but before turning to them it is worth noting that the size and strength of the boatswain's hands, and his hairiness, are echoed in the description of Captain MacWhirr 'clutching in his powerful, hairy fist an elegant umbrella' (4). Jeremy Hawthorn, writing about the expressive body in *Under Western Eyes*, notes the importance of hands as (along with eyes) the 'most communicatively significant parts of the human body' (*NT*, 244), and identifies 'chains of association', linking the 'strong' hands of the morally strong Natalia to those of her brother, in contrast to the 'white shapely hand' of Prince K—, the 'skeleton hand' of Madame de S— and the 'soft hand' of Peter Ivanovitch, all indicative of the moral inadequacies of these characters (*NT*, 243–5). Hands, of course, are not only particularly expressive but are crucial to manual work, and it is not surprising that Conrad, as a sailor, should value strong hands as he valued work itself. The similarity between the hands of the Captain and the boatswain, then, might be taken as indicative of the democracy of labour as Conrad sees it. Conrad's vision of shipboard life (which at times functions as a form of paradigm of society) is hierarchical and authoritarian on the one hand, and yet on the other hand stresses the communality of work and duty in the face of hardship: the sense of the existential equality of all in the face of the sea.

MacWhirr's 'sturdy' body, with a face which simply reflects his character, and dressed in a manner which makes no compromise with the influences of the Far East, its weather and culture (T, 3), has a solidity of presence which is implicitly contrasted with the exotic, enigmatic, undisciplined bodies of the Chinese coolies:

> The fore-deck, packed with Chinamen, was full of sombre clothing, yellow faces, and pigtails, sprinkled over with a good many naked shoulders, for there was no wind, and the heat was close. The coolies lounged, talked, smoked, or stared over the rail; some, drawing water over the side, sluiced each other; a few slept on hatches.
>
> (6–7)

The racist high–low binary is mapped onto the geography of the ship. Jukes, talking to the leader of the Chinese coolies,

> was gruff, as became his racial superiority, but not unfriendly. The Chinaman, gazing sad and speechless into the darkness of the hatchway, seemed to stand at the head of a yawning grave.
>
> (13)

The story neither endorses this assumption of racial superiority nor clearly repudiates it, though the rendering of the Chinese leader's perspective ('who concealed his distrust of [Jukes's] pantomime under a collected demeanour' (13)) tends towards the latter. The following passage describes the 'coolies' fighting for their money below decks as the violent storm tosses them and the ship around:

> With a precipitated sound of trampling and shuffling of bare feet, and with guttural cries, the mound of writhing bodies piled up to port detached itself from the ship's side and sliding, inert and struggling, shifted to starboard, with a dull, brutal thump. The cries ceased. The boatswain heard a long moan through the roar and whistling of the wind; he saw an inextricable confusion of heads and shoulders, naked soles kicking upwards, fists raised, tumbling backs, legs, pigtails, faces.
>
> (58)

The 'coolies' are alternately united into a single body – a writhing mound of flesh – and separated out into body parts:

> Jukes saw a head bang the deck violently, two thick calves waving on high, muscular arms twined round a naked body, a yellow-face, open-mouthed and with a set wild stare, look up and slide away ... The hatchway ladder was loaded with coolies swarming on it like bees on a branch ... The ship heeled over more, and they began to drop off: first one, then two, then all the rest went away together, falling straight off with a great cry.
>
> (62–3)

The logic of this passage, in which Jukes observes, not persons, but 'a head', 'two thick calves' and 'muscular arms', suggests that 'a yellow-face' should read 'a yellow face'.[37] It is characteristic of the denigrated body that it is dispersed or fragmented on the one hand, or coalesces into an indifferent mass on the other. The former is how pornography habitually represents women: as a sum of body parts fetishized. The latter is how class hatred habitually represents the working class politicized: the mass, the threatening mob. Both fragmented and coalesced bodies suggest a loss of individual autonomy, of a discrete, active, willing self located within the boundaries of a separate body.[38] The description of the Chinese men closely resembles Karl Marx's description of the lumpenproletariat as 'the whole indefinite, disintegrated mass thrown hither and thither' (the same paradox of conglomeration and fragmentation, both feared).[39] This similarity is indicative of the fact that, as Stallybrass and White argue, 'transcodings between different levels and sectors of social and psychic reality are effected through the intensifying grid of the body' (*PPT*, 26) – the transcodings in this case being between race and class. The idea of the Chinamen as *only* body also appears in one of Jukes's many racist conceptions: 'they say a Chinaman has no soul' (T, 101).

The vision of the hold as a 'yawning grave' hints at the abjection of the dead body, and that association of the labourers with abjection becomes stronger near the end of the story, in Jukes's description of their possessions: 'We ... shovelled out on deck heaps of wet rags, all sorts of fragments of things without shape, and that you couldn't give a name to, and let them settle the ownership themselves' (102). James Hansford links this to the theme of language and meaning in the story, and particularly to MacWhirr's confidence in the 'clear and definite language' (T, 15) of facts. Hansford contrasts the dollars, which are 'named, shaped, distributable items', and which MacWhirr takes the trouble to distribute equally, with the 'bits of nameless rubbish' (T, 7) (identified as such even before the damage wrought by the storm).[40] It might at first sight seem hyperbolic to apply Kristeva's concept of the abject to the damaged possessions of the Chinese labourers, but such an application becomes plausible and even necessary when the description of those possessions is seen in terms of the inscription of meanings – social, sexual, political – onto bodies: the bodies of individual men, bodies of men in a collective sense (the crew, the Chinese labourers), the body of the ship. The 'nameless' quality of the damaged possessions (always bearing in mind that this description is part of Jukes's letter, and therefore explicitly filtered through a racist mind) associates them both with the excluded quality of the abject and with abjection as the loss or failure of meaning: they are seen as *merely* material, matter devoid of meaning, in contrast to the significant and signifying dollars. Like the bodies of the Chinese men, rolled together in the hold, the possessions have become indistinct, a mass, an abject arousing fear and desire. They thus partake of the material and bodily (bearing in mind that they include 'clothes of ceremony') (T, 7), as that which falls outside or is excluded by rationality and signification. Yet, bringing to bear the analysis of discourses of high and low made by Stallybrass and White, and the insights of postcolonial theory into the construction of the Eastern 'mass' as Other to the Western imperial subject, we can see this

meaninglessness as itself a form of meaning: a construction of otherness which bears the marks of a particular ideological project.

Desire perhaps provides, not a resolution of this paradox of the
meaningful and the meaningless, but a way of thinking through it.
Stallybrass and White maintain that

> The top *includes* that low symbolically, as a primary eroticized
> constituent of its own fantasy life. The result is a mobile, conflict-
> ual fusion of power, fear and desire in the construction of
> subjectivity: a psychological dependence upon precisely those
> Others which are being rigorously opposed and excluded at the
> social level.
>
> (*PPT*, 5)

If we join with this a Lacanian understanding of desire as founded on
lack and therefore necessarily failing of its object, it is perhaps possible
to see how the 'low' body can be at once desired for what it means, and
yet exceed, or fall away from, that role as meaningful signifier. The low
body can flicker between object and abject. In the role of object, this
body 'settles me within the fragile texture of a desire for meaning', as
the Chinese Other defines for Jukes his own colonial, white, masterful
identity and as the valueless personal 'rubbish' confirms the universal
exchange value of the dollars.[41] In the role of abject, the low body
'draws me toward the place where meaning collapses'.[42]

To what extent does desire figure in 'Typhoon'? There are, of course,
those odd and striking overtones of homoeroticism between the officers:

> He poked his head forward, groping for the ear of his commander.
> His lips touched it—big, fleshy, very wet.
>
> (44)

This somehow seems to go beyond the no-doubt desirable situation of
a chief mate having the ear of his Captain. If the 'top' depends upon
the low and includes the low symbolically , 'as a primary eroticized
constituent of its own fantasy life' (*PPT*, 5), then the practical,
economic dependence upon a racial Other (ideologically represented
as subordinate or inferior) is evident in the very function of the
'coolies' and their money, as well as in the Siamese owner of the ship
and the Siamese flag which, like the arrival of the boatswain on the
deck, so irritates Jukes. The symbolic inclusion of the 'low' as eroticized fantasy appears in irruptions of the grotesque body (orifices,

physicality) into the relations between the officers. The presence in 'Typhoon' of suggestions of desire between men is an unsettling possibility within the structure of moral and psychological insights into matters such as duty, courage, fear and imagination that the story overtly offers the reader. Mark Wollaeger, commenting on the importance of physical proximity in the story, argues that MacWhirr's 'self-possession' counters the loss of self which threatens Jukes. He instances Jukes's contact with MacWhirr which produces 'an access of confidence, a sensation that came from outside like a warm breath' (T, 89) (*FS*, 124). However, rather than reconfirming the autonomous, defended male self/body, such a process implies an opening of self to other via a physical closeness.

If the idea of thinking through the body bears more explicitly on 'Typhoon', it is perhaps in respect of MacWhirr's notorious lack of imagination and his consequent impressive but dangerous lack of fear of the tropical storm into which he steers his ship. Imagining what an experience would be like, as opposed to simply recognizing the fact that it may occur, frequently involves a form of thinking through the body – anticipating and perhaps even experiencing in advance, psychosomatic responses – a rush of adrenaline perhaps, a dry mouth and even an unsettled stomach. The major role attributed to sexuality by feminist thinkers attempting to think through the body is surely in part because sexuality in humans so amply involves the imagination: sexual arousal does not require the physical presence of a sexual object. Here again MacWhirr would seem to be initially lacking. We are told, in the account of his earlier life, that his 'young woman' was 'called Lucy', but that it 'did not suggest itself to him to mention [to his parents] whether he thought the name pretty' (6). Of MacWhirr's response to gaining his first command, we are told that 'the view of a distant eventuality could appeal no more [to MacWhirr] than the beauty of a wide landscape to a purblind tourist' (8). Presumably, the sexuality of sailors is subjected to particular pressures by the circumstances of long absences from home. Jeremy Hawthorn comments on MacWhirr's inability to communicate meaningfully in his letters to a wife who lacks the imagination to read between the lines just as he lacks the ability to imagine what might interest her. Ironically, she fails to read a letter which is 'for once ... worth reading, one written by a sadder and wiser MacWhirr' (*NT*, 225). What, then, of MacWhirr's sexuality? For a man incapable of responding to that which is not immediately present, prolonged absence from a sexual partner would have to imply, not merely frustration, but the total disappearance of the sexual self – unless of course MacWhirr carries his unfurled umbrella to Far Eastern brothels (which is the sort of information Conrad tends not to give us) or finds objects of desire on board his ship. Hawthorn argues that 'a significant change has taken place in MacWhirr during the typhoon', in that he is 'able to *imagine*' the situation of the Chinese men below decks (*NT*, 230–1). In this empathy, however limited, with the physical trauma of the 'low', Other, exoticized/denigrated body within the body of his own ship, MacWhirr has, then, acquired some ability to think through his own body. This is perhaps one reason for that emphasis on the bodily throughout the story from the opening description to all those gropings during the storm.

The reading of *The Secret Agent* which follows will explore the meaning (and resistance to meaning) of the body of Stevie in the terms which have been outlined: the grotesque, the hysterical, the abject. Showing how the status and ultimate fate of Stevie's ambivalently masculine body and identity is interwoven with Conrad's moral and political critique of urban Western society, it will suggest that this critique can be read through the body to reveal the importance of masculinity as a part of that social structure, implicated with class, economic exchange, law and crime, domination and struggle. Stallybrass and White identify and analyse the construction of the 'low' urban Other, involving ideas of the body and the social formation, in nineteenth-century discourses, including 'the parliamentary report, the texts of social reform, the hysterical symptom of the psychoanalyst's patient ... the poet's journal and the novel' (*PPT*, 125). The urban low is prominent in *The Secret Agent* from the start. The Dickensian scene-setting of the early pages includes description of Verloc's house as 'one of those grimy brick houses which existed in large quantities before the era of reconstruction dawned' (3), of visitors to his shop with 'traces of *mud* on the *bottom* of their *nether* garments' (4, emphasis added) and of Verloc himself, with his 'air of having wallowed, fully dressed, all day on an unmade bed' (4). Thus early links are established between the slums of late nineteenth-century London, the lower bodies of the anarchists and Verloc's own complex disreputableness (lacking a respectable occupation, but having several of the other sort). Verloc's association with an 'unmade bed' hints at sexual decadence. The association of slums with darkness is present ('before ... reconstruction *dawned*'), even if tinged with irony; so too, later in Chapter 1, is the rhetoric which reshapes the causal link between poverty and disease into a metaphorical identity between the low social body and infection: '[Verloc] generally arrived in London (like the influenza) from the Continent' (6). Stallybrass and White comment that 'in the bourgeois imagination the slums opened (particularly at night) to let forth the thief, the murderer, the prostitute and the germs' (*PPT*, 133). *The Secret Agent* inhabits the discursive world of the nineteenth-century urban 'low' to the point where it is tempting to find a reflexive joke in the embarrassed young customers of Verloc's shop who buy marking ink and then drop it into the gutter (5) (writing in the gutter?). Indeed, in an unusual intrusion the otherwise anonymous narrator ironically places himself in the role of a slightly fastidious Mayhew or other middle-class social investigator:[43]

> There was also about [Verloc] an indescribable air ... common to men who live on the vices, the follies, or the baser fears of mankind; the air of moral nihilism common to keepers of gambling hells and disorderly houses; to private detectives and inquiry agents; to drink sellers and, I should say, to the sellers of invigorating electric belts and to the inventors of patent medicines. But of that last I am not sure, not having carried my investigations so far into the depths.
>
> (13)

The grotesque is obviously one of the dominant modes of *The Secret Agent*. How important is the grotesque body, in the sense defined by Bakhtin and elaborated by Stallybrass and White? And how do masculinity and the body bear upon each other in this 'simple tale'?[44]

The narrative voice of *The Secret Agent* is strongly characterized by its tones of irony, cynicism and contempt, although it is not consistent, nor does it belong to any identified person. This voice is obsessively and excessively concerned with the body, in particular with the body seen under certain aspects: as grotesque, distorted, unhealthy, deformed; as subject to violence or fragmentation; as object of disgust and fascination; as expressive of character and as ironically inappropriate to character; as enigmatic text which others seek to read. As well as the more obvious examples of descriptions of Verloc, Mrs Verloc, Stevie, Ossipon, Michaelis and the Professor, these obsessions are manifest in the depictions of more minor characters, such as the cab driver, with his 'bloated and sodden face of many colours' (*SA*, 157), the mother of Stevie and Winnie, with her 'big cheeks [which] glowed with an orange hue' (159), and even the cab-driver's horse, whose 'little stiff tail seemed to have been fitted in for a heartless joke' (166).

The narrative voice also has a peculiar fixation on idleness, seen as unhealthy, unhygienic and morally corrupt. Idleness and the grotesque body are linked by this voice, both being seen as implicitly threatening to, or subversive of, masculinity. If we term the notional owner of this unidentified voice 'the narrator', then the point of view of this unnamed narrator remains slightly hazy, because of his tendency to blend his own comments into the thoughts of characters via the use of free indirect discourse.[45] Nevertheless, the narrator is a somewhat dominating presence in the novel, not only because of his tone, but also because of his unpleasant views, prejudices and tendency to what might be called hysterical animosity.

Idleness is particularly associated with Verloc, whose body is throughout treated with a distaste which centres on his alleged laziness. He is described, for example as 'burly in a fat-pig style' (13) and the narrator observes that 'his idleness was not hygienic ... He had embraced indolence from an impulse as profound as inexplicable and as imperious as the impulse which directs a man's preference for one particular woman in a given thousand' (12). One of the disturbing features of the narrator's attitude to Verloc is that it is shared with Vladimir, who reflects (and comments) unfavourably on Verloc's 'fleshy profile' and 'gross bulk' (24). The narrator's perspective has a habit of merging at points with that of singularly unsympathetic characters, such as Vladimir or the Professor. One might argue that this implies that there *is* no narrator, only a set of narrative devices; yet we are obliged to depend, at least initially, on this narrative voice for many facts and judgements. It is unclear how far it can be relied upon even factually. For example, it claims that Verloc 'was too lazy even for a mere demagogue, for a workman orator' (12), yet Verloc claims with apparent plausibility that his powerful voice has been 'famous for years at open-air meetings and at workmen's assemblies in large halls' (23). The possibility is implied of a contrast between the hard-working, upright, bounded, morally responsible male body and the idle, recumbent, grotesque, degenerate body. This contrast is along the lines of the classical versus grotesque body antithesis described by Stallybrass and White. But in *The Secret Agent* this antithesis seems unable to maintain itself, as grotesque features invade the realm of the 'classical' dominant male body. In Chapter 5, Inspector Heat's chance meeting with the Professor in the street frames a retrospective account of Heat's inspection of the horrible mangled remains of Stevie. In both scenes Heat appears superficially as the classical body in contrast to the grotesque body of the 'miserable and undersized' (81), 'unwholesome-looking' (83) Professor and in contrast to the dispersed body of Stevie. Heat looms up 'stalwart and erect' with a 'swinging pace' (82), with 'a good deal of forehead, which appeared very white in the dusk', and eyeballs which 'glimmered piercingly' (83). The allusion to his forehead emphasizes his upper body/mind, his piercing eyes suggest mental perspicacity and his 'whiteness' implies (in terms of the racist discourses of the time) a lack of degeneracy, in contrast, for example, to the association of Ossipon with racial otherness ('A bush of crinkly yellow hair topped his red, freckled face, with a flattened nose and prominent mouth cast in the rough mould of the negro type' (44)). An attitude of body fascism, partially endorsed by the narrator through the use of free indirect discourse, emerges in the observation: 'To the vigorous, tenacious vitality of the Chief Inspector, the physical wretchedness of that being, so obviously not fit to live, was ominous' (94). One might or might not sympathize with the view that the Professor is unfit to live on the grounds of his morals and actions, but the assertion that he is not fit to live because of his poor physique is characteristic of the unpleasant way in which *The Secret Agent* treats the body as a site for the inscription of narratorial judgement. Yet in both these scenes, and in the interview between Heat and the Assistant Commissioner, the separation of high and low, inside and outside, health and degeneracy, white and black, upon which the self-image of the European male 'classical' body depends is subtly eroded. Both the Greenwich bomb and the anarchists in general disturb Heat because he perceives them as outside the established social order (which includes respectable criminals such as thieves). To Heat 'as criminals, anarchists were distinctly no class, no class at all' (97) – that is they lack a place in the hierarchies of the social body, whereas thieves and police are 'products of the same machine' (92). While Heat thus regards police work and burglary as related forms of labour (91–2), the Professor describes terrorism and police work, revolution and legality as 'forms of idleness at bottom identical' (69), where idleness seems a bizarre choice of epithet. In a different configuration of outside and inside, Heat is annoyed at the Greenwich explosion happening out of the blue, and assumes that it must be the work of a 'rank outsider' (i.e. not one of the revolutionaries known to him): 'Outsiders are the bane of the police as of other professions' (86). Heat has partially fitted even anarchists into his idea of social order through his belief that he can observe and monitor them all, which the narrator informs us is a fallacy because of the appearance of 'sudden holes in space and time' (85) when the police will lose the

trace. Another sort of hole in space and time threatens Heat's professional detachment and his rationality when he is confronted with
Stevie's remains:

> His reason told him the effect must have been as swift as a flash of
> lightning ... Yet it seemed impossible to believe that a human body
> could have reached that state of disintegration without passing
> through the pangs of inconceivable agony ... Heat rose by the force
> of sympathy, which is a form of fear, above the vulgar conception
> of time ... He evolved a horrible notion that ages of atrocious pain
> and mental torture could be contained between two successive
> winks of an eye.
>
> (87–8)

This response to Stevie's body also brings Heat closer to Stevie's mind,
since fear and unsettling sympathy with the suffering of others are
characteristic of Stevie. Furthermore, this rapprochement of the representative of social order with the destroyed body and hysterical
personality of the 'idiot' or 'degenerate' unsettles the superiority
which Heat desires to feel over the puny Professor. When the Professor
threatens him with joint destruction by the bomb which he always
carries, Heat's recent view of Stevie's remains gives a horrible effectiveness to the Professor's words: 'you may be exposed to the
unpleasantness of being buried together with me, though I suppose
your friends would make an effort to sort us out as much as possible'
(93). The abjection of the body in becoming a mutilated corpse and
the confusion of inside and outside threaten the autonomy of the classical male body. Furthermore, in the scene which follows these, the
Assistant Commissioner sees Heat in terms which associated him with
the grotesque, idle Verloc, and in terms which question his 'whiteness'. He notes that Heat's physiognomy, though 'determined' is
'marred by too much flesh' (116) and, observing that Heat is 'a big
man', is reminded of 'a certain old fat and wealthy native chief in the
distant colony' [where the Assistant Commissioner had begun his
career] (118). These effects, in which the classical male body is threatened by irruptions of the grotesque, come about largely through
attempts by characters to read each other's bodies: the Assistant
Commissioner trying to read Heat's living body just as Heat tries to
read Stevie's remains. The implication seems to be that normative
masculinity depends upon the male body not being read, or read only
in certain terms. These terms accord with the theories cited earlier,

that interiority and fluidity are threatening to the normative representation of the male body. Stevie's insides are literally turned out, while the Assistant Commissioner, his detective instincts aroused by his suspicion that Heat is concealing something, thinks with pleasure 'I'll turn him inside out like an old glove' (119).

Stevie is the key figure for a consideration of masculinity and the body in *The Secret Agent*, but Stevie's body, its meaning and its recalcitrance to meaning are best approached through the body of his mother (significantly unnamed in the text). The mother's first appearance in the text is as a grotesque body whose physical attributes, socio-economic status and topographical location are closely connected:

Winnie's mother was a stout, wheezy woman, with a large brown face. She wore a black wig under a white cap. Her swollen legs rendered her inactive. She considered herself to be of French descent, which might have been true; and after a good many years of married life with a licensed victualler of the more common sort, she provided for the years of widowhood by letting furnished apartments for gentlemen near Vauxhall Bridge Road in a square once of some splendour and still included in the district of Belgravia. This topographical fact was of some advantage in advertising her rooms.

(6)

Verloc visits her 'downstairs where she had her motionless being' (7), and when he marries Winnie 'the married couple took her over with the furniture' (8). The move 'from the Belgravian square to the narrow street in Soho affected her legs adversely. They became of an enormous size. On the other hand, she experienced a complete relief from material cares' (8). The location of the mother's legs in space (space inscribed with social meaning: Belgravia vs. Soho) is grotesquely mapped by their internal transformations. Her body is described in terms which accord with those of grotesque realism, which 'images the human body as multiple, bulging, over- or under-sized, protuberant and incomplete' (*PPT*, 9), but the tone is black humour rather than carnivalesque laughter. Rather than functioning as a resistance to, or subversion of, the capitalist order, the grotesque mother's body marks her place within systems of economic exchange and constraint. In a Bakhtinian transcoding between the body and the social sphere, her legs get wider as her place of residence becomes more constrained, and with her daughter's marriage of convenience she is both rendered a mere object or chattel (like the furniture) and dematerialized (her enormous legs are contrasted with her relief from material cares, as if her legs were immaterial). Those material cares are, of course, her children, whose bodily needs (food, warmth, shelter, etc.) are a source of anxiety, because one of them is a woman, the other limited in his mental powers and thus 'a terrible encumbrance' (8), so that both are destined in this society for forms of dependence. The simultaneous existence of the body as recalcitrant physical object and as discursive sign is at issue here, emphasizing the ways in which the constraints and needs of the body are inscribed in social discourse and social practice. In *The Secret Agent* the extent and sharpness of Conrad's satire on the institutions of European society reveal a radicalism which also impinges on his representation of gender relations. While it would seem unlikely that Conrad started out with any intention of making a critique of gender oppression, his understanding of the effects of poverty, vulnerability and need on the individual leads him to write a novel in which a woman and an unmanly man are poignantly shown as the actual and symbolic victims of a corrupt and deadening system. These two victims are Winnie Verloc (who is identified in Conrad's 'Author's Note' as central to the novel) and her brother Stevie.

A problematic of the masculine body is developed in this novel through the figure of Stevie, who begins and remains in a condition of dependence, dependent on a woman who is herself dependent on a man. This situation is emphasized in the very first sentences of the novel: 'Mr. Verloc ... left his shop nominally in charge of his brother-in-law. It could be done, because there was very little business ... And, moreover, his wife was in charge of his brother-in-law' (3). Stevie thus occupies when Karen Klein calls 'the feminine predicament' ('the sense of the body as not under one's own control, but subject to the force and will of others') (FP, 104). This condition is acted out in his lack of bodily control as such: 'A brusque question caused him to stutter to the point of suffocation. When startled ... he used to squint horribly' (9). Stevie's lack of bodily autonomy culminates, of course, in the tragic and repellent radical fragmentation of his body. The early pages of the novel contain many examples of Conrad's proleptic irony in the form of allusions to Stevie's later fate. His mother's reflection that 'he was difficult to dispose of, that boy' (8) prompts her satisfaction in disposing of him along with the furniture, a link which then serves to contrast disposal with confinement, implying that these are two alternative fates of the subjected body:

Mr. Verloc was ready to take [Stevie] over together with his wife's mother and with the furniture ... The furniture was disposed to the best advantage all over the house, but Mrs. Verloc's mother was confined to two back rooms.

(10)

The furniture seems to come off best out of this arrangement; only in retrospect, or on second reading, are we struck by a parallel with Stevie's body, 'disposed' (though hardly 'to the best advantage') over Greenwich Park, 'disposed of' all too effectively in one sense, but also hard to dispose of, since the police have to scrape it up with a shovel.

Given the tension in theories of the body between the sense of the body as site of social meaning, and the idea of it as resistant to such meaning, there is a significant oscillation in the novel between the ideas of Stevie's body as meaningful or meaningless. Masculinity itself constitutes an attribution of meaning to the body, marked as male. Stevie is ambiguous in this respect, an ambiguity which is introduced in the context of writing itself: 'He was delicate and, in a frail way, good-looking, too, except for the vacant droop of his lower lip ... He had learned to read and write, notwithstanding the unfavourable aspect of the lower lip' (8). Though his bodily limitations do not prevent him learning to write, it is what is already written on his body that is to determine the course of his life. His positive attributes ('delicate and, in a frail way, good-looking') tend to the conventionally feminine, while his marks of conventional masculinity are partial and ambivalent: 'a growth of thin fluffy hair had come to blur, like a golden mist, the sharp line of his small lower jaw' (10). His negative attributes inscribe on his body his lack of rational subjecthood ('the vacant droop of his lower lip'). The only form of inscription in which we see him engaged is the drawing of circles with compass and pencil (45). While Stevie's ability to write indicates a degree of rational subjecthood, his drawing seems only to confirm his status as symbolic victim, since the circles suggest, among other things, the circles of deceit and conspiracy that lead to his death and the symbolic central-ity of the place of that death (the meridian at Greenwich). Mark Wollaeger sees Stevie's circles, and other geometric details in the text (such as Verloc's code 'name', which is a triangle) in terms of a 'play between geometry and chaos', and associates this with 'the attack on the body' in the novel, which he sees as an expression of Conrad's 'desire for order' (*FS*, 150–1). Wollaeger's argument is that a certain fantasy of rational order requires complete control of others, and a complete transparency of individuals. This desire to control and see into others finds expression in the destruction of the body, as well as in an authorial imprinting of meaning on characters via their appearance and physical fate.

A number of discourses are evoked or alluded to in ways that bear on the problematic meaning of Stevie's body. Theories of degeneracy overload the body with meaning, and this is one of a number of ways in which Stevie's body is linked to that of his sister. As Rebecca Stott argues, Conrad mobilizes 'the discourses of criminology and degeneracy' in this text which 'teems with references to Lombroso and Nordau and their studies of degenerate types', and 'although Stevie is chosen initially as the degenerate subject, Winnie becomes progressively the site of Ossipon's (and the text's) investigations into degeneracy'.[46] Stott's conclusion is that, through the association of Mrs Verloc and other female characters in Conrad with the 'linguistic and epistemological void' of London (or of the jungle, or of the abyss), Conrad associates the female body, and especially the maternal body, with disruption and dissolution.[47] Hence at the end of the novel 'Winnie slips back into the interstices of that black, atavistic space ... a temporal and spatial alterity whose presence in the text is itself part of a breakdown of "configurations of sexual, racial and political asymmetry underlying mainstream modern Western culture"'.[48] While the marks of degeneracy inscribed on Stevie become transferred to his sister, her association with a disruptive bodily alterity also reflects back onto him, through their bodily closeness, which extends from their physical resemblance to Stevie's idyllic memory of sharing Winnie's bed as a child, 'a heaven of consoling peace', which generates 'a symbolic longing' (167) to take to bed with him any objects of his compassion. This memory has all the hallmarks of the pre-Oedipal, since Winnie plays a maternal role in relation to Stevie. Such pre-Oedipal closeness to the mother is arguably what is repressed in constructions of the normative masculine body, which Stevie thus doubly transgresses by his continued symbiotic closeness to and dependence on his mother/sister, and by his own identification with the maternal body, as in his tragic-comic desire to take the cabman and horse to bed with him to comfort them for their sufferings.

Stevie's remains are also subjected to the forensic gaze of the police, and such investigations, whether by police, detectives or amateurs, function in many Victorian fictional narratives to highlight the attribution of meaning to the material and to the body.[49] Foucault's account of nineteenth-century configurations of power and knowledge stresses the internalization of control and surveillance as part of the displacement of the spectacular physical subjugation of the body. Stevie is always subject to surveillance; there is, or should be, always someone keeping an eye on him, as when he sits at the kitchen table drawing circles, while Winnie 'glanced at him from time to time with maternal vigilance' (10). He is, however, incapable of fully internalizing the rational constraints of bourgeois normality, and is liable to succumb to a revolutionary and explosive indignation at cruelty or injustice, shrieking, stuttering or (on one occasion) letting off fireworks (9). His cruel fate is, then, in part a symbolic destruction of the indisciplined and undisciplinable body. His remains yield up meaning only in the form of his address, inscribed on his coat by the loving care of his sister. Initially Inspector Heat, despairing of identifying the body, characterizes it specifically as 'unreadable' (89), but the address on Stevie's coat does indeed lead Inspector Heat to the unravelling of the mystery, so that in narrative terms Stevie's dead body does provide meaning. Yet Stevie's remains are also described as 'a heap of *nameless* fragments' (87, emphasis added). This paradox – that Stevie's remains yield up both the marker of an identity and the nameless – points towards the aporia of the body, towards the sense of the body as enigma articulated by Jane Gallop. Stevie's name is the marker of his marginal but nevertheless acknowledged social and legal identity. The body, as what Braidotti terms 'one's primary location in the world', is the site of this identity.[50] Yet, as philosophical speculations and science-fiction fantasies about organ-exchange have revealed, we remain uncertain about precisely where and how that identity inheres in the collection of organs and parts which in a physical sense constitutes the body. Borrowing the structuralist distinction between sign and index, we might argues that as index Stevie's remains are meaningless (they are no longer recognizable in ordinary terms as the location of a person). Only through the arbitrary sign of the address, as bureaucratic identification of location, does the trace of the meaningful body remain.[51]

Banting claims that the body resists in some measure society's constructions of it: 'As material substance, that is, as non-name and nonsense, the body resists and displaces the official order'.[52] The death of Stevie separates his location in society from his material substance, as if violently to wrench apart the discursive meaning granted by subjectivity from the recalcitrance of the material. Banting cites hysteria as a prime example of the body which 'goes on strike'.[53] We may detect elements of the hysteric in the figure of Stevie: 'his attention being drawn to this unpleasant state, Stevie shuffled his feet.

His feelings were habitually manifested by the agitation of his limbs' (176). Even Winnie is not fully competent at reading her brother's bodily signs. The narrator informs us that Stevie's 'immoderate compassion' is always succeeded by 'innocent but pitiless rage' (169), and the latter is harnessed by Mr Verloc to set Stevie on his fatal anarchistic mission. However, the unreadability of Stevie's body is again manifest, since 'those two states expressing themselves outwardly by the same signs of futile bodily agitation, his sister Winnie soothed his excitement without ever fathoming its twofold character' (169). Like the signs of 'degeneracy', the hysterical effect is shared in muted form by his sister, significantly in response to the depersonalized male gaze of her husband: 'At the sound of his wife's voice he stopped and stared at her with a somnambulistic, expressionless gaze so long that Mrs. Verloc moved her limbs slightly under the bedclothes' (177). Yet Mr Verloc himself can also respond in this way, in the face of the bullying sarcasm of Mr Vladimir: 'This perfectly gratuitous suggestion caused Mr. Verloc to shuffle his feet slightly' (35). Like the grotesque body, the hysterical body is associated with the feminine or with dubious masculinity, but this dubiety extends more widely than first appears.

Another way of understanding the status of Stevie's remains would be in terms of Kristeva's concept of the abject. The macabre or gothic black humour with which Conrad treats Stevie's fate links the dead body with repulsive ideas of eating. Kristeva cites food loathing as 'perhaps the most elementary and most archaic form of abjection', going on to associate this with the more absolute abject quality of a corpse. In rejecting or expelling food 'I expel *myself*, I spit *myself* out, I abject *myself* within the same motion through which "I" claim to establish *myself*.' Yet a corpse, which '*show[s] me* what I permanently thrust aside in order to live', is 'the most sickening of wastes ... a border that has encroached upon everything. It is no longer I who expel, "I" is expelled ... The corpse, seen without God and outside of science, is the utmost of abjection.'[54] Since neither God nor science is treated with much faith in *The Secret Agent*, the abject quality of Stevie's remains is perhaps appropriate: they are described as 'that heap of mixed things, which seemed to have been collected in shambles and rag shops' (87), and as 'an accumulation of raw material for a cannibal feast' (86). They are inspected by Heat with 'the slightly anxious attention of an indigent customer bending over what may be called the by-products of a butcher's shop with a view to an inexpensive Sunday dinner' (88). Furthermore, the park keeper 'was as sick as a dog' (87) when he heard the policeman collecting up the bits, and Heat is unable to eat for the rest of the day.

Stevie's fate is, then, is some ways a culmination of the always-abject state of his partial masculinity. Two of the conditions which Katherine Judith Goodnow notes as tending to provoke horror of the abject apply here: the 'feminization' of the male body and an association with the pre-symbolic authority of the maternal.[55] Stevie lives under the authority of his mother and sister, until he is taken off by Verloc to take up, as Winnie hopes, his place in the patriarchal symbolic order. When she succeeds in persuading Verloc to take Stevie out with him, she proudly reflects that they 'might be father and son' (187), and congratulates herself on the sacrifices she has made to bring this about (specifically, by implication, her toleration of Verloc as a sexual partner in pragmatic preference to the butcher whom she loved). Stevie's ultimate inability to become a 'man' is signalled in his fate: his body cannot escape from its abject gender ambiguity and dependence on the maternal, and so the contact with the father figure only leads to it being flung into the more extreme abjection of violent death.

If Stevie is the abject of the capitalist social order, then the anarchists and revolutionaries (with the exception of the Professor) are its object, using the term 'object' as Kristeva does in distinguishing it from the abject: 'If the object … through its opposition, settles me within the fragile texture of a desire for meaning, which, as a matter of fact, makes me ceaselessly and infinitely homologous to it, what is *abject*, on the contrary, the jettisoned object, is radically excluded and draws me toward the place where meaning collapses.'[56] The social order, which the novel portrays as largely destructive, defines itself in contradistinction to the forces of supposed disorder represented by the anarchists. Conrad's fierce contempt for the anarchists allows him to present as symmetrical and mutually supportive the relationship between them and the social order which they claim to oppose, and which claims to stand against them. As already noted, the Professor sees Revolutionaries and Police as part of the same system (69) and Heat sees burglar and policeman as recognizing the same conventions (92). Only Stevie, with his ungovernable body, and the Professor, with his grotesque body, are presented as radical, unassimilable threats to that system. Both are associated with the violent dispersal of the body: this is Stevie's fate, and this is the threat which gives the Professor his special status and ability to unsettle Heat.

4
Gender and the Disciplined Body: *Nostromo*

In *Nostromo* Conrad deploys stereotypes of gender and race, which is not to say that he merely *reproduces* such stereotypes, since I shall argue that they form part of the novel's critique of false consciousness, and its associated deconstruction of certain illusions of masculinity. These stereotypes involve both body and character, and imply their correspondence. It is a novel in which heroic male moustaches are much in evidence. Gould and Nostromo are characters that draw upon two stereotyped versions of normative masculinity, Anglo-Saxon and Latin. Gould is the ideal English gentleman colonial administrator: resolute, dignified, restrained, inscrutable, knowledge-able in the ways of his adopted country yet indelibly English (*N*, 47–8). This crucial Englishness, which initially seems to hold him apart from what is seen as the mad farce of South American politics, is presented as a bodily characteristic:

> Born in the country [Sulaco] ... spare and tall, with a flaming mous-tache, a neat chin, clear blue eyes, auburn hair, and a thin, fresh, red face, Charles Gould looked like a new arrival ... He looked more English than ... anybody out of the hunting-field pictures in the numbers of *Punch*.
>
> (46–7)

Gould even conforms to the 'mad dogs and Englishman' cliché, a fact recognized and gently mocked by Don José Avellanos: 'Carlos, my friend, you have ridden from San Tomé in the heat of the day. Always the true English activity. No? What?' (51). Nostromo is the ideal Latin heroic male adventurer of the people: strong, brave, resourceful, admired and vain, a casual and confident wooer, with his 'unapproachable

style' of dress (125). These two men are matched by female stereotypes. Mrs Gould, who, 'with her little head and shining coils of hair,
sitting in a cloud of muslin and lace ... resembled a fairy' (52),
dispenses 'the small graces of existence ... with simplicity and charm',
being 'highly gifted in the art of human intercourse which consists in
delicate shades of self-forgetfulness and in the suggestion of universal
comprehension' (46). A late incarnation of the Victorian 'Angel in the
House', Mrs Gould mitigates somewhat but also facilitates her
husband's essentially ruthless political manoeuvrings and economic
ambitions. The objects of Nostromo's romantic attentions include 'the
Morenita' and Giselle Viola. The former, whether passionate, pouting,
angry or tearful, is essentially an amalgam of some clichés of Latin sex
appeal:

> Her arms and neck emerged plump and bare from a snowy
> chemisette; the blue woollen skirt, with all the fullness gathered in
> front, scanty on the hips and tight across the back, disclosed the
> provoking action of her walk. She came straight on and laid her
> hand on the mare's neck with a timid, coquettish look upwards out
> of the corner of her eyes.
>
> (127)[1]

Giselle is a mere 'girlish figure' (546), 'beautiful' but 'incapable of
sustained emotion' (547).

This sort of characterization has obvious limitations – notably in
respect of the female characters – and Nostromo, while an interesting
exemplum of the fate of a certain sort of masculinity, is not generally
felt to be an interesting character, in the sense of having any complex
inner life. This view was shared by Conrad, who wrote in a letter:

> But truly N[ostromo] is nothing at all—a fiction—embodied vanity
> of the sailor kind—a romantic mouthpiece of 'the people' which (I
> mean 'the people') frequently experience the very feelings to which
> he gives utterance. I do not defend him as a creation.[2]

Clearly these stereotypes are used knowingly by Conrad and, to
varying degrees, with what seems a critical intent. Conrad obviously
intended Nostromo as a semi-allegorical figure, though his claim that
Nostromo gives utterance to the feelings of the people shows a blind-
ness to the markedly masculine nature of Nostromo's feelings (or an
assumption that women are not significant). Similarly, it is apparent

throughout his work that Conrad took great interest in what he saw as the characteristics of different nations. In the same letter he explained that he had gone to some trouble to differentiate Nostromo, as an Italian, from Spanish or South American ways of behaving ('As to his conduct generally and with women in particular').[3] However, Fredric Jameson identifies a political subtext beneath this apparent concern for accuracy. He points out that the novel effectively takes the side of the aristocrats in South America by demonizing the Monterists, for which, purpose they must be sharply distinguished from the tradition of European popular revolution associated with Nostromo's friend and surrogate father, Viola, and thus with Italy. Jameson argues that

> Conrad never went further politically than in this sympathetic portrayal of the nationalist-populist ideal; at the same time, it must be said that he contains and carefully qualifies this pole of his new historical vision, primarily by separating off one genuine Latin (but *European*) revolutionary impulse – the Italian, which is here exotic and foreign – from the indigenous Monterista variety.
>
> (*PU*, 274)

Nevertheless, the novel not only calls into question the implicit moral claims underlying Gould's Englishness, but also demonstrates the moral and emotional vacuity of ideals of normative masculinity, since Gould and Nostromo are both revealed as hollow men of modernity. Imagining themselves to be heroic leaders and moulders of events, they discover themselves to be the tools of impersonal and often destructive forces. In the case of the women characters Conrad seems rather more in the thrall of the stereotypes, less ironical in deploying them. As Karen Klein judiciously concludes, in probably the most telling study of the role of the body in Conrad,

> Not the least of the ironies ... however, is that [Conrad's] authorial attitude toward Mrs. Gould as a female – an idealization that masks his deep condescension based on his sense of superiority – is precisely the attitude of the men in power to Nostromo and is the basis of their exploitation of him.
>
> (*FP*, 115–16)

Mrs Gould is given moral insights into the cruelty and futility of much political action and economic development in this colonial society.

However, the narrator's view of her as a 'little lady' tends to make her impotence seem a natural part of her femininity[4]: 'the woman's instinct of devotion' in contrast to 'the man's instinct of activity' (74). It is true, of course, that the novel tends to show the ultimate impotence of all individuals in the face of economic and historical forces, and that Mrs Gould is shown as doing good within the limited sphere allowed her. Nevertheless, her earlier and greater understanding of the illusory nature of her husband's ideals is denied effective outlet in action. This is of course plausible, historically, socially and psychologically. The limitation of the portrayal is that the narrator seems to share and endorse the idea of women's role which set such limits. Klein refers to Conrad's 'authorial attitude', whereas I have been referring to the attitude of the narrator. This is not because I regard Conrad as clearly distancing himself from or ironizing the narrator but because, as in *The Secret Agent*, the relationship of narrator and author is uncertain. In each novel the primary narrator is uncharacterized (extradiegetic and heterodiegetic) but adopts attitudes and tones of voice which are coloured by the setting, mood and characters of the particular novel.[5] Thus the narrator of *Nostromo* tends to Olympian detachment, tinged with contempt or admiration, while the narrator of *The Secret Agent* seems misanthropic and vindictively ironical.[6] The narrative voice of *Nostromo* is, however, much more variable. In addition to the use of characters (such as Decoud and Mitchell) as homodiegetic subsidiary narrators, the narrative voice sometimes mitigates its detachment by adopting a form of free indirect discourse with respect to the Sulaco community in general, as in the account of the legend of the lost Gringos of Azuera (*N*, 4–5). As Wollaeger aptly puts it, 'these modulations create the illusion of sometimes attending to the mediated voice of a narrator, sometimes to the voice of the author' (*FS*, 139). This uncertainty creates problems but also opportunities for the reader, since it tends to break down the illusion of total authorial control, such control being a crucial philosophical issue in *Nostromo*, as Wollaeger shows.[7]

Despite the element of stereotyping, Conrad's treatment of the Goulds does not lack psychological depth. Gould's character, and more specifically the form taken by his masculinity, are shown to be formed by the vicarious experience of his father's frustration and defeat, when the latter had the seemingly useless mine concession forced on him by the corrupt government of Costaguana. In response to his father's futile rage, Gould develops that restraint and understated determination which is one familiar form of heroic English masculinity (a version, in fact, of the 'stiff upper lip'). His response to his father's anguished letters denies emotional identification with his father, a denial which is justified in terms of bodily separation: 'The view he took of it was sympathetic to his father, yet calm and reflective. His personal feelings had not been outraged, and it is difficult to resent with proper and durable indignation the physical or mental anguish of another organism, even if that other organism is one's own father' (58–9). Here, as in *The Secret Agent*, the attitude of the impersonal narrator is problematic. The above could conceivably be free indirect discourse (that is, Gould himself could reflect thus about the separation of organisms), but it seems unlikely. If the generalization belongs to the narrator or narrative voice, then that voice is inconsistent or short of memory, since Mrs Gould does not find it difficult to resent the physical and mental anguish of others, whether her husband, Dr Monygham or the oppressed peoples of Costaguana.

Arguably, what the narrative voice here does is less to adopt Gould's point of view than to adopt a male point of view: taking as universal an emphasis on bodily separation, a resistance to penetration by the feelings of others and a concomitant suppression of sympathy which are typically male. Indeed, in its attitude to Mrs Gould, the narrative seems (as Klein notes) consistently to adopt the attitude of a patronizing and idealizing male. Rather like Gould, the narrator seems, in respect of Mrs Gould, 'the most anxious and deferential of dictators' – an attitude, we are told, that 'pleased her immensely' (62) when they were courting. The observation quoted above concerning Gould's response to his father's anguish is only superficially accurate: since a desire to make the mine profitable becomes the guiding obsession of Gould's life, his 'calm and reflective' view of it conceals an excessive identification with his father, which involves a diversion of his sympathy from humans to mines: 'Abandoned workings had for him strong fascination. Their desolation appealed to him like the sight of human misery' (59). His relationship with the future Mrs Gould is (fatally for her future happiness) formed via the mediation of this obsession. We are told that her delight in him takes wings when she discovers it (59), and that much of their courting involved discussion of the Gould concession, 'because the sentiment of love can enter into any subject and live ardently in remote phrases' (60). When she agrees to go with him to Costaguana as his wife, her enthusiasm for the plan offers him an unprecedentedly 'fascinating vision of herself' (65), yet this vision is really a reflection of his own enthusiasm. Gould perhaps never does achieve a clear vision of her as an autonomous person. In

the characteristic pattern of homosocial exchange, Mrs Gould serves
to mediate the relationship between Charles Gould and his father: to
experience the emotion, desire, excitement which Gould cannot allow
himself to feel at the prospect of symbolically joining with and
displacing his father. This is very evident in their responses to news of
the death of Mr Gould senior. The son sweats and stares fixedly, the
woman cries in sympathy for both father and son, and the patronizing voice of the narrator, obsessed as ever with the smallness of the
woman, describes her as 'very small in her simple, white frock, almost
like a lost child ... while he stood by her, again perfectly motionless in
the contemplation of the marble urn' (62). Charles Gould is really the
lost child here, turning to her and to the mine to rediscover his lost
father. The mine involves extraction of material from the body of the
earth, a symbolically sexual penetration of 'a wild, inaccessible, and
rocky gorge of the Sierra' (54). Such a Freudian reading might seem
glib, were it not supported by the fact that, as Jeremy Hawthorn points
out, 'the mine ... becomes as a mistress to [Gould], usurping the place
of his wife in his thoughts and affections'.[8] One might develop this
insight: if women serve as forms of mediation and tokens of exchange
in the homosocial economy of a patriarchal society, then the mine,
accorded the place of the women, may do the same for Gould. In
Nostromo the natural landscape, rather than the city, is the object of
transcodings of the human body: the 'great body of motionless and
opaque clouds' (5) smothering the quiet gulf, clouds which the sun
can later be seen 'eating ... up' (6); the 'cool purity' of Higuerota with
its 'white dome' (26); the pain of Mrs Viola, the gnawing of which 'for
years ... had been part of the landscape embracing the glitter of the
harbour under the wooded spurs of the range' (25). If Gould has
cathected (to use the Freudian term for attaching a quantity of psychic
energy to a particular object) the mine more than his wife, this is
indicative of a masculinity which has to find obscure routes to bodily
and emotional closeness with other men: the body of the earth is also
the body of his father, since the mine and his father have become
profoundly identified in his psyche. The cool, white purity of Mr
Gould's family allies itself with a South American aristocracy claiming
racial purity, itself a form of (delusory) physical separation: 'The name
of Gould has always been highly respected in Sulaco', Gould tells his
future wife:

> My uncle Harry was chief of the State for some time, and has left a
> great name amongst the first families. By this I mean the pure

Creole families, who take no part in the miserable farce of govern-
ments. Uncle Harry was no adventurer. In Costaguana we Goulds
are no adventurers. He was of the country, and he loved it, but he
remained essentially an Englishman in his ideas. He made use of
the political cry of his time.

`   (64)

This passage is replete with proleptic ironies, most notably bearing
on Gould's later realization that his family are indeed adventurers,
and that he himself has been made use of by the material interests
which he imagined himself to 'make use of' (83): 'with his English
parentage and English upbringing, he perceived that he was an
adventurer in Costaguana, the descendant of adventurers ... [with]
something of an adventurer's easy morality' (365). As we have seen,
Gould remains an Englishman, in his body as well as his ideas, but
the novel reveals that the colonial fantasy of the moral purity of the
English male body has no more substance than the fantasy of racial
purity underlying the above comments by Gould, in which the
'essentially' English gentlemen, with the help of the 'pure' Creoles,
take power, while imagining themselves above politics, and exploit
the body of the land and the bodies of its people, while imagining
themselves above adventuring.

Gould's eventual realization of this is the revenge of the 'cool
purity' of Higuerota, which makes men physically appear like dwarfs
(26–7), and this symbolically corresponds to the historical and
economic forces which dwarf them morally. Furthermore, Gould's
masculinity, and the complacent masculinity (at least at times) of the
narrative voice, are implicitly rebuked too. Wollaeger points to a deep
fear of 'a dissolution of self' in *Nostromo*, which he reads in terms of
philosophical scepticism (*FS*, 124).   He cites Monygham's awareness
of the 'most dangerous element' of physical dangers, 'the crushing,
paralyzing sense of human littleness, which is what really defeats a
man struggling with natural forces, alone, far from the eyes of his
fellows' (*N*, 433), and Arnold Bennett's sense that Higuerota is 'the
principal personage in the story'.[9] Wollaeger concludes that 'society
and consciousness alike ... are endangered by "the majesty of inorganic nature" (*SA*, 14)' (*FS*, 125). Yet is it not rather normative
masculinity which is endangered? – that masculinity which cannot
bear to feel little and so insists on Mrs Gould being little, which desires
to conquer the body of nature while retaining the firm boundaries of
its own body, which, like the chairman of the railway, shows 'the

indifference of a man of affairs to nature, whose hostility can always be overcome by the resources of finance' (39).

Karen Klein sees *Nostromo* as concerned with 'many forms and degrees of oppression', of which bodily subjection is both a symbol and a powerful instance, so that the suspended body of the tortured and murdered Hirsch is 'the core symbol of this novel'. But, as she rightly points out, the 'most iterated' image of the novel is that of the San Tomé mine – which is both symbol and instance of economic and productive forces as the engine of history (FP, 114). A coherent reading of masculinity and the body in *Nostromo* needs to relate the various constructions of masculinity in the novel to its account of historical and social change. Klein bases her analysis of *Nostromo* on a distinction between the 'masculine situation', involving 'the sense of one's body as autonomous' and 'a security based on the knowledge of the cultural assignment of superiority to males in the hierarchy of values' (FP, 104) and 'the feminine predicament', characterized by 'the sense of the body as not under one's own control, but subject to the force and will of others' (FP, 104) and 'the sense of the self as inferior in the hierarchies of status and power' (FP, 106). Arguing that it is possible for men and women to occupy either situation in certain contexts and situations, she reads Nostromo's realization that he has become the tool of the '*hombres finos*' as a shift from the masculine situation to the feminine predicament. In the scene where he gives his buttons to the Morenita he is in the former, she in the latter, but 'in the course of the narrative, Nostromo comes to occupy the place of the Morenita in relation to the real power-brokers: the English, the Spanish, American interests' (FP, 110). Nostromo's awareness of this is triggered by his confrontation with Monygham and with the body of the tortured and murdered Hirsch. The latter, as a Jewish victim of extreme cruelty, has experienced the worst consequences of the feminine predicament, while Monygham is a past victim of torture (FP, 111–12). Klein's rationale for describing such events in terms of gender is Engels's claim that 'women represent the first oppressed group'. Hence she argues that 'gender oppression ... precedes other forms of group oppression ... and serves as the paradigm for them', and is also the most pervasive form of such oppression, as women are found in virtually all groups (FP, 102–3).

I find Klein's argument convincing and thought-provoking, including her claims that the ending of the novel evades, through contrived ironies, the truths which have been revealed. (The unsatisfactory nature of the novel's ending is also a result of its attempt to reinstate

Nostromo's heroic status through unconvincing romantic hyperbole.)
However, Klein's account raises two problems concerning masculinity
and the body. First, the priority which she gives to gender oppression
as a paradigm paradoxically ends up by risking dilution of its specificity to the point where the issue of gender tends to disappear. Klein
argues that 'the feminine predicament pertains to all females', but
modifies this with the suggestion that 'many appear to escape the
component of hierarchical inferiority through economic class' (FP,
107). However, she implies that men move between the masculine
situation and the feminine predicament according to their access to
power. There is thus a tendency in her argument for 'masculine' and
'feminine' to become merely markers for degrees of power or powerlessness. In practice the relationship to power inscribed in masculinity
seems more recalcitrant. The second and related problem pertains
more specifically to *Nostromo*. If Nostromo is shown to be the tool of
Gould and the aristocrats, then ultimately Gould is shown to be the
tool of his American backers and their 'material interests'. Is Gould,
then, also in the feminine predicament by the end of the novel? If so
– if, that is, a wealthy, successful, powerful colonial mine-owner and
power-broker, with a fine house, a supportive wife and many servants,
is seen to lack bodily autonomy and status –, then it begins to seem
almost like a universal human condition. What happens in Klein's
article, I think, is that a liberal, feminist concern for the rights of the
individual overlaps with a Marxist view of society in terms of large-
scale impersonal power-structures, and this generates a
methodological aporia. The account of the pervasive influence of
'material interests' in *Nostromo* makes it highly conducive to Marxist
readings.[10] In terms of the body, though, Foucault would be equally
relevant. In *Discipline and Punish* he sees power in modern society as
operating upon the body through what he terms 'disciplinary
methods'.[11] These methods involve the detailed analysis and regulation of bodily and mental activity characteristic of prisons, hospitals,
factories, schools, barracks and other such institutions in the modern
period (i.e. since the late eighteenth century). They produce 'docile
bodies': that is, bodies that are productive and subjected to social
control without the need for overt coercion or violence.[12] As Foucault
specifies in *The History of Sexuality*, his concept of power does not
attribute it to particular groups:

> By power, I do not mean 'Power' as a group of institutions and
> mechanisms that ensure the subservience of the citizens of a given

state ... [nor] a general system of domination exerted by one group over another ... power must be understood ... as the multiplicity of force relations immanent in the sphere in which they operate and which constitute their own organization [and] as the process which, through ceaseless struggles and confrontations, transforms, strengthens, or reverses them.[13]

Here Foucault offers a concept of power which is not limited to individuals or groups having power over each other, but emphasizes impersonal processes and forces. When Klein states that Nostromo comes to occupy the feminine predicament, she describes this in terms of his being used by certain individuals and groups: 'Persons in this power axis of economics and politics control Nostromo, too ... He is their man and they use him as carelessly as he used the Morenita' (FP, 110). Yet beyond the violation or exploitation of individual bodies by other individuals or groups, the novel seems to reveal the existence of structures of power which discipline bodies in a way which is impersonal, although it may be 'intentional' as Foucault explains:

> Power relations are both intentional and nonsubjective ... There is no power that is exercised without a series of aims and objectives. But this does not mean that it results from the choice or decision of an individual subject ... neither the caste which governs, nor the groups which control the state apparatus, nor those who make the most important economic decisions direct the entire network of power that functions in a society (and makes *it* function); the rationality of power is characterised by tactics ... (the local cynicism of power), tactics which ... end by forming comprehensive systems: the logic is perfectly clear, the aims decipherable, and yet it is often the case that no one is there to have invented them.[14]

This seems strikingly apt in relation to Sulaco, with its governing class (the Blancos, during certain periods), its groups controlling the state apparatus (the Monterists, during other periods), its individuals making economic decisions (Gould, Holroyd), all of whom are powerful in different ways, yet none of whom seem to control or determine the ultimate consequences of power,[15] and with its local cynicism (Nostromo, Sotillo, Fuentes). These elements make up a system beyond the understanding of those who operate it.

Nostromo depicts a pre-modern society (the old Costaguana of aristocrats and bandits) emerging into modernity (the new Occidental

Province of railroads, tramcars, organized industry and domination by American capital).[16] The disciplining of the body – and specifically the male working body – is crucial to this process and the silver mine, which is the central, symbol of the novel, provides the clearest example of this. Foucault distinguishes discipline from slavery: slavery was based upon 'a relation of appropriation of bodies' whereas discipline 'could dispense with this costly and violent relation by obtaining effects of utility at least as great'.[17] Rather than violent appropriation of the bodies of others, deploying physical force and punishment, discipline is

> a policy of coercions that act upon the body, a calculated manipulation of its elements, its gestures, its behaviour ... so that they [the bodies of others] may operate as one wishes, with the techniques, the speed and the efficiency that one determines. Thus discipline produces subjected and practised bodies, 'docile' bodies.[18]

It is the difference, say, between flogging men to make them work, and using time and motion studies, training, rules and human resource policies to induce them to employ their bodies to maximum productive effect. The San Tomé mine does not get as far as time and motion studies during the period depicted in the novel, but Gould's transformation of the mine, and hence of the society of Costaguana, is precisely achieved through a move towards such disciplinary methods:

> Worked in the early days mostly by means of lashes on the backs of slaves, its yield [i.e. that of the mine] had been paid for in its own weight of human bones. Whole tribes of Indians had perished in the exploitation; and then the mine was abandoned, since with this primitive method it had ceased to make a profitable return, no matter how many corpses were thrown into its maw.
>
> (52)

In contrast, Gould transforms the mine into an economic success and a political power base through the creation of a disciplined body of men: disciplined in both the normal sense and in Foucault's sense. He introduces numbered villages (100), an informal uniform emerges (97), and the miners are subject to surveillance and categorization by the representatives of Capital, Church and Medicine in the persons of Don Pepé ('El Señor Gobernador' (99)), Father Roman and Dr Monygham:

[Don Pepé] was in charge of the whole population in the territory of the mine ... He affirmed with humorous exaggeration to Mrs Gould—

'No two stones could come together anywhere without the Gobernador hearing the click, señora.'

... Even when the number of the miners alone rose to over six hundred he seemed to know each of them individually ... He seemed able ... to classify each woman, girl, or growing youth of his domain ... He and the padre could be seen frequently side by side, meditative and gazing across the street of a village at a lot of sedate brown children, trying to sort them out, as it were, in low, consulting tones.

(99–102)

However benign, such surveillance and categorization, constituting the individual as object of detailed control and knowledge, is, according to Foucault, typical of the operation of power in a modern 'disciplinary' society, in contrast to the relative anonymity of traditional society, where 'power was embodied in the person of the monarch and exercised upon a largely anonymous body of subjects'.[19] In the disciplinary society, effects of power circulate 'through progressively finer channels, gaining access to individuals themselves, to their bodies, their gestures and all their daily actions'.[20] Don Pepé's work of surveillance is described with detailed reference to the body, in a passage which has affinities with the descriptions of fragmentary bodies in *Lord Jim* (the pilgrims on the *Patna*), and 'Typhoon' (the 'coolies' on the *Nan-Shan*):

He could distinguish them not only by their flat, joyless faces ... but apparently also by the infinitely graduated shades of reddish-brown, of blackish brown, of coppery-brown backs, as the two shifts ... mingled together with a confusion of naked limbs.

(100)

They [Don Pepé and Father Roman] would together put searching questions as to the parentage of some small, staid urchin met wandering, naked and grave, along the road with a cigar in his baby mouth, and perhaps his mother's rosary ... hanging in a loop of beads low down on his rotund little stomach.

(102)

The organization of the mine also extends to a system of watchmen, themselves watched over by Don Pepé (103) and regular structured convoys for the transportation of the silver (86–7). As Foucault shows, the humanitarian liberal claims of such modern institutions enable more subtle and efficient forms of coercion over the body. Through organizational structures, routines of behaviour, markers of identity and control, combined with self-interest and a sense of belonging, the miners become an organized and unified body of men, capable of marching on the town to intervene in a political crisis and the mine becomes 'an institution, a rallying point for everything in the province that needed order and stability to live' (110).

A comparable but lesser process takes place with the Cargadores or dockworkers led by Nostromo, whose effectiveness under his influence is contrasted with the 'revolutionary rabble' of the Monterists (12). The evolution of modern industrial practices leads eventually to what the narrator, with a hint of mock pride, terms 'quite serious, organized labour troubles' (95). In the early days, however, the effectiveness of the Cargadores is crucially dependant upon the prestige of Nostromo: that is, it works by a more traditional model, centred on the display of the body of the leader (rather than on the disciplining of the body of the followers) and crude physical coercion. These are dramatized in the scene where Nostromo cuts off his buttons to placate the Morenita, at the centre of an admiring crowd (127–30), and in the description of Nostromo's methods for rousing the Cargadores after a fiesta (95–6). So Nostromo's realization that he has been exploited and is regarded as ultimately disposable (what Klein terms his fall into the feminine predicament) can be seen in Foucauldian terms as his discovery that a changing social order has rendered his methods of control outdated: the old order in which prestige and punishment were both written on the body has been displaced by a bureaucratic modernity of disciplined, docile bodies.

What Gould discovers is not that his methods are outdated (quite the contrary) but that they are, in respect of his personal (partly unconscious) aims, self-defeating. The events of the novel clearly belong to what Chris Bongie terms the age of the 'New Imperialism' when, the opportunities for exploration as such being more or less exhausted, the Great Powers competed for control over lands which had already been mapped out (*EM*, 17–18).[21] Gould himself is an agent of New Imperialist 'progress', helping to establish the dominance of the USA over South America. He affects to understand and accept this from the start: 'the great silver and iron interests shall survive, and some day shall get hold of Costaguana along with the rest of the world' (82). Yet the unconscious fantasy that he is engaged in working out (as a consequence of his identification with his father) is one of heroic individuality: 'the secret of it was that to Charles Gould's mind these uncompromising terms were agreeable. Like this the mine preserved its identity, with which he had endowed it as a boy; and it remained dependent on himself alone' (82). It is entirely in accord with Foucault's account that Gould's belief in his individual autonomy is the product of his subjection to the disciplinary powers of modernity, and serves those powers. For Foucault individuality as conceived in modern society is 'an effect and an object of discipline', so that our sense of ourselves as individuals is constituted through the processes which constrain us: 'The man described for us [by humanism], whom we are invited to free, is already in himself the effect of a subjection much more profound than himself'.[22] Both Gould and Nostromo, in their different class and racial positions, are in this sense subjected, and what they are subjected to is, primarily, productivity:

> Discipline increases the forces of the body (in economic terms of utility) and diminishes these same forces (in political terms of obedience) ... It dissociates power from the body; on the one hand, it turns it into an 'aptitude', a 'capacity', which it seeks to increase; on the other hand, it reverses the course of the energy, the power that might result from it, and turns it into a relation of strict subjection.[23]

Bongie and Foucault concur in dating a new dispensation from the late eighteenth century. For Bongie this is modernity, characterized by a sense of the loss of 'authentic experience' following 'the political and technological revolutions of the late-eighteenth and early-nineteenth centuries' (*EM*, 9). For Foucault it is the new configuration of power and knowledge which he terms discipline, involving the human sciences and social institutions in a combined construction of a relatively docile human subject. Both see this dispensation of the last two centuries as involving a deceptive form of individuality. Bongie traces the disappearance of a form of subjectivity 'typical of traditional communities' (*EM*, 9) and pertaining to 'the old subject of experience' who was supposedly 'able to apprehend others concretely' within a context where value was not called into question. This disappearance, he argues, has generated in compensation 'the modern (Romantic) *individual*'. This modern subject, while 'desirous of experience, is nonetheless constituted by the impossibility of that experience', and 'although aware of his own alienation and in search of a remedy for it ... cannot admit that this alienation is what actually constitutes him' (*EM*, 10). For Foucault 'subject' and 'subjection' are, as we have seen, closely related terms: that which forms us as modern subjects or individuals also subjects us to disciplinary power. Exoticism, according to Bongie, is a strategy for maintaining 'the illusion of spontaneous desire' and of autonomous subjectivity, by seeking a realm of experience outside an alienating modernity (*EM*, 10). He distinguishes two forms of exoticism: 'whereas imperialist exoticism affirms the hegemony of modern civilization over the less developed, savage territories, exoticizing exoticism privileges those very territories and their peoples, figuring them as a possible refuge from an overbearing modernity' (*EM*, 17). *Nostromo* is dominated by the former fantasy and Gould in particular embodies its paradoxical project. Discovering in Costaguana (a colonial context where modernization and urbanization come relatively late) a field for the assertion of individual autonomy over against an Other seen as inferior he nevertheless directs that assertion towards the establishment of a modernity which will erode that autonomy (or reveal it to have always been illusory).

Bongie notes the possibility that 'modern individualism and masculist ideology feed into each other' (*EM*, 10), a possibility illuminated by Christine Buci-Glucksmann's account of the late nineteenth century as the moment when an alienation of men from their bodies is matched by an excessive identification of women with the body.[24] This also suggests one way in which the male and female roles in *Nostromo* are connected to its theme of economic and social change. The process of 'confiscation' of the male working body by industrialization and urbanization underlies the alienation of Gould and Nostromo, revealing their respective versions of heroic male masculinity (encoded in their bodies) to be increasingly outmoded or delusionary. One thing which distinguishes the subjection of Gould and Nostromo from that of the female characters is the displacement of the idea of the body onto the women. Mrs Gould, the Morenita and Giselle Viola 'overrepresent' (to use Buci-Glucksmann's term) the body, while the fictive heroic autonomy of Gould and Nostromo is invested in their power and will. The narrator, particularly liable to take a position of sexist condescension when led into generalization (a quality which is shared with narrators elsewhere in Conrad's work, notably Marlow), betrays such an identification of women with the body when he opines that:

It must not be supposed that Mrs. Gould's mind was masculine. A woman with a masculine mind is not a being of superior efficiency; she is simply a phenomenon of imperfect differentiation—interestingly *barren* and without importance.

(66–7; emphasis added)

'Barren', with its suggestion of childlessness, implies that for a woman to challenge men in the sphere of the mind would detract from her body (an idea commonly used by the reactionary side in the 'New Woman' debate of the 1890s). Yet a symbolic reading of the Goulds' childlessness would more plausibly relate it to the barrenness of Gould's heart rather than the liveliness of his wife's intelligence. The identification of women with the body helps to generate the feminine predicament: to constrain the possibilities for women of attaining even limited autonomy and status. But the identification of men with mind and will and the overidentification of women with the body conceals the existence of masculinity and femininity as correlative though unequal forms of bodily discipline. Gould, Mrs Gould and Nostromo all find themselves trapped within systems of meaning which determine them. All three have believed that their way of being bodied forth their inner selves, but discover that their bodies have been written upon by history and ideology (a fact of which Hirsch is the symbol). All three have taken pleasure in others' attribution of meaning to their bodies: Mrs Gould has enjoyed being admired and condescended to by Gould; Nostromo has enjoyed the physical display of his status and reputation; Gould has enjoyed the admiration of Holroyd and others for his imperturbability. In each case this pleasure turns bitter. However, the narrator seems more complicit with the inscription of Mrs Gould's body. The identification of the males with mind and will and the overidentification of the females with the body has the further consequence, perhaps unintended by Conrad, that the novel's progressive revelation of the subjection of the male characters to 'material interests' implies a deconstruction of their masculinity. This masculinity is revealed as, borrowing Althusser's words, an 'imaginary relationship of individuals to their real conditions of existence', and therefore a form of ideology.[25]

The ending of the novel expresses an unwillingness to accept this deconstruction. The traditional romantic troping of nature and landscape as female represents a displacement of the body parallel to the displacement of the body onto women. By exerting mind and will in an effort to dominate nature, men deny their bodily existence as part of the natural. However, the landscape in *Nostromo* tends to sound rather male, from the domineering Higuerota to the Golfo Placido which 'goes to sleep under its black poncho' (6). The ending of the novel, however, reinscribes the landscape under the sign of (Linda's) lost romantic love:

> In that true cry of undying passion that seemed to ring aloud from Punta Mala to Azuera and away to the bright line of the horizon, overhung by a big white cloud shining like a mass of solid silver, the genius of the magnificent Capitaz de Cargadores dominated the dark gulf containing his conquests of treasure and love.
>
> (566)

Both Linda and the landscape appear as feminine objects of Nostromo's heroic conquest, and the key fact that Nostromo was (morally) conquered *by* the treasure is seemingly forgotten. Invoking romantic cliché, this ending serves to repress the homosocial: the fact that Gould's primary desire has been formed around the figure of his father, while Nostromo's primary desire has been to impress other men, whether the Cargadores or the '*hombres finos*'.

A Foucauldian account of *Nostromo* seems most effective, then, in relating the fate of the body in *Nostromo* to its themes of social and historical change. However, Foucault's theory needs to be supplemented by feminist writing, including Cixous's concept of *écriture féminine*. Foucault is widely seen as neglecting the importance of gender. As Sandra Lee Bartky notes: 'Women, like men, are subject to many of the same disciplinary practices Foucault describes. But he is blind to those disciplines that produce a modality of embodiment that is peculiarly feminine.'[26] Bartky suggests one reason for this neglect: despite his insistence that power is diffused and does not 'belong' to institutions, she suggests that his analysis of its operations (in *Discipline and Punish*) is carried out too exclusively with respect to institutions:

> Foucault tends to identify the imposition of discipline upon the body with the operation of specific institutions, for example, the school, the factory, the prison. To do this, however, is to overlook the extent to which discipline can be institutionally *unbound* as well as institutionally bound. The anonymity of disciplinary power and its wide dispersion have consequences that are crucial to a proper understanding of the subordination of women ... The social construction of the feminine body ... at its base ... is discipline ...

and discipline of the inegalitarian sort. The absence of formally identifiable disciplinarians and of a public schedule of sanctions only disguises the extent to which the imperative to be 'feminine' serves the interest of domination.[27]

A seemingly paradoxical implication of this is, I would suggest, that Foucault also neglects masculinity as a disciplinary practice, even while he analyses some of the institutions that produce it. This is an example of a general effect in which the sort of masculinist discourse that simply takes as universal what is in fact specifically male is blind to the specificity of masculinity as a social construction. Neglecting the issue of gender, Foucault analyses (for example) the army or prison as disciplines producing a certain form of docile body, but does not look at the implications of these as institutions which have operated through and upon males, so that he does not consider elements peculiar to masculinity in the forms of embodiment which he describes. This is not to claim that male forms of embodiment are *equally* subjected, not a manoeuvre to undermine Bartky's feminist point. Indeed, an advantage of Foucault's idea of a 'microphysics of power', dispersed and acting through those subjected to it, is that it offers, as I have suggested, a way out of the dilemma implicit in Klein's reading of *Nostromo*: how do we reconcile an awareness of the relative empowerment of men with an awareness of the subjection of many men to economic and political oppression? In arguing that power is not *possessed* by groups, Foucault does not, I take it, mean to deny that some groups have much greater power. The discipline that constructs masculinity is still a form of subjection, though one which accords relatively greater autonomy, while also promoting forms of aggressive and violent behaviour. We thus arrive at a reading of the masculine body in the novel: masculinity as a discipline òr technology of normalization. Stereotypes are in one sense only exaggerated versions of such a technology: parodic accounts of how individual bodies in a (proto-)modern state are self-disciplining. Here, as elsewhere, Conrad's work seems more radical in its view of masculinity than in its view of femininity. I agree with Klein that *Nostromo* is patronizing to women; yet the vision of normative masculinity in the novel approaches that of masquerade or parody. If Gould and Nostromo at times seem like stereotypes, this reveals the way in which masculinity itself is a form of stereotype. Yet the narrative seems complicit with the stereotyping of women, rather as Conrad is often conservative and indeed reactionary in his view of radical politics, yet subversive in his view of the establishment. Jeremy Hawthorn argues that Conrad succumbs to pessimistic determinism in *Nostromo*, because he is unwilling to entertain 'the possibility of human beings changing their social relationships so as to alter their material interest'.[28] This tendency of the novel would accord with its amenability to Foucauldian analysis, since Foucault's account of power, like Conrad's account of 'material interests', can tend to make change seem impossible because of the pervasiveness of trans-human forces. In Chapter 3 I contrasted Cixous's celebratory account of a coinherence of body and meaning with Foucault's emphasis on the body as a site of social inscription. A vision of the liberation of the male body from masculinity as a discipline would then seem to require a male version of writing the body. However, Stephen Heath argues that, because of male power, there can be no equivalent for men of the political validity of women's emphasis on writing the body and a gendered discourse:

> The truth about men and their bodies *for the moment* is merely repetitive ... the régime of the same, the eternal problem of the phallus, etc. ... Taking men's bodies away from the existing representation and its oppressive effects will have to follow women's writing anew of themselves.[29]

The 'moment' of Heath writing this was 1986, since which time there have been many developments in society, in feminist theory, in gay and lesbian theory, and in the study of masculinity. It is therefore an open question whether the situation described by Heath has changed: whether, alongside a continuing analysis and critique of phallic constructions of masculinity, there is now a place for the developing of alternative models. The route to a writing of the male body would seem to be through an understanding of homosexual desire and homosocial bonds, and the complex relations between them. There is a need, then, to examine traces of desire between men, as well as the very various forms of bond between men, in Conrad's fiction. This is not in order to hint at some revelation about the 'reality' of Conrad's sexuality, but because same-sex desire is the excluded and repressed term of normative masculinity – an excluded term which determines many of its features. These issues will be taken up in more detail in Chapters 7 and 8. At this point it is enough to observe the importance of a number of homosocial bonds in *Nostromo*: Gould and his father (*N*, 63, 66, 73); Nostromo and his surrogate father, Viola (548); Gould and Holroyd (65).

As I indicated in the Introduction, a consideration of masculinity in Conrad's work is by no means limited to the question of Conrad's *opinions* on the issue, nor even to those opinions in combination with any reactions and assumptions which he might betray unconsciously (though all of these are of course of interest). Fictional texts of the complexity and richness of Conrad's reveal meaning on many different levels and in many different ways other than as an expression of the author's intention. Furthermore, since masculinity is, among other things, a way of relating to others and a way of conceiving of oneself, the voices and narrative personae which Conrad projects and the way in which these interact with characters and (implied) readers are crucial. Both Klein and Wollaeger are led by their discussions of *Nostromo* to address the author's attitude to his characters. Klein, as we have seen, accuses Conrad of a patronizing attitude towards Mrs Gould. Wollaeger, who deals interestingly with what he terms 'the attack on the body' (*FS*, 150) in *The Secret Agent*, does not look at issues of gender, but like Klein considers subjection and the author's attitudes to his characters in *Nostromo*. Pointing to the occurrences of torture in the novel, and to the way in which the narrative tends to impose on characters the author's moral scheme (outlined by the fable of the gringos in Chapter 1), Wollaeger, again like Klein, reads the torture of Hirsch as an instance of loss of autonomy. Arguing that characters strive for an autonomy (in relation to economic forces, to historical change and to other individuals) which the author seems unwilling to grant them, he claims that Conrad's vision insists on the power of external determination, but that 'making the text turn back on itself, Conrad criticizes his own complicity in the many instances of torture his text recounts, and this reflexive commentary saves the story from becoming reductively fatalistic or even sadistic' (*FS*, 141). Wollaeger's evidence for such a reflexive critique lies in the 'verbal and structural connections ... between Decoud's suicide and Hirsch's murder [which] suggest the author's awareness of the extent to which the narrative machinery of *Nostromo* may exist in order to torture its characters' (*FS*, 140–1). I find this a compelling reading of the novel, but would wish to introduce both the issue of gender and the fate of the body considered in more specific terms than merely as indicative of autonomy or its lack. For the voice which narrates much of the novel, whether considered as an implied or 'secondary' author, or as an extradiegetic and heterodiegetic narrator, is crucially *disembodied*, and therefore not subject to the risk of bodily subjection.[30] The Bakhtinian ideal of polyphony, to which Wollaeger alludes, imagines a degree of equality between author and characters in which 'each character embodies an autonomous perspective that carries the same authority as the discourse of the author' even though 'each character is at the same time determined by the all-encompassing intention of the author as realized in the design of the fiction' (*FS*, 131). In Wollaeger's summary here, the language encodes an inequality between the characters who can only '*embody*' a '*perspective*' (subjectivity as residing in the body and comprehension metaphorically represented as vision) and the author, whose authority is that of discourse and is '*realized*' through a grand '*design*'. One might make an analogy with film here. Kaja Silverman argues that:

> There is a general theoretical consensus that the theological status of the disembodied voice-over is the effect of maintaining its source in a place apart from the camera, inaccessible to the gaze of either the cinematic apparatus or the viewing subject – of violating the rule of synchronization so absolutely that the voice is left without an identifiable locus. In other words, the voice-over is privileged to the degree that *it transcends the body*. Conversely, it loses power and authority with every corporeal encroachment, from a regional accent or idiosyncratic 'grain' to definitive localization in the image. Synchronization marks the final moment in any such localization, the point of full and complete 'embodiment'.[31]

This formulation is very suggestive in relation to the Marlow of 'Heart of Darkness', who becomes a voice speaking in the darkness, as he talks of Kurtz, whom he describes in turn as 'A voice! a voice!' (147). 'Heart of Darkness' might be considered as a text where the embodiment of the homodiegetic-intradiegetic narrator Marlow (the most important narrator in that text) varies in degree in a way which is symbolic of his identification with Kurtz and his confrontation with a loss of self. In that case the shift from 'Heart of Darkness' to *Nostromo* would be rather in accord with Wollaeger's suggestion that the lack of a Marlow-type figure interceding between Conrad and his characters leads to a more coercive attitude on the part of the secondary author. The textual equivalent of synchronization would be a correspondence between the narrating instance (the time in which the telling of the story takes place) and the narrated instance (the time of the story which is narrated). In 'Heart of Darkness' there is a temporal distance between these two, but it is fairly regular and stable, whereas in *Nostromo* it varies wildly, so that in Silverman's terms the narrator of *Nostromo* is less embodied and more transcendent. The narrative voice of the novel flirts with embodiment when it speaks the popular wisdom of Costaguana, analogous to a 'regional accent or idiosyncratic "grain"', but it retains the ability to transcend the body at will. Silverman notes that disembodied female voice-overs are virtually unknown in Hollywood film.[32] This marks the distinction between a disembodied, transcendent, unsynchronized male voice and the speaking from and with the body which Cixous describes as characteristic of a woman who 'physically materializes what she's thinking'.[33]

Disembodied writing is of course precisely what French feminism has identified as a male form of discourse, in response to which *écriture féminine* seeks a writing closer to the body of the author. Does Conrad in any sense write his own body? As we have seen, while Cixous argues that it is possible for male writers to do so (instancing a gay male writer), Heath argues that there can be no equivalent for men of the political validity of writing the body (though tentatively excepting gay male writing). Not only have men been less likely to write in an embodied manner, but if they do it does not have the same political meaning, since, as Gallop points out, 'men are more able to venture into the realm of the body without being trapped there'.[34] Certainly if one thinks of the narrative voice(s) of *Nostromo* in terms of the distanced superiority of Higuerota, towering in somewhat phallic manner over the characters, or if one takes the force of Wollaeger's analysis of the coercive, controlling stance of the implied/secondary author, then Conrad's strategies here would seem in accord with Gallop's point that 'men have their masculine identity to gain by being estranged from their bodies and dominating the bodies of others'.[35] We might ask, though, whether the reflexive critique which Wollaeger detects in *Nostromo* embraces a critique by Conrad of the power which he gains from being disembodied. Reilly argues that

> *Nostromo* is not merely a self-conscious, but actually a self-critical text. It acknowledges a possibly debilitating paradox at the heart of its own project in that it attempts to analyse the historical development of capitalism and its correlative colonialism, while being itself a strand within the discourse of capitalism/colonialism and hence disposed to endorse its values.[36]

Does the novel similarly acknowledge its complicity with a masculinist denial of the body in order to subjugate the bodies of others? Within the text itself the only suggestion of such an acknowledgement comes from reading, as Guerard does, the inconsistencies or waywardness of the narrative voice as a form of self-betrayal by Conrad. If the novel is read in relation to other texts by Conrad, including the non-fictional, then some wider sense of anxiety about embodiment and complicity is revealed. The link seems to be immobility and passivity, desired as forms of indulgence and feared as forms of subjection. Guerard suggests that Conrad unfairly projects his own scepticism onto Decoud and proposes that *Nostromo* 'was written by an even more skeptical Decoud who recognized, to be sure, the immobilizing dangers of skepticism'.[37] In *The Secret Agent*, as I have already shown, the narrator attacks laziness in an excessive and obsessive manner. In the 'Author's Note' to *Victory* Conrad associates himself with his protagonist Heyst by describing an experience of observing an attractive and perhaps victimized female, an experience which provided material for Heyst's rescue of Lena from the orchestra. In the novel Heyst learns too late to overcome passivity, but he does at least rescue Lena; Conrad admits to having been too idle to take any active interest in the women he saw ('Author's Note', *V*, xvii). Here lack of activity is presented as part of the pleasant indulgence of a sophisticated *flâneur*. However, in many passages of Conrad's fiction lack of activity is sinister.[38] The apotheosis of this sinister passivity in *Nostromo* is the body of Hirsch, an uncanny, abject corpse, initially taken for a living man by Nostromo, when the latter sees 'the distorted shadow of broad shoulders and bowed head. He was apparently doing nothing, and stirred not from the spot, as though he were meditating' (423–4). Later Nostromo perceives 'his constrained, toppling attitude — the shoulders projecting forward, the head sunk low upon the breast ... The rigid legs ... the feet hanging down nervelessly' (427). In a passage from a letter of 1891, Conrad complains that he is vegetating and not thinking, and plays with the idea that he does not exist. His image of himself here partakes of the black humour of his fictional descriptions of Hirsch and comparable dead figures (such as Kayerts at the end of 'An Outpost of Progress'). He imagines himself as a Punch doll:

> l'échine casée en deux le nez par terre entre les pieds; les jambes et les bras raidement écartés, dans cette attitude de profond désespoir, si pathétiquement drôle, des jouets jétés dans un coin.

[his spine broken in two, his nose on the floor between his feet; his legs and arms flung out stiffly in that attitude of profound despair, so pathetically droll, of dolls tossed in a corner.][39]

Passivity as non-being, as bodily subjection, as loss of identity: the author as abject, in the feminine predicament, grotesque. Perhaps only in such fragmentary self-revelation and in the oblique manoeuvres of his narrators can Conrad tentatively embody his own masculinity.

5
Epistemology, Modernity and Masculinity: 'Heart of Darkness'

Conrad's exploration of the epistemological uncertainty of the modern condition has been discussed by many critics, who vary in the degree of scepticism which they attribute to his work. Ian Watt describes Conrad's use of disrupted chronology as reflecting his 'sense of the fragmentary and elusive quality of individual experience' and analyses what he terms Conrad's 'subjective moral impressionism' in 'Heart of Darkness': that is to say, his use of a narrative form which asserts 'the bounded and ambiguous nature of individual understanding'. Watt suggests a moderate form of modernist uncertainty, involving subjectivity, fragmentariness and ambiguity.[1] J. Hillis Miller goes further in suggesting that 'the special place of Joseph Conrad in English literature lies in the fact that in him the nihilism covertly dominant in modern culture is brought to the surface and shown for what it is.'[2] Daphna Erdinast-Vulcan argues plausibly for a pervasive tension in Conrad's work between, on the one hand, a quest for epistemological and ethical certainty and, on the other, a relativistic scepticism about the possibility of such certainty.[3] There is general agreement, however, that Conrad's fiction emphasizes the problematic nature of questions of what we can know, how we can know it and what degree of certainty is possible. These questions are raised in particular in terms of the relationship of language to truth and reality and in this form locate Conrad's work within literary modernism.[4] However, until recently relatively little attention has been paid to how epistemological issues in Conrad's work are inflected by gender: the ways in which knowledge, ideas about knowledge and symbols of truth are differentially distributed among male and female characters (and implied readers) and the ways in which such knowledge, ideas and symbols are themselves used to set up, construct, reinforce or modify gender differences. Nina Pelikan Straus's article 'The Exclusion of the Intended from Secret Sharing in Conrad's *Heart of Darkness*', as it became widely known in the early 1990s, helped to spark a debate on these issues.[5]

Such an investigation has significance that goes beyond questions of Conrad's own attitudes. Conrad is widely regarded as a major literary modernist and as a prophet and critic of the condition of social modernity. While modernity (a social phenomenon) and modernism (a movement in the arts) are by no means identical or co-extensive, modernist experiment in the arts can be understood as a response to the experiences of modernity.[6] The modernist techniques of writing which Conrad used and in certain respects pioneered, such as the use of multiple narratives, unreliable narrators and non-linear narrative, also enabled him, as Ian Watt argues, to represent what have been seen as some of the key philosophical dilemmas of modernity or the modern condition: principally epistemological and ethical doubt. But feminist writing has questioned the universalizing assumptions of many accounts of the problems of 'modern man', and suggested that women's experience of modernity and women's relations to issues of knowledge and truth were significantly different from those of men.[7] Many of the grounds for asserting such a difference are very applicable to Conrad's work. It has been pointed out that many of the archetypal figures of modernism as traditionally conceived are necessarily male. For example, Janet Wolff argues that 'the literature of modernity describes the experience of men', citing the example of the *flâneur*, the idler or stroller with the 'freedom to move about in the city, observing and being observed, but never interacting with others'.[8] As Wolff points out, women did not enjoy such freedom during the second half of the nineteenth century, since an idling woman might be taken for a prostitute, while the exchange of anonymous gazes in which the *flâneur* indulges was one which the conventions of respectability did not allow to women.[9] While these conventions were increasingly challenged and gradually eroded during the period of literary modernism (c. 1890–1930), the city wanderers of Joyce's *Ulysses*, Eliot's early poetry, Knut Hamsun's *Hunger* and other modernist classics remained crucially male (a version of the *flâneuse* appears in 1925, in Woolf's *Mrs Dalloway*). Conrad's fictional settings are prior to the First World War and Victorian conventions of female respectability remain potent (though open to challenge in a novel such as *Chance*). Such a construction of femininity can be understood in terms of a sexual politics which made women the object of the male gaze. The wanderer in the city plays a role in certain of Conrad's works, in particular *Under Western Eyes*, *The Secret Agent* and *Chance*. The *flâneur* as described by Walter Benjamin in his writings on Baudelaire is a figure indicative of modernity yet also 'on the margins both of the great city and of the bourgeois class'.[10] The *flâneur* has affinities with the detective, with the victims and murders of Poe's stories which Baudelaire translated as well as with Baudelaire himself as alienated poet.[11] Razumov and the language-teacher in *Under Western Eyes*, Verloc, Ossipon, Heat and the Professor in *The Secret Agent* and Marlow in *Chance* all adopt at certain points a role like that of the *flâneur*, while women characters, such as Mrs Verloc and Flora de Barral, are placed in such a situation only at moments of risk or vulnerability. Furthermore, many of Conrad's central figures occupy roles which were characteristically or exclusively male during that period: sea-captain, trader, entrepreneur, spy, detective. This gives a decisively gendered inflection to the experience of modernity which he represents. The availability to men of certain sorts of experience and knowledge, and the exclusion of women from these, must be understood as systematic, and therefore integral to the epistemological basis of the novels, rather than as merely contingent upon plot and setting. If we see one reason for Conrad's interest and importance as a writer as being his representation of the epistemological position of the subject of modernity, then the gendering of that subject must crucially determine the form of modernity which his work presents.

An account of the gendered epistemology of Conrad's work requires a model of the interaction between knowledge, power, sexuality and gender within late nineteenth-century and early twentieth-century European society. The basis for such a model is found in the work of Nietzsche and Foucault, as read and revised by feminist critics, in particular Eve Sedgwick. Nietzsche's radical understanding of knowledge as something produced, and as a tool of power rather than as a neutral description of the world, is developed by Foucault, who asks 'what is at stake in the will to truth, in the will to utter this "true" discourse, if not desire and power?'[12] Eve Sedgwick argues that

> many of the major nodes of thought and knowledge in twentieth-century Western culture as a whole are structured – indeed, fractured – by a chronic, now endemic crisis of homo/heterosexual definition, indicatively male, dating from the end of the nineteenth century.
>
> (EC, 1)

She does so on the basis of Foucault's view that, in Sedgwick's words:

> modern Western culture has placed what it calls sexuality in a more
> and more distinctively privileged relation to our most prized
> constructs of individual identity, truth and knowledge ... [so that]
> the language of sexuality not only intersects with but transforms
> the other languages and relations by which we know.
>
> (*EC*, 3)

Sedgwick also points out that 'ignorance and opacity collude or
compete with knowledge in mobilizing the flows of energy, desire,
goods, meanings, persons' *(EC*, 4). This observation serves to emphasize the need to attend to complementary structures of knowledge and
ignorance in Conrad's fiction.[13] Luce Irigaray's analyses of patriarchal
structures of exchange have identified the functional need for women
to be deprived of knowledge (or placed in the role of the 'ignorant'):
'In a relationship established between (at least) two men, the ignorant
young woman is the *mediation prescribed by society*' (*TS*, 199).

Drawing some of these threads together, I would suggest that the
epistemology of Conrad's work is explicable in terms of (social) structures of male power and (psychic) structures of male desire. A
discourse of knowledge, truth and ignorance plays a crucial part in the
maintenance of these structures, reinforcing both masculine identity
and male access to empowering knowledge, while enabling the
symbolic, psychic and social exploitation of women. This discourse
does not simply attribute knowledge to men and ignorance to women
but variably associates women with particular forms of ignorance and
knowledge in such a way as to make them available as symbols of a
mysterious truth and objects of a secret knowledge while largely
depriving them of the role of knowing subject. Conrad's texts participate in an ideological discourse which both produces 'truths' about
women and produces a concept of femininity constructed as the
Other of male knowledge. This Other is simultaneously, and paradoxically, the complementary ignorance against which male knowledge
defines itself and a symbol of the ultimate truth which, though unattainable, represents a structurally important horizon of metaphysical
knowledge. This discourse, like many discourses which evoke 'woman'
as an archetype, is sustained by a willed ignorance concerning particular women. Conrad's work does not always uncritically reproduce
such a discourse. In inviting the reader to empathize with women
characters and with male characters who temporarily occupy a 'femi-

nized' position, the fiction offers some critical purchase on these structures of exploitation, without ever fully analysing or stepping outside them.

Many of Conrad's novels and short stories can be understood in terms of a circulation of various types of knowledge. These include, for example, knowledge of the sea, of 'the world' (i.e. social practices), of oneself, of specific other people, of human nature in general and various forms of professional knowledge (such as that of the merchant officer, the policeman, the spy, the entrepreneur). All these forms of knowledge are evoked at what one might term a mundane or pragmatic level, the level of facts, insights and opinions. But all are seen at some point or other in the texts as leading towards an ultimate form of knowledge or metaphysical truth: that form of knowledge which is the most highly-valued and the most charged with stylistic and emotional intensity. This inscrutable truth is evoked through rhetorical questions, professions of incomprehension, references to what is better not considered, gestures towards an ultimate experiential truth, refusals of apparent common sense:

> Is he satisfied – quite, now, I wonder? ... Was I so very wrong after all? ... Who knows? He is gone, inscrutable at heart.
>
> (*LJ*, 416)

> What sort of peace Kirylo Sidorovitch Razumov expected to find in the writing up of his record it passeth my understanding to guess.
>
> (*UWE*, 5)

> Yes, that's what it amounts to ... Precious little rest in life for anybody. Better not think of it.
>
> (*SL*, 132)

> Haven't we, together and upon the immortal sea, wrung out a meaning from our sinful lives?
>
> (*NN*, 173)

> Yes; I see it ... but I'll be hanged if it is yet as real to me as ... as the other thing ... say, Karain's story.
>
> (K, 55)

As critics have pointed out, the nature of Conrad's rhetoric is both to evoke the idea of ultimate, metaphysical truth and to question its possibility.[14] My attention will be primarily directed, not towards what the substance of such a truth might be for Conrad, but towards the structural significance and symbolic associations with which his texts endow the idea of such truth, as well as less exalted forms of knowledge. In terms of structural significance, I am concerned with the way in which knowledge circulates among characters, is passed on or withheld, is shared or competed for. In terms of symbolic associations, I consider the symbolic identification of certain characters at key points in the fictions with an idea of truth.

One advantage of considering the texts in this light is that it enables the inclusion of the author, readers and critics (as well as implied author and implied reader) since the acts of writing, reading and interpreting are themselves a form of circulation of knowledge.[15] Conrad's fictional self-consciousness (evident in the many references in his work to the acts of reading, writing, telling, listening and interpreting) serves to project the processes of circulation of knowledge outside the confines of the text. The gendering of knowledge and truth within Conrad's texts deeply implicates the aesthetic and didactic status of those texts. In representing 'truths' about gender and in representing a relationship between truth and gender, Conrad's fictions are also, in Foucault's terms, participating in the production and distribution of knowledge and truth via the institution of literature. Readers and critics are not, however, passive in this process. They may repeat or change the modes of circulation set up within the text. In discussing masculinity in Conrad's fiction I would hope to resist certain gendered modes of circulation rather than to perpetuate them.

The process of circulation may be analysed in terms of the literary forms and modes of communication employed by his homodiegetic narrators. The principal literary forms are: the telling of stories (e.g. Marlow in 'Heart of Darkness'); the writing of letters (e.g. MacWhirr and Jukes in 'Typhoon', Decoud in *Nostromo*, Marlow in *Lord Jim*), the keeping of a diary (Razumov in *Under Western Eyes*) and the writing or speaking of narratives which claim not to be fictional, but which must involve elements of fictionalization, at least in the form of shaping and selecting material (Marlow in *Lord Jim*, the language-teacher in *Under Western Eyes*). Two important modes of communication in Conrad's fiction are confessing and overhearing (or its written equivalent – reading a text intended for someone else). These two modes combine in various ways with the literary forms which have been mentioned. Storytelling, letter-writing and journal-writing may all have elements of confession in them and may all be overheard or read by those other than their intended hearers or readers. For example, Verloc's confession to Inspector Heat, and Heat's response, are overheard by Mrs Verloc, with dramatic consequences. On another level, Marlow's story-telling in 'Heart of Darkness', addressed to his listeners on the *Nellie*, is 'overheard' by the reader. This placing of us as readers in relation to the storytelling act materially alters our response.

A third important mode of communication in these works is lying. It may at first sight seem perverse to describe lying as the communication of knowledge. However, a believed lie involves the circulation of false knowledge, while a lie which is perceived as such, whether tentatively or with confidence, provides the hearer with some complex information both about the substance of the lie and about the liar. The ambivalence which obviously applies to lying in fact extends to confession and overhearing as well. I shall suggest that both of these are likely to involve misinterpretation. Thus in respect of all three modes, what is circulated is not simply knowledge as such, but forms of knowledge and ignorance, interpretation and misinterpretation.

Confession typically involves a complex interaction of the impulse to reveal and the impulse to conceal, of articulation and repression of knowledge. Both impulses, however, are communicative in effect, since the confessional situation constitutes the listener or reader as one who interprets the repressed or unstated as well as the stated. This view of confession is familiar from the psychoanalytical process, in which the analysand comes to sessions in order to speak but often communicates with silence, and from the religious confession, in which what must be spoken is, almost by definition, what one might wish to conceal. Rousseau illustrates this mingling of motives at the point in his *Confessions* where he first embarks on the subject of his sensuality and sexual preferences. Describing the awakening of his sensuality in response to his first experience of corporal punishment, he claims that his embarrassment at this revelation has only been overcome sufficiently for him to write it down by his sense of its didactic value: 'The magnitude of the lesson to be derived from so common and unfortunate a case as my own has resolved me to write it down.'[16] Since, however, what he has to confess is his pleasure in an experience conventionally regarded as in itself humiliating and embarrassing, the reader is liable to suspect that he enjoys the embarrassment of the confession as well.

Overhearing is similarly ambivalent, since many utterances are aimed at a specific audience. Marlow's narration in 'Heart of Darkness' is directed towards a group of male professionals, united by 'the bond of the sea' (45) which makes them 'tolerant of each other's yarns—and even convictions' (46). This places the reader in the position of an overhearer, and when Marlow says that 'you fellows see more than I could then' (HOD, 83) this does not necessarily apply to the reader. Are we to count ourselves one of these perceptive 'fellows'? Such a question clearly carries a different inflection for male and female readers: it seems to exclude women readers, without necessarily including all men readers. In *Under Western Eyes*, the language-teacher tells us parts of Razumov's story on the basis of the latter's journal (which was not, of course, written for his eyes) and expresses his inability to comprehend aspects of the story. This again sets up a dynamic of differential interpretative ability between reader and homodiegetic narrator. Do we see more or less than the language-teacher, or do we simply see differently? Keeping these points in mind, I now turn to examine the processes by which knowledge circulates in certain works of Conrad's middle period and more especially to reveal the gendered inflection of this process.

The epistemological structure of 'Heart of Darkness' involves a pair of men (Marlow and Kurtz), a group of men (Marlow and his listeners on board the Nellie) and a pair of women (the African woman at the Inner Station and the 'Intended'). The pair of men is the locus of the discovery of a hidden truth; the pair of women represent the complementary exclusion, necessary to maintain the men's belief in the secrecy and power of that truth; the group of men foregrounds the problematics of interpretation but also the possibility of a wider circulation of that truth among men. The two women, in different ways, are excluded by the text from the subject-position of knowledge (that of the knower) and are made into its object (that which is known). The African woman might, it seems, possess secret knowledge (of Kurtz and his 'unspeakable rites') (HOD, 118). However, she is allowed no voice, but only the pseudo-eloquence of gestures which allow the narrative voice of Marlow to assimilate her to the jungle. The Intended does speak in the text, but is excluded from this supposedly precious knowledge. At the point where it might be passed to her (and thereby transformed or demystified), a rhetorical move by Marlow bypasses her as the subject of knowledge and utterance and reinstates her as the object of (his own) utterance and (his listeners') knowledge. There is some slippage in the roles occupied by the women, but this slippage is between three roles, each of which is conceived as the antithesis to the powerful, knowing, speaking male

subject of knowledge. The knowing subject is opposed to: (1) the ignorant; (2) the known, the object of knowledge; (3) the unknowable.

'Heart of Darkness' is a story about the gaining and passing on (or
failure to pass on) of knowledge and about relationships between
men. This knowledge is rhetorically structured in terms of the transgression of boundaries; the supposed insight of Kurtz's final words,
'The horror! The horror!' (149), is a result of his having gone beyond
various notional boundaries – of 'civilization', of self-restraint, of
taboo, finally of death, of his having 'made that last stride ... stepped
over the edge' (151). Marlow's sharing of something of this insight is
possible because he too has 'peeped over the edge' (151). Marlow
attempts to pass on this (partial) knowledge to his male listeners
through the medium of language, but again this is only partly possible. Marlow's confidence that 'you fellows see more' is set against his
sense that 'No, it is impossible; it is impossible to convey the life-
sensation of any given epoch of one's existence—that which makes its
truth, its meaning' (82). Many versions of what this knowledge is are
possible: knowledge of the self (as Marlow suggests at one point)
(150), of the Other, of the unconscious, of the violence and oppression of colonialism, of the corruption of European civilization, of evil
within human nature. I would suggest that, while at the realist level
the story makes, for example, a (limited) critique of colonialism, at the
symbolic level the 'truth' which is at its centre is primarily an empty
signifier, generated by what Sedgwick terms 'representationally
vacant, epistemologically arousing place-markers' (*EC*, 95). Examples
are 'the incomprehensible' (50), 'dark places' (48), 'misty halos' (48),
'subtle and penetrating essence' (82), 'dream' (82), 'The horror!' (149),
'a moral victory paid for by innumerable defeats, by abominable
terrors' (151), 'an immense darkness' (the last words of the story, 162).
These terms, in other words, generate a rhetorical and narrative intensity around the idea of something to be known, without ever
specifying what that something is. Sedgwick points out the associations of such a technique with a homophobic discourse which treats
same-sex desire as something which cannot be spoken of. In 'Heart of
Darkness' the technique also produces racist and sexist effects, since
Africa, African people and women are drawn into this symbolic black
hole. The empty signifier is empty only in terms of the story's symbolic
self-understanding; ideologically, it has a history and a meaning.

To say that ideologies underlie the text would be the wrong
metaphor, borrowing its own figurative register of hidden metaphysical truth. Rather, ideologies structure the text, so that it may be

profitable to examine, not what the 'empty' signifier might mean (what is the knowledge that Marlow obtains?), but rather the structural distribution of that signifier (how is that knowledge circulated?). Such an analysis of the discourse of power/knowledge within the text may reveal another sort of meaning, through the homologies of this discourse with historically identifiable discourses (such as the male homosocial and homophobic discourse identified by Sedgwick, or the colonialist discourse of civilization, light and knowledge versus the primitive, darkness and ignorance). To an extent this is reading against the grain of the text, which presents itself as about metaphysical and personal truths mapped onto geographical and spatial metaphors (the journey, the heart, the way in, the edge). Where, however, the text encourages and assists a reading in terms of political and ideological structures is in its narrative technique, its use of the frame of Marlow and his listeners, which focuses attention on an economy of knowledge and power extending to the reader. That this frame is both part of the ideological structure and provides a critique of it should not surprise us, being indicative of the condition of Conrad's work which makes it a continuing subject of political debate. This condition, I would suggest, is that of working within a set of historical and ideological discourses, but offering footholds for the critique of these discourses through a reflexive relativism embodied in narrative structure.[17]

The much-debated lie to the Intended seems an inevitable point of departure for a discussion of knowledge in 'Heart of Darkness'. The very term 'the Intended' is an example of the way in which the text tempts interpretation into ideological acceptance: it is difficult to refer to the woman whom Marlow meets at the end of the story other than by this term, which involves the critic in replicating her objectification and the subordination of her subjectivity to Kurtz's will. There is another suppression, as well as Marlow's lie to her about Kurtz's last words: the suppression by the text of the name (her name) which he pretends had been those last words. Marlow's lie also associates her (unspoken) name with the idea of horror.[18] In realist terms, the lie needs little explanation. Faced with Kurtz's grieving fiancée, whom he has only just met and who seems to be keeping going psychologically by idealizing her dead lover, is it surprising that Marlow does not risk causing embarrassment and trauma by telling this woman that her lover had become a brutalized mass murderer? What encourages the reader to go beyond such a realist account is the linguistic, symbolic and emotional excess of the passage which includes the lie, the near-

hysteria with which Marlow overloads his description of the meeting.
The effect is cumulative, and therefore not easily rendered by quotation, but consider the following examples:

> The sound of her low voice seemed to have the accompaniment of
> all the other sounds, full of mystery, desolation, and sorrow, I had
> ever heard—the ripple of the river, the soughing of the trees swayed
> by the wind, the murmurs of the crowds, the faint ring of incom-
> prehensible words cried from afar, the whisper of a voice speaking
> from beyond the threshold of an eternal darkness.
>
> (159)

> I heard a light sigh and then my heart stood still, stopped dead
> short by an exulting and terrible cry, by the cry of inconceivable
> triumph and of unspeakable pain.
>
> (161–2)

This cry bears comparison with Linda's cry at the end of *Nostromo*
which, as I suggested in Chapter 4, is part of a repression of the
homosocial. In 'Heart of Darkness' the rhetorical excess would
suggest that highly rational explanations of Marlow's motives – or
even highly coherent explanations of his behaviour in symbolic
and/or unconscious terms – may distract us from a key fact: the
combined panic and excitement produced in Marlow and in the text
itself by the proximity of a woman to an utterance (Kurtz's last words)
which evokes, by its very hollowness, an idea of ultimate truth. As the
above quotations show, this proximity calls forth a veritable barrage
of those epistemologically arousing place-markers: 'mystery', 'incomprehensible', 'beyond the threshold', 'eternal darkness': the
unspeakable in pursuit of the inconceivable. Famously, or rather infa-
mously, Marlow has earlier claimed that truth is generally
unavailable to women :

> It's queer how out of touch with truth women are. They live in a
> world of their own, and there had never been anything like it, and
> never can be. It is too beautiful altogether, and if they were to set
> it up it would go to pieces before the first sunset. Some confounded
> fact we men have been living contentedly with ever since the day
> of creation would start up and knock the whole thing over.
>
> (59)

Marlow's patronizing attitude to women here has been extensively criticized.[19] What has been less noticed is the sheer incongruity of
Marlow's description of the world inhabited by men.[20] We have
learned, quite rightly, to read 'Heart of Darkness' as a document of epistemological, existential and ethical uncertainty, of dreams dreamt
alone, of truth and meaning which, if they can be found, can never be
conveyed. The pragmatism of Marlow the practical sailor, with his
belief in work, serves only to keep at bay, when necessary, Marlow the
spinner of spectral enigmas. Yet suddenly, in the face of his naively
idealistic aunt, Marlow sees himself as the contented inhabitant, with
other men, of a commonsense, positivistic world of 'facts'. It would
seem that one purpose of women, for a man like Marlow, is to make his
own world seem epistemologically secure. This may motivate his decision to protect the idealism of Kurtz's 'Intended'. Yet for Marlow the
latter also represents (but does not possess) a truth beyond mere 'facts'.

Marlow's account of his motives for visiting the Intended makes it
clear that he is not willing for her to occupy a subject position, either
of knowledge or of emotional possession, but wishes her to remain as
that which is known or possessed. Marlow conceives his activities
back in the 'sepulchral city' (152) as expressing his loyalty to Kurtz. He
feels that he has acquired from Kurtz a knowledge which makes him
contemptuous of the inhabitants of the city and he also has a number
of Kurtz's possessions. He sets about a grudging distribution of these:
'some family letters and memoranda' (154) are given to a cousin,
while the report on the 'Suppression of Savage Customs', after being
offered to a company official, is passed to a journalist. Marlow
comments:

> Thus I was left at last with a slim packet of letters and the girl's
> portrait ... I concluded I would go and give her back her portrait
> and those letters myself.
>
> (154–5)

This seems at first to be a continuation of the process of distributing
Kurtz's possessions. Then, however, Marlow continues:

> Curiosity? Yes; and also some other feeling perhaps. All that had
> been Kurtz's had passed out of my hands: his soul, his body, his
> station, his plans, his ivory, his career. There remained only his
> memory and his Intended—and I wanted to give that up, too, to
> the past, in a way—to surrender personally all that remained of

him with me to that oblivion which is the last word of our common fate.

(155)

What is most striking here is perhaps the extent of Marlow's fantasy identification with Kurtz, combined with a fantasy of possessing him, body and soul (points to which I shall return). Equally significant, however, is the subtle shift made by 'I wanted to give that up too', where 'that' seems to refer, ungrammatically, both to 'his memory' and to (the portrait of) 'his Intended'. The shift is from the idea of giving up a bit of Kurtz *to* the woman (treating her as a possible subject of knowledge/possession) to the idea that she is herself one of Kurtz's possessions, to be given up to 'oblivion'. This shift seems to be achieved via the portrait, which Marlow sees as a reified and idealized image of truthfulness itself:

> One felt that no manipulation of light and pose could have conveyed the delicate shade of truthfulness upon those features.
>
> (154–5)[21]

In a metonymic slippage, giving up the portrait becomes giving up the woman herself. The woman becomes the portrait, a portrait which Marlow interprets as a visual image of truth, not an image of a mind capable of being told the truth. The Intended becomes one of the things, like Kurtz's station, body, soul and so on, which Marlow is ready to give up, although he has never possessed them, except in fantasy.[22]

Telling stories about someone is not the usual way of consigning them to oblivion: the Intended is surrendered, less to 'oblivion' than to Marlow's fantasies about her and to his male listeners. This brings us back to the nature of the male bonds in 'Heart of Darkness'. Nina Pelikan Straus argues that

> In *Heart of Darkness* women are used to deny, distort, and censor men's passionate love for one another. Projecting his own love on to the form of the Intended, Marlow is able to conceal from himself the dark complexity of his own love—a love that strikes him with horror—for Kurtz.
>
> (EI, 134)

This version of the familiar idea of a 'doubling' between Marlow and Kurtz in terms of passionate love between men is best understood via

Sedgwick's argument that the visibility of the homosocial–homosexual continuum has been 'radically disrupted' in the case of men in modern Western society (*BM*, 1–2). So if we follow Straus in seeing Marlow's fascination with Kurtz in terms of desire between men which excludes women from a secret knowledge, this is not necessarily to say that the story is primarily about repressed homosexual desire. Rather the argument is that the relationship between Marlow and Kurtz takes place within a whole matrix of inter-male relationships involving competitiveness, desire, bonding, the sharing and appropriation of power and knowledge, and that this matrix of relations has characteristically functioned in modern Western society through the setting up of powerful barriers between sexual and other forms of inter-male relationship. Women, by functioning as objects of exchange (literal or psychic) and of shared desire, have been used to maintain such a barrier, male desire being channelled through women. This involves the exclusion of women from the subject positions of power, knowledge and desire. They are established as that which is desired, that which is the object of knowledge, that which is exchanged or controlled.

However, an interpretation of 'Heart of Darkness' in terms of male homosexual desire can undoubtedly be made, building on Straus's article. The secret knowledge which Marlow and Kurtz come to share (or rather, which Marlow comes to imagine he has shared with Kurtz), the metaphors of transgressing a boundary with which Marlow glosses the relationship of this knowledge to death, the 'unspeakable rites' (HOD, 118) which Kurtz has practised, all have distinctively sexual overtones within the discourse of sexuality/knowledge that Sedgwick identifies in late nineteenth-century Europe. Furthermore, certain of Sedgwick's observations on *Billy Budd* (written in 1891, the year following Conrad's own visit to the Congo but before his own novella was written) are strikingly relevant to the rhetoric employed by Marlow:[23]

> In the famous passages of *Billy Budd* in which the narrator claims to try to illuminate ... the peculiarly difficult riddle of 'the hidden nature of the master-at-arms' Claggart ... the answer to the riddle seems to involve not the substitution of semantically more satisfying alternatives to the epithet 'hidden' but merely a series of intensifications of it. Sentence after sentence is produced in which, as Barbara Johnson points out ... 'what we learn about the master-at-arms is that we cannot learn anything': the adjectives applied to

him ... include 'mysterious,' 'exceptional,' 'peculiar,' 'exceptional'
again, 'obscure,' 'phenomenal,' 'notable,' 'phenomenal' again,
'exceptional' again, 'secretive' ... [These are combined with] a parallel and equally abstract chain of damning ethical designations –
'the direct reverse of a saint,' 'depravity,' 'depravity,' 'wantonness
of atrocity,' 'the mania of an evil. nature.'

(*EC*, 94–5)

This whole description is remarkably relevant to the way in which
Kurtz, and Marlow's relationship with Kurtz, are defined, or rather left
undefined. Kurtz is described to Marlow as 'a very remarkable person'
(69), as a man who will 'go far, very far' (70) (a richly ironical phrase,
with the benefit of hindsight), as 'an exceptional man' (75), 'a
prodigy', 'an emissary of pity, and science, and progress, and devil
knows what else', 'a special being' (79). Marlow comments: 'I had
heard Mr. Kurtz was in there ... Yet somehow it didn't bring any image
with it—no more than if I had been told an angel or a fiend was in
there' (81). Later we find Kurtz referred to as 'that man' (89), and, in
Marlow's conversation with the 'harlequin' (122), as one who has
'enlarged my mind' (125). The harlequin tells Marlow that he and
Kurtz 'talked of everything ... Of love, too', although 'It isn't what you
think' (what does Marlow think?), but 'It was in general. He made me
see things—things' (127). The harlequin claims that 'you can't judge
Mr. Kurtz as you would an ordinary man' (128). Marlow himself
describes Kurtz as 'a remarkable man' (138) and as 'very little more
than a voice' (115), a fate which he shares himself within the narrative frame as it becomes darker on the *Nellie* – one aspect of the crucial
rapprochement or doubling between Marlow and Kurtz. As well as
these 'intensifications' of the mystery surrounding Kurtz, there are
many 'damning ethical designations': Kurtz, we are told, 'lacked
restraint in the gratification of his various lusts' (131); 'there was
something wanting in him' (131); 'he was hollow at the core' (131);
he is 'an atrocious phantom' (133), a 'shadow' (141), 'like a vapour
exhaled by the earth' (142), a 'wandering and tormented thing' (143),
marked by 'exalted and incredible degradation' (144), and whose soul
'had gone mad' (145), possessed by 'diabolic love and ... unearthly
hate' (147) and, of course, in his own words, 'the horror!' (149).

Faced with this barrage of mystification and condemnation, it is
worth briefly being literal minded as an experiment. What has Kurtz
actually done? He has murdered and brutally exploited African
people, but this he has in common with the others involved in the

imperialist project. What were his 'unspeakable rites' (118), bearing in mind that they involved 'various lusts' (131) and that Marlow apparently cannot bring himself to be specific about them? Cannibalism? Perhaps, but Marlow seems ready enough to discuss that in relation to the Africans on board the river steamer. Human sacrifice? The heads on stakes might imply this, but, again, Marlow is frank enough about these, and finds them an expression of a 'pure, uncomplicated savagery' (132) which is more tolerable than the imagined details of the ceremonies involving Kurtz. Some form of magic? The witch doctors who appear on the shore are made to appear pathetically powerless. All of these activities might be involved, but none seems adequate to explain the mystique of the unspeakable attributed to Kurtz's practices. The conclusion, I think, has to be that what Kurtz has done is precisely the non-specified or unspeakable: it is less any set of actual actions than a symbolic location of taboo-breaking. As such, and in the historical context of the turn of the century, it can hardly fail to evoke the homophobic taboo of 'the love that dare not speak its name'.[24] Perhaps the closest that Marlow comes to identifying the unspeakable is when he finds it intolerable to hear about 'the ceremonies used when approaching Mr. Kurtz' (131–2), which seem to involve crawling. This is one of a number of references to the idea of idol-worship, and suggests the harlequin's adoration and idealization of Kurtz, which Marlow mocks but in some degree comes to share. The focus of horror is thus on Marlow's intense emotional desire to meet Kurtz and identification with him after his death, although this focus is masked by the projection of the 'horror' onto the imagined primitive of Africa. Marlow's own feelings for Kurtz (tinged as they are with idol-worship) are themselves the horror. It is in sexual terms, as well as in terms of imperialist exploitation, that the darkness which Marlow imagines he finds in Africa is reflected back into the heart of the culture inhabited by Marlow and his respectable male listeners.

In her discussion of the characterizations of Claggart in *Billy Budd*, Sedgwick notes that two elements give some 'semantic coloration' (*EC*, 95) to the enigmatic terms used of the master-at arms. The first is the series of 'damning ethical designations' for which I have already identified a parallel in 'Heart of Darkness'. The second is 'the adduced proximity ... of three specific, diagnostic professions, law, medicine, and religion, each however said to be reduced to "perplexing strife" by "the phenomenon" that can by now be referred to only, but perhaps satisfactorily, as "it"' (*EC*, 95). This phenomenon is Claggart's 'wracking juncture of same-sex desire with homophobia'

(*EC*, 100). In 'Heart of Darkness', we find Marlow's experience framed by members of a comparable, but significantly different, set of professions: law, medicine, accountancy and commerce. Medicine is represented by the doctor who measures Marlow's head in the continental city, and the other professions by the lawyer, accountant and company director who (together with the frame narrator) form his audience on the *Nellie*. Whether these men are enlightened or perplexed by what they learn from Marlow is not clear, but they occupy the role of trying to understand the unspeakable. If accountants and company directors are not diagnosticians of psychology, they are of economy – and it is economies, both of imperialism and of male desire, which Marlow sets out to conceal and reveal at the same time.

The case for a reading of 'Heart of Darkness' in terms of homosexual desire may be summarized as follows. It concerns a story told by one man to a group of men with whom he feels a close bond, a bond necessary for them to understand his story, although he nevertheless feels part of it cannot be communicated. His story concerns his growing fascination, disgust and identification for another man, centred on his realization that this man has been involved in taboo practices about which the story-teller (Marlow) will not be specific. This realization creates, at least in the mind of the story-teller, an enduring intimacy with the other man, despite his death, an intimacy involving the sharing of a disgraceful yet exciting knowledge from which the dead man's fiancée must be protected.

I am not, however, arguing that 'Heart of Darkness' is simply a concealed narrative of male homosexual desire. Like many literary texts, it is multiply over-determined. My argument is that the rhetorical and symbolic structures of Conrad's novella constantly evoke discourses of sexual knowledge and ignorance, which, as Sedgwick shows, focused with particular intensity at that period (and since) on a crisis of heterosexual/homosexual definition. The male homosocial relations which are prominent at all levels of 'Heart of Darkness' are structured by this crisis, just as they are structured by the denial of power and utterance to women and by the economics of empire. In terms of the politics of literary interpretation, to neglect a reading of the text in terms of homosexual desire would be to repeat the processes of exclusion and denial which have been so prominent in the discourse of male sexuality, just as to read the text's overt marginalization of women as merely social realism is to replicate a sexist discourse, and to defend the text's representation of Africa on the grounds that Africa is used here only as a symbol of the European psyche is to replicate a racist discourse.

The central instance in the story of the structuring of homosocial relations by the problematics of homosexual/heterosexual definition is the doubling between Kurtz and Marlow, which has been extensively discussed by critics.[25] Doubles are a recurrent feature of Conrad's fiction, crucial to the symbolic meaning of this and other stories, most notably 'The Secret Sharer' and *Under Western Eyes*. In the triangular situation which exists in Marlow's mind after Kurtz's death, and especially during the scene with the Intended, there is a notable confusion between identification and desire. His fantasy that he possesses Kurtz, body and soul, is also a fantasy of *being* Kurtz, echoing as it does Kurtz's own obsessional possessiveness:

All that had been Kurtz's had passed out of my hands: his soul, his body, his station, his plans, his ivory, his career. There remained only his memory and his Intended.

(155)

You should have heard him say, 'My ivory' ... 'My Intended, my ivory, my station, my river, my— 'everything belonged to him. It made me hold my breath in expectation of hearing the wilderness burst into a prodigious peal of laughter ... Everything belonged to him—but that was a trifle. The thing was to know what he belonged to.

(116)

This fantasy is enacted in the ambiguity of Marlow's wish to surrender 'his memory' (155): does this mean Marlow's memory of Kurtz, or Kurtz's own memory? To Marlow they have become almost the same. Does Marlow know what he himself 'belonged to'? Sedgwick refers to Freud's list of the transformations, under a 'homophobic regime of utterance', of the sentence 'I (a man) *love him* (a man)' (*EC*, 161): (1) 'I do not *love* him – I *hate* him'; (2) 'I do not love *him*, I love *her*'; (3) 'I do not love him; *she* loves him'; (4) 'I do not love him; I do not love anyone'. All of these seem to be in play in Marlow's scene with the Intended. Number 3 ('*I* do not love him; *she* loves him') is readily available as a defence, since it happens to be true that the Intended loves Kurtz (though Marlow seems keen to stress the enduring and transcendent power of her love on limited evidence). Number 2 ('I do not love *him*, I love *her*') is implied in Marlow's talk of the beauty of the Intended and his hinting at an undisclosed or unconscious reason for visiting her. Number 1 ('I do not *love* him – I *hate* him') has always been implicit in Marlow's mixed attitude of fascination, admiration, fear and disgust towards Kurtz. Number 4 ('I do not love him; I do not love anyone') would illuminate Marlow's continuing bachelor status, which becomes a theme and problem only in *Chance*. Most evident of all, however, is a fifth transformation which Sedgwick adds, observing that it is characteristic of Nietzsche and underlies Freud's project so intimately that it does not occur to him to make it explicit: 'I do not *love* him, I *am* him' (*EC*, 162). Sedgwick's perception that the emergence in the nineteenth century of a definition of the 'homosexual' in terms of sameness offered a way of concealing and expressing same-sex desire through images of self love (*EC*, 160–1), opens the possibility of alternative interpretations of many of the pairs of male doubles that are found in Conrad's work. In the case of 'Heart of Darkness', Marlow's placing of the Intended as one of Kurtz's possessions, comparable to the ivory in which he traded, is revealed as part of an economy of repressed same-sex desire, complicit with both the structures of patriarchy and with the economies of empire. This link is elucidated by Irigaray:

> The use of and traffic in women subtend and uphold the reign of masculine hom(m)o-sexuality, even while they maintain that hom(m)o-sexuality in speculations, mirror games, identifications, and more or less rivalrous appropriations, which defer its real practice ... The exchange of women as goods accompanies and stimulates exchanges of other 'wealth' among groups of men.
>
> (*TS*, 172)[26]

Conrad's text continues this traffic on the level of epistemology, by offering to male readers a rich series of mirror games and identifications, involving the exchange of women as the objects of knowledge.

'Heart of Darkness', then, suggests a possible symbolic structure or paradigm in which the key terms are: women, men, knowledge or truth, confession or revelation, lying or concealment. This structure can be found in many of Conrad's works, although it is by no means invariable or omnipresent. The next chapter will consider some of the ways in which subsequent works of fiction by Conrad repeat this structure but in ways which are more critical, more inclined to question its validity.

6

Masculinity, 'Woman' and Truth: *The Secret Agent, Under Western Eyes, Chance*

The gendered circulation of knowledge, which I have described in 'Heart of Darkness', reappears in several of Conrad's later works, notably *The Secret Agent, Under Western Eyes* and *Chance*, but in each it is disrupted or questioned to a greater degree. The basic paradigm is one in which knowledge, both literal knowledge of particular facts and events and existential knowledge, is sought, shared, competed for and otherwise circulated among groups of men, including the implied author, male narrators (such as Marlow or the language-teacher in *Under Western Eyes*), male narratees and implied male readers. This circulation involves and is facilitated by the exclusion of women from such knowledge, combined with a tendency to identify them symbolically with it. The women represent the truth, particularly ungraspable metaphysical truth, but they do not possess it. Another way of putting this would be to say that the exclusion of women from the space within which men's knowledge circulates encourages the identification of the truth 'beyond', ultimate or unattainable truth, with the feminine. Jacques Derrida, summing up both the paradox and the logic of Nietzsche's gendered epistemology, has commented on this incompatibility between representing and possessing truth:

> How is it possible that woman, who herself is truth, does not believe in truth? And yet, how is it possible to be truth and still believe in it?[1]

One might gloss this with the observation that no one (at least no one sane) regards themselves as a symbol of ultimate truth or unattainable wisdom. Such a role is a projection of someone else's fantasies and needs. To maintain the identification of women with the ideal, the unattainable, the metaphysical ultimate requires that they be seen from a distance. This identification draws on traditional myths such as the Sphinx and appears most clearly in 'Heart of Darkness' in Kurtz's painting of a veiled woman carrying a lighted torch. However, the possibility of women gaining possession of knowledge exists as a focus of fear and desire. At key points in many texts the truth or a truth is somehow revealed to an important female character, or such a revelation is threatened. These points are moments of crisis, often identified with violence and death. Examples are: Marlow's lie to the Intended in 'Heart of Darkness'; Winnie Verloc's overhearing of the story of Stevie's death in *The Secret Agent*; Razumov's confession to Natalia Haldin in *Under Western Eyes*; the concealing from Flora of her father's attempt to murder her husband in *Chance*. Each of these events is followed and/or preceded by violence and/or death, or associated symbolically with death. In each of these texts this moment threatens to disrupt a pattern of knowledge circulating primarily or exclusively among men: Kurtz, Marlow and his male audience in 'Heart of Darkness'; the world of police, anarchists, spies, civil servants and diplomats in *The Secret Agent*; the network of understanding, deceit and misunderstanding involving Razumov, Haldin, Mikulin, General T., the students, the revolutionaries and the language-teacher in *Under Western Eyes* (Sophia Antonovna is an interesting exception to the largely male character of this network); the chain of men with designs on Flora, including her father, her husband, Powell and Marlow in *Chance*. We may even see a shadow of this paradigm in Nostromo's deathbed confession to Mrs Gould. The association of women gaining knowledge with death can be explained in terms of the inconsistency between woman as an image of truth and a woman as the subject or possessor of knowledge. When these two collide, at moments of revelation and confession, it is a system of distances, prohibitions and barriers that collapses, and that collapse threatens the death of a masculine heterosexual self constructed in imaginary opposition to the feminine. Another way of putting this would be to say that for a woman to both represent truth and possess it would give her an aura of omnipotence, since the maintenance of male power requires a separation between the idea of 'woman' and women. Sedgwick has pointed out that ignorance can be a source of power as well as knowledge and has suggested that 'ignorance and opacity collude or compete with knowledge in mobilizing the flows of energy, desire, goods, meanings, persons' (*EC*, 4). The power relations among the groups of men in Conrad's work are maintained by a circulation of knowledge homologous with the circulation of women themselves and corresponding to a double ignorance: an ignorance attributed (with some historical and social plausibility, but also in excess of such plausibility) to women; an ignorance about women, their experience and their understanding, on the part of men. One of the main questions for us as readers and critics of Conrad seems to me to be in what way this gendered economy of knowledge functions in the exchange of knowledge and uncertainty which is the act of reading and interpreting, the question of our own place in this economy. In this chapter I shall briefly examine the dynamics of knowledge circulation in *The Secret Agent* before looking in more detail at *Under Western Eyes* and *Chance*.

The world of *The Secret Agent*, one of police, anarchists and *agents provocateurs*, is, in an obvious way, one in which knowledge is a valued commodity. Yet the woman whose story is, according to Conrad's 'Author's Note', central to the novel is excluded from knowledge of this world, both by her husband's protective caution and habitual secretiveness, and by her own incuriousness. Verloc tells his wife approvingly that she had 'no business to know' about his work and its risks (238), while Winnie, described as a woman of 'philosophical, almost disdainful incuriosity' (237), takes an attitude to his work which seems to resemble her general attitude to life: 'Without "troubling her head about it," she was aware that it "did not stand looking into very much"' (241). This exclusion of the woman from knowledge does not appear, in *The Secret Agent*, as the direct fulfilment of a fantasy of male power as it does in 'Heart of Darkness'. This is in part because, in *The Secret Agent*, the exclusion is subjected to the critical force of Conrad's coruscating irony and is used to satirical purpose. The habitual secrecy and restraint of the Verlocs' marriage – which in a sense kills them both – is clearly a parody of the secrecy and restraint of the corrupt and suffocating bourgeois society of which Verloc is a servant. But a further and important difference between the two texts is that the revelation of truth to the woman – an abyss which Marlow, loading his language with images of the deathly, approaches but never reaches in 'Heart of Darkness' – actually takes place in *The Secret Agent*, bringing death in its train. The figurative and descriptive language surrounding this revelation invests the situation with symbolic resonances. In the long and skilful build up from the moment when Winnie learns of Stevie's death to the moment when she stabs her husband, she is described in terms which associate her with a sphinx-like figure, a veiled image of inscrutable truth: 'as though the skin had been a mask' (212); 'sorrow with a veiled face' (232). When she dresses to go out, her metaphorical veil becomes a literal one – her husband tears it off, but only reveals 'a still unreadable face' (256).[2] Here, as in 'Heart of Darkness', it is the descriptive excess which may alert us to the intensity of desire and fear focused on the idea of a woman gaining knowledge: the obsessive repetition of words (such as 'immobility'), and the need to heighten and emphasize qualities of the dramatic: 'prolonged immobility' (232); 'a frozen, contemplative immobility' (241); 'her immobility amazing' (246); 'The perfect immobility of her pose expressed the agitation of rage and despair, all the potential violence of tragic passions, better than any shallow display of shrieks, with the beating of a distracted head against the walls, could have done' (212).[3] The descriptive evocation of Mrs Verloc as terrifying sphinx, as angel of destructive passion, after she has overheard Verloc's confession to Heat, is matched by an earlier evocation of her as ideal angel of the domestic sphere, statuesque embodiment of a private realm from which secret knowledge of the male world must be excluded. This evocation is prompted by an impulse on Verloc's part to confess everything to her. This impulse is, however, forestalled by the threat which it poses, in his mind, to this ideological construction of her as pure domestic woman:

> At that moment he was within a hair's breadth of making a clean breast of it all to his wife. The moment seemed propitious. Looking out of the corners of his eyes, he saw her ample shoulders draped in white, the back of her head, with the hair done for the night in three plaits tied up with black tapes at the ends. And he forbore. Mr. Verloc loved his wife as a wife should be loved—that is, maritally, with the regard one has for one's chief possession. This head arranged for the night, those ample shoulders, had an aspect of familiar sacredness—the sacredness of domestic peace. She moved not, massive and shapeless like a recumbent statue in the rough; he remembered her wide-open eyes looking into the empty room. She was mysterious, with the mysteriousness of living beings. The far-famed Secret Agent ... was not the man to break into such mysteries.
>
> (179–80)

This amounts to a powerful ironic statement of the close connection between the idealization of woman as mysterious and sacred and her oppression as a possessed object. As in 'Heart of Darkness', confessing to a woman is a tempting but terrifying possibility. The woman is held to represent a 'sacred' or metaphysical truth and to protect this role as living embodiment of an 'ultimate' truth she must be denied knowledge of mundane truths, of men's truths. Here, though, it is not the potentially sympathetic figure of Marlow who seeks to enforce such protection, but the corrupt and grotesque Verloc. Male critics (or readers) are unlikely to 'identify the imaginative autobiography of their masculinity' with that of Verloc, as Straus argues they do with that of Marlow (EI, 130).

In *Under Western Eyes* as in 'Heart of Darkness' we find an idealized figure of a beautiful young woman, from whom the truth of a male crime must be kept. However, in this case the concealment becomes unbearable to the man who knows of that crime. The result is the novel's climactic double confession, to Natalia Haldin and to the assembled Russian revolutionaries. It is the latter confession which, in literal and realistic terms, leads to the deafening and crippling of Razumov. Nevertheless, symbolically this punishment, leading to his anticipated early death, seems to confirm the taboo established in 'Heart of Darkness' on the passing of male secrets to a woman. The parallel with 'Heart of Darkness' is evident when, for example, Natalia expresses the hope of learning from Razumov some of her brother's last words (137), just as the Intended asks Marlow for Kurtz's last words, and also when the language-teacher describes Natalia as 'a frank and generous creature, having the noblest—well—illusions' (192). The crime that Razumov confesses is his own, not that of another, and we know what that crime was: the betrayal of Natalia's brother to torture and execution at the hands of the Russian state. It is not a question, as with Kurtz and Marlow, of some unspeakable transgression with sexual overtones. Or is it? Razumov has something worse to confess (he feels) even than his betrayal of Victor Haldin to the authorities:

Listen—now comes the true confession. The other was nothing. To save me, your trustful eyes had to entice my thought to the very edge of the blackest treachery ... Victor Haldin had stolen the truth of my life from me, who had nothing else in the world, and he boasted of living on through you on this earth where I had no place to lay my head. She will marry some day, he had said—and your eyes were trustful. And do you know what I said to myself? I shall steal his sister's soul from her ... If you could have looked then into my heart, you would have cried out aloud with terror and disgust.

(359)

In a brilliant analysis of the novel, Terence Cave shows how the reader is drawn into complicity with 'Razumov's almost unspeakable fears and desires'.[4] This complicity is established through the mediating role of a male narrator, the restrained and middle-aged teacher of languages. The function of his narration as a 'medium of transference' for those fears and desires depends upon Conrad's intricate disposition of knowledge and ignorance in relation to narrative voice (who speaks, when they speak, and their relation to the action) as well as narrative tense (particularly order, the relationship between the chronological order of events and the order in which they are disclosed in the narrative).[5] Cave summarizes it thus:

> The language-teacher is a first-person narrator whose discourse – the novel as it stands – is written in retrospect, from a position of full knowledge and saturated interpretation. Within that discourse, he appears as a participator in the action, ignorant of Razumov's imposture until the last moment. Even after the confession, it is still necessary for him to read Razumov's diary.[6]

The language-teacher's ignorance, during the course of the action, of Razumov's betrayal, allows him to indulge vicariously his own desires: 'He depicts Natalia as a woman ripe for seduction and clearly regards Razumov as a likely candidate; his own sexual interest in Natalia endows him with the prurience necessary for him to act as a kind of pander.'[7] Yet his knowledge of Razumov's betrayal, at the time that he writes his narrative, makes his discourse a sort of trap for the reader's own vicarious pleasure in reading the story:

> The language-teacher as a character in his own story is already contaminated; his narration doubly so, since *it* knows what the language-teacher didn't then know, namely that Razumov has betrayed Haldin. And because it knows, we know, so that if we want Razumov to seduce Natalia, we side with treachery and moral violation. This is where the lure of evil is most deeply ingrained in the plot.[8]

Not only do the language-teacher's restraint and avowed imaginative limitations draw us into accepting what might otherwise seem an

implausibly sensational plot, but his 'imperfect censorship leaves
blanks we are bound to fill, which means we in our turn are contam-
inated by the narrator's epistemophilia'.[9]
For Cave, the confession at the climax of *Under Western Eyes* is
indeed a confession of an (intended) sexual crime and an illicit desire:

> The very fact that Razumov articulates this further confession (the
> 'true' one), and thus writes into the story a narrative future fore-
> stalled by the confession scene itself, sufficiently demonstrates that
> some such ultimate twist *is* the object of our narrative desire ...
> The imaginary rape, the violence that would have made Natalia
> '[cry] out aloud with terror and disgust', is the melodramatic scene
> that the narrative conjures up without having to take responsibility
> for it.[10]

So the knowledge which is ultimately revealed to Natalia has something in common with that which is forever withheld from Kurtz's
Intended. Like 'Heart of Darkness', *Under Western Eyes* is a fiction
about men's knowledge and understanding of themselves and
other men, and the ways in which such knowledge circulates, articulating relationships between men. And again women serve as
objects of male competitiveness and as such mediate relationships
between men. However, several factors operate to modify and
complicate the homosocial male economy, resulting in a work
which is ultimately more rich and satisfying than 'Heart of
Darkness', less in thrall to a certain masculinist ideology and more
able to explore and question it.
As indicated in the Introduction, the basic model of the male
homosocial economy is established in the various, but to some extent
convergent, work by Gayle Rubin, René Girard, Eve Sedgwick and Luce
Irigaray:

> If it is women who are being transacted, then it is the men who give
> and take them who are linked, the woman being a conduit of a rela-
> tionship rather than a partner to it.
>
> (TW, 174)

> The impulse toward the object is ultimately an impulse toward the
> mediator; in internal mediation this impulse is checked by the
> mediator himself since he desires, or perhaps possesses, the object.
>
> (DD, 10)

The male-homosocial structure whereby men's 'heterosexual desire' for women serves as a more or less perfunctory detour on the way to a closer, but homophobically proscribed, bonding with another man.[11]

In a relationship established between (at least) two men, the ignorant young woman is the *mediation prescribed by society*.

(*TS*, 199)

A possible confusion arising from different terminology needs to be sorted out. Girard, who does not consider issues of gender and assumes a symmetry in the erotic triangle, unaffected by the gender of those involved, uses the term 'mediator' for the role model/rival (person A) who prompts in another (person B) a shared desire for the object (person C).[12] For Rubin, Sedgwick and Irigaray, A and B are characteristically men, while C is characteristically a woman. Where Girard refers to A (the rival) as the 'mediator', Irigaray refers to C (the woman as avowed object of desire) as the prescribed 'mediation' between men. Girard and Irigaray are thus using the term 'mediate' in different ways.

Natalia Haldin is indeed 'transacted' between her brother Victor and Razumov. Having already explained that he chose Razumov to turn to because the latter has no family who might be put at risk (*UWE*, 19), Haldin evokes the idea of patriarchal inheritance, in which a woman serves to continue the male line of succession, which 'passes through' her body without ever alighting on her:

'Yes. Men like me leave no posterity,' he repeated in a subdued tone. 'I have a sister though. She's with my old mother—I persuaded them to go abroad this year—thank God. Not a bad little girl my sister. She has the most trustful eyes of any human being that ever walked this earth. She will marry well, I hope. She may have children—sons perhaps. Look at me. My father was a Government official in the provinces.'

(22–3)

It is this speech that Razumov recalls, in the confession to Natalia quoted above, as the starting point of his own desire for her (before he has even met her). Thus Haldin's (unconscious?) incitement of Razumov's desire accords with Girard's idea of the rival who, possessing/desiring the object, incites desire in another. Haldin does not literally desire his sister, at least not in a sexual sense, but he possesses her through her devotion and admiration, and imaginatively places her in the role of his partner by implicitly seeing her as the mother of his spiritual posterity. Indeed, the fact that it is Natalia's brother who, as it were, offers her to Razumov, places the situation more firmly within the structure outlined by Rubin, in which the incest taboo serves to establish relations of kinship between men through the exchange of women. All this, of course, takes place in a context which is both ironic and tragic, in which the exchange is also to become an (intended) revenge on Razumov's part.

However, it does not seem appropriate to describe Razumov's heterosexual desire for Natalia in Sedgwick's terms as 'a more or less perfunctory detour on the way to a closer, but homophobically proscribed, bonding' with her brother (and this is not merely because her brother is by this time dead). Razumov's desire in relation to Victor Haldin seems primarily one of identification: the desire to *be* him, or to be in his place. Chosen because he has no family of his own, Razumov is tempted to steal Haldin's family, to take his place as the idolized heroic young male in the eyes of Natalia and her mother. Haldin had boasted of 'living on through' Natalia's children; instead Razumov, his betrayer, would appropriate this patriarchal line of succession. The Conradian theme of the double operates between Haldin and Razumov, given the tinge of the uncanny by Razumov's (imagined) vision of Haldin lying corpse-like on his (Razumov's) bed (32) and his (hallucinatory) vision of Haldin's body in the snow (36-7). Of course Kurtz and Marlow also have aspects of doubling, and Marlow's fascination with Kurtz is an inextricable blend of identification and desire (as well as repulsion). It would, in principle, be possible to make the same argument that I made in relation to Marlow and Kurtz in respect of Razumov and Haldin: to read Razumov's wish to be Haldin in terms of Sedgwick's fifth transformation/denial of male homosexual love: 'I do not *love* him, I *am* him' (see Chapter 5 above). However, the argument does not seem convincing in relation to *Under Western Eyes*. There are no evident overtones of the sexual in Razumov's response to Haldin. Rather Razumov's primary desire seems to be for a family and a place in the patriarchal succession: to that extent, and for those reasons, he would like to *be* Haldin, or to be his brother, as he would perhaps have liked to be brother to the two privileged girls who are in fact his half-sisters. All this is of course traceable to his virtually orphaned position as an illegitimate child, and to the figure of Prince K——. The latter, Razumov's biological father, has, prior to the crisis with Haldin, only appeared in Razumov's life once, and then as a fragmented and somewhat feminized set of body parts and sensations: 'a white shapely hand' which is 'soft and passive', 'a distinct pressure of the white shapely hand just before it was withdrawn' (12) and (reasserting his role as the father) 'grey silky side-whiskers' (13). When Razumov comes to know Natalia, it seems as if her brother serves as a token of exchange between them; that the other man, the man who was there first (the object of Natalia's sisterly devotion and of Razumov's supposed friendship) is the conduit or detour in a heterosexual relationship, rather than the women serving as the detour in any denied homosexual bond. The case then seems to support the possibility of the symmetry which Girard assumes. Whereas the Intended in 'Heart of Darkness' is treated as a sort of cipher, lacking name or personality, a mere object in the psychological exchange of Marlow and Kurtz, Natalia, although a somewhat simplified and idealized figure, has some access to subjecthood and agency. Furthermore, she does not remain permanently in ignorance: the moment of disclosure arrives.

Masculinity, and a masculine homosocial economy, are culturally variable, and *Under Western Eyes* benefits from a more subtle treatment of cultural difference than 'Heart of Darkness', where the Africans are so strongly identified as primitive Other that the possibility of a different, African form of masculinity arises only in the form of colonialist exoticizing fantasy of the 'natural' man.[13] The language-teacher's generalizations about the Russian temperament have of course an element of obtuse stereotyping about them, but they are clearly presented as a product of his imaginative and intellectual limitations, even if they also reflect aspects of Conrad's own views.[14] The language-teacher and Razumov have certain affinities with two different ideals of masculinity: the language-teacher with the ideal of a restrained, chivalrous, protective, self-abnegating gentleman, and Razumov with the ideal of the strong, taciturn, seemingly imperturbable man of action. One difference of course is that the former ideal represents the language-teacher's self-image, whereas the latter is thrust quite inappropriately onto Razumov by the perceptions of others. Both ideals, however, are ironized. Even if we do not share Richard Ruppel's reading of the language-teacher as a closet homosexual, we strongly suspect some self-deception and denial of his real feelings.[15] In the case of Razumov we are privy to his tormented mental state and unfulfilled need to express his feelings. Thus, as often in Conrad's work, certain rather stereotypical ideas of

masculinity are treated ironically almost as a byproduct of his exploration of existential uncertainty. Ideas of cultural difference come
into play as part of this ironization, as when Haldin calls Razumov 'a
regular Englishman' (22) because of his brevity of speech and seeming
coolness (22), or when the language-teacher talks of Natalia's 'characteristically Russian exploit in self-suppression' (375) just at the
moment when his own (characteristically English?) self-suppression is
most in evidence. (He is evidently in love with Natalia, yet comments
that 'I gathered this success to my breast' (373) when he learns of
Natalia's decision to return to Russia, which means that he will never
see her again.)

The most crucial difference between 'Heart of Darkness' and *Under
Western Eyes* is perhaps that what is exchanged between men in *Under
Western Eyes* is less knowledge (even, as in 'Heart of Darkness', secret
and enigmatic knowledge) than ignorance and misunderstanding.
This offers a more troubled and uncertain view of the male homosocial economy, and implicates both author and reader in that
uncertainty. I want to focus particularly on the relationship of
speaker to listener (or writer to reader), and on narratological chains
whereby the listener/reader of one narrating relationship also serves
as the speaker/writer for another narrating relationship, and so on.
These chains are of particular interest in the study of masculinity
within narrative fiction. They seem to project constructions of
masculinity outside the text, to implicate implied author and implied
reader (and perhaps even actual readers) in a series of exchanges and
transferences of desire. Particular modes of the communicative act
can be passed along these chains, and these modes carry with them
aspects of masculinity. In the case of *Under Western Eyes* the mode of
communication concerned is almost a mode of non-communication,
in that misinterpretation is always involved. Whereas in 'Heart of
Darkness' an enigmatic, veiled knowledge is passed among men, the
epistemological structure of *Under Western Eyes* involves a series of
confessions which are dogged by the failure to understand, or by
incorrect understanding.

Aspects of the narrative chain are thematized in the novel.
Immediately after deciding to give Haldin up to the authorities,
Razumov says to himself, 'I want to be understood' (39), and in his
interview with Mikulin, Razumov seizes on the word 'misunderstood'
in an attempt to avoid the word 'mistrusted', and expresses the fear of
having been misunderstood by the authorities (87). In fact he is afraid
of being understood, that is to say, of his ambivalence (which led him

initially to search for Ziemianitch to aid Haldin's escape) being revealed. Somewhat later, as the oppression of his lonely situation bears in on him, he becomes equally afraid of *not* being understood:

> Yet he could not defend himself from fancying that Councillor Mikulin was, perhaps, the only man in the world able to understand his conduct. To be understood appeared extremely fascinating.
>
> (297)

At the same time he realizes the impossibility of understanding. This is partly a political point, in that it is the context of suspicion and political oppression that makes attempts at honest disclosure both futile and dangerous. However, ultimately it is also a psychological and even an existential point:

> The idea of going back and, as he termed it to himself, *confessing* to Councillor Mikulin flashed through his mind.
>   Go back! What for? Confess! To what? 'I have been speaking to him with the greatest openness,' he said to himself with perfect truth. 'What else could I tell him? That I have undertaken to carry a message to that brute Ziemianitch? Establish a false complicity and destroy what chance of safety I have won for nothing—what folly!'
>
> (297)

The existential implication here is that the truth of the self can never be ultimately revealed. Razumov acted first to help Haldin and then to betray him. Behind these actions is no ultimate truth of Razumov's identity but rather a contingent and circumstantial confusion. Since Natalia Haldin, Sophia Antonovna and Tekla are, in their various ways, presented as relatively admirable characters with firm convictions and resolute in their behaviour, Conrad's destabilizing of the self bears most on the masculine self. It is the masculine self which both needs and fears to confess, which both wants to be understood and yet lacks the substance necessary for final understanding. The political aspects have already been pointed out to Razumov by Mikulin, who comments that 'abstention, reserve, in certain situations, come very near to political crime' (294). This observation shows the insufficiency of the language-teacher's stereotypically 'English' code of masculinity as reserve and restraint. Under certain forms of political oppression, one must confess, and one cannot confess to innocence, only to guilt.

The philosophical keynote to this element in the story is set by the statement (which seems to belong to the language-teacher as narrator): 'A man's real life is that accorded to him in the thoughts of other men by reason of respect or natural love' (14). 'Man' and 'men' here are ambiguous in the way that they so often are in English before the later twentieth century: they might be generic (meaning people) or gender specific (meaning just men). The effect is generally to imply that the latter is the privileged instance of the former: that is to say, women are not *necessarily* excluded from such formulae, but often the masculine instance is taken as the important or indicative one. There is another measure here, though, of the difference between 'Heart of Darkness' and *Under Western Eyes*. The real life of Marlow and Kurtz most assuredly does not lie in the thoughts of the Intended. In 'Heart of Darkness' women's knowledge is not valued. In *Under Western Eyes* Natalia's 'respect' and (potential) 'natural love' are indeed important to Razumov, while Sophia and Tekla are also characters whose understanding and love count for something.

These key scenes between Razumov and Mikulin establish misunderstanding as a theme, as well as instigating its role as the mode of communication and interaction between the characters. Razumov is misunderstood by his fellow students, his silence interpreted as unshakeable integrity. He goes on to be misunderstood by Natalia Haldin and the revolutionaries in Geneva, where the veiled confessions which he cannot help making are systematically misinterpreted so as to protect him and conceal his guilt. Most crucially as regards the narrative structure, Razumov is misunderstood (though in a rather different manner) by the language-teacher, the narrator on the next diegetic level. The teacher repeatedly stresses his own inability to comprehend the Russian temperament and Razumov's nature and motives in particular. For example, he professes himself unable to understand why Razumov wrote his diary, his textual confession:

> It would be idle to inquire why Mr. Razumov has left this record behind him. It is inconceivable that he should have wished any human eye to see it ... What sort of peace Kirylo Sidorovitch Razumov expected to find in the writing up of his record it passeth my understanding to guess.
>
> (4–5)

Why, one might in turn wonder, does the language-teacher write his own narrative? He stresses his inability to understand his material, his inadequacy to the task of creating for the reader an impression of Razumov's personality, and his distaste for words themselves ('Words, as is well known, are the great foes of reality' (3)). His incomprehension of Razumov's need to write passes up to the next diegetic level, posing for the implied reader the mystery of the language-teacher's need to narrate. Indeed, since this mystery is implicitly raised by the carefully structured ironies of the book as a whole, it resounds up a further diegetic level, to implicate Conrad, or more strictly speaking, the implied author of the text as a whole. Why has the author written a book about the language-teacher misunderstanding Razumov? The answer may lie in the nature of the confessional mode. The language-teacher's inability to understand Razumov's confession is in itself a confession of his own feelings, his own desires. It is, indeed, in the nature of the confession that communicative success and failure are closely bound together. This appears, for example, in the interpretative work of the psychoanalyst, who interprets the analysand's failure to communicate as a form of communication. The perpetual deferment of the total revelation of inner truth that is the ultimate and unreachable goal of the confession is represented metonymically in the novel as Razumov passes from being a character who listens but does not speak (when he is a student) to being one who speaks well but cannot hear (after he is deafened). He thus moves from one subject position of the confessional situation to the other, from the silent interpreter who allows others to disclose themselves (even while they misinterpret that silence) to the garrulous discloser who (if we take Razumov's deafness symbolically rather than realistically) is unable to interpret. The temporal rupture that allows Razumov to occupy these positions only separately, across a chronological divide, figures the impossibility of ideal self-presence, of simultaneously confessing and interpreting one's own confession, so that one might know exactly to what one was confessing.

In several respects, *Under Western Eyes* addresses explicitly the topic of gender roles. One such is via the person of Peter Ivanovitch, the Russian revolutionary and visionary 'feminist'. Like Conrad's other portrait of a 'feminist' (the governess in *Chance*), this is a savage caricature. Peter Ivanovitch exploits and bullies women and his mystical idealization of 'woman' is presented as typical of a deluded Russian love-affair with hollow words. As regards the theme of knowledge – what women know, what they should know, and how they stand in relation to 'ultimate' knowledge – the effect is, however, more subtle. Peter Ivanovitch's idealization of women serves as a self-parodic shadow to some of Conrad's own idealizing tendencies. Madame de S—, prime object of Peter Ivanovitch's encomiums, is presented as corrupt and grotesque. However, Natalia Haldin is presented in serious terms as possessing some of those qualities which Ivanovitch implausibly attributes to Madame de S— ('a noble and peerless spirit') (129–30) and, more plausibly, to the Russian girl who helps him escape from captivity ('the sacredness of self-sacrifice and womanly love') (121). Might Conrad be working through some of his own idealistic simplifications of 'woman' by projecting them onto a derided so-called 'feminist', just as he projects onto Russians some of his own ambivalent love of vague and portentous language? Furthermore, the novel contains a number of women characters who, while not necessarily free of illusions, are strong and admirable. The language-teacher admires Natalia, not merely for conventional feminine charms, but for 'collected independence' and 'the strength of her nature' (373), while Sophia Antonovna is an independent woman of strong intellect, confident of her political role and her emancipated sexuality, as appears in her long conversation with Razumov (238–64). This conversation returns often to the theme of gender roles, with a certain ironic needling from both parties, from Razumov's 'Verily, without women we can do nothing. So it stands written, and apparently so it is' (239–40) to Antonovna's 'you like other men are fastidious, full of self-love and afraid of trifles' (243), her allusion to 'petty masculine standards' (248) and numerous similar comments. Like the language-teacher's view of Russians, Sophia Antonovna's views of men are neither endorsed nor rejected: they carry some force and conviction and in certain ways fit various of the male characters, yet her judgement is called into question by her seemingly unshakeable admiration for the egotistical Peter Ivanovitch. The novel ends with a collision between the respective prejudices of the language-teacher and Antonovna, as the former expresses the hope that Peter Ivanovitch will be beaten by his peasant girl, while Antonovna insists to the last that he is 'an inspired man' (382).

The fear attached to the disclosure, to a woman, of knowledge (especially knowledge of the male self and of male secrets) is represented in partly comic form in relation to the supposed discernment of Madame de S—. The scenes involving Razumov and the Russian revolutionaries in Geneva are packed with double-edged allusions to understanding, to truth and to trust. In one, Peter Ivanovitch momentarily alarms Razumov by portentously warning him of the supposed powers of discernment of Madame de S—: 'Nothing can remain obscure before that—that—inspired, yes, inspired penetration, this true light of femininity'. 'You don't object to being understood...?' (213), he asks (precisely what Razumov would object to, of course). In fact, Madame de S—, a hysterical spiritualist, is the least likely of anyone in Geneva to perceive the truth. There is the shadow here of the classic duality in the representation of women: the beautiful, charming, sincere, idealistic Natalia counterpoised to Madame de S—, a symbol of falsity and physically repulsive, like 'a corpse galvanized into harsh speech and glittering stare by the force of murderous hate' (222) (a description strongly suggestive of the Freudian uncanny).[16] A conventional misogynist paradigm lurks in the background (the beautiful virgin and the ugly witch), but reworked within a complex ironic structure.

If we consider the triangle of desire and knowledge formed by Razumov, Natalia and the language-teacher, we can observe an unsettling of the paradigm which I outlined in relation to 'Heart of Darkness'. The paradigm is clearly present, at least in the situation as perceived by the language-teacher (and to an extent by Natalia). The teacher sees her as admirable but innocent in the ways of the world, as the 'ignorant young girl' specified by Irigaray as the approved mediator between men. At the same time his idealization of Natalia hints at an association of her (in his mind) with metaphysical or ultimate truth. This view of her is neatly encapsulated in his description of her as 'so true, so honest, but so dangerously inexperienced!' (142): in his view she *is* 'true' (trustworthy, honest, full of integrity) but she cannot *know* the truth (being inexperienced). Natalia also describes herself (to Razumov) as ignorant but trustworthy (181). The teacher is clearly aware, with the voyeurism and vicarious excitement identified by Cave, of some sort of transaction between himself and Razumov, involving him passing Natalia over to the younger man:

> In my fear of seeing the girl surrender to the influence of the Château Borel revolutionary feminism, I was more than willing to put my trust in that friend of the late Victor Haldin.
>
> (164–5)

He imagines their growing intimacy with an evident mixture of pleasurable identification with the young man and suppressed jealousy (see 170–6).

However, as the reader knows, and as the language-teacher himself knows by the time that he writes his narrative, his idea of Razumov is mistaken. Like the students in St Petersburg, he takes taciturnity as a sign of sincerity (173). Although one of the novel's psychological subtleties is that Razumov remains at some level one of the most sincere characters, his situation does not allow him to be sincere in practice. The transaction between two men of the world, in which the elder passes on a young woman to the younger in return for vicarious satisfaction of his repressed desires, is traversed by a hidden fracture. The language-teacher's knowledge of the world will not serve him here, because he has to deal with the unknown in the form of Russia. This, at least, is how he comes to explain his own ignorance and failure of understanding: in terms of the incomprehensibility of Russia to a Westerner. (How far is this a *post-hoc* justification of his own dubious role? After all, he lived in St Petersburg until the age of nine, speaks fluent Russian and seems to know quite a lot about Russian politics.) He expresses his ignorance in a phrase which echoes the much quoted passage in 'Heart of Darkness', where women are said by Marlow to be 'out of it' (HOD, 115):

> I perceived that she was not listening. There was no mistaking her expression; and once more I had the sense of being out of it — not because of my age, which at any rate could draw inferences — but. altogether out of it, on another plane whence I could only watch her from afar.
>
> (170)

Is Conrad making a conscious reference back to 'Heart of Darkness' here? Not necessarily, since the phrase itself could easily enough recur by accident (when, a little later, Peter Ivanovitch calls Razumov 'one of *us*' (208), an ironic echo of *Lord Jim* is more inescapable). Nor do I think that Conrad, in *Under Western Eyes*, is offering an explicit critique of male bonds and their consequences for women. What seems to me to be happening here, as often in Conrad's work, is that his basic social conservatism is deflected from what might otherwise have been its routine course by his experience of cultural dislocation, and his resulting confrontation with alienation and the relativity of social values. This experience clearly informs his portrayal of the language-teacher, though in complex ways, not as direct representation. The teacher gives voice to some of Conrad's own suspicion of the Russian temperament and fear of revolutionary ardour, yet is also ironized and revealed as lacking in self-knowledge. Conrad's ideas about male and female roles, which are fairly conventional, cannot remain untouched by the strain of radical scepticism about identity and truth that is found in his thought. In *Under Western Eyes* the knowledge that circulates between men is deeply flawed by misunderstanding, misinterpretation, failure of communication and betrayal of trust.

In Conrad's late work gender becomes a more explicit theme. *Chance*, published two years after *Under Western Eyes* (though it had been long in the writing) was a marked departure for Conrad. Not only does it have a happy ending (uniquely among his novels), but it also, by design, pays more attention to women's lives. Conrad wrote to his literary agent, James Pinker, 'It's the sort of stuff that *may* have a chance with the public. All of it about a girl and with a steady run of references to women in general all along, some sarcastic, others sentimental, it ought to go down.'[17] The novel did indeed sell better than any of its predecessors.[18] Despite Conrad's implication of a deliberate strategy of populism, the novel has a highly intricate narrative structure.[19] As Martin Ray observes, 'Marlow is called upon to collect and collate the reports of six or more observers in the chain of narration and to trace his way through seven different temporal levels in the course of the story, whose time-span covers some seventeen years, concluding in the dramatic present.'[20] As I have argued in greater detail elsewhere, the terms of exchange along this narrative chain between a series of male figures involve a competitive arrogation of superior knowledge of an essentialized 'woman' or 'women'.[21] In a sense this is also a mode of misinterpretation, both because of the inherent falsification of such gender essentialization, and because the claim to superior interpretative powers by each male figure collapses by virtue of the reflecting effect of the chain: each individual's claim to understanding is supported by the dismissal of the claims of another. The figure of Marlow in *Chance* is distinctly different from his earlier avatar in 'Heart of Darkness'. However, as part of the deliberate focus on women in *Chance*, Marlow's tendency to generalizations about women is extended via his comments to the frame-narrator. The following is one of his more striking pronouncements on the subject of female passivity:

And this is the pathos of being a woman. A man can struggle to get a place for himself or perish. But a woman's part is passive, say what you like, and shuffle the facts of the world as you may, hinting at lack of energy, of wisdom, of courage. As a matter of fact, almost all women have all that—of their own kind. But they are not made for attack. Wait they must. I am speaking here of women who

are really women. And it's no use talking of opportunities either. I
know that some of them do talk of it. But not the genuine women.
Those know better. Nothing can beat a true woman for a clear
vision of reality.

(*C*, 281)

Here, as elsewhere, Marlow seems to combine some understanding of
the social oppression which forced certain roles onto women ('a man
can struggle') with a rather patronizing essentialism ('wisdom ... of
their own kind. But they are not made for attack'). Also typical of a
number of his assertions about women is his passing reference to
possibilities for emancipation ('talking of opportunities') which he
dismisses by means of a circular argument: women who are interested
in opportunities are not the 'genuine women', so that women are
proved to be essentially passive by only counting as women those who
conform. Interestingly, though, Marlow associates this supposed
passivity with 'a clear vision of reality'. In *Nostromo* the narrator
observes that 'action is consolatory. It is the enemy of thought and
the friend of flattering illusions' (66). Presumably, then, women's
'clear vision of reality' may, in Marlow's theory, derive from their
inability to act.[22] Such a vision might be reached through 'attention
[which] originated in idleness', a phrase which Conrad uses to
describe his own creative meditation on the figure of Lena in *Victory*
('Author's Note', *V*, xv). Thus Marlow's definition of the otherness of
the female rebounds on itself, for not only is Marlow's own role in the
events that he narrates in *Chance* largely a passive one of observing
and waiting, but he repeatedly claims for himself, on the basis of this
detachment from the action, precisely that 'clear vision of reality'
which, on his own account, is denied to those men more involved in
the action of the story than he. In relation to the climax of events on
board the *Ferndale*, recounted to Marlow by the second mate, Powell,
Marlow claims that:

The inwardness of what was passing before his eyes was hidden
from him [i.e. Powell], who had looked on, more impenetrably
than from me who at a distance of years was listening to his words.

(426)

Marlow's language here, as in many places, suggests a strong voyeuristic element: the scene to which he refers culminates in the sexual
consummation of Captain Anthony's marriage to Flora, a woman

whom both Powell and Marlow find very attractive. Marlow, while acknowledging Powell's voyeuristic priority ('who had looked on'), claims for himself, using diction appropriate to male sexual fantasy, a superior power of penetrating the inwardness of events. But the main point here is that, despite the egregiously male nature of the rhetoric of penetration which Marlow uses, his 'clear vision' of events is based on the passive waiting that he identifies as female. It is true that Marlow does play a part in the action of the main story in that he encourages Fyne to go along with his wife's wishes and to interfere in the relationship between Anthony and Flora. But even this element of action on Marlow's part accords well with his own description of the woman's role:

> In this world as at present organized women are the suspected half of the population ... The part falling to women's share being all 'influence' has an air of occult and mysterious action, something not altogether trustworthy like all natural forces.
>
> (327)

Marlow's influence on Fyne, who quite commendably is unwilling to 'push under the head of a poor devil of a girl quite sufficiently plucky' (190), is indeed suspect. Marlow's confident assertion that Fyne might as well humour his wife, by seeking to intervene between Flora and Captain Anthony, since it will be 'not the slightest use' (191) turns out to be quite wrong. Fyne's interference, effectively engineered by Marlow and Mrs Fyne, the misogynist and the feminist (though for quite different motives), has a disastrous effect on the Anthonys' marriage. Marlow conveniently forgets the part played in this disaster by his own supposed perceptiveness when he subsequently seems to blame a combination of chance and feminism. Marlow's role in the events of the novel closely resembles that which he seeks to attribute to women: overt passivity combined with covert influence. My object in pointing this out is not to use Marlow's definitions of femininity, which are in any event inconsistent and largely specious, to define him as somehow 'feminine', but to consider the narrative significance of the process by which he constantly sets up gender-based distinctions that undo themselves.

Marlow also identifies 'female' traits in other male characters. In relation to Captain Anthony in particular, Marlow expresses both fear and contempt of the passive. To Mrs Fyne he says, of her brother:

It's difficult to imagine a victim as passive as all that; but granting
you the (I very nearly said: imbecility, but checked myself in time)
innocence of Captain Anthony...

(158)

During the incident of the near-collision on board the Ferndale, the
marital dilemma in which Anthony finds himself is expressed by his
lack of motion: 'He stirred not ... Why is it that the stillness of a
human being is often so impressive, so suggestive of evil?' (321–2).
This comment, which may remind us of the sinister immobility of the
jungle in Conrad's earlier works, alludes to more than a passing
moment. Shortly before, Powell has stamped on the starboard side of
the deck to summon his Captain to deal with the emergency, but
contrary to 'the immemorial custom and usage of the sea' (316)
Anthony is not sleeping in the starboard cabin (because Flora is sleeping there). The danger of the lack of sexual action on board the
Ferndale is symbolically reinforced by this incident, in which the ship
is nearly lost because the Captain is not sleeping with his wife. Powell
is also in danger of failing sexually because of passivity. At one point
in his narration Marlow opens a Pandora's box of Freudian symbolism
when he develops the fancy of a young girl as 'something like a
temple', musing that 'the privileged man, the lover, the husband, who
are given the key of the sanctuary do not always know how to use it'
(311). Near the end of the book, when Marlow suggests to Powell that
he declare his love to the widowed Flora, Powell's eyes light up 'like
the reflection of some inward fire tended in the sanctuary of his heart
by a devotion as pure as that of any vestal' (441). It seems that middle-
aged sailors, as well as young girls, may resemble temples. Thus
Marlow repeatedly attempts to constitute femininity as an Other in
terms that associate it with passivity, with covert action, or with the
enigmatic and unreadable, but these strategies are repeatedly
subverted as such qualities become associated with Marlow himself, or
with other male characters.

Marlow's narrative in *Chance*, like that in 'Heart of Darkness', is a
heuristic process, a process of exploration and discovery, but what is
here explored is a more open form of masculinity, as opposed to the
discovery of a secret knowledge confirming a masculinist ideology. As
in 'Heart of Darkness', a certain truth is concealed from the young
woman, in this case the fact that her father tried to murder her
husband (Captain Anthony) out of jealousy. In this way some of the
intensity of the male competitiveness circulating around Flora is

hidden from her. However, the murder attempt is rapidly followed by her father's suicide and (in narrative time though not in story time) by the accidental drowning of her husband, who insists on Powell leaving the sinking ship before him.[23] The latter disaster has to be reported to her by Powell, the same young man who has helped to conceal the murder attempt and who himself secretly desires her. Thus Powell, though devoted to Captain Anthony, unwittingly participates in and announces the death of the older man who, in Girard's terms, stands as the mediator of, and obstacle to, his desire. In almost the last scene of the novel we find an echo of Marlow's lie to the Intended. Some years after Anthony's death Marlow is alone with Flora, whom he comes to visit partly in order to facilitate some expression of the love he detects between her and Powell. She alludes to the night of the murder attempt (which remains unknown to her):

> '"That night when my poor father died suddenly I am certain they had some sort of discussion about me. But I did not want to hold out any longer against my own heart! I could not."
> She stopped short, then impulsively—
> "Truth will out, Mr. Marlow."
> "Yes," I said.'

(444)

Again Marlow conceals a male horror from an idealistic woman. Yet the psychological and ethical implications are very different. The truth of the Intended's heart was, we are led to believe, a delusion. Flora may not realize the depths to which her father sank, but the truth of her heart has been shown to be superior to the male delusion of chivalry (under which Anthony laboured) as well as to her father's vicious competitiveness. The end of the novel, with a marriage between Powell and Flora in prospect, is a triumph for Flora's sort of truth. Furthermore, rather than Marlow protecting his own masculine heroic identification, his masculinity is called into question by that ending. He has himself enough understanding of 'the heart' generously to bring Powell and Flora together in the face of their mutual inhibition. He suggests to Flora that Powell has given up the sea because of his love for her (445). But this echoes the frame-narrator's puzzlement as to why Marlow seems to have given up the sea himself: 'The sea is the sailor's true element, and Marlow, lingering on shore, was to me an object of incredulous commiseration like a bird, which, secretly, should have lost its faith in the high virtue of flying' (34). We are left wondering what Marlow's secret might be, what sort of love (or fear) might be keeping him away from the sea. His own desire for Flora remains in evidence in the final scenes, a mediated desire for which Powell provides vicarious fulfilment.

What Marlow is exploring, in a manner half-conscious and half-unconscious, is not so much the nature of women as the nature and psychological significance of his own ideas of the feminine. In returning obsessively, during his narration, to his theories as to the nature of women, Marlow is achieving two ends, both of which are matters of oblique or covert self-examination. First, his assumed tone of knowledgeableness about women and their ways, in contrast to Captain Anthony's idealism, little Fyne's imperceptiveness and Powell's innocence, masks a profound identification with these other men, in their shared lack of understanding and their shared inability to engage with women other than through the distorting medium of complementary sets of male idealizations and condemnations. Whereas Straus identifies in 'Heart of Darkness' a shared, male secret knowledge, I find in *Chance* a secret sharing of male ignorance, a covert fellowship of fear and desire in relation to the feminine. The anonymous frame-narrator plays an important role here. His presence enlarges the potential field of male identification: Conrad, implied author, frame-narrator, Marlow, Powell, Anthony, the (male) reader (the question of gender-specific reading will be taken up again shortly). The frame-narrator serves to distance and control Marlow through his occasional mockery of Marlow's portentous utterances. He is in particular an object of Marlow's defensive projections, in that Marlow is continually attributing to him a dissent (on the subject of women) that he rarely expresses. The following exchange occurs after Marlow's statement about female passivity which was quoted earlier:

> 'Nothing can beat a true woman for a clear vision of reality: I would say a cynical vision if I were not afraid of wounding your chivalrous feelings—for which, by the by, women are not so grateful as you may think, to fellows of your kind . . . .'
> 'Upon my word, Marlow,' I cried, 'what are you flying out at me for like this?'
>
> (281)

Marlow's pre-emptive attacks on the supposed views of the frame-narrator suggest that Marlow himself is uneasily aware of the inadequacy and inconsistency of his own formulations, and that even while he attempts to use the frame-narrator as he uses the other men in the novel, as naive foil for his own superior penetration, he defensively attributes to the frame-narrator his own doubts. Their interaction is at times strikingly like that of analyst and analysand, as the frame-narrator uses silence to allow Marlow's internal conflicts to surface by projection onto him. Significantly, this occurs in relation to one of Marlow's claims to knowledge:

> 'I did not ask Mr. Powell anxiously what had happened to Mrs. Anthony in the end. I let him go on in his own way, feeling that no matter what strange facts he would have to disclose, I was certain to know much more of them than he ever did know or could possibly guess . . . .'
>
> Marlow paused for quite a long time. He seemed uncertain as though he had advanced something beyond my grasp. Purposely I made no sign. 'You understand?' he asked.
>
> (310–11)

Just as Marlow let Mr Powell 'go on in his own way', so the frame-narrator allows Marlow to 'go on in his own way', perhaps also feeling that 'no matter what strange facts he would have to disclose, I was certain to know much more of them than he ever did'. Subsequently the frame-narrator responds with mockery of Marlow's self-image as an 'honest backwoodsman with his incomparable knowledge' (311). What is interesting here is Marlow's evident and uneasy competitiveness with other men, both Powell and the frame-narrator, over knowledge and penetration into the supposed mysteries of the female. In this novel so centred on women, the 'inwardness' of events becomes symbolically female, so that knowledge (and ignorance) of women function as paradigms of all knowledge and ignorance.

Marlow's first hidden motivation as narrator, then, is to compete with the other men for the knowledge and, symbolically, for the sexual possession of women. The frame-narrator seems to express his awareness of this by his 'sarcastic' grin on the novel's last page, in response to which Marlow defensively denies such competitiveness: 'I am not afraid of going to church with a friend' (447). No one has suggested that he is afraid, so it is clearly Marlow's own idea. Marlow's second and more complex motive is to consider a duality in his own self and life by the familiar psychological process of projecting aspects of oneself with which one is not fully at home onto some Other (here onto women in general). Marlow has a contemplative, meditative, listening aspect, evident in his quiet dealings with Powell (which contrast with his assertive loquacity in relation to the frame narrator). Yet the suggestions of passivity in such an aspect and the associated fear of a clear view of a possibly unbearable reality make his relationship to such qualities necessarily ambivalent. Despite his misogynistic clichés, Marlow also exhibits intermittently a power of sympathetic identification with Flora's psychological traumas as a repeated victim and an interest in the idea of himself as feminine, as evinced in his comment that 'there is enough of the woman in my nature to free my judgement of women from glamorous reticency' (53). As in 'Heart of Darkness', the act of narrating in *Chance* is an open-ended process, involving the potential for Marlow to move beyond his existing conceptual and ideological limitations.

It is in *Chance* that the presence of narrative chains implicates the male reader and critic most challengingly. If Marlow constitutes his role as story-teller by the arrogation of a largely spurious superiority of insight into women as against Anthony, Fyne, Powell and the frame-narrator (while the frame-narrator may return the favour), I cannot analyse this process without implicitly constituting myself as reader and critic through the assumption that I know more about women than Marlow does, that I 'know much more of them [the facts] than he ever did know or could possibly guess' (311) – perhaps an equally spurious claim. One effect of this implication of the male reader or critic is to make *Chance* a gender-specific text in the way that Straus claims 'Heart of Darkness' to be (a text that women will read differently) (EI, 130–5), yet with a greater questioning of the status of masculinity. Another effect is to make it a very interesting text for the male reader concerned with his own relation to ideas of self and femininity, and this despite the fact that the overt treatment of women is heavily reliant on idealization and cliché. For it draws the male reader, through its narrative strategy, into a dialectic of understanding and ignorance, of superiority and self-accusation in relation to the gender conceptions of other men – a dialectic of liberating self-criticism and inescapable complicity.[24] The possibility of this relation extending to the author is implied by Erdinast-Vulcan's idea that Conrad felt himself 'being forcibly drawn into his own fiction', an idea which she convincingly deduces from the changes between the serial and book versions of the novel.[25]

Chance is a revealing, if uneven, study of certain aspects of male figuration and representation of women and the dynamics of the circulation of these representations among men. How far this is within the author's control, and how far it is something that happens despite what we deduce to have been his 'intentions' is an interesting question but not one which necessarily determines the interest .or value of the text, since *Chance* involves male characters, male readers and the male author in a process of struggle between conscious formulations and opinions, on the one hand, and unconscious assumptions and identifications, on the other.

7
Vision, Power and Homosocial Exchange: *The Arrow of Gold*

In examining the interaction of gender with colonialist ideologies of race in Conrad's early work, Chapters 1 and 2 noted a number of examples of the articulation of power relations through visual exchanges between characters. Eyes, looking, appearance and other aspects of the visual remain significant elements in Conrad's characterization and symbolic patterns of meaning throughout his career.[1] However, in Conrad's late novels the visual again assumes particular importance in relation to gender. The early novels and stories set in the Far East share a number of features with late work such as *Victory*, *Chance* and *The Arrow of Gold*: an ambivalent relationship to popular genres such as adventure and romance, a focus on sexuality and strong representations of women as sexual and visual objects.[2] This objectification is, however, more critically presented in the late works, as a role projected onto the women characters by men, and one that they resist, whereas in the earlier work the texts themselves present women in that way, not, certainly, as passive or powerless, but primarily as the focus of male sexual desires and fears. This chapter and the next will examine more systematically the place of the visual in Conrad's late representations of masculinity.

'You fellows see more than I could then' (83), remarks Marlow to his small group of male listeners in 'Heart of Darkness'. It is one of Marlow's reflections on the problems of understanding his own experiences in Africa and an acknowledgement that he may not have grasped the full implications of those experiences at the time. It implies that his listeners may understand more, or understand differently, the meaning of the events that he is describing to them, but also perhaps that he himself now interprets them differently. As listeners or narratees, the group of men on board the *Nellie* locate the position (or at least a possible position) for the reader. Furthermore one of them relays and frames Marlow's story. Is the implied reader, then, someone who would fall into the category of 'you fellows'? Will he see more than Marlow? Is there any possibility of a female implied reader? The use of 'see' to mean 'understand' or 'realize' is a familiar idiom; this and a whole set of related metaphors (such as 'perceive', 'perspective', 'illuminate', 'insight') are a product of a tradition in Western thought that privileges sight as a model for knowledge and understanding.[3] Marlow's use of the metaphor of vision not only evokes this tradition but is also indicative of the important role played by metaphors of sight and vision in Conrad's fiction and critical writings.

Marlow's comment is part of a major area of philosophical concern for Conrad, that of the problematic relations between experience, truth and interpretation. In *Chance*, Marlow makes the same assumption, though he himself occupies the inverse subject-position: referring to another man's experience which he is recounting at second hand, he claims for himself the greater penetration of the retrospective gaze: 'The inwardness of what was passing before his eyes was hidden from him, who had looked on, more impenetrably than from me who at a distance of years was listening to his words' (*C*, 426). Conrad's most characteristic metaphor for the problems of interpretation and understanding is that of vision, particularly the metaphor of seeing into things, but also, for example, the famous image of the 'haze' in 'Heart of Darkness', where the quest for the meaning of a story is figured as looking at 'one of these misty halos that sometimes are made visible by the spectral illumination of moonshine' (48). Ideas of penetrative vision ('insight') and of the mental 'vision' of understanding are frequent in Conrad's fiction. Examples include: 'And then my eyes became opened to the inwardness of things and speeches the triviality of which had been so baffling and tiresome' (*SL*, 26); 'I strained my mental eyesight only to discover that, as with the complexion of all our actions, the shade of difference was so delicate that it was impossible to say' (*LJ*, 197). It is, however, in Conrad's comments on his own writings that the visual metaphor for understanding is most pervasive. His 'Author's Notes' refer frequently to his 'vision': .

It was only then that I had the first vision of a twilight country which was to become the province of Sulaco.

('Author's Note', *N*, ix)

I don't know whether I really felt that I wanted a change, change
in my imagination, in my vision and in my mental attitude.

('Author's Note', *SA*, ix)

In a manner testifying to the clearness of my vision and the correct-
ness of my judgement.

('Author's Note', *UWE*, vii)

These notes also represent the creative process in terms of Conrad's
ability to see his characters, but here a gendered distinction is apparent. Conrad presents his heroines as objects of his enquiring or loving
gaze:

That's why I long sometimes for another glimpse of the 'beautiful
Antonia' (or can it be the Other?).

('Author's Note', *N*, xiv)

Slowly the dawning conviction of Mrs. Verloc's maternal passion
grew up to a flame between me and that background, tingeing it
with its secret ardour and receiving from it in exchange some of its
own sombre colouring.

('Author's Note', *SA*, xii)

It was at her, whom I call Lena, that I have looked the longest and
with a most sustained attention.

('Author's Note', *V*, xv)

His heroes, however, he presents rather as collaborators, as sustainers
of the creative impulse, as fellow watchers, seers, actors. So he
describes his wish to glimpse Antonia Avellanos once more as 'the
idlest of dreams' since 'I did understand perfectly well ... that the
moment the breath left the body of the Magnificent Capataz ... there
was nothing more for me to do in Sulaco' ('Author's Note', *N*, xiv–xv).
The male protagonist authorizes Conrad's presence, while the female
motivates his creative desire. Similarly he confesses that 'I have lived
longest with Heyst' ('Author's Note', *V*, xv), and that 'I let her [Lena]
go with Heyst, I won't say without a pang but certainly without
misgivings' (xvii). The language-teacher of *Under Western Eyes* is
described as an essential 'eye-witness' since otherwise Miss Haldin
'would have had no one to whom she could give a glimpse of her
idealistic faith, of her great heart, and of her simple emotions'

('Author's Note', *UWE*, ix). Conrad identifies with a male figure and hints at a certain rivalry with him: who will see more, who will be afforded those exciting glimpses of the female? A statement from Conrad's Preface to *The Nigger of the 'Narcissus'*, often taken as his artistic credo, refers to the role of the novelist in terms of vision:

> My task which I am trying to achieve is, by the power of the written word to make you hear, to make you feel—it is, before all, to make you *see*! That—and no more, and it is everything! If I succeed, you shall find there according to your deserts: encouragement, conso-lation, fear, charm—all you demand—and, perhaps, also that glimpse of truth for which you have forgotten to ask ... The task ... is to hold up unquestioningly, without choice and without fear, the rescued fragment before all eyes in the light of a sincere mood ... One may perchance attain to such clearness of sincerity that at last the presented vision of regret or pity, of terror or mirth, shall awaken in the hearts of the beholders that feeling of unavoidable solidarity.
>
> (x)

Edward Said contrasts the ideal of community and clarity evoked here with the agonized sense of writing alone in the darkness that emerges from some of Conrad's letters. Said also points to the way in which Marlow, in the act of narrating, fades into darkness in 'Heart of Darkness' (and in *Lord Jim*), so that his listeners lose sight of him.[4] Marlow's comments, quoted above from 'Heart of Darkness' and *Chance*, about the relative understanding achieved by himself and others, are also indicative of a more problematic relation of narrator and narratee than the Preface to *The Nigger of the 'Narcissus'* might suggest. The idea of a fragment of life held up 'before all eyes' suggests a free sharing of vision, unobscured and unmediated. In fact, the evocation of the visual in Conrad's fiction generally occurs within mediated and fractured narratives, involving a differential circulation of the image and of the truth it is held to embody. Certain characters have greater insight (or claim to have greater insight) than others; there may be an impulse of solidarity but there are also impulses of competitiveness and these, I shall argue, extend to implied author and readers. A politics of the visual is involved, in the sense of a power differential between seer and seen, subject and object of the act of vision. In Conrad's fiction the act of seeing frequently serves to estab-lish a power relation, because this act is a product of the desire, control or supervision of the one who sees (or, in certain cases, of the one who is seen). Since the visual image is here encoded in narrative discourse, a politics (and an economics) of narration are also involved: in so far as value is invested in the visual, that value circulates between characters, narrators, author, readers. Such circulation is not open and frictionless, but works according to laws of desire and repression. So, especially in a situation where the one who sees is also the one who narrates, while the object of the look remains silent, the power relation of the look is itself put into circulation.

For example, the presentation of the African woman in 'Heart of Darkness' embodies such a power-relation. Informed by the projection of cultural and sexual fantasies, Marlow's description of her as 'savage and superb, wild-eyed and magnificent' (HOD, 135–6) is overtly about her power – the power over Kurtz which she shares with the wilderness. But her lack of comprehensible voice within his narrative – the one time she is heard we are told only that she 'shouted something' (146) – combined with the elaborate description of her visual appearance, renders her the passive object of a masterful gaze, and transforms her into an image which Marlow makes available to his listeners and Conrad to his readers. The status of the visual in Conrad's fiction is a matter of the conjunction between the metaphor of vision as knowledge and the way in which the narrative seeks to convey visual impressions or describe the process of looking. Indeed, the Preface to *The Nigger of the 'Narcissus'* seeks to unite these: to suggest that by offering the reader a representation of the seen, the text can also present inner truth. As Ian Watt notes, this is a philosophically weak part of Conrad's argument, since the basis for this link is not articulated.[5] Furthermore, Conrad presupposes a universal subject of vision although, as has been noted, in the case of several novels the 'Author's Note' distributes the roles of subject and object of the gaze according to gender. By the same token, it is frequently women who, in Conrad's fiction, are presented as aestheticized objects of desiring contemplation. However, as has been noted in relation to the early fiction, such a gaze is directed towards certain male characters, presenting a more complex sense of gender roles. Furthermore, as Wayne Koestenbaum has noted, *Romance* (a collaborative novel written jointly by Conrad and Ford Madox Ford), is full of seemingly eroticized visual images of 'near-naked men, in postures of threat and repose'.[6]

Much Western thought since Plato has tended to link reason, truth, knowledge and goodness with light, while associating darkness or blackness with irrationality, falsity, ignorance and evil. This metaphorical binary has appeared in many different forms of discourse and has been inflected in various ways.[7] Building on the contradiction that Said notes between the Preface and the letters, one might note that the light and clarity invoked in the former suggest Enlightenment ideals of writing as transparent, lucid and communal, whereas Conrad's fictional style is modernist, elusive, ambiguous and suggestive of epistemological isolation. In the nineteenth century the light/darkness binary gave support to the discourse of racist imperialism: a philosophical metaphor made it easier for Europeans to identify Africans with ignorance or evil. Conrad's appeal to 'the light of a sincere mood' appears in the Preface to a novel the title of which (*The Nigger of the 'Narcissus'*) immediately evokes such racism. Furthermore, the story deploys a metaphorical rhetoric of dark and light, with a black man as a symbol of dissolution and death. As noted in Chapters 1 and 2, the power relations of looking crucially implicate gender with race in Conrad's early work, and traces of this remain in his late fiction, as when the hero of *The Arrow of Gold* remarks of a (European) woman that her face 'made you think of remote races' (66): a cross-substitution between forms of constructed 'otherness'. The dark/light binary has a particularly prominent place in Conrad's fictional metaphorical register. Much feminist theory, notably post-1960s French feminism, has linked ocularcentrism and phallocentrism and such arguments would imply that Conrad's ideal of clear visual presentation in the Preface has its roots in a specifically male discourse.[8] Similarly, Conrad's rhetoric of darkness, uncertainty and scepticism is, on one view, a projection of the fear of the Other, comparable to Freud's allusion to 'the sexual life of adult women' as 'a "dark continent" for psychology'.[9]

Fredric Jameson identifies a class politics of the visual in Conrad's fiction. The significance of the visual in Conrad's work is often seen in terms of 'impressionism', a concept which has been carefully charted by Ian Watt in art historical and literary historical terms.[10] He also considers what he terms 'subjective moral impressionism', which serves to indicate 'the bounded and ambiguous nature of individual understanding'.[11] Jameson introduces political questions into this discussion. Analysing a passage from *Lord Jim*, he points out that, as Jim contemplates the factory chimneys of urban capitalism from the apparently external location of a sea-going ship, Conrad's style serves to transform material realities into aesthetic impressions (*PU*, 210). Thus Jameson sees impressionism as contributing to a displacement, within Conrad's fiction, of awareness of the process of production and of 'its class content under capitalism' (*PU*, 215). Jameson's analysis is very revealing of Conrad's use of the sea, paradoxically seen both as a place of work and as an escape from the social world which that work organizes, as a microcosm of society and as an alternative to it. However, the politics of the visual, of distance and of aestheticization involve gender as well as class, as many feminist writers have argued. One way in which the visual has been related to gender is by the claim that heterosexual male sexuality, as modern Western society shapes it, is marked by a wish to look which is also a wish to dominate. This claim has both sociological and psychological bases. The analysis of 'images of women' in the visual arts, the media and pornography, combined with the knowledge of the extent of male violence and discrimination, provides a strong basis for the argument that:

> Whether it is a man looking at women on the street, the male artist's gaze at the model, or the male audience for a blue movie, women do not share in the culture of looking in the same way ... This gender difference in who has the power to look and at whom is embedded in cultural forms.[12]

At the same time a theory of looking as a controlling or sadistic male activity can be evolved from the Freudian concept of 'scopophilia'. Feminist accounts draw on Freud's theories of childhood voyeurism and the castration complex, while criticizing Freud's 'law of the self-same': his reading of female development in terms of male development.[13] Thus Toril Moi suggests that 'the *gaze* enacts the voyeur's desire for sadistic power, in which the object of the gaze is cast as its passive, masochistic, feminine victim.'[14] One feminist reaction to this, and to the inadequacy with which Freud deals with the desire of girls and women, has been to assert the radically different structure of women's desire, as does Luce Irigaray, stressing the other senses:

> Investment in the look is not as privileged in women as in men. More than other senses, the eye objectifies and masters. It sets at a distance, and maintains a distance. In our culture the predominance of the look over smell, taste, touch and hearing has brought about an impoverishment of bodily relations. The moment the look dominates, the body loses its materiality.[15]

Questions of looking, gender and desire as they bear on cultural arte-
facts have been developed most extensively in the field of film theory,
particularly in relation to the structures of looking constructed by the
cinematic apparatus, by the use of the camera and by the manipulation of narrative and image. A recurrent point of reference and
departure for such theory has been Laura Mulvey's article 'Visual
Pleasure and Narrative Cinema', which argues that:

> In a world ordered by sexual imbalance, pleasure in looking has
> been split between active/male and passive/female. The determin-
> ing male gaze projects its phantasy on to the female figure which is
> styled accordingly. In their traditional exhibitionist role women are
> simultaneously looked at and displayed, with their appearance
> coded for strong visual and erotic impact so that they can be said
> to connote *to-be-looked-at-ness*.[16]

Mulvey's paradigm is psychoanalytical. She sees pleasure in looking
(scopophilia) as basic to cinema and as divisible into 'pleasure in using
another person as an object of sexual stimulation through sight' and
narcissistic 'identification with the image seen'. She basically follows
Freud in seeing these two (desire and identification) as in tension,
although 'interacting and overlaying each other'.[17] Mulvey argues
that mainstream cinema displays 'the woman as icon ... for the gaze
and enjoyment of men, the active controllers of the look' but that
these images of women also provoke castration anxiety.[18] Filmic structures represent two unconscious reactions to this anxiety: fetishistic
scopophilia (disavowal of castration), associated with the static, the
aesthetic and the idealization of women, and voyeuristic scopophilia
(an investigative, controlling response), associated with narrative,
denigration of women and sadism. Subsequent critiques and revisions
of Mulvey's article (by herself as well as others) have focused on such
issues as its neglect of the female spectator and her pleasure in
looking, its failure to consider gay and lesbian desire, its conflation of
the looks of the spectator, the camera and the male protagonist, and
on the validity or otherwise of its psychoanalytical basis.[19] Certain of
these critiques and elaborations of Mulvey's account are particularly
helpful for an analysis of the relationship of masculinity to the visual
in Conrad's fiction.

Steve Neale distinguishes between a general and a gender-specific
application of the Lacanian concept of castration:

A theoretical distinction needs to be made .,. between the relations between any human subject, any drive or desire, and any instance of representation, on the one hand, and the points at which (and the ways in which) sexual difference is inscribed and constructed across these relations on the other. This distinction hinges funda-mentally on a further distinction between Symbolic castration, and the place of castration within the Symbolic specification of sexual difference. Symbolic castration is marked by a splitting of the subject and by the radical lack of any object for any drive. It is something to which both men and women are subject. However, the Symbolic in addition marks lack and castration as distinct for male and female in its specification of sexual difference. Here, the female comes to signify castration and lack vis-à-vis the male.

(SD, 129)

I have certain reservations about this general concept of Symbolic castration, to which I shall return. Given, however, the prevalence and productivity of the concept in much film theory, its implications are worth following through. Neale points out that Mulvey's account, which attends only to the association of the female with castration, thereby identifies men as wholly controllers of the look, ignoring cross-gender identification via fantasy. He argues that 'the logic of a fantasy scenario can produce "male" characters in "female" positions and vice versa, cutting across the distribution of gender identity constructed at other levels and in other ways by the cinematic text' (SD, 126). His complication of Mulvey's model draws on the ques-tioning of gender essentialism by gay and lesbian theory and provides a valuable way of analysing the complexities and ambiguities present in Conrad's construction of gender. Neale notes that the male body as well as the female body can be fetishized, but according to different conventions: 'the male body can be fetishised ... inasmuch as it signi-fies masculinity, and, hence, possession of the phallus, the absence of lack'. On the other hand, the male body can also 'function as the object of voyeuristic looking', that is, it can signify castration and lack, but only if it is 'marked', whether by disfigurement, or racial or cultural otherness. (SD, 130). This paradoxical set of possibilities, in which the male body can signify either castration or its absence, and in which male and female roles may be exchanged in fantasy, illumi-nates some of the instabilities in Conrad's representation of masculinity. 'Marking' in the form of racial or cultural 'otherness' is illustrated by Kaja Silverman in her discussion of the presentation of an Arab character in Fassbinder's film *Fear Eats the Soul* (*MS*, 137–45). As I have suggested in Chapters 1 and 2, such an effect comes into play in Conrad's Malay fiction, where the racial otherness of male characters both signifies castration (in the Lacanian sense) and enables fetishization of the male body as the absence of castration. Neale's stress on the mobility of fantasy also assists a more nuanced account of how effects of narrative focalization offer shifting possibilities of gender-identification to the reader of Conrad's fiction. The technical means are different (verbal narrative as against camera) but fruitfully analogous at many points. By reading elements of narrative technique through analogies with film theory I hope to import into my interpretation of Conrad's fiction some of film theory's sensitivity to the power/vision nexus, while avoiding a reductive a priori identification of masculinity, power and the gaze.

Kaja Silverman distinguishes between the gaze and the look, emphasizing the alterity of the gaze and its independence of any particular viewer. According to Lacan, she argues, the male voyeur may possess the look, but he is at risk of being shamed by his sense of the gaze, which remains outside desire and constitutes the subject as someone perceived (*MS*, 129–30). Thus she argues that particular individuals or groups may temporarily act as carriers of the gaze in relation to some other person, but that the gaze is never the property of a person, nor of a gender. The gaze, in Lacan's words, 'determines [the subject], at the most profound level, in the visible' and is therefore a manifestation of the power of the social, or the symbolic order, in constructing subjectivity.[20] Silverman's distinction between gaze and look is helpful for distinguishing the manifestations of collective social power-systems from the manifestations of individual desire. It is then possible to analyse how these two sorts of vision converge when the look masquerades as the gaze (in the desiring look of a character whose desire is reinforced by the power to name the subjectivity of the desired person) or diverge (for example when the desire of a relatively powerless character is given expression in looking).

Both Neale and Silverman seek to complicate a simple identification of the viewing subject with the male and the seen object with the female, without denying that looking constitutes a crucial form of patriarchal power. At certain points in her argument Silverman is in danger of allowing the abstract intricacies of Lacanian theory to obscure the pervasive presence of power differentials: the extent to which the gaze, even if it cannot belong to any individual, implicates the power of men in society. For example, she attacks as a 'gross misunderstanding' the form of feminist critique which regards dominant cinema as damaging because it presents women as the object of desire, against which Silverman argues that 'we all function simultaneously as subject and object' (*MS*, 143–4). This may be true in terms of the Lacanian definitions of those terms, but does not necessarily recognize that the social consequences of a man or a woman functioning as an object are not the same. This elision is arguably a consequence of the logic of the same which Irigaray reveals in Lacanian thought.[21] Lacanian concepts such as the Law of the Father or Symbolic castration tend to subdue all psychic phenomena to transcendent laws which are also male laws. However, Silverman's alternative to the 'objectification' critique of dominant cinema is a suggestive and subtle one: 'If feminist theory has reason to lament that system of representation [dominant cinema], it is ... because the male look both transfers its own lack to the female subject, and attempts to pass itself off as the gaze' (*MS*, 143–4). The problem here is that the concept of 'lack' is closely connected to Symbolic castration and thus to the centrality of the phallus in Lacanian theory, so that this position has built into it a male law masquerading as a universal law.

In what follows, then, the psychoanalytically-based paradigms of Mulvey, Neale and Silverman are used provisionally. In so far as the centrality of the phallus in such theory reflects the existing cultural unconscious, these paradigms aid the analysis and critique of that cultural unconscious, of its representations and of the social practices which it supports. However, in so far as such a critique leads us to look, however tentatively, beyond the existing order, we need to reject the transcendent or universal status which Lacanian theory is inclined to attribute to male-centred concepts. Notable among feminist film critics who have argued for such a rejection is Teresa de Lauretis, who observes that: 'In the psychoanalytic view of signification, subject processes are essentially phallic ... they are *subject* processes *insofar* as they are instituted in a fixed order of language – the symbolic – by the function of castration.' As a result, the female subject 'finds herself in the empty space between the signs, in a void of meaning, where no demand is possible and no code available', while the place of the female spectator in the cinema is 'between the look of the camera (the masculine representation) and the image on the screen (the specular fixity of the feminine representation), not one or the other but both and neither'.[22] These conceptions – of a void or an impossible site of subjectivity – find suggestive analogies in Conrad's fiction.

There is, then, a well-established body of theory and criticism which links the dominance of vision to male power. However, to equate pleasure in looking with masculinity would be simplistic and the association of seeing with mastery needs to be treated with some caution. The configuration of vision and power varies in different periods and cultures. Foucault distinguishes in *Discipline and Punish* between a mode in which 'power was what was seen, what was shown and what was manifested' while 'those on whom it was exercised could remain in the shade' and the disciplinary mode of power, which 'is exercised through its invisibility; at the same time it imposes on those whom it subjects a principle of compulsory visibility.'[23] The former would characterize, for example, a Renaissance court, while the latter would be more typical of bureaucratic systems of control such as modern penal and educational practices. This distinction is of some relevance to Conrad's portrayal of non-Western cultures. Psychoanalytical and feminist theories of the gaze which stress its masterful, sadistic and objectifying nature can themselves be placed in a historical context, a project undertaken by Martin Jay in his study of the denigration of sight in twentieth-century thought (especially French thought), in contrast to its earlier celebration as 'the "noblest" of the senses'. Jay comments that Foucault (one of the key figures in the linkage of power and vision along with Freud, Sartre and Irigaray) 'resisted exploring [vision's] reciprocal, inter-subjective, communicative function, that of the mutual glance'. Jay notes that '*le regard*', strongly associated in Sartre's *Being and Nothingness* with 'the alienating and objectifying power of the Other's gaze', 'never assumed [in French] its alternative meaning in English of caring or esteeming'.[24] Furthermore, the Lacanian distinction between eye (or look) and gaze supports the view that 'true reciprocity is only an illusion': the look of the Cartesian eye can never harmoniously balance the gaze of the 'objective other'.[25]

It is precisely a 'communicative function' and a mood of caring or esteem with which Conrad seeks to invest vision by his references to sincerity and solidarity in the Preface to *The Nigger of the 'Narcissus'*. He evokes hearing ('to make you hear') and feeling ('to make you feel') – omitting smell and taste which are, indeed, not greatly in evidence in his fiction – but privileges sight ('to make you see') as the culmination. While this is no doubt partly because of a particular interest in the visual image, it also results from the traditional Romantic association of 'vision' with genius, understanding, power, knowledge. Here there is again a point of purchase for a feminist critique, since that association is itself part of the male-dominated cultural history that has been described by Irigaray.[26] The use of the words 'charm' and 'glimpse' in the passage quoted earlier from the Preface hint at a feminization and eroticization of truth which, as I suggested in Chapters 5 and 6, is a frequent configuration of truth and vision in Conrad's work (again drawing on a long tradition in male writing, especially male Romanticism). Just as there is a tension between Conrad's ideal of clarity and light and his sense of working in the darkness, so his aspiration to vision as a faculty of sharing and mutuality is shadowed by patterns of rivalry, structures of power and the gendered history of the aesthetic discourses which he evokes.

In specific fictional texts or films the details of construction determine whether these general ideological features of the visual are reinforced or resisted. Whether a look objectifies or establishes a caring reciprocity must depend on a complex range of material and psychological conditions. The most obvious condition is that of equality: whether a mutual look on equal terms is possible. But here the question of medium intervenes. Mulvey's article has been very influential because it identifies a tripartite structure of looks in conventional cinema, involving camera, characters and spectators. In fiction there is a similarly complex structure, rendered more oblique by the verbal medium. The writer wishing to evoke visual images is likely to think in terms of the mind's eye, since he or she must depend in part on the imagination of the reader. The duality identified by Evelyn Fox Keller and Christine Grontowski between physical and mental 'sight' is peculiarly present to the reader of fiction, who looks at the physical page while imaginatively 'seeing' the content of the story.[27] Perhaps the difficulty of controlling the conditions of such looking and seeing prompts a certain anxiety in Conrad's tone and slipperiness in his words in the Preface. Can the artist really work 'unquestioningly' (especially a sceptic such as Conrad) or 'without choice'? Whose 'sincere mood' is claimed or requested by the phrase 'in the light of a sincere mood' – that of writer or reader or both? Looking from a distance and a one-way gaze are likely to involve a power differential, while a close, mutual regard is more suggestive of care and communication. It is uncertain which category embraces the work of the fiction writer as Conrad represents himself. Writing alone and in the darkness of introspection, any sense of closeness and mutuality felt by the writer must depend on imaginative projection. That Marlow, as narrator, is partly a dramatization of this dilemma is a familiar idea. Marlow's rhetoric and his sense of difference and competition between different viewers, introduce an economy of the gaze (as in Mulvey's tripartite structure). When looking is an activity shared among men looking at a woman or at a feminized object, matters of power, desire, fantasy and control are inescapably present.

I now turn to look more closely at one of Conrad's late fictions in order to consider such structures of looking and to illustrate the gendering of the visual. It is worth pausing, however, to note that my last sentence is itself firmly within the discourse of vision as knowledge or mastery: the phrases 'to look more closely' and 'to illustrate' rest on a model of criticism or interpretation as the result of visual scrutiny on the part of the critic, and as an invitation to visual scrutiny on the part of the reader. The same would be true of many alternative phrasings: to examine, to illuminate, to offer some insights into, to review, to reflect on, to reveal. Literary criticism has tended to figure texts as objects of the critic's inquiring gaze. When writing as a male critic about gender issues in the work of a male author, one must necessarily be concerned with the question of one's own participation in the economy of text and interpretation. In this context reflexivity (a sustained awareness of one's own writing practice) is integral to understanding.

Conrad's late novel *The Arrow of Gold: A Story between Two Notes* (1919) contains a curious scene of dramatized narration, mixed with conversation (20–61), in which three men, Mills, Blunt and the young protagonist (referred to as Monsieur George), sit up together most of the night, and Blunt tells the story of the life of Rita de Lastaola, the novel's central female character. She is referred to as the epitome of charm, beauty and sexual desirability. In one corner of the room in which they sit a tailor's dummy, without head or hands, cowers in what seems like a posture of embarrassment or fear. From time to time the eyes of the men stray towards this dummy. The visual plays a central role in the novel, and in the male attitudes which it explores. In particular the denial of autonomous subjectivity to Rita involves the visual fixing of her by the male look masquerading as the gaze. Related to this are various other responses: an idea of her as an object, in particular some sort of art object; a repression of her voice, manifested in a tendency to ignore what she says in favour of contemplating her appearance; an emphasis on her stillness, lack of movement; a denial that she exists at all outside the mind of the male observer.

The theme of voyeurism and the gaze is decisively established in this episode of night narration. The tailor's dummy, we learn, had been used by Allègre, the painter who was Rita's lover, as a substitute model for Rita. Later in the novel, this dummy becomes a substitute for Rita in the minds of other characters; most crucially, that of M. George himself. Here is how it is first introduced:

> Mills without a word flung himself on the divan and, propped on his arm, gazed thoughtfully at a distant corner where in the shadow of a monumental carved wardrobe an articulated dummy without head or hands but with beautifully shaped limbs composed in a shrinking attitude seemed to be embarrassed by his stare.
>
> (21)

This dummy functions as a symbolic projection of a male sadistic fantasy, in a way which would accord with Toril Moi's conception of the male gaze. Although it does retain its limbs, which, like Rita's are 'beautifully shaped', it otherwise resembles William Faulkner's formulation of such a fantasy in *Mosquitoes*: 'a virgin, with no legs to leave me, no arms to hold me, no head to talk to me'.[28] What threatens it is the male gaze, since it appears 'embarrassed' by Mills's stare, and is later described as 'lurking in the shadows, pitiful and headless in its attitude of alarmed chastity' (48). In one of those odd, indicative moments of gender instability in Conrad's fiction, this description occurs as a gloss on how one man refers to another: Blunt alludes to Mills (who is present at the time) 'as though ... he had been as much a dummy as that other one lurking in the shadows ...' When M. George first enters the room, he finds that his 'eyes kept on straying towards that corner' (22). Its status as an object for sadistic fantasy is apparent from M. George's later reference to it as 'that amazing, decapitated, mutilated dummy of a woman lurking in a corner' (122). This reference occurs in a conversation during which he tells Rita that he supposed she might have been 'a product of Captain Blunt's sleeplessness' (123); that is to say, that he wondered whether Blunt had simply invented her and the story of her life. Here there is a strong suggestion that the effect of the narration has been to mutilate Rita's identity (at least in M. George's mind) and to construct her as a dummy, an object but not a subject.

The first direct appearance of Rita (that is, the first time M. George sees her himself, as opposed to hearing about her) immediately connects his tendency to regard her as an aesthetic object with his difficulty in recognizing her autonomous subjectivity and his compulsive imagining of her as 'woman' (in Teresa de Lauretis's sense) rather than as a woman:[29]

My first sensation was that of profound astonishment at this evidence that she did really exist. And even then the visual impression was more of colour in a picture than of the forms of actual life ... The white stairs, the deep crimson of the carpet, and the light blue of the dress made an effective combination of colour to set off the delicate carnation of that face, which ... made you think of remote races, of strange generations, of the faces of women sculptured on immemorial monuments.

(66–7)

As Robert Hampson notes, the effect given is that of 'the organisation and evaluation of a description in painterly terms'. He suggests that 'the reader's attention is drawn, not to an aesthetic object, but to an aesthetic way of seeing', thus emphasizing the relativity of perspective and interpretation.[30] That is true, but what is made clear by M. George's remark that 'the visual impression was more of colour in a picture than of the forms of actual life' is that his 'aesthetic way of seeing' reduces Rita to an object: not simply an object of desire but a lifeless object, like the dummy. M. George's responses to Rita construct her as a visual object as relentlessly as they deny her an independent voice. There are so many instances of this that it would be tedious to enumerate them, but the following are two of the more striking examples. In a scene where Rita expresses her sense of claustrophobia, she says that she would like to escape to the sea with M. George, away from the oppressive manipulation of Blunt and others. M. George does not consider what experience might lie behind such a longing, despite the great emotional significance that the sea has for him. Instead, he responds in aesthetic terms, constructing in detail a setting and pictorial effects:

What a charming, gentle, gay, and fearless companion she would have made! ... It would be a new occasion for me, a new viewpoint for that faculty of admiration she had awakened in me at sight—at first sight—before she opened her lips—before she ever turned her eyes on me. She would have to wear some sort of sailor costume, a blue woollen shirt open at the throat ... Dominic's hooded cloak would envelop her amply, and her face under the black hood would have a luminous quality, adolescent charm, and an enigmatic expression. The confined space of the little vessel's quarterdeck would lend itself to her cross-legged attitudes, and the blue sea would balance gently her characteristic immobility.

(149)

It is presumably on the basis of such responses that Gary Geddes sees M. George as set apart from 'the false world of culture' by his 'genuinely artistic sensitivity', and claims that M. George and his sailing companion Dominic 'are both artists in the purest sense, natural men whose sensitivity enables them to perceive the form and the beauty that may underlie the commonest experience or enterprise'.[31] Yet as an emotional or human response to Rita's statement M. George's line of thought is woefully inadequate. He goes on to say vaguely 'Yes, you ought to come along with us for a trip' (149), but the proposal is clearly not a serious response to Rita's original statement, which was essentially an expression of constraint and an appeal for help.

Laura Mulvey's distinction between sadistic voyeurism and idealizing fetishism corresponds to the Manichean overt structure of *The Arrow of Gold* noted by Daphna Erdinast-Vulcan.[32] On this scheme the dummy serves as the object of sadistic voyeuristic looking for Blunt and for Ortega (who has pursued Rita with savage violence since her childhood), whereas fetishism is the strategy of the inexperienced and idealistic M. George and is expressed in the aestheticized images of Rita. However, Mulvey identifies voyeurism and fetishism as two responses to the same male anxiety and my own argument is that these two apparently opposed responses to Rita are complementary. M. George's aestheticizing denies Rita 'the forms of actual life' (66) and the sadistic lurks beneath the idealizing. The connection is implied by M. George's realization of fellowship with Ortega: 'She penetrated me, my head was full of her ... And his head, too, I thought suddenly with a side glance at my companion' (274).[33]

The aestheticizing aspect of M. George's response reaches its peak during a scene where he is in a locked room with Rita, defending her from the manic attentions of Ortega. He admits that: 'All I wanted was to keep her in her pose, excited and still, sitting up with her hair loose, softly glowing, the dark brown fur making a wonderful contrast with the white lace on her breast ... I cared for nothing but that sublimely aesthetic impression' (304). This moment, when M. George most explicitly evokes the aesthetic, is also the moment when his language is most sexually suggestive. This applies not only to 'excited' and 'glowing' but also to the 'dark brown fur' which, placed in contrast to the white lace associated with her breast, suggests a mapping onto the female body of the duality of sexualized and pure woman, in the form of the 'dark' genitals contrasted to the white breast. The situation here is also highly charged with sexual sadism, since Rita is under threat from a violent would-be rapist (Ortega) and M. George's chivalrous impulse to protect Rita does not prevent him from gaining a certain illicit excitement from the situation. His aesthetic fetishization of Rita is a repression of a sadistic voyeurism, so that the dummy (the mutilated, punished woman) might be seen as the unconscious of M. George's desire.

Although Geddes associates Rita's tendency to freeze into immobility with the fact that she has been a victim of what he terms Allègre's 'Olympian indifference' he does not seem to recognize the extent to which M. George is implicated in the reductive and oppressive nature of an exclusively aesthetic response to another person, especially a person in difficulty.[34] The dummy acts as a link between M. George and Allègre, signalling a further complicity. Both treat Rita as an aesthetic object and both use the dummy as a substitute for her. Geddes's discussion of the novel illustrates the way in which this circulation of Rita as object may extend to the author and to male critics and readers. Geddes comments on the 'quality of *caught* life' in *The Arrow of Gold*, and goes on to quote Conrad's letter to Sidney Colvin, where he calls the novel: 'a study of a woman, *prise sur le vif*'. He glosses the French phrase as 'very life-like', or, more literally, 'taken alive', 'caught on the quick'.[35] There are worrying connotations here, for did not Allègre, who so damaged Rita psychologically, 'take her alive', 'catch her on the quick'? Bickley and Hampson defend the novel as 'not a clumsy piece of autobiographical writing but rather a serious attempt to create an aesthetic *object*'.[36] Like Geddes's comment, and the words from Conrad's letter, this would seem to implicate the author, and by extension the male reader, in the treatment and mistreatment of Rita, her construction by men as an aesthetic object for their own pleasure, and the pleasure or envy of other men.

The dummy may be contrasted with another marginal, but symbolically significant, female figure: the girl taking the part of Night in the carnival masque in Chapter 1 of Part I. Subjected to the male gaze, this girl is not shrinking, motionless and embarrassed, but challenging, mobile and a cause of embarrassment to the male observer:

> They filed past my table; the Night noticed perhaps my fixed gaze and throwing her body forward out of the wriggling chain shot out at me a slender tongue like a pink dart. I was not prepared for this, not even to the extent of an appreciative 'Trés joli,' before she wriggled and hopped away. But having been thus distinguished I could do no less than follow her with my eyes.

(9)

Carnival is traditionally a time for the licensed transgression of normal social and sexual roles, and this passing girl offers an image of female sexuality which is the inverse of the masochistic male fantasy represented by the dummy. The mask which she wears both invites and rejects the male gaze, since it covers the upper half of her face, protecting her identity, while leaving exposed 'her uncovered mouth and chin', which, M. George notes, 'suggested refined prettiness' (9). Instead of shrinking back before the power of M. George's voyeuristic gaze, she throws her body forward and sticks out her tongue in a mocking but sexually provocative gesture. If M. George is abashed, however, Blunt knows how to treat such behaviour with an appropriately patronizing response. Faced with the same provocation, he 'with great presence of mind chucked her under the chin' (9), at the same time flashing his white teeth like a villain out of melodrama, a habit he also indulges with the dummy (122) and with Rita (148). Rita too reacts to M. George's fixed gaze: after her quarrel with Blunt, and the latter's departure, the first words she says to M. George are 'Don't stare at me' (150).

The scene of the night-time narration is a scene in which the idea of a woman as a visually-defined object of desire is circulated among men. M. George envies Mills and Blunt, not because they know Rita, but because they have seen her: 'For these two men had *seen* her, while to me she was only being "presented," elusively, in vanishing words, in the shifting tones of an unfamiliar voice' (31). In this scene Rita is persistently imagined as a figure in a picture, 'a feminine figure which to my imagination had only a floating outline ... She was being presented to me now in the Bois de Boulogne' (31). The recurrence of the idea of Rita as being 'presented' to M. George by the other men is also significant, suggesting the circulation of an image of the female among several male psyches, with a combination of competitiveness and sharing. What is being passed around among them is both an object of desire and a possession, as is made apparent at the first mention of her:

Mills was also emphatic in his reply ...
'I am not an easy enthusiast where women are concerned, but she was without doubt the most admirable find of his amongst all the priceless items he had accumulated in that house.'

(23)

An object acquires economic value if it is both scarce and in demand.

So the form of male sexuality which constitutes a woman as a price-less commodity requires that she be seen as unusual, or preferably unique, and that she be desired by other men. The second require-ment makes voyeurism integral to this sexual complex. In order to be sure of the value of his possession, the male needs other males to look on, and envy him. Blunt, who is in pursuit of Rita, betrays this need by his impulse to impress Rita's desirability on Mills and M. George and in passages such as the following:

> 'An intimacy,' began Mr. Blunt, with an extremely refined grimness of tone, 'an intimacy with the heiress of Mr. Allègre on the part of . . . on my part, well, it isn't exactly . . . it's open . . . well, I leave it to you, what does it look like?'
> 'Is there anybody looking on?' Mills let fall, gently, through his kindly lips.
> 'Not actually, perhaps, at this moment. But I don't need to tell a man of the world, like you, that such things cannot remain unseen. And that they are, well, compromising, because of the mere fact of the fortune.'
> ... [Mills replies:]
> 'Whereas the woman herself is, so to speak, priceless.'
> Mr. Blunt muttered the word 'Obviously.'
>
> (59)

There is a certain irony here, in that Blunt, so concerned to protect his good name from the imputation of fortune-hunting, betrays the fact that his desire for Rita is an economic desire, for the possession of a rare commodity. The antithesis between the 'fortune' and the 'price-less' woman is based on the contrast between that which has a price, and that which doesn't. But the word 'priceless' is incurably contam-inated by its use for objects which are beyond price only in the sense of being extremely valuable, and which obey the laws of supply and demand. Blunt returns elsewhere in the novel to his unconscious concern with voyeurism. During a quarrel with Rita he refers to M. George as 'our audience' (147). Indeed, this concern with the third party is encoded in one of his habits of speech, which M. George describes as 'his particular trick of speaking of any third person as of a lay figure' (148), a comment which oddly recalls the dummy.

M. George presents himself as the representative of 'a perfect fresh-ness of sensations and a refreshing ignorance' (31) and Hampson interprets *The Arrow of Gold* as a novel of initiation into passion.[37] Yet the fact that the scene of night-time narration precedes M. George's first meeting with Rita serves to emphasize that what he is initiated into is the homosocial exchange system of patriarchy. Although the passion which Rita awakes in him is, in one sense, fresh, it is in another sense firmly inscribed in the always-already existing discourse of desire. M. George sees the dummy (a substitute for Rita) before he sees Rita, so that the relationship of substitution is reversed: the dummy occupies a subject-position between the three men into which Rita is then inserted. Robert Hampson interprets Rita's behaviour partly in terms of a 'morbid psychology', arising from her childhood trauma at the hands of Ortega. He further suggests that Allègre's actions have produced in her what R. D. Laing terms a 'false-self system'. This interpretation is valid in its own humanist terms, but I prefer to develop Hampson's suggestive comment that 'the art-world of the novel [its emphasis on the aesthetic aspect of perception] acts as a metonym for European bourgeois society: its alienation, its reification of others, its exchange-relations'.[38] Since gender was an important factor in all these processes, Rita's responses to her treatment as an aesthetic object may usefully be interpreted in terms of a feminist and gender politics rather than a humanist psychology. Such an interpretation would suggest, not that she possesses a 'false-self' and therefore needs to acquire a 'true' one, but that her mode of self-assertion in a patriarchal context is necessarily through the evasion of a 'true' self, since such a self (socially constructed) could only internalize her own objectification. That is, the system of exchange-relations and its discourse of reification interpellates a 'true self' which is subjected to the ideology of aestheticization. What Hampson, quoting Paul Wiley, terms Rita's 'hysterical gesture[s]' of desperate self-transformation may be interpreted according to a feminist understanding of hysteria and madness as resistance to an oppressive construction of female subjectivity.[39] Hampson interestingly points to M. George's experience of being treated as an instrument or object by Mills and Blunt as parallel to the treatment of Rita by Allègre.[40] M. George's slightly ambiguous role in the gender system of the novel is, in realist terms, a product of his youth. However, it also illustrates Kaja Silverman's observation that 'we all function simultaneously as subject and object' (*MS*, 144) and Steven Neale's emphasis on the mobility of fantasy identification. M. George's intense fantasy investment in the Rita whom Blunt discursively 'creates' for him aligns his subjectivity with the male subject who looks at and exchanges the female object. Yet his boyish admiration for the experience and self-assurance of Mills and Blunt hints at a slightly different role. He remarks: 'I knew very well that I was utterly insignificant *in these men's eyes*' [emphasis added], continuing:

> Yet my attention was not checked by that knowledge. It's true they were talking of a woman, but I was yet at the age when this subject by itself is not of overwhelming interest. My imagination would have been more stimulated probably by the adventures and fortunes of a man. What kept my interest from flagging was Mr. Blunt himself. The play of the white gleams of his smile round the suspicion of grimness of his tone fascinated me like a moral incongruity.
>
> (31)

A little earlier M. George has been impatiently hanging around in the streets hoping to meet Mills, rather as if he were in love with him and he is chaffed by his companions who 'wanted to know whether she, whom I expected to see, was dark or fair' (11). As elsewhere in Conrad's work, the conventional social construction of masculinity is unsettled when there is a suggestion of desire between men unmediated by the exchange of women. However, Blunt's narrative of vision and desire relocates M. George's subject position from that of the object of the gaze ('in these men's eyes') to that of its subject and redirects his imagination and desire from men to women, or rather to a relationship with men via a woman.

Given the prominence of voyeurism and the aestheticization of the woman in *The Arrow of Gold*, it is intriguing that the novel is notionally based on 'a pile of manuscript which was apparently meant for the eye of one woman only' (3), although this manuscript has been edited by the frame-narrator, whose identity and sex remain unspecified. Indeed, the very existence of the text is the result of a woman's desire to see, if not a man, then at least the textual record of his life: 'she wrote to him: "... I confess to you I should like to know the incidents on the road which has led you to where you are now." ... He succumbed' (3–4). The shared male discourse of 'Heart of Darkness' is emphasized by the allusions, during the course of Marlow's narrative, to his circle of male listeners and their possible responses. Tantalizingly, the equivalent allusions to M. George's relations with his intended female reader have been removed by the frame-narrator, who tells us that: 'In the form in which it [M. George's story] is presented here it has been pruned of all allusions to their common past, of all asides, disquisitions, and explanations addressed directly to the friend of his childhood' (4). Thus a female reader is notionally implied, hinting at a reversal, in the narrative frame, of the hierarchy of vision and power in the main body of the text. While Rita is narrated to M. George before she is seen by him (a narration which installs her as the object of male looks that hesitate between fetishism and voyeurism), M. George himself is called into textual existence by a women's desire to see. Feminist film critics have identified the exclusion of the desiring look of the woman as central to patriarchal structures of looking. Here that desiring look appears, in a crucial yet also marginal location, as the instigating moment of the text yet set aside in a 'note'. The concluding 'second note' reveals no more about this excluded female reader, but admits a further excision in that M. George's account of his affair with Rita is omitted and replaced by the sententious generalizations of the editor: 'Whether love in its entirety has, speaking generally, the same elementary meaning for women as for men, is very doubtful' (337). Conrad fails to develop the possibilities for a radical revision of the structures of gender exclusion which are present in 'Heart of Darkness'. Indeed, as Hampson notes, the editor's address to 'those who know women' in the second note (338) seems to imply a male reader, so that 'the editor has suppressed the female addressee and appropriated the revised text for a male audience'.[41] The final chapter will examine how this male homosocial exchange interacts with the economic and psychic structures of imperialism (with the visual again playing a crucial role) in a novel which surrounds masculinity with philosophical scepticism and sexual ambiguity.

8

Vision and the Economies of Empire and Masculinity: *Victory*

In the penultimate chapter of *Victory: An Island Tale* (1915) the reader is offered a tableau of the male gaze, bringing together sexuality, death and the female body and comparable in this respect to the night-time narration scene in *The Arrow of Gold*. Lena lies dying from a bullet wound which Heyst has just discovered by tearing open the top of her dress. Davidson, who has arrived just too late to avert the tragedy, stands by him:

> They stood side by side, looking mournfully at the little black hole made by Mr. Jones's bullet under the swelling breast of a dazzling and as it were sacred whiteness. It rose and fell slightly—so slightly that only the eyes of the lover could detect the faint stir of life. Heyst, calm and utterly unlike himself in the face, moving about noiselessly, prepared a wet cloth, and laid it on the insignificant wound, round which there was hardly a trace of blood to mar the charm, the fascination, of that mortal flesh.
>
> (405)

This is only the culmination of a number of scenes in which Lena is presented as an aestheticized and sexualized object of contemplation:

> 'Look! Is that what you mean?'
>   Heyst raised his head ... in the brilliant square of the door he saw the girl—the woman he had longed to see once more—as if enthroned, with her hands on the arms of the chair. She was in black; her face was white, her head dreamily inclined on her breast.
>
> (391)

The duality of black and white here is matched by the way in which she is both enthroned in the chair and thus elevated as an image of purity (that is, fetishized) and framed in the doorway as an object of surveillance and desire (that is, subject to voyeuristic looking). In the later death-bed scene death and sexual desire are explicitly juxtaposed, placing it in a long and well-documented tradition of images of dead or dying beautiful women. In her study of death, art and femininity in Western culture, Elisabeth Bronfen takes as the epitome of 'the modes of figuration of death and its linkage to femininity' a painting, *Der Anatom*, which has notable affinities with the image of the dying Lena.[1] *Der Anatom* shows an anatomist looking at a dead woman but a dead woman whose beauty is as yet unaffected, almost alive as Lena is almost dead. The focalizing gaze of the anatomist directs the eyes of the viewer to one white breast of the woman, just uncovered by his hand. Similarly the reader of *Victory* finds.his or her gaze directed by that of Heyst and Davidson towards the 'fascination' of Lena's breast. This scene lends itself readily to a Freudian reading. The 'sacred' white breast, both sexual and idealized, suggests the fantasy body of the mother, the perfect, unattainable object of desire, while the small black hole, unmarred by blood, suggests the female genitals, fearfully associated with death and castration. Such a reading, however, tends to presume a male reader. Bronfen identifies the fetishization of the dead woman as a way of expressing but also repressing the knowledge that the spectator will also die, just as in Freud's conception the fetish serves both to record and to repress the knowledge of the absence of the female phallus. An obviously phallic fetish is present, since Lena at this point demands to be given the dagger which she won from Ricardo and 'which Davidson was still holding unconsciously' (405).[2] This dagger is described as 'the symbol of her victory', and its masculine associations are fairly explicit: from her early position as a victim of men Lena has gained power over both Ricardo and Heyst, though at the cost of her life. It seems that a woman who symbolically possesses the phallus must die. As often in Conrad's fiction, a Freudian reading is not so much unconvincing as too obvious. The scene is also a set piece of homosocial visual exchange. Two men gaze down at the body of a woman, its sexual allure and physicality are stressed and the reader is invited to share their contemplation. To analyse the scene in these terms allows a theorization of the gendering of the implied reader, rather than a replication of this gendering by critical discourse. Lena dies the subject of the male gaze: 'she breathed her last, triumphant, *seeking for*

his glance in the shades of death' (407, emphasis added). She herself
internalizes this role by imagining herself as seen by another:
'Exulting, she saw herself extended on the bed, in a black dress' (407).
So, while a female reader might be invited to empathize with Lena,
this empathy would be recruited to the service of male desire. Steve
Neale's account of the potential fluidity and mobility of fantasy identification in cinema is revealing if applied by analogy to Conrad's
narrative technique here. Neale identifies three intersecting levels on
which sexual difference is constructed and on which a tension may be
operative between the mobility of identificatory processes on the one
hand, and the organization and systematization generated by narrative structures on the other:

> 1) positions and identifications constructed from moment to
> moment in a film through its organisations of point of view, 2)
> positions and identifications as these are systematised in relation to
> the story thus narrated (character identification would be particu-
> larly important here), and 3) positions and identifications available
> to the subject across the structure of the fantasy scenario.
>
> (SD, 125)

Neale also identifies various configurations of gender, power and
looking involving the spectator's look at the screen, the look of the
camera and the look of the protagonist. If we consider the scene of
Lena's death in relation to these three levels and three looks then
what emerges is the closing down of the possibilities of identification
established earlier in the novel. In this culminating, penultimate
chapter, levels of identification and looks are aligned into a single
structure. The narrative, long concentrated on a small group of characters on the island, now further narrows with the defeat of the
villains, whose death we hear about in retrospect in the final chapter.
Lena and Heyst assume their full centrality, with Davidson present as
a representative of the outside world. The organization of point of
view structures the relationship between Neale's three looks which,
translated into fictional terms, are the looks of reader, narrator and
character. All the characters are looking at the iconic image of Lena:
Heyst and Davidson orienting the look of narrator and reader towards
her body. Even Lena, at the moment of her death, imagines herself as
seen by a male other. Although the narrator allows us to know a little
more than any of the characters (in that we are allowed glimpses into
the minds of both Heyst and Lena), the 'positions and identifications

available' are concentrated, on all three levels. We are offered the possibility of identifying with Heyst's look, or of identifying with either Davidson or Lena, both of whom are themselves, in different ways, identifying with Heyst's look.

Earlier in the novel, however, the fluid possibilities of subject identification are developed through more diverse patterns of looking. Heyst's relationship with Lena, which ends with her seeking his glance, also begins with that glance: 'She had captured Heyst's awakened faculty of observation ... He looked at her anxiously, as no man ever looks at another man' (71). In between, their interaction is continually described in terms of eyes, gazes and glances. The presentation of the heroine of *Victory*, as in other late Conrad works, shows a combination of fetishization with certain hesitant signs of an understanding of what might underlie the male need (Conrad's need, the male reader's need) to fetishize a heroine. Sight is of course a traditional focus of interest and source of tropes in the literature of love but the sustained frequency of such references to the visual in *Victory* is striking, and can be demonstrated only by rather extensive quotation:[3]

> She was astonished almost more by the near presence of the man himself ... the kindly expression of the man's blue eyes looking into her own.
>
> (72–3)

> They looked at each other ... with a surprised, open gaze ... it was a long time before they averted their eyes; and very soon they met again, temporarily, only to rebound, as it were. At last they steadied in contact ... Heyst had been interested by the girl's physiognomy ... the features had more fineness than those of any other feminine countenance he had ever had the opportunity to observe so closely.
>
> (74)

> 'What else did you mean when you came up and looked at me so close?'
>
> (86)

> 'I understand that women easily forget whatever in their past diminishes them in their eyes.'
> 'It's your eyes that I was thinking of ...'
>
> (88)

Next day ... she managed to give him a glance of frank tenderness, quick as lightning, and leaving a profound impression, a secret touch on the heart.

(92)

His tone was playful, but his eyes, directed at her face, were serious ... She remained silent for a while, returning his gaze till he removed it ... His gaze travelled up her figure and reached her face, where he seemed to detect the veiled glow of intelligence ... Heyst spoke just to say something rather than to gaze at her in silence.

(191)

He felt intensely aware of her personality, as if this were the first moment of leisure he had found to look at her.

(192)

Looking towards him with a movement of her eyes only, the girl noticed the strong feeling on his face ... he remained staring ... observing her indefinable expression of anxiety.

(202–3)

Heyst came out with an abrupt burst of sound which made her open her steady eyes wider ... She could understand him better then than at any moment since she first set eyes on him ... 'I assure you I could see much more than you could tell me. I could see quite a lot that you don't even suspect yet; but you can't be seen quite through.'

(209–10)

His eyes rested on her, inquisitive, ready for tenderness.

(214)

In Chapters 3 and 4 of Part 3 (describing a morning in the life of Lena and Heyst on Samburan, just before the intrusion of the villains) we find a sort of visual duel between the two characters, beginning and ending with oblique allusions to their sexual relations. At the start of Chapter 3 we are told that 'Heyst came out on the veranda and spread his elbows on the railing, in an easy attitude of proprietorship' (185). This sense of proprietorship, overtly of the bungalow and the island, implicitly extends to Lena. At the end of Chapter 4 Conrad employs what was later to become a clichéd film technique to indicate sex, as his narrative passes discretely over a period of time in between Heyst kissing Lena and his retrieving her cork helmet 'which had rolled a little way off', while she does up her hair 'which had come loose' (216). Framed by these two allusions to sex is a long scene in the forest during which their relationship develops through growing intimacy, misunderstanding and reconciliation, uncertainty and desire. Themes of power and desire are articulated through visual exchange. At the start of Chapter 4 Heyst declares himself 'willing to sit here and look at you till you are ready to go' and the narrative voice explains:

> He was still under the fresh sortilege of their common life, the surprise of novelty, the flattered vanity of his possession of this woman; for a man must feel that, unless he has ceased to be masculine. Her eyes moved in his direction, rested on him, then returned to their stare into the deeper gloom at the foot of the straight tree-trunks ... The warm air stirred slightly about her motionless head. She would not look at him, from some obscure fear of betraying herself. She felt in her innermost depths an irresistible desire to give herself up to him more completely, by some act of absolute sacrifice. This was something of which he did not seem to have an idea.
>
> (201)

A play of looks is in evidence here: a steady, untiring, unembarrassed male gaze at a posed and 'possessed' woman and, by contrast, a brief, hesitant returned look by the woman, quickly averted for fear of 'betraying herself' – either disclosing her feelings or being untrue to her own interests. While this passage specifically alludes to the 'irresistible desire' of the woman, it can hardly be taken as constructing the 'conditions of visibility for a different [female] social subject' or as repositioning the subject in relation to pleasure in looking – tasks which de Lauretis ascribes to feminist cinema – since Lena's desire here is a desire for loss of subjectivity to a man, and is appropriately expressed by *not* looking.[4] There is a double-bind for Lena: a need for intimacy and a need to be needed, combined with a sense that this is on offer only through a certain role as possessed object. Lena's vulnerability (a result of her hard childhood, her poverty, her lonely position and her mistreatment by the Zangiacomos, Schomberg and others) has made her sense of herself, now that Heyst has rescued her, peculiarly depend upon him. She feels that she would no longer be 'in the world' (187) if Heyst stopped thinking about her and says 'I can only be what you think I am' (187). By contrast, when Heyst is faced by the possibility of being what Lena might think he was (someone who cast off Morrison), he is very angry, and solaces himself by having sex with her (212–15). Lena herself seems to indulge in a fantasy of having been recreated by Heyst, a fantasy which fits in with the occasionally Edenic overtones of the situation.[5] She tells him that she has been called Alma and Magdalen, and asks him to give her a new name, in accordance with his desire: 'you can call me by whatever name you choose ... Think of one you would like the sound of—something quite new. How I should like to forget everything that has gone before' (88). Yet Heyst (who earlier in his life has mentally criticized in himself the Adamic impulse to action or naming (173–4)) calls her Lena (186), which recalls rather than forgets her earlier names. These names are obviously loaded with associations. Magdalen suggests the stereotype of the 'fallen woman'. 'Alma', as Susan Gubar points out, means 'soul' but is also a word for an Egyptian dancing girl, hinting at the classic male-constructed duality of woman as idealized soul or as sexual commodity (a duality corresponding to the fetishistic/voyeuristic duality).[6] Heyst's choice of name raises the question of how different he is from Schomberg and the other men who have pestered or exploited Lena. Though he is very different in character, his genuine kindness does not free him from the sexual dynamics of his society. Despite his philosophical scepticism and pessimism he cannot repress the 'original Adam' (173) in himself, nor can he escape entirely from the snares of 'the world'. Heyst saves Lena out of chivalry (but also in order to fulfil his own repressed needs, sexual and emotional). Heyst is a gentlemen, but Lena is still dependent on her sexual role to maintain his support. Here we may usefully evoke Silverman's distinction between the gaze – the social construction of subjectivity – and the desiring look of the individual. Both Heyst and Lena can act as subjects of the look: when Lena looks at Heyst it is not always hesitantly, for we find statements such as 'For a long time the girl's grey eyes had been watching his face' (196). The point is that the social power of the man enables the male look to appropriate, and masquerade as, the gaze, a process by which it 'transfers its own lack to the female subject, and attempts to pass itself off as the gaze' (*MS*, 144). Heyst's rescue of Lena saves her from the Zangiacomos' attempts to capitalize on her sexual desirability. But in appropriating that desirability for himself, temporarily removing it from commodified circulation, Heyst also takes upon himself the role of reconstituting Lena's subjectivity, which has been so much inscribed in that circulation that she is uncertain of her identity outside it. Her situation in this respect resembles that of Rita in *The Arrow of Gold*, who has been treated as a sexual / aesthetic commodity since her childhood. On the island, Heyst (until the arrival of the villains) in effect becomes the sole embodiment of the gaze for Lena, the only source from which her subjectivity can be maintained, supported or undermined.

The process which Silverman terms the transferral of male lack to the female subject is also in evidence in the relationship of Heyst and Lena at this stage. Irigaray regards the specularization of the woman – her objectification by the male gaze – as an exertion of male power and a means by which male anxiety is relieved and male ego-identity supported, while the ambiguities of masculinity are concealed or repressed (*S*, 54). In the passage quoted above ('He was still under the fresh sortilege ...'), the narrative voice seems to be reassuring itself in the face of a certain hesitancy as regards Heyst's masculinity. His gaze at a possessed woman bolsters up his allegiance to a conventional masculinity, threatened by his passivity and perhaps his involvement with Morrison.

After Lena's long look at Heyst, she realizes that 'addressing her, he was really talking to himself'. Then:

Heyst looked up, caught sight of her as it were, and caught himself up ... 'All this does not tell you why I ever came here. Why, indeed? It's like prying into inscrutable mysteries which are not worth scrutinising ...'. He looked fixedly at her, and with such grave eyes that she felt obliged to smile faintly at him, since she did not understand what he meant. Her smile was reflected, still fainter, on his lips.

(196–7)

There is a sense of a mutual regard, of exploration and a quest for understanding, although limited by Heyst's self-absorption and marked by traces of power ('she felt obliged'). Here Heyst proposes himself as incomprehensible, but elsewhere in this scene it is Lena's firm gaze that is constructed or interpreted, not as an expression of her desire or need, but as a mark of her incomprehensibility and the occasion for the stimulation of male desire:

In the intimacy of their life her grey, unabashed gaze forced upon him the sensation of something inexplicable reposing within her; stupidity or inspiration, weakness or force—or simply an abysmal emptiness, reserving itself even in the moments of complete surrender.

(192)

She turned and looked at him attentively ... Heyst stood the frank examination with a playful smile, hiding the profound effect those veiled grey eyes produced—whether on his heart or on his nerves, whether sensuous or spiritual, tender or irritating, he was unable to say.

(193)

'But why are you looking so hard at me? Oh, I don't object, and I shall try not to flinch. Your eyes—'

He was looking straight into them, and as a matter of fact had forgotten all about the late Morrison at that moment.

'No ... What an impenetrable girl you are, Lena, with those grey eyes of yours! Windows of the soul, as some poet has said ... Well, nature has provided excellently for the shyness of your soul.'

(204)

The above passages explicitly render Heyst's point of view, but at one point the narrative voice shares his conception: 'She turned upon him her veiled, unseeing grey eyes in which nothing of her wonder could be read' (214). These passages recall Marlow's assumption in *Chance* that what is mysterious to him in a woman must be blankness.[7] But why should the Conradian rhetoric of the incomprehensible be brought into play merely because a woman looks at a man without being 'abashed'?

Susan Gubar places Heyst's renaming of Lena in the context of a Western cultural myth of male primacy which identifies female sexuality with textuality and fears the female body 'for its power to articulate itself':[8]

Converted from artist to accompanist to accomplice, she seems 'like a script in an unknown language' or 'like any writing to an illiterate.' Looking at her Heyst feels like 'a man looking this way and that on a piece of writing which he was unable to decipher, but which may be big with some revelation'.[9]

The process of renaming hints at a Frankenstein-like assemblage out of parts, though these are parts of language rather than body parts: 'the girl—to whom, after several experimental essays in combining detached letters and loose syllables, he had given the name of Lena' (186). It is as if Heyst is unable to write her identity in a new, Edenic language, but can only reassemble elements of the patriarchal ideology which has already named her. Lena herself is aware of not having escaped. The phrase 'abysmal emptiness' (192), used to describe Heyst's sense of her gaze, resonates with a moment in which Lena perceives starkly her dependence on Heyst:

> The girl, from her position a little above him, surveyed with still eyes the abstracted silence of the man on whom she now depended with a completeness of which she had not been vividly conscious before, because, till then, she had never felt herself swinging between the abysses of earth and heaven in the hollow of his arm.
>
> (209)

This vertigo of powerlessness recalls and explains Lena's fear of the sight of the empty sea which 'was to her the abomination of desolation' (190) and which reminds her of childhood trauma in the loss of a mother figure (192) and of the deluge (191), figuring the destruction of life, and hence of identity. This 'flaming abyss of emptiness' which makes Lena 'long for the friendly night' (216) frames the scene in the forest since they pass it on their way up and on their way back. While Lena perceives in the empty sea an image of the fragility of her own identity, dependent upon a sexual relationship with a man, Heyst identifies her firm gaze with the abyss, with nothingness, with the inexplicable; in short, with ideas of the enigmatic and threatening which are conventionally projected onto women by puzzled or fearful men.

Mary Ann Doane analyses the negation of the female gaze via a still photograph by Robert Doisneau, in which we see a man looking and the picture (of a naked woman) at which he is looking, so that we are invited to share his gaze. This gaze crosses that of the woman standing by his side, who is looking with great interest at a picture which has its back to us, so that:

> not only is the object of her look concealed from the spectator, her gaze is encased by the two poles defining the masculine axis of vision. Fascinated by nothing visible – a blankness or void for the spectator – ... the female gaze is left free-floating, vulnerable to subjection. The faint reflection in the shop window of only the frame of the picture at which she is looking serves merely to rearticulate, *en abŷme*, the emptiness of her gaze, the absence of her desire in representation.[10]

Heyst's sense of an abyss within Lena would seem to express his need for her dependence, his need for her to remain the object of his desiring gaze, rather than the subject of her own desire. Like the woman in the photograph, Lena does (sometimes) look firmly in a way that might make manifest her desire. But the narrative of the novel finally endorses Heyst's desire by setting her up as an iconic sexual object and by ending in her death and the effacement of her subjectivity. The negation of the female gaze in art, cinema and literature is often achieved through the death of the woman. Doane cites Claire Johnston's view of death as the 'location of all impossible signs', and reads three mainstream films of the 1940s as demonstrating that 'the woman as subject of the gaze is clearly an impossible sign'.[11] Irigaray argues that the effacement of women's desire is a condition for the working out, by men, of the death drive, in that women are taken to represent the death drive and serve as a mirror to support the male ego in the process of building itself up and warding off death (S, 54–5). In fulfilling this function, woman is inscribed in a specular economy of the same:

> Now, if this [male] ego is to be valuable, some 'mirror' is needed to reassure it and re-insure it of its value. Woman will be the founda-tion for this specular duplication, giving man back 'his' image and repeating it as the 'same'.
>
> (S, 54)[12]

In accordance with this economy Heyst, talking to Lena, is talking to himself and, faced with her look, can read it only as the seductive veil over absence, death, castration, the abyss. Though Heyst also dies, it is Lena's death that is presented as a symbolic sacrifice, made in order to rescue Heyst from his alienation and disengagement. After her death he is able belatedly to acknowledge to Davidson the importance of hope, love and trust in life (410). Lena has taken on the role of representing the death drive: this is one meaning of that death-bed scene. Irigaray writes that 'in order to trans-form his death drives and the whole instinctual dualism, in order to use his life to ward off death for as long as it takes to choose a death, man will have to work on building up his ego' (S, 54). Lena frees Heyst from the legacy of deathly detachment that his father forced upon him, enabling Heyst to take up an identity and to choose a death.

Irigaray's use of an economic model in her reinterpretation of Freudian theory can elucidate the gender relations in *Victory*, since it is within an economy of masculinity that Lena's role is worked out.[13] The tableau of her death is presented, not just to Heyst, but to Davidson and to the reader, while her relationship with Heyst is preceded and shadowed by his relationship with Morrison. Furthermore, the plot is fuelled by male relationships and desires: Schomberg's lust and jealousy, Ricardo's relationship with Jones, Heyst's maverick position in the society of European males. An economic model is helpful in interpreting these complex patterns, not only because of the theoretical efficacy such a model has been shown to have by Eve Sedgwick's analyses of homosociality, but also because of the ways in which Conrad's fiction interweaves social and psychic economies with the economies of empire, commerce and financial speculation. The novel begins with materiality, commerce, sameness and difference: 'There is, as every schoolboy knows in this scientific age, a very close chemical relation between coal and diamonds' (3). The fact that coal and diamonds are the same element was famously used by D. H. Lawrence as a metaphor for the transformation of the self, for the absence of the 'old stable ego' in his fiction.[14] Might Conrad's opening bear on human as well as chemical relations? On the second page Heyst is assessed in terms of likeness and difference: 'He was not mad. Queer chap—yes, that may have been said, and in fact was said; but there is a tremendous difference between the two, you will allow' (4). Later we are told again that Heyst was 'generally considered a "queer chap"' (91) and in the final pages of the novel Davidson says that Heyst 'was a queer chap. I doubt if he himself knew how queer he was' (408). Wayne Koestenbaum has noted the marked use of the word 'queer', with sexual connotations, in Conrad's and Ford's *Romance*.[15] One should be cautious about reading in later usage: queer would probably not have meant homosexual to Conrad.[16] On the other hand, within a regime of masculinity which combined widespread same-sex sexual activity with widespread denial and homophobia, homosexuality was a likely form which being 'queer' might take. Homosexuality is strongly implied in the homophobic portrait of the misogynist Jones, while Davidson reflects that Heyst 'never talked of women, he never seemed to think of them, or to remember that they existed' (42). The outward contrast and inner connection of coal and diamond might suggest that being a 'queer chap' and being an ordinary one, while overtly contrasted, are connected in a concealed manner. The opening passage about coal, and about the collapse of The Tropical Belt Coal Company of which Heyst was local manager, continues in a vein of ponderous Conradian irony:

The Tropical Belt Coal Company went into liquidation. The world of finance is a mysterious world in which, incredible as the fact may appear, evaporation precedes liquidation. First the capital evaporates, and then the company goes into liquidation. These are very unnatural physics, but they account for the persistent inertia of Heyst, at which we 'out there' used to laugh among ourselves—but not inimically. An inert body can do no harm to anyone.

(3)

Heyst, previously a detached wanderer and observer, had been drawn into the mine project by his relationship with Morrison and this commercial activity temporarily rendered him less different from the other European men 'out there'. However, after the death of Morrison and the collapse of the company, an unnatural process transforms Heyst back into an 'inert body', passive and remote. As manager Heyst had been engaged in active, productive activity, working the material body of the earth, but 'unnatural physics' reduce him to a body himself. A subtext of gender and sexuality seems present in these ironic manoeuvres around the nature of a man who is seen as a queer, passive body, rather than a 'normal', active will and mind. Irigaray describes the ideological formation that represents men as active and women as passive:

> Man is *the* procreator ... sexual *production-reproduction* is referable to his 'activity' alone, to his 'pro-ject' alone. Woman is nothing but the receptacle that passively receives his *product*, even if sometimes, by the display of her passively aimed instincts, she has pleaded, facilitated, even demanded that it be placed within her. Matrix – womb, earth, factory, bank – to which the seed capital is entrusted so that it may germinate, produce, grow fruitful, without woman being able to lay claim to either capital or interest since she has only submitted 'passively' to reproduction.
>
> (*S*, 18)

Heyst assumes a role of 'normal' masculinity when he becomes the agent of European investment in the mine. This financial and cultural relationship parallels the gender relation described by Irigaray, since the European financial interests exploit the resources of the Malay Archipelago while retaining capital and profit for themselves. The transformation of Heyst, from observer to manager and back again, is, however, only a shift between different forms of speculation. Heyst's odd character reflects the influence of his father's philosophical ideas. His father's mind gave Heyst 'a special insight into its mastery of despair' (196), and as a result Heyst became a spectator of life: 'I could not take my soul down into the street to fight there. I started off to wander about, an independent spectator—if that is possible' (196). Rejecting 'the streets', Heyst nevertheless becomes a sort of *flâneur* of the world in general.[17] He sees his involvement with Lena as 'his latest departure from the part of an unconcerned spectator' (185), but 'at the same time he could not help being temperamentally, from long habit and from set purpose, a spectator still' (185). He tells Davidson: 'At one time I thought that intelligent observation of facts was the best way of cheating the time which is allotted to us ... but now I have done with observation, too' (54). However, it is his 'faculty of observation' (71) that leads to his involvement with Lena and he continues to observe her intensely (if not always intelligently).

While Heyst's previous detachment from the world had been a matter of observation and speculation, his involvement, with the mine and then with Lena, is a matter of new forms of speculation and observation: financial speculation and sexual observation. When the mining company collapses, Heyst tries to reconvert commercial speculation into philosophical speculation, staying on Samburan no longer as manager but as a hermit philosopher lounging on his lonely veranda. However, the two forms of speculation are re-enmeshed by the presence of a woman. Heyst's lone presence on the island was the subject only of idle speculation among the European community, not exactly philosophical speculation but without a profit-motive (unless one counts Schomberg's resentment at Heyst's failure to patronize his restaurant). However, once Lena is with him, the pair become the subject of malevolent and interested speculation. Schomberg invests his jealousy in the greed of Jones and Ricardo, setting them going on a speculative journey to rob Heyst of his supposed wealth and of Lena. The plot manifests the homology between a psychic economy of masculinity (with woman as the object of exchange) and the financial economy of imperial capitalism (in which money or commodities are exchanged). The possibility of the reader (specifically the male reader) being drawn into this specular economy is indicated by Robert Secor's observation that the novel's narrative method (beginning with narration by an unspecified European man) makes the reader 'share the cognitive methods of the Schombergian world', with Heyst and Lena as enigmatic objects of speculation and investigation.[18]

Victory involves a contest between philosophy and 'woman', more specifically between Schopenhauerian pessimism and detachment and a woman who is symbolically identified with sexuality, passion, involvement, life – and death.[19] The philosophical scepticism of Heyst senior involves a loss of faith in words and ideals:

> I suppose he began like other people; took fine words for good, ringing coin and noble ideals for valuable banknotes ... Later he discovered—how am I to explain it to you? Suppose the world were a factory and all mankind workmen in it. Well, he discovered that the wages were not good enough. That they were paid in counterfeit money.
>
> (195–6)

Heyst learns the barrenness of life without hope, love and trust, so we have here a version of the Conradian theme of the saving illusion: for life to be of value, it is necessary to believe in ideals, even though they may be philosophically untenable or illusory. But in this novel scepticism is identified with the intellectual speculations of the detached male philosopher, while ideals are identified with the woman as object of voyeuristic observation and sexual speculation. Heyst senior's loss of faith in a semantic gold-standard generates irony on two levels. First, he nevertheless uses words to pass on his scepticism to his son: 'He dominated me ... I have heard his living word. It was irresistible' (196). Second, a meta-level of irony bears on Conrad's text itself, which, in accordance with Heyst senior's view, would be engaged in passing a false coin to us as readers. If gender is a constructed set of differences, then semantic scepticism might also question masculinity and femininity. Jacqueline Rose links language, gender identity and the visual image as systems in which certainty is a fantasy. She observes that for both Freud and Lacan 'our sexual identities as male or female, our confidence in language as true or false, and our security in the image we judge as perfect or flawed, are fantasies.'[20] Heyst senior did not question the gold standard of sexual difference so far as we know, but his son is drawn into a battle which revolves around precisely that: Lena figures as a treasure, competed for, but also as a coin, circulated, while her identity hovers between that of the 'essence' of 'woman', evoked in images of idealized femininity, and that of token of exchange in a contest of male desire, jealousy, revulsion and repression, involving Schomberg, Ziacomo, Heyst, Ricardo, Jones and Davidson.

Heyst's existence as an 'inert body' after the failure of the mine company suggests a passivity at odds with conventional, active masculinity, a passivity from which he is aroused by his observation of Lena. When Conrad, in the 'Author's Note' to *Victory*, recalls the experience which gave him the idea of her character, he stresses both idleness and vision:

> It was at her, whom I call Lena, that I have looked the longest and with a most sustained attention. This attention originated in idleness for which I have a natural talent ... Having got a clear line of sight I naturally (being idle) continued to look at the girl through all the second part of the programme.
>
> (xv–xvi)

Unlike Heyst, however, Conrad was not stirred into action by the sight of this girl being pinched on the arm:

> I believe that those people left town the next day.
> Or perhaps they had only migrated to the other big café ... I did not go across to find out. It was my perfect idleness that had invested the girl with a peculiar charm, and I did not want to destroy it by any superfluous exertion.
>
> (xvii)

Here Conrad sets up a homosocial relationship between himself and Heyst, with Lena (elided with her real life model) as an object of exchange between himself and his male character: 'I let her go with Heyst, I won't say without a pang but certainly without misgivings' (xvii).

While homosocial exchanges structure many of Conrad's fictions, *Victory* is unusual in making relatively overt reference to homosexuality. The relationship between 'Mr. Jones' and Martin Ricardo is a combination of criminal partnership, feudal master–servant bond and barely denied sexual attachment. Jones's hatred and fear of women and his murderous jealousy when Ricardo pursues Lena are fairly obvious indicators of his homosexuality, though the portrait is much distorted by a homophobia which can represent same-sex desire among men only negatively, as misogyny and a male couple only as a criminal partnership. Ricardo pursues women but shows a Sweeney-like inclination to murder them: 'Take 'em by the throat or chuck 'em under the chin is all one to me—almost' (166) (one might recall Blunt's gesture of chucking a girl under the chin in *The Arrow of Gold*). He claims to have no feelings, but he clearly does have strong feelings about Jones. These are apparent from his tedious idealization of Jones, but are made most explicit during his long

afternoon conversation with Schomberg. This conversation, a
turning point in the plot and the initiating moment of the disastrous trip of the three criminals to Samburan, is a visual duel
between the two men to match that between Heyst and Lena. In
this male duel, and in the descriptions of Jones, Ricardo and Pedro
on their arrival at the hotel, there is an equally extraordinary
number of references to eyes. These include references to Ricardo's
'eyes that gleamed and blinked' (100), Jones's 'sunken eyes', 'long,
feminine eyelashes' (102) and 'spectral intensity of ... glance' (112),
Pedro's 'queer stare of his little bear's eyes' (116) and Schomberg's
attempt 'to keep within bounds the enlargement of his eyes' (129),
as well as passages such as the following:

> Schomberg, raising his eyes, at last met the gleams in two dark
> caverns under Mr. Jones's devilish eyebrows, directed upon him
> impenetrably.
>
> (115)

> [Ricardo confesses a passionate love for cards, and] the effect of this
> outburst was augmented by the quiet lowering of the eyelids, by a
> reserved pause as though this had been a confession of another
> kind of love.
>
> (124)

> Ricardo blinked slowly for a time, then closed his eyes altogether,
> with the placidity of the domestic cat dozing on the hearth-rug. In
> another moment he opened them very wide.
>
> (148)

> The greenish irises which had been staring out of doors glided into
> the corners of his eyes nearest to Schomberg and stayed there with
> a coyly voluptuous expression.
>
> (152)[21]

Most striking, however, is Ricardo's description of his first meeting
with Mr Jones:

> It was only then that he looked at me—quietly, you know ... He
> seemed to touch me inside somewhere. I went away pretty quick
> from there ... I wasn't frightened. What should I be frightened for?
> I only felt touched—on the very spot. But Jee-miny, if anybody had

told me we should be partners before the year was out—well, I
would have—

(127–8)

After a string of oaths, Ricardo then sits 'dumb with a stony gaze as if
still marvelling inwardly' (128). Thus an intimate gaze, so intimate that
it seems like an internal touching, initiates Ricardo's devoted loyalty
and retrospectively provokes in him an internal gaze of wonder.
Ricardo's comments on Jones are an odd mixture of servility, admiration and coy innuendo: 'It was the first time he called me Martin ... I
let him know very soon that I was game for anything ... in his
company' (130); 'A gentleman's just like any other man—and something more' (130); 'That's where a gentleman has the pull of you. He
don't get excited' (141); 'That's another thing you can tell a gentleman
by—his freakishness' (150). Ideas of sameness and difference occur in
relation to Jones and Ricardo and to Jones and Heyst. During Ricardo's
narration it 'flashed through Schomberg's mind that these two were
indeed well matched in their enormous dissimilarity, identical souls in
different disguises' (130). R.B. Lewis has noted the link between Heyst
and Jones set up by the idea that they are both 'gentlemen'.[22]
   Questions of same-sex desire appear with greater subtlety in the
relationship of Heyst and Morrison, which attracts a sense of uncertainty: 'Heyst became associated with Morrison on terms about which
people were in doubt. Some said he was a partner, others said he was
a sort of paying guest, but the real truth of the matter was more
complex' (10). The narrator of this part of the novel, who appears to
be an unnamed member of the European community in that area, is
close enough to omniscience to reveal the real origin of their partnership, but nevertheless implies limits to his understanding of Heyst:
'One day Heyst turned up in Timor. Why in Timor, of all places in the
world, no one knows. Well, he was mooning about Delli ... possibly in
search of some undiscovered facts' (10). We learn that the relationship
between Heyst and Morrison originated in the former's financial
rescue of Morrison and continued because of Heyst's delicacy of
feeling but we may suspect that this delicacy masked a certain unacknowledged need for company on the part of the isolated Heyst. This
pattern is repeated by Heyst in respect of Lena and this parallel creates
a certain sexual ambiguity. Heyst's concern for Morrison draws him
into a potentially enriching though finally disastrous financial project
– the coal mining. Heyst's concern for Lena draws him into a sexual
relationship which greatly enriches his life but is similarly short-lived,

ending in the death of both him and Lena. Heyst's father has not destroyed his son's human needs, but has repressed his ability to acknowledge them; only the needs of others enable him to seek company, active employment, or emotional and sexual fulfilment.

The connection between the two relationships is explicitly made by Heyst talking to Lena, but is prefigured when he first meets her. In each case an ambiguity is raised about the relationship with Morrison. On first seeing Lena, Heyst looks at her 'as no man ever looks at another man' (71). Yet in the next paragraph, when he gets up to speak to her, we are told that: 'It was the same sort of impulse which years ago had made him ... accost Morrison, practically a stranger to him then ... It was the same impulse. But he did not recognize it' (71–2). Shortly afterwards the narrator adds:

> It is very clear that Heyst was not indifferent. I won't say to the girl, but to the girl's fate. He was the same man who had plunged after the submerged Morrison ... But this was another sort of plunge altogether, and likely to lead to a very different kind of partnership.
>
> (77)

The look is different, the 'plunge' is different, yet the impulse is the same. This pattern, of similarity and difference, is repeated in Heyst's account to Lena of the Morrison affair. Lena describes her horror of Schomberg's sexual harassment, and says that she was 'cornered' (195). This is as much a literal as a metaphorical term, since we have earlier been told that Schomberg has 'assailed her in quiet corners' (79). Heyst is quite clear what she is talking about, dealing tactfully with her embarrassment as she refers to their own sexual relations (195). He nevertheless picks up her term to describe his relations with Morrison: 'One day I met a cornered man. I use the word because it expresses the man's situation exactly, and because you just used it yourself. You know what that means?' (197). Lena is startled by this, and when Heyst explains that 'I mean in his own way', she responds 'I knew very well it couldn't be anything like that' (197). Heyst also refers to his friendship with Morrison, based on the fact that 'one gets attached in a way to people one has done something for' (199), as constituting 'a germ of corruption' (200). Lena is understandably upset, since this might equally apply to her relationship with Heyst.

Twice, then, the idea of a sexual element in Heyst's relationship with Morrison is evoked and then put aside. It might be argued that these are unsurprising effects in a fiction about a social context where men worked and lived closely together often without women, but where open homosexuality was taboo. Conversely, Jeffrey Meyers takes Heyst's relationship with Morrison as clearly a 'homosexual friendship'. While this seems a possible reading, Meyers's conception of what such a relationship would imply leads him to claim that Heyst 'never desires Lena' and is impotent in their sexual encounters.[23] The former seems to me difficult to argue, given passages such as: 'He remembered that she was pretty, and, more, that she had a special grace in the intimacy of life' (215); 'He looked at her figure of grace and strength, solid and supple, with an ever-growing appreciation' (218). Heyst's alleged impotence Meyers deduces from phrases such as 'He stopped, struck afresh by the physical and moral sense of the imperfections of their relations' (222). Yet the sentence continues, '—a sense which made him desire her constant nearness', and the overall effect on Heyst of the relationship suggests a growing love, desire and jealousy. Furthermore, Heyst's allusion to their sexual relations prompts from Lena 'a stealthy glance of passionate appreciation' (195). Meyers goes on to the yet more dubious assertion, that Lena's supposed previous sexual experience 'lends substance to Ricardo's claim ... that he and Lena have a great deal in common'.[24] Here Meyers seems in danger of succumbing to the misogyny which he (rightly) sees in Jones and Ricardo and (more debatably) in Heyst. Why would sexual experience give a woman a great deal in common with a violent professional criminal and would-be rapist? In point of fact, when Lena says that only since being with Heyst has she realized 'what a horror it might have been' (195) if she had succumbed to Schomberg, she clearly implies that her sexual experience was very limited. Most disturbingly, Meyers suggests that Ricardo must in fact ('despite Conrad's explanations' to the contrary) have succeeded in raping Lena and that 'since the passionate Lena is a "bad girl" with considerable sexual experience and Heyst is clearly unable to satisfy her emotional or physical needs, she subconsciously responds to Ricardo's sexual assault.'[25] This is a very literal-minded reading of the haze of ambiguity and transgression that Conrad creates around questions of sexuality in *Victory*: Meyers assumes that a character either is or isn't homosexual, and if he is, he cannot be attracted to a women. As with 'Heart of Darkness', I would argue that, instead of trying to determine a definite but hidden homosexuality, it may be more useful to notice the literary, moral and political implications of the effect of ambiguity, the presence of hints and uncertainty. Eve Sedgwick has shown some of the distorting effects of homophobia in literary discourse. I would suggest that the traces of homosexuality in Conrad's work are important primarily because of the pressure they exert on the homosocial structures which dominate the narratives. As Sedgwick points out, patriarchal homosexual structures are often homophobic as well: in her terms, 'the potential unbrokenness of a continuum between homosocial and homosexual' (*BM*, 1) is obscured or rendered invisible within structures of power involving the exchange of women among men. The hints of homosexual feeling in Heyst's relationship with Morrison unsettle the homosocial structures present in plot and narrative, as do the suggestions of a feminization of Heyst and the presence at certain moments between Heyst and Lena of a gaze of mutuality rather than of power. Visual processes, of looking and being looked at, of self-confident scrutiny and anxious self-consciousness, play a major part, together with the articulation of gendered antitheses, such as that of activity and passivity. While the interaction of Heyst and Davidson in the penultimate chapter fits a pattern of homosocial exchange, notably in their contemplation of the dying Lena, the Morrison–Heyst–Lena triangle is not one in which the men exchange the woman or her image, but one in which a man (Heyst) relates in comparable ways to another man and to a woman. At this stage of the novel Lena is more a substitute for Morrison (or vice versa) than a token of exchange.

Both *Victory* and *The Arrow of Gold* end with nothingness, absence or loss. *Victory* ends in death: 'There was nothing to be done there ... Nothing!' (412) and *The Arrow of Gold* with M. George's loss of both Rita and the arrow, symbol of romantic love. These endings reflect the strong strains of scepticism and pessimism in Conrad's work: a scepticism that doubts the possibility of knowing either reality or oneself and a consequent pessimism as to the achievement of fulfilment or tranquillity. A common and persuasive reading of these endings would therefore be in existential or epistemological terms. For example R. W. B. Lewis stresses epistemological concerns when he suggests that *Victory* is 'intimately concerned with questions of truth and reality, as it is with lies and illusion' and that it 'achieves the conditions of art; for the manifold *and* unitary truth of things is just what Conrad succeeds in making real and visible.'[26] At the same time his account focuses on the fate of characters considered in broadly existential terms. For example: 'Between the two kinds of failure, Lena's victory is squeezed out in a way that is a victory both for her and for the novel in which she has her being', a novel which 'never fails to take account of the variable and highly unpredictable character of individual human beings'.[27]

Such a reading is illuminating in the broadly humanist terms that it employs but we may also ask how far the doubts, losses and absences of Conrad's work reflect the structures of gender and cultural difference as constructed in the societies he knew and represented. Humanist readings do not necessarily neglect questions of gender or cultural difference, but tend to essentialize these, so that the final meaning of the absence or the abyss is referred back to a dilemma of general human experience. As against this, feminist and postcolonial theory would encourage us to consider whether the absence or abyss is not integral to the forms of subjectivity and the discourses of knowledge that Conrad's characters deploy. In both novels the absence or loss is strongly connected with characters' sense of their own identity, and specifically masculine identity. In *The Arrow of Gold* the gift of the arrow is associated with Rita being 'very much of a woman' (348), with her destruction of the young man's romantic dreams, with a 'something' ('lives which seem to be meant for something' (350)) which is the ineffable purpose of life. In a sense it is a gift of masculinity, as emancipation from the experience of being 'penetrated' by the woman (274), an emancipation which enables M. George's return to the male life of the sea. In *Victory* nothingness is the legacy of Heyst's father, who 'considered the universal nothingness' (219). Heyst carries that abyss within him and when Lena is brought into his world she sees the void of her dependence on him, but rescues him from his nothingness by making him love her, though at the cost of her own life. Lewis identifies an association of visibility and nothingness with Jones: 'Mr Jones is perhaps the most fascinating instance in the novel of the motion towards visibility, if only because it is the most paradoxical. What becomes full and finally visible about him is a kind of absence, a nothingness.' Lewis, however, develops this idea in terms of Jones's devilish qualities, his role as 'the source of nonbeing' rather than his ambivalent relation to conventional masculinity.[28]

Problems of masculinity expressed in terms of absence, loss and of 'nothing to see' fit readily, and perhaps too readily, an interpretation in terms of Freudian castration anxiety or Lacanian theories of lack and Symbolic castration. If the absences and lacks in Conrad's fiction are read as expressions of this alleged general 'Symbolic castration', signifying radical alterity within the self and the finally unfulfillable nature of desire, the implications are ultimately not so different from those of humanist readings of Conrad. The latter have frequently responded to Conrad's sense of the problematic and divided nature of identity and his portrayal of human life as a quest that cannot succeed.[29] Lacan's idea of lack as constitutive of desire is a fruitful one, but not wholly new and there seems no good reason to call it castration, other than as a way of perpetuating phallocentrism. Even if it be demonstrated that Lacanian theory, fully and correctly understood, is opposed to phallocentrism, the theory is so formed as to restrict such understanding to a very few, and one of the effects of its influential status is to ensure that issues of desire, including a supposedly non-gender-specific lack, continue to be discussed in terms of the presence or absence of a structure metaphorically named after the male organ. The idea that the Symbolic (the social and linguistic order) marks the female as lacking or castrated is, however, one which can be widely supported from a wide range of discourses and representations. If one understands a general 'Symbolic castration' as the way in which a patriarchal society represents to itself an experience of self-division, then this may serve a critical and feminist analysis.

I would suggest, then, that there are situations, moments, aspects of Conrad's texts which could appropriately be described in terms of the fear of castration. One of the significations of the absence or loss with which these and many other Conrad texts end may be the experience, by certain characters, of a threat to their sense of masculinity, for which threat castration is the conventional metaphor. However, the concept of castration seems to me limited as a way of analysing the processes that generate that threat, precisely because it installs the presence or absence of the phallus as ultimate signifier. If one seeks to move from analysing the self-representations of masculinity (the way in which men have traditionally understood their masculinity) to proposing models for current reinterpretation, then a Freudian or Lacanian model is liable to be unhelpful, and even reactionary in the sense of serving to smuggle in the same old ideology in a new guise. As Stephen Heath argues:

> Where the conception of the symbolic as movement and production of difference, as chain of signifiers in which the subject is effected in division, should forbid the notion of some presence from which difference is then derived, Lacan instates the visible as the condition of symbolic functioning, with the phallus the standard of the visibility required: seeing is from the male organ.

> The constant limit of the theory is the phallus, the phallic function, and the theorization of that limit is constantly eluded, held off ... for example, by collapsing castration into a scenario of vision.[30]

Defenders of Lacanian theory usually rely on the radical distinction between phallus (a structure) and penis (an organ), a defence which Heath describes as 'pure analogical rationalisation' and which de Lauretis persuasively undermines by quoting Lacan's association of lack with a 'particular organ'.[31]

What is at issue when applying such theory is the performativity of literary critical discourse (or film criticism, or cultural studies): the extent to which, in writing about masculinity, one may be enacting a version of masculinity, putting it into circulation, or recirculating it. I have already quoted (in Chapter 2) elements of Gayle Rubin's analysis of such a process: 'In the cycle of exchange manifested by the Oedipal complex, the phallus passes through the medium of women from one man to another ... women go one way, the phallus the other. It is where we aren't' (TW, 192). There is a danger that analyses of masculinity in terms of the phallus and castration will, in performative terms, act as a continuing circulation of the phallus, a continued marking out of a place of critical discourse where women are not. This brings me back to the need for a reflexive self-awareness in a male critical discourse on masculinity. The risk is that such a discourse, even (or especially) if inspired by feminist thought, may put feminism in the position of 'woman' and circulate it through homosocial discursive structures.[32] The concepts of the phallus, of castration and of lack are necessary to an understanding of much feminist theory and film theory, yet a male critic needs to try to stand outside the paradigm they support even while writing from within it (a women critic is, in one sense, always already outside it).

I would, then, like to conclude by returning to one of the most intense moments of Heyst's desiring look at Lena, and to the observation about masculinity that accompanies and props up his pleasure in possessing and seeing her: 'for a man must feel that, unless he has ceased to be masculine' (201). Here the abyss opens under the logic of the same: a woman serves to constitute and confirm a man's masculinity, but through a painfully apparent tautologous logic: Heyst feels vanity (in 'possessing' a woman) because he is masculine and he is masculine because he feels vanity. Psychoanalytic theory provides us with a way of naming this abyss but perhaps, in a utopian spirit, we should leave it unnamed. Margaret Whitford defends Irigaray's utopianism on the grounds that 'imagining how things could be different is part of the process of transforming the present in the direction of a different future'.[33] She quotes Irigaray's answer to someone who claimed not to understand the meaning of 'masculine discourse': 'Of course not, since there is no other. The problem is that of a possible alterity in masculine discourse – or in relation to masculine discourse.' Whitford comments:

> Irigaray is trying to 'imagine the unimaginable' and it is in this light that we should understand her view that to aim for a state 'beyond sexual difference' without rearticulating our present organization of male and female would only maintain the deceptive universality of the male.[34]

This view combines the aspiration towards a presently unimaginable future with an imperative to rearticulate the social institutions of the present. Such a rearticulation must rest on an understanding of the history and development of those institutions. A re-examination of the work of Conrad, some of which is now a century old, in terms of how it represents, is shaped by but also refigures the institution of masculinity, may contribute to that understanding and thus to the imagining of a different future. On the other hand, anyone who reads Conrad with attention and appreciation will be particularly wary of imagining that words have the power to transform social reality, and similarly wary of seeking utopias, since these two activities are particular objects of Conrad's corrosive scepticism.[35] Yet, paradoxically, Conrad is also a champion of the need for ideals, even while he shows the tragic tendency for such ideals to be degraded in action.[36] Indeed, *Victory* ends with two forms of 'last words' corresponding to these two aspects of the Conradian world-view. The first is the often quoted words which are almost Heyst's final words before his death: 'woe to the man whose heart has not learned while young to hope, to love— and to put its trust in life!' (410). The second is the last word of the text: 'Nothing!' (412). Perhaps we cannot at present imagine the absence of masculinity without evoking ideas of lack or loss, a formation which seems to lead only back to the phallus. I am inevitably writing a masculine discourse, in Irigaray's sense. When the male critic's act of seeing, examining, representing is so firmly trapped within the gendering of the aesthetic, how can he claim to see, or try to reveal, an alterity in masculine discourse? At the risk, then, of what may seem a gesture of transcendence, I would like to offer an imagining of the Conradian abyss or nothingness, not as negation, death or loss, but as an alterity of the masculine which was for Conrad, and remains for many men today, unspeakable.

Notes

Introduction

1 For the view that Conrad's portrayal of women is unsuccessful see Thomas Moser, *Joseph Conrad: Achievement and Decline* (Cambridge, MA: Harvard University Press, 1957). Gordon Thompson and Susan Lundvall Brodie, who both seek to defend Conrad's representation of women, recognize that the idealization of women in Conrad's fiction represents a projection of male needs and fantasies, but nevertheless tend to perpetuate this idealization in their own critical discourse. See Gordon Thompson, 'Conrad's Women', *Nineteenth-Century Fiction*, 32 (1978), 442–65; Susan Lundvall Brodie, 'Conrad's Feminine Perspective', *Conradiana*, 16 (1984), 141–54.

2 Nina Pelikan Straus, 'The Exclusion of the Intended from Secret Sharing in Conrad's "Heart of Darkness"', *Novel*, 20 (1987), 123–37; Karen Klein, 'The Feminist Predicament in Conrad's Nostromo', in *Brandeis Essays in Literature*, ed. John Hazel Smith (Waltham, MA: Department of English and American Literature, Brandeis University, 1983), 101–16.

3 For example, Wendy Moffat, 'Domestic Violence: The Simple Tale within *The Secret Agent*', *English Literature in Transition 1880–1920*, 37.4 (1994), 465–89. Two books on Conrad's representations of women seek to defend him from the charge of sexism, using humanist rather than theoretical approaches: Ruth L. Nadelhaft, *Joseph Conrad* (Feminist Readings) (Hemel Hempstead: Harvester, 1991); Heliena Krenn, *Conrad's Lingard Trilogy: Empire, Race and Woman in the Malay Novels* (New York and London: Garland Publishing, 1990).

4 For the developing debate on masculinity in Conrad, see the books by Koestenbaum (1989), Hawthorn (1990), Showalter (1991), Bristow (1991), Lane (1995), Stott (1992), the chapters by Mongia, McCracken, Roberts, Hampson and Elbert in *CG*, and the articles by Roberts (1992, 1993, 1996), Hampson (1996) and Bonney (1991), all listed in the bibliography.

5 Jeffrey Meyers, *Homosexuality and Literature: 1890–1930* (London: Athlone Press, 1977); Robert R. Hodges, 'Deep Fellowship: Homosexuality and Male Bonding in the Life and Fiction of Joseph Conrad', *Journal of Homosexuality*, 4 (Summer 1979), 379–93; Robert J.G. Lange, 'The Eyes Have It: Homoeroticism in *Lord Jim*', *West Virginia Philological Papers*, 38 (1992), 59–68; Wayne Koestenbaum, *Double Talk: The Erotics of Male Literary Collaboration* (New York and London: Routledge, 1989), pp. 166–73; Richard Ruppel, 'Joseph Conrad and the Ghost of Oscar Wilde', *The Conradian*, 23.1 (Spring 1998), 19–36.

6 See Joseph Bristow, *Empire Boys: Adventures in a Man's World* (London: Harper Collins, 1992).

7 See Bristow, pp. 153–66.

8 Laurence Davies, 'Conrad, *Chance* and Women Readers', in *CG*, 75–88 (p. 78). Davies cites Conrad's letter to *The Times* of 15 June 1910, *CL*, IV, 327.

9   See Elaine Showalter, *Sexual Anarchy: Gender and Culture at the Fin de Siècle* (1990; London: Bloomsbury, 1991). Also Eve Kosofsky Sedgwick, who argues for 'a chronic, now endemic crisis of homo/heterosexual definition, indicatively male, dating from the end of the nineteenth century' (*EC*, 1).

10   See Showalter, *Sexual Anarchy*, pp. 14, 171 and Ruppel, pp. 21–2.

11   The exception is the 'Author's Note' to *Almayer's Folly*, a note which was written by early 1895 but not published until 1920. The 'Author's Notes' for the other works were written in the period leading up to 1920.

12   Todd K. Bender, Preface to Krenn, p. vi.

13   Bernard C. Meyer claims that Conrad's attitude to women was marked by particular fear and mistrust. *Joseph Conrad: A Psychoanalytic Biography* (Princeton, NJ: Princeton University Press, 1967), p. 289.

14   The debate about racism in Conrad has largely taken the form of responses to Chinua Achebe, 'An Image of Africa: Racism in Conrad's *Heart of Darkness*', in *Hopes and Impediments: Selected Essays 1965–1987* (London: Heinemann, 1988), pp. 1–13. My own brief discussion of the issues is found in *Joseph Conrad (Longman Critical Reader)*, ed. Andrew Michael Roberts (London and New York: Longman, 1998), pp. 8–12 and 109–10.

15   Herbert Sussman's distinction between 'maleness' ('fantasies about the essential nature of the "male"') and 'masculinity' ('those multifarious social constructions of the male current within the society') is thought-provoking, but not easy to maintain, since fantasies about maleness are surely integral to social constructions of masculinity. Herbert Sussman, *Victorian Masculinities: Manhood and Masculine Poetics in Early Victorian Literature and Art* (Cambridge: Cambridge University Press, 1995), pp. 12–13.

16   For a discussion of the range of meaning of 'ideology', see Jeremy Hawthorn, *A Glossary of Contemporary Literary Theory*, 3rd edn (London: Arnold, 1998), pp. 158–64.

17   Terry Eagleton, *Ideology: An Introduction* (London: Verso, 1991), p. 30.

18   Louis Althusser, *Lenin and Philosophy and Other Essays*, trans. Ben Brewster (London: New Left Books, 1971), p. 152.

19   Juliet Mitchell, *Psychoanalysis and Feminism* (1974; Harmondsworth: Penguin, 1975), p. 413.

20   Margaret Whitford, *Luce Irigaray: Philosophy in the Feminine* (London and New York: Routledge, 1991), pp. 13, 19.

21   Stephen Heath, 'Male Feminism', in *Men in Feminism*, eds Alice Jardine and Paul Smith (1987; New York and London: Routledge, 1989), pp. 1–32 (p. 26).

22   Heath, 'Male Feminism', p. 26.

23   Heath notes that the only politically progressive project of male writing that he can envisage is 'in and from areas of gay men's experience' ('Male Feminism', p. 25).

24   Edward Said, *Culture and Imperialism* (London: Chatto & Windus, 1993), p. 79.

25   The term 'Strong Poet' alludes to the influence theory of Harold Bloom, according to which 'Poetic Influence – when it involves two strong, authentic poets – always proceeds by a misreading of the prior poet, an act of creative correction that is actually and necessarily a misinterpretation'.

Harold Bloom, *The Anxiety of Influence: A Theory of Poetry* (Oxford: Oxford University Press, 1973), p. 30.

26 Ruppel, p. 35.
27 Ruppel, pp. 23–34.
28 Ruppel, p. 24.
29 Heidi Hartmann, 'The Unhappy Marriage of Marxism and Feminism: Towards a More Progressive Union', in *Women and Revolution: A Discussion of the Unhappy Marriage of Marxism and Feminism*, ed. Lydia Sargent (Boston: South End Press, 1981), pp. 1–41 (p. 14); quoted *BM*, 3.
30 See *BM*, 26 and *EC*, 36n, 154.
31 For a discussion of the 'achievement and decline' thesis, derived from Thomas Moser's *Joseph Conrad: Achievement and Decline* (Cambridge, MA: Harvard University Press, 1957), see Gary Geddes, *Conrad's Later Novels* (Montreal: McGill-Queen's University Press, 1980), pp. 1–10 and *passim*; Hampson, *Betrayal and Identity*, pp. 1–2 and *passim*.

Chapter 1 Masculinity, 'Race' and Empire

1 Paul Gilroy, 'White Man's Bonus', review of Richard Dyer, *White*, *Times Literary Supplement*, 29 August 1997, p. 10.
2 Kwame Anthony Appiah, 'Race', in *Critical Terms for Literary Study*, eds Frank Lentricchia and Thomas McLaughlin (Chicago and London: University of Chicago Press, 1990), pp. 274–87 (p. 276).
3 Appiah suggests that 'there is a fairly widespread consensus in the sciences of biology and anthropology that the word "race," at least as it is used in most unscientific discussions, refers to nothing that science should recognize as real' (Appiah, p. 277). While the debate concerning race within biology is clearly outside the scope of the present discussion, it may be of interest to note that a 1998 international conference of biologists and palaeontologists was reported as showing growing support for the thesis that so-called racial differences 'are the product of comparatively recent, and therefore superficial, adaptations to environment'. A 'leading geneticist', Walter Bodmer, was quoted as stating that 'most of the genetic variation in human populations is found within any population, and a minority of it relates to difference between them. You can take a population of 1,000 from anywhere and they will have as much variation, almost, as a population of 1,000 sampled from all over the world. The differences between populations is far less than the differences within them. There is no credence to a demarcation of human populations into clearly separated population groups.' *The Guardian*, 6 July 1998, p. 11.
4 This includes the affirmative use of a form of 'racial' identity by groups which have been oppressed on racist grounds (for example forms of black identity).
5 'Karain', together with 'The Lagoon' which is a shorter work with some related features, was collected in the 1898 volume *Tales of Unrest*. Of the other stories in that volume, 'The Idiots' and 'The Return' have European settings, while 'An Outpost of Progress', set in Africa, is a much more directly satirical piece than Conrad's other early 'imperial' fiction.

6 Homi K. Bhabha, *The Location of Culture* (London and New York: Routledge, 1994), p. 39.

7 Bristow, pp. 163–4.

8 Bristow, p. 164.

9 The term 'Other' or 'other' has a wide currency in contemporary academic discourses, including radical philosophy, Lacanian psychoanalysis, and feminist and postcolonial theory. The specific senses in which it is used are quite diverse, although they have in common the idea of that which is excluded, marginalized, repressed or seen as divergent from the norm. Certain theories (e.g. Lacanian) distinguish between 'the Other' and 'the other' but the significance of capitalization is not consistent across different theories and writers. In the present book (which draws primarily on feminist and postcolonial theory in its treatment of otherness) I capitalize the word as 'Other' where a general principle or representation of otherness is implied.

10 Bongie implies the link between exoticism and the ideology and fantasies of masculinity when he deliberately uses the masculine pronoun for the 'Romantic individual', but he adds that he will not be considering 'the extent to which modern individualism and masculist ideology feed into each other' (*EM*, 10).

11 Hélène Cixous, 'Sorties: Out and Out: Attacks/Ways Out/Forays', in Hélène Cixous and Catherine Clément, *The Newly Born Woman*, trans. Betsy Wing (Manchester: Manchester University Press, 1986), pp. 63–132 (p. 71).

12 Homi Bhabha, 'The Other Question', in *Contemporary Postcolonial Theory: A Reader*, ed. Padmini Mongia (London: Arnold, 1996), pp. 37–54 (p. 38). Reprinted from *Screen* 24.6 (1983), 18–36.

13 Luce Irigaray uses the phrase 'the other of the other' (in the context of gender rather than race) for a female economy, not subject to the male realm of the Semblance. See Whitford, p. 104. Andrew Bennett and Nicholas Royle suggest that black women's writing 'being marginalized twice over, figuring the other of the other, reinforces a sense of the polymorphic nature of identity in all discourse'. Andrew Bennett and Nicholas Royle, *An Introduction to Literature, Criticism and Theory: Key Critical Concepts* (Hemel Hempstead: Prentice Hall/Harvester Wheatsheaf, 1995), p. 162.

14 Bhabha, *The Location of Culture*, p. 4.

15 On Manichean values of good and evil attached to this binary structure see Abdul R. JanMohamed, *Manichean Aesthetics: The Politics of Literature in Colonial Africa* (Amherst: University of Massachusetts Press, 1983), pp. 3–4.

16 Jonathan Dollimore, 'Homophobia and Sexual Difference', in *The Oxford Literary Review*, special issue on *Sexual Difference*, ed. Robert Young, 8.1–8.2 (1986), 5–12 (p. 5).

17 White's argument for Haggard as representing the 'shift towards subversion' relies on identifying liberal and democratic tendencies within British politics as the 'status quo' (*AT*, 99), so that Haggard's reactionary militarism is seen as oppositional. This ignores other strands within British culture, including the militarism which connects Haggard's vision to the approaching First World War. As White herself notes, Paul Fussell argued that Henty and Haggard 'prepared a generation of young men for war in

1914' (*AT*, 88). See Paul Fussell, *The Great War and Modern Memory* (London: Oxford University Press, 1975), p. 155.

18 H. Rider Haggard, *King Solomon's Mines* (1885; London: Cassell, 1893), p. 9.

19 Conrad himself expressed a comparable sentiment in a letter: 'the Secret Sharer, between you and me, is *it*. Eh? No damned tricks with girls there.' Letter of 5 November 1912 to Edward Garnett, *CL*, V, 128.

20 *King Solomon's Mines*, p. 282.

21 *King Solomon's Mines*, p. 301.

22 See Ann Laura Stoler, *Race and the Education of Desire: Foucault's* History of Sexuality *and the Colonial Order of Things* (Durham, NC and London: Duke University Press, 1995).

23 The editors of the World's Classics edition note that her white teeth merely mean that she does not chew betel. *An Outcast of the Islands*, eds J.H. Stape and Hans van Marle (Oxford: Oxford University Press, 1992), p. 375.

24 See Watt, *Conrad in the Nineteenth Century*, p. 37.

25 See Ann Laurer Stoler, who comments that the '"vast theoretical and legislative edifice" that was the theory of degeneracy secured the relationship between racism and sexuality'. Stoler, *Race and the Education of Desire*, p. 31.

26 See Ronald Hyam, *Britain's Imperial Century 1815–1914: A Study of Empire and Expansion* (London: Batsford, 1976) and 'Empire and Sexual Opportunity', *Journal of Imperial and Commonwealth History*, 14.2 (1986), 34–89.

27 Ann Laurer Stoler, 'Carnal Knowledge and Imperial Power: Gender, Race and Morality in Colonial Asia', in *Gender at the Crossroads of Knowledge: Feminist Anthropology in a Postmodern Era*, ed. Micaela di Leonardo (Berkely: University of California Press, 1991), pp. 51–101 (p. 52). For another critique of the hydraulic model, see Christopher Lane, *The Ruling Passion: British Colonial Allegory and the Paradox of Homosexual Desire* (Durham, NC and London: Duke University Press, 1995), p. 2.

28 Stoler, 'Carnal Knowledge and Imperial Power', p. 56.

29 Sander L. Gilman, 'Black Bodies, White Bodies: Toward an Iconography of Female Sexuality in Late Nineteenth-Century Art, Medicine, and Literature', in *'Race', Writing and Difference*, ed. Henry Louis Gates (Chicago and London: University of Chicago Press, 1986), pp. 223–61 (p. 256).

30 Lane, p. 2.

31 Gilman, p. 256.

32 Stoler, *Race and the Education of Desire*, p. 46; 'Carnal Knowledge and Imperial Power', p. 58.

33 Stoler, 'Carnal Knowledge and Imperial Power', p. 60.

34 Bhabha, *The Location of Culture*, p. 37.

35 Bhabha, *The Location of Culture*, pp. 38–9.

36 To say that Haggard's fiction is ideological is not, of course, to imply that its representation of masculinity is monolithic and unproblematic. The paradoxical structure of masculinity to which I refer in the Introduction is apparent in Haggard's idea that the highest ideal to which a boy can aspire is to become an English gentleman. Unless Haggard has in mind upward class mobility (which seems unlikely), his remark implies that secure gender and national identity are ideals which must be struggled for.

However, one knows that Haggard's heroes (unlike Conrad's) will succeed in this aim. See H. Rider Haggard, *Allan Quatermain* (1887; London: George Harrap, 1931), dedication, p. 5.

37   *King Solomon's Mines*, p. 283.

38   Edward Garnett, Introduction to *Letters from Conrad 1895 to 1924* (London: Nonesuch, 1928), ed. Edward Garnett, p. xiii.

39   Robert Young, *White Mythologies: Writing History and the West* (London and New York: Routledge, 1990), p. 124.

40   Young, p. 125.

41   Gail Ching-Liang Low, *White Skins, Black Masks: Representation and Colonialism* (London and New York: Routledge, 1996), p. 48.

42   Jeremy Hawthorn, who has examined in detail the ideological implications of Conrad's use of free indirect discourse, discusses the variety of terminology used to identify the different ways of representing speech and thought. See *NT*, Chapter One. What I am calling interior monologue might also be termed direct discourse, while what I am terming 'narratorial comment' is usefully defined by Hawthorn as 'an extra-mimetic narrative perspective': that is, a narrative voice from 'outside the created world of the fictional text', 'from a different level of reality from that in which the characters live' (*NT*, 2, 62).

43   Ruth L. Nadelhaft, *Joseph Conrad* (Feminist Readings Series) (Hemel Hempstead: Harvester Wheatsheaf, 1991), p. 31.

44   Terry Eagleton, *Criticism and Ideology: A Study in Marxist Literary Theory* (London: Verso, 1976), p. 135.

45   Linda Ruth Williams, *Critical Desire: Psychoanalysis and the Literary Subject* (London: Edward Arnold, 1995), p. 157.

46   Sigmund Freud, *The Ego and the Id*, in *The Standard Edition of the Complete Psychological Works of Sigmund Freud*, trans. under the general editorship of James Strachey in collaboration with Anna Freud, assisted by Alix Strachey and Alan Tyson, 24 vols (London: Hogarth Press, 1953–74), XIX, pp. 1–66 (p. 54).

47   Williams, p. 159.

48   Freud, *Beyond the Pleasure Principle*, in *The Standard Edition of the Complete Psychological Works of Sigmund Freud*, XVIII, pp. 1–64 (p. 38).

49   Elizabeth Bronfen, entry on 'death-drive (Freud)', in *Feminism and Psychoanalysis: A Critical Dictionary*, ed. Elizabeth Wright (Oxford and Cambridge, MA: Blackwell, 1992), p. 56.

50   My thinking on this point goes back to a conference paper given by Padmini Mongia at the 1992 conference of the Joseph Conrad Society (UK), subsequently published as 'Ghosts of the Gothic: Spectral Women and Colonized Spaces in *Lord Jim*', *CG*, 1–15. In the paper and the ensuing discussion she pointed out the inability of Conrad's texts to represent female sexual desire with conviction.

51   Hampson, *Betrayal and Identity*, p. 26.

52   On focalization, see Gérard Genette, *Narrative Discourse*, trans. Jane E. Lewin (1980; Oxford: Blackwell, 1986), pp. 189–94. The conclusion of Chapter One of *Almayer's Folly* (pp. 19–20) is an example of external focalization on Nina, describing what she sees, but only the references to her looking 'eagerly' and with 'a steady and anxious gaze' hint at what her

thoughts might be. In contrast, we are regularly given Almayer's thoughts and feelings in some detail.

53 Teresa de Lauretis, *Alice Doesn't: Feminism, Semiotics, Cinema* (London: Macmillan, 1984), p. 68.

54 The Cambridge edition of the novel amends the second 'dress' here to 'kriss' (a dagger), so that it reads 'I have seen his kriss. It shines! What jewels!' *Almayer's Folly: The Story of an Eastern River*, eds Floyd Eugene Eddleman and David Leon Higdon, with an Introduction by Ian Watt (Cambridge: Cambridge University Press, 1994), p. 40. This both improves the sense and emphasizes the phallic presentation of Dain.

55 Suzanne Raitt, *Virginia Woolf's To The Lighthouse* (Hemel Hempstead: Harvester Wheatsheaf, 1990), p. 65.

56 Annette Kuhn, *Women's Pictures: Feminism and Cinema* (1982; London: Verso, 1993), p. 53.

57 Constance Penley, 'Feminism, Film Theory and the Bachelor Machines', *m/f*, 10 (1985), 39–59 (p. 54), quoted SD,123.

58 Mary Ann Doane, 'Film and the Masquerade: Theorizing the Female Spectator', in *The Sexual Subject: A Screen Reader in Sexuality*, ed. Screen Collective (London: Routledge, 1992), pp. 227–43 (p. 231).

59 *An Outcast of the Islands*, eds J. H. Stape and Hans van Marle, introduction by J. H. Stape (Oxford and New York: Oxford University Press, 1992), pp. xvii–xviii.

60 Stape, p. xvi.

61 Letter of 24 September 1895 to Edward Garnett, *CL*, I, 247, quoted Stape, p. xvii.

62 Hélène Cixous, 'Sorties', p. 71.

63 Stape, p. xiii.

64 Stape, p. xv.

65 Stape, p. xv.

66 See Morag Shiach, 'Their "Symbolic" Exists, It Holds Power – We, the Sowers of Disorder, Know it Only Too Well', in *Between Feminism and Psychoanalysis*, ed. Teresa Brennan (London and New York: Routledge, 1989), pp. 153–67 (p. 156).

67 Stape, p. xv.

68 Stape, p. xix.

69 Nadelhaft, pp. 33, 32.

70 Nadelhaft, p. 34.

71 Heath, 'Male Feminism', p. 16.

72 Claire Pajaczkowska, 'The Heterosexual Presumption: A Contribution to the Debate on Pornography', *Screen*, 22.1 (1981), 79–94 (p. 92), quoted in Heath, 'Male Feminism', p. 2.

Chapter 2 Imperialism and Male Bonds

1 The popular phrase 'male bonding' derives from Lionel Tiger's *Men in Groups* (New York: Random House, 1969), described by R. W. Connell as 'a complete biological-reductionist theory of masculinity based on the idea that we are descended from a hunting species': R. W. Connell, *Masculinities* (Cambridge: Polity Press, 1995), p. 46. However, the repeated use of the

phrase has given it a certain ironic edge more appropriate to construction-
ist theories of masculinity.

2 Elaine Showalter's study of the *fin de siècle* crisis in masculinity does discuss
Conrad, but only 'Heart of Darkness' (*Sexual Anarchy*, pp. 95–104). Robert
Hampson links Conrad's late novel *Chance* to *Dr Jekyll and Mr Hyde* in
terms of secret male bonds ('Chance and the Secret Life: Conrad,
Thackeray and Stevenson', in *CG*, 105–22).

3 Daniel Bivona, *Desire and Contradiction: Imperial Visions and Domestic
Debates in Victorian Literature* (Manchester: Manchester University Press,
1990), pp. vii–viii.

4 Letter of 18 February 1894 to Marguerite Poradowska, *CL*, I, 148. The original is in French: 'il me semble que tout est mort en moi'.

5 Letter of 5 December 1903 to Kazimierz Waliszewski, *CL*, III, 89.

6 'Nothing' is also the highly significant final word of Conrad's *Victory*.

7. Quoted Sussman, p. 39.

8 Conrad first met Garnett either on 8 October 1894 at the office of T. Fisher
Unwin or soon afterwards (in Unwin's company) at the National Liberal
Club (Owen Knowles, *A Conrad Chronology* (Basingstoke: Macmillan,
1989), p. 19). A few weeks later Conrad and Garnett spent an evening
alone together, in an Italian restaurant and Conrad's rooms at 17
Gillingham Street. Conrad's 'Author's Note' appears to refer to this second
meeting ('One evening when we had dined together') as the occasion
when Garnett said 'why not write another [novel]?' (*OI*, viii), prompting
him to start *An Outcast of the Islands* that very evening. Garnett suggests
that Conrad has 'misdated this conversation, which took place at our first
meeting', which Garnett places in the National Liberal Club in November
1894, and says that at their second meeting Conrad showed him the
manuscript opening of the novel (Garnett, viii). However, since Conrad
reports in a letter of August 1894 that he has started 'Two Vagabonds' (later
to become *An Outcast of the Islands*), even his first meeting with Garnett
postdates the inception of the novel (Letter of 18? August 1894 to
Marguerite Poradowska, *CL*, I, 171). However, the fictional nature of
Garnett's role as begetter of the text only gives it more significance in
terms of the feelings and fantasies of the two men.

9 Koestenbaum, pp. 166–73.

10 Garnett, pp. vii, x, xxv.

11 Sussman, p. 39.

12 Ford Madox Ford, *Ford Madox Brown: A Record of his Life and Work* (London:
Longmans, 1896), p. 190, quoted Sussman, p. 41.

13 See Sussman p. 42 on Carlyle's identification of 'his literary project with
that of the Captain of Industry'.

14 Ford Madox Hueffer, *Ancient Lights and Certain New Reflections: Being the
Memories of a Young Man* (London: Chapman & Hall, 1911), p. 243.

15 Compare the dissatisfaction with modernity expressed in Rider Haggard's
Allan Quatermain, where the character-narrator escapes to Africa from the
'sinks of struggling, sweltering humanity' (p. 15); as Gail Ching-Liang Low
observes, 'he can only escape contamination by his dreams of empowered
masculinity in the wild open land of the African outback': Low, p. 37.

16 Koestenbaum, p. 168.

17 'Stephen Crane', *LE*, 103–4.
18 'Fourmillante cité, cité plein de rêves, / Où le spectre en plein jour raccroche le passant!' ('O swarming city, city full of dreams, where ghosts accost the passers-by in broad daylight!'): Baudelaire, 'Les Sept Vieillards' ('The Seven Old Men'), from *Les Fleurs du Mal*, in *Baudelaire: Volume 1: The Complete Verse*, bilingual edition, ed. and trans. Francis Scarfe (London: Anvil Press, 1986), p. 177.
19 Richard Dyer, 'Don't Look Now: The Male Pin-Up', in *The Sexual Subject*, pp. 265–76 (p. 275).
20 The filmic effect here was pointed out to me by Paul Kirschner.
21 Cedric Watts, 'Conrad and the Myth of the Monstrous Town', in *Conrad's Cities: Essays for Hans van Marle*, ed. Gene M. Moore (Amsterdam and Atlanta, GA: Rodopi, 1992) pp. 17–30 (p. 22).
22 Jim Reilly, *Shadowtime: History and Representation in Hardy, Conrad and Eliot* (London and New York: Routledge, 1993), p. 146.
23 Geoffrey Galt Harpham, *One of Us: The Mastery of Joseph Conrad* (Chicago and London: University of Chicago Press, 1996), p. 176.
24 Harpham, p. 115.
25 Tony Tanner, Introduction to *The Oxford Book of Sea Stories* (Oxford and New York: Oxford University Press, 1995), p. xiv, quoted Harpham, p. 112.
26 Harpham, p. 111. Conrad's comment (quoted by Harpham, p. 55), is found in his foreword to the 1914 Doubleday 'Deep Sea' edition. This foreword, entitled 'To My Readers in America', is reprinted in *The Nigger of the 'Narcissus'*, ed. Robert Kimbrough (New York: W. W. Norton, 1979), pp. 167–8 (p. 168). Elsewhere Conrad also describes Nostromo as 'nothing', though with the somewhat different implication that he is a representative figure, rather than a mirror for others. See Chapter 4, note 2, below.
27 Scott McCracken, '"A Hard and Absolute Condition of Existence": Reading Masculinity in *Lord Jim*', in *CG*, 17–38 (p. 25).
28 A heterodiegetic narrator is one who is absent from the story that he or she tells. See Genette, p. 245. The concept of the Ideological State Apparatus is found in the work of Althusser, who applies the term to institutions which maintain the class structure through ideologically-produced consensus. See *Lenin and Philosophy and Other Essays*, pp. 127–86.
29 See Low, p. 35.
30 Jules de Gaultier, *Bovarysme*, quoted *DD*, 5.
31 Richard Ruppel argues that Jim provokes a homoerotic response in Marlow and others: Ruppel, p. 27.
32 Sussman traces back to Carlyle this 'masculinist idea of a separate male knowledge that must be hidden from the female and communicated in secret, often in darkness, among men': Sussman, p. 39.

Chapter 3 Masculinity and the Body

1 Hélène Cixous, 'The Laugh of the Medusa', trans. Keith Cohen and Paula Cohen, in *New French Feminisms*, eds Elaine Marks and Isabelle de Courtivron (Hemel Hempstead: Harvester Wheatsheaf, 1981), pp. 245–64 (p. 251).

2   Cixous, 'The Laugh of the Medusa', p. 253. *Écriture féminine* 'describes how women's writing is a specific discourse closer to the body, to emotions and to the unnameable, all of which are repressed by the social contract': Maggie Humm, *The Dictionary of Feminist Theory* (Hemel Hempstead: Harvester Wheatsheaf, 1989), p. 59.

3   See especially Michel Foucault, *Discipline and Punish: The Birth of the Prison*, trans. Alan Sheridan (Harmondsworth: Penguin, 1977) and *The History of Sexuality: An Introduction*, trans. Robert Hurley (1978; Harmondsworth: Penguin, 1981).

4   Michel Foucault, *Power/Knowledge: Selected Interviews and Other Writings, 1972–1977*, ed. Colin Gordon, trans. Colin Gordon, Leo Marshall, John Mepham and Kate Soper (Hemel Hempstead: Harvester Wheatsheaf, 1980), p. 56.

5   Jane Gallop, *Thinking Through the Body* (New York: Columbia University Press, 1988), pp. 3–4.

6   Michel Foucault, *Power/Knowledge*, pp. 57–8.

7   *The Body: Social Process and Cultural Theory*, eds Mike Featherstone, Mike Hepworth and Bryan S. Turner (London, Thousand Oaks, CA and New Delhi: Sage Publications, 1991), p.1.

8   Rosi Braidotti, *Patterns of Dissonance: A Study of Women in Contemporary Philosophy*, trans. Elizabeth Guild (Cambridge: Polity Press, 1991), p. 219.

9   A call for papers for a seminar series at the University of Aberdeen during 1996 stated that 'the seminar is an attempt to move beyond theories and critical practices which orbit around the homogenizing concepts of the "body" and the "subject"'. Publicity of the Aberdeen Critical Theory Seminar (acts), 1996.

10   'Feminists have stressed that the generic category "*the* body" is a masculinist illusion. There are only concrete bodies, bodies in the plural, bodies with a specific sex and colour. This counterbalances psychoanalysis's tendency to phallocentrism, especially the ways it understands the female body': Elizabeth Grosz, in *Feminism and Psychoanalysis*, ed. Elizabeth Wright, p. 39

11   Pamela Banting, 'The Body as Pictogram: Rethinking Hélène Cixous's écriture féminine', *Textual Practice*, 6.2 (Summer 1992), 225–46 (p. 227).

12   Cixous, 'The Laugh of the Medusa', p. 247.

13   Rosalind Coward, *Female Desire: Women's Sexuality Today* (London: Paladin, 1984), p. 227.

14   Gallop, p. 7.

15   Sussman, pp. 10–11, 13, 20–1, 25.

16   Mary Ann Doane, *Femmes Fatales: Feminism, Film Theory, Psychoanalysis* (London and New York: Routledge, 1991), p. 2, summarizing and quoting from Christine Buci-Glucksmann, *La raison baroque de Baudelaire à Benjamin* (Paris: Édition Galilée, 1984), pp. 203–4.

17   This moment is persuasively analysed by Fredric Jameson as indicative of 'the impulse of Conrad's sentences to transform such [political and social] realities into impressions' (*PU*, 210).

18   'Ocean Travel', *LE*, p. 38.

19   John Fletcher, 'Forster's Self-Erasure: *Maurice* and the Scene of Masculine Love', in *Sexual Sameness: Textual Differences in Lesbian and Gay Writing*, ed.

Joseph Bristow (London and New York: Routledge, 1992), pp. 64–90 (pp. 68–70).

20 Cixous, 'Sorties', pp. 85–6.

21 Carole Pateman, quoted Showalter, *Sexual Anarchy*, p. 8; see Showalter, Chapter 1, 'Borderlines', pp. 1–18.

22 Showalter, *Sexual Anarchy*, p. 133–4.

23 Tim Armstrong, *Modernism, Technology, and the Body: A Cultural Study* (Cambridge: Cambridge University Press, 1998), p. 5.

24 Christine Battersby, 'Her Body/Her Boundaries: Gender and the Metaphysics of Containment', in *Journal of Philosophy and the Visual Arts: The Body*, ed. Andrew Benjamin (London: Academy Edition; Berlin: Ernst & Sohn, 1993), 31–9 (p. 34). Battersby is citing the work of Paul Smith and Michèle Montrelay.

25 Julia Kristeva, *Powers of Horror: An Essay on Abjection*, trans. Leon S. Roudiez (New York: Columbia University Press, 1982), pp. 1–2.

26 Kristeva, p. 3.

27 Kaja Silverman, *The Acoustic Mirror: The Female Voice in Psychoanalysis and Cinema* (Bloomington and Indianapolis: Indiana University Press, 1988), p. 81.

28 See Sandra M. Gilbert and Susan Gubar, *The Madwoman in the Attic: the Woman Writer and the Nineteenth-Century Literary Imagination* (New Haven, CT and London: Yale University Press, 1979), pp. 53–64; *In Dora's Case: Freud, Hysteria, Feminism*, eds Charles Bernheimer and Claire Kahane (London: Virago, 1985), especially the Introduction by Kahane, pp. 19–32; Elaine Showalter, *The Female Malady: Women, Madness and English Culture, 1830–1980* (1985; London: Virago, 1987), pp. 129–34, 147–62.

29 Banting, *passim*; Showalter, *The Female Malady*, pp. 133, 157; Kahane, in Bernheimer and Kahane, p. 31; Dianne Hunter, 'Hysteria, Psychoanalysis, and Feminism: The Case of Anna O.', *Feminist Studies*, 9 (1983), 465–88 (p. 484).

30 Banting, pp. 230–1.

31 Jonathan Dollimore, *Sexual Dissidence: Augustine to Wilde, Freud to Foucault* (Oxford: Clarendon Press, 1991), pp. 26–7.

32 Gallop, pp. 3–4.

33 Roland Barthes, *Roland Barthes par roland barthes* (Paris: Seuil, 1975), p. 121, quoted and trans. Gallop, p. 12.

34 Gallop, pp. 12–13.

35 F. R. Leavis, *The Great Tradition* (1948; Harmondsworth: Penguin, 1972), pp. 214–15.

36 Francis Mulhern, 'English Reading', in *Nation and Narration*, ed. Homi Bhabha (London and New York: Routledge, 1990), pp. 250–64 (pp. 255–6).

37 The reading of 'yellow-face' is found in the Dent's Collected and World's Classics Editions, but the Penguin edition alters it to 'yellow face'. *Typhoon and Other Stories*, ed. Paul Kirschner (London: Penguin, 1992), pp. 40, 100.

38 On the crowd as object of Orientalist and colonialist fear, see Douglas Kerr, 'Crowds, Colonialism and *Lord Jim*', *The Conradian*, 18.2 (Autumn 1994), 49–64.

39 Karl Marx, *Marx-Engels Selected Works* (London: Lawrence & Wishart, 1951), vol. 1, p. 267, quoted *PPT*, 125.

40 James Hansford, 'Money, Language and the Body in "Typhoon"', *Conradiana*, 26.2/26.3 (Autumn 1994), 135–55 (p. 136).
41 Kristeva, pp. 1–2.
42 Kristeva, p. 2.
43 Henry Mayhew, a writer, journalist and editor, was the author of the sociological study, *London Labour and the London Poor* (1861–2).
44 *A Simple Tale* is the subtitle of *The Secret Agent*.
45 The masculine pronoun is used here since this narrative voice seems to me clearly male, as evidenced, for example, by its comments on women.
46 Rebecca Stott, 'The Woman in Black: Race and Gender in *The Secret Agent*', in *CG*, 39–58 (p. 48).
47 Stott, in *CG*, 55–6.
48 Stott, in *CG*, 56, quoting Benita Parry, 'Problems in Current Theories of Colonial Discourse', *Oxford Literary Review*, 9 (1987), 27–58 (p. 54).
49 Compare Wilkie Collins, *The Moonstone*, Arthur Conan Doyle's Sherlock Holmes stories, Charles Dickens, *Bleak House*, *Our Mutual Friend*.
50 See note 8.
51 In an index there is a causal relationship between signifier and signified (Jonathan Culler gives the example of smoke signifying fire), whereas 'in the sign proper as Saussure understood it the relationship . . . is arbitrary or conventional': Jonathan Culler, *Structuralist Poetics: Structuralism, Linguistics and the Study of Literature* (London: Routledge & Kegan Paul, 1975), p. 16
52 Banting, p. 231.
53 Banting, p. 231.
54 Kristeva, pp. 2, 3, 3–4.
55 Katherine Judith Goodnow, *Kristeva in Focus: From Theory to Film Analysis*. PhD thesis, University of Bergen, 1994, pp. 5, 66.
56 Kristeva, pp. 1–2.

Chapter 4 Gender and the Disciplined Body

1 As Karen Klein notes (FP, 110), her anonymity is emphasized by the references to her as 'a pretty Morenita' (N, 127), although she refers to herself as 'your Paquita'.
2 Letter of 31 October 1904 to R. B. Cunninghame Graham, *CL*, III, 175.
3 *CL*, III, 175.
4 The phrase 'little lady' is used by the engineer-in-chief of the railway (42), but, as discussed below, the narrative voice at certain times shares this attitude.
5 An extradiegetic narrator carries out the primary or first-level act of narrating, while a heterodiegetic narrator is absent from the story that he or she tells, in contrast to a homodiegetic narrator such as Marlow, who recounts a story in which he himself took part. Genette, pp. 228–31, 245.
6 Mark Wollaeger sees the absence of a homodiegetic narrator such as Marlow or the teacher of languages (in *Under Western Eyes*) as allowing Conrad's scepticism a freer reign in these novels. See *FS*, Chapter 5.
7 Wollaeger argues that the questions about existence raised by philosophi-

cal scepticism are reflected in struggles for personal autonomy in *Nostromo* and *The Secret Agent*, 'played out as the revolt of characters against how others within the fiction attempt to define or control them and ... as the resistance of characters to the narrative design itself' (*FS*, 122). Albert Guerard notes the uncertain status of the narrator of *Nostromo*, and offers an interesting metafictional reading when he suggests that there is 'a marked discrepancy between what Decoud does and says and is, and what the narrator or omniscient author says about him' and that 'Conrad may be condemning Decoud for a withdrawal and skepticism more radical than Decoud ever shows; which are, in fact, Conrad's own': A. J. Guerard, *Conrad the Novelist* (Cambridge, MA: Harvard University Press, 1958), pp. 199–200. Jameson suggests that 'Conrad is here premodern in that he has not been able to discover the transpersonal standpoint of, say, Joycean narrative, or even that of Flaubert' (*PU*, 271).

8   Jeremy Hawthorn, *Joseph Conrad: Language and Fictional Self-Consciousness* (Lincoln: Nebraska University Press, 1979), p. 61.
9   Arnold Bennett, letter of 22 November 1912 to Conrad, in *Twenty Letters to Joseph Conrad*, ed. G. Jean-Aubry (London: The First Edition Club, 1926), quoted *FS*, 125.
10 See *PU*, 269–80; Hawthorn, *Joseph Conrad: Language and Fictional Self-Consciousness* p. 56; Reilly, pp. 133–71.
11 Foucault, *Discipline and Punish*, p. 137.
12 Foucault, *Discipline and Punish*, pp. 135–69.
13 Foucault, *The History of Sexuality: An Introduction*, p. 92.
14 Foucault, *The History of Sexuality: An Introduction*, pp. 94–5
15 Holroyd might seem the exception, but as Gould observes, the 'great silver and iron interests' will continue their progress even if Holroyd dies or has to give up (*N*, 82).
16 See *N*, 95. My argument is broadly in accord with Jameson's view that Conrad's work can be seen as the product of what Weber identifies as the 'crucial transitional stage' between traditional and rationalized forms of social institution (*PU*, 249).
17 Foucault, *Discipline and Punish*, p. 137.
18 Foucault, *Discipline and Punish*, p. 138.
19 Sandra Lee Bartky, 'Foucault, Femininity, and the Modernization of Patriarchal Power', in *Feminism and Foucault*, eds Irene Diamond and Lee Quinby (Boston: Northeastern University Press, 1988), pp. 61–86 (p. 79).
20 Foucault, *Power/Knowledge*, pp. 151–2.
21 Chronologically this would seem correct: Bongie states that the period of exploration was largely over by the 1880s; Ian Watt suggests 1890 as a plausible date for the main events of the novel: Ian Watt, *Joseph Conrad: Nostromo* (Cambridge: Cambridge University Press, 1988), chronology (no page number).
22 Foucault, *Discipline and Punish*, pp. 161, 30.
23 Foucault, *Discipline and Punish*, p. 138.
24 Buci-Glucksmann, pp. 203–4.
25 See Introduction, note 18.
26 Bartky, p. 64.
27 Bartky, pp. 75–6.

28   Hawthorn, *Joseph Conrad: Language and Fictional Self-Consciousness*, p. 71.
29   Heath, 'Male Feminism', p. 26.
30   Wollaeger suggests that 'the only author we can discuss with complete certainty' in the context of 'the coercive presence of the author *in the text*' is 'what Bakhtin has called the "secondary author", "the image of the author" created within the text by the "primary" or historical author' (*FS*, 130–1).
31   Silverman, *The Acoustic Mirror*, p. 49.
32   Silverman, *The Acoustic Mirror*, p. 48.
33   See Chapter 3 above, note 1.
34   Gallop, p. 7.
35   Gallop, p. 7.
36   Reilly, p. 143.
37   Guerard, pp. 199–202 (p. 200) and see note 7 above.
38   On this see Andrew Michael Roberts, 'Action, Passivity and Gender in Conrad's *Chance*', in *CG*, 89–104.
39   Letter to Marguerite Poradowska, 16 October 1891, *CL*, I, 97–9.

Chapter 5 Epistemology, Modernity and Masculinity

1   Watt, *Conrad in the Nineteenth Century*, pp. 357, 174.
2   J. Hillis Miller, *Poets of Reality: Six Twentieth-Century Writers* (London: Oxford University Press, 1966), p. 5.
3   Daphna Erdinast-Vulcan, *Joseph Conrad and the Modern Temper* (Oxford: Clarendon Press, 1991).
4   On the elements of scepticism and nihilism in Conrad's 'conscious philosophy' and their connection to 'the climate of thought in the late nineteenth century' see C. B. Cox, *Joseph Conrad: The Modern Imagination* (London: Dent, 1974), p. 8. On Conrad's scepticism concerning language see Hugh Epstein, 'Trusting in Words of Some Sort: Aspects of the Use of Language in *Nostromo*', *The Conradian*, 12.1 (May 1987), 17–31.
5   See, for example, Padmini Mongia, 'Empire, Narrative and the Feminine in *Lord Jim* and *Heart of Darkness*', in *Contexts for Conrad*, eds Keith Carabine, Owen Knowles and Wieslaw Krajka (East European Monographs; Boulder: University of Colorado Press, 1993), pp. 135–50, rpt. in *Under Postcolonial Eyes: Joseph Conrad After Empire*, eds Gail Fincham and Myrtle Hooper (Rondebosch: University of Cape Town Press, 1996), pp. 120–32. See also the chapters by Mongia and Roberts in *CG* and *Joseph Conrad: Contemporary Critical Essays*, ed. Elaine Jordan (London: Macmillan, 1996), Introduction, pp. 6–9.
6   For a survey of some of the critical views of Conrad's relationship to modernity, see *Joseph Conrad* (Longman Critical Reader), ed. Andrew Michael Roberts (London and New York: Longman, 1998), pp. 20–4.
7   Bonnie Kime Scott (ed.), *The Gender of Modernism: A Critical Anthology* (Bloomington and Indianapolis: Indiana University Press, 1990); Juliet Flower MacCannell, *The Regime of the Brother: After the Patriarchy* (London: Routledge, 1991), Chapter 1, 'The Primal Scene of Modernity' (pp. 9–30) and Chapter 2, 'Modernity as the Absence of the Other: the General Self'

(pp. 31–40); Alice A. Jardine, *Gynesis: Configurations of Woman and Modernity* (Ithaca NY: Cornell University Press 1985); Alison M. Jagger and Susan R. Bordo (eds), *Gender/Body/Knowledge: Feminist Reconstructions of Being and Knowing* (New Brunswick, NJ and London: Rutgers University Press, 1989); Gabriele Griffin, *Difference in View: Woman and Modernism* (Basingstoke: Taylor & Francis, 1994).

8 Janet Wolff, 'The Invisible *Flâneuse*: Women and the Literature of Modernity', in *The Problems of Modernity: Adorno and Benjamin*, ed. Andrew Benjamin (London: Routledge, 1989), pp. 141–56, 141, 146.

9 Griselda Pollock quotes Jules Michelet's *La Femme*: 'How many irritations for the single woman! She can hardly ever go out in the evening; she would be taken for a prostitute': *Oeuvres completes* (Vol. XVIII, 1858–60) (Paris: Flammarion, 1985), p. 413, quoted Griselda Pollock, *Vision and Difference: Femininity, Feminism and the Histories of Art* (London and New York: Routledge, 1988), p. 69.

10 John Rignall, 'Benjamin's *Flâneur* and the Problem of Realism', in *The Problems of Modernity*, pp. 112–21 (p. 112).

11 The *flâneur* is the stroller or idler whose home is the streets and arcades of the city and who 'goes botanizing on the asphalt': Walter Benjamin, *Charles Baudelaire: A Lyric Poet in the Era of High Capitalism*, trans. Jarry Zohn (London and New York: Verso, 1983), p. 36. On the association of the *flâneur* with the alienated individual and with victims, murderers and detectives, see pp. 40–6, 170.

12 Michel Foucault, 'The Order of Discourse', in *Untying the Text: A Post-Structuralist Reader*, ed. Robert Young (London: Routledge & Kegan Paul, 1981), pp. 48–78 (p. 56).

13 On the complementary nature of truths and errors within a discourse, see Foucault, 'The Order of Discourse', p. 60.

14 For example, Jacques Berthoud argues that Conrad is 'dramatizing the need for a metaphysics that can't exist': Jacques Berthoud, *Joseph Conrad: The Major Phase* (Cambridge: Cambridge University Press, 1978), p. 190. Edward Said puts it in more complex terms: 'Conrad's goal is to make us see, or otherwise transcend the absence of everything but words, so that we may pass into a realm of vision beyond the words ... For Conrad the meaning produced by writing was a kind of visual outline, which written language would approach only from the outside and from a distance that seemed to remain constant'; 'by using substance instead of words the Conradian hero, like Conrad himself, aims to vindicate and articulate his imagination. Every reader of Conrad knows how this aim too is bound to fail': Edward Said, *The World, The Text and the Critic* (1983; London: Faber, 1984), pp. 95, 110.

15 'The term implied author ... comes from Wayne C. Booth's *Rhetoric of Fiction* (1961) ... [It] is used to refer to that picture of a creating author behind a literary work that the reader builds up on the basis of an image put in the work ... by the author him or herself. The implied author may be very different from the real-life individual responsible for writing the work.' 'By extension the term "implied reader" was coined to describe the reader which the text (or the author through the text) suggests that it expects'; Jeremy Hawthorn, *A Glossary of Contemporary Literary Theory*, (3rd

edn (London: Edward Arnold, 1998), pp. 24, 284.

16 Jean-Jacques Rousseau, *The Confessions*, trans. J. M. Cohen (Harmondsworth: Penguin, 1953), p. 25.

17 Jim Reilly makes a comparable point when he argues that *Nostromo* offers a critique of 'conservative positions and capitalist/colonialist assumptions ... from *inside*', since both text and author are 'enmeshed within' those positions and assumptions: Reilly, p. 145.

18 It happens on several occasions in Conrad's fiction that the real name of a woman is obscure or never revealed, as in the cases of Lena in *Victory* (see Chapter 8) and Jewel in *Lord Jim*.

19 See, for example, Nadelhaft, p. 46.

20 But for an account which has affinities with my own, see Joanna M. Smith, '"Too Beautiful Altogether": Patriarchal Ideology in *Heart of Darkness*', in *Joseph Conrad, Heart of Darkness: A Case Study in Contemporary Literature*, ed. Ross C. Murfin (New York: St. Martin's Press; London: Macmillan, 1989), pp. 179–98.

21 This aspect of Marlow's attitude is even more evident in the manuscript and magazine versions of the novella, where the words quoted are preceded by 'that face on paper seemed to be a reflection of truth itself'. Norton Critical Edition of *Heart of Darkness*, ed. Robert Kimbrough, 2nd edn (New York and London: W. W. Norton, 1971), p. 74.

22 Rebecca Stott notes that ivory, the object of Kurtz's exploitation of Africa, appears in Brussels only in the keys of the Intended's grand piano, so that 'just as the source of the ivory in the white woman's drawing-room is the darkness of the African wilderness, the source of the white woman herself is the savage mistress, correlated in the final pages through the motif of the outstretched arms of both women': Rebecca Stott, *The Fabrication of the Late Victorian Femme Fatale: The Kiss of Death* (London: Macmillan, 1992), pp. 150–1.

23 *Billy Budd* was not published until 1924, so any links are not a matter of influence but of comparable social and discursive contexts.

24 Sedgwick suggests that 'What *was* new from the turn of the century was the world-mapping by which every given person, just as he or she was necessarily assignable to a male or a female gender, was now considered necessarily assignable to a homo- or a heterosexuality, a binarized identity that was full of implications, however confusing, for even the ostensibly least sexual aspects of personal existence. It was this new development that left no space in the culture exempt from the potent incoherences of homo/heterosexual definition' (*EC*, 2).

25 C. B. Cox argues that 'Kurtz in *Heart of Darkness* ... in certain ways reflects the unconscious urges of Marlow's soul' (Cox, p. 7). See also David Thorburn, *Conrad's Romanticism* (New Haven, CT: Yale University Press, 1974), p. 143.

26 Sedgwick argues that 'Irigaray's writing about the "hom(m)osexual" is the locus classicus of this trajectory ... according to which authoritarian regimes or homophobic masculinist culture may be damned on the grounds of being *even more homosexual* than gay male culture', a trajectory which, Sedgwick claims, leads to 'terrible commonplaces about fascism' (*EC*, 154). Without attempting to arbitrate this point, let me say that the

view I am deriving from Irigaray is emphatically not that homosexuality is complicit with patriarchy and empire, but that a homophobic discourse is complicit with these structures – a homophobic discourse which prescribes a notional absolute barrier between male homosocial bonds and male homosexual bonds, leading men to use women in order to conduct certain relations with other men while assuring themselves and each other than these are not homosexual relations. This would presumably apply less to men the more they regarded themselves as being overtly homosexual. The terms of the argument must be subject to the contentions of what Sedgwick terms universalizing and minoritizing definitions of homosexuality (*EC*, 1).

Chapter 6 Masculinity, 'Woman' and Truth

1 Jacques Derrida, *Spurs: Nietzsche's Styles/Éperons: Les Styles de Nietzsche*, parallel text with English translation by Barbara Harlow (Chicago and London: University of Chicago Press, 1978), p. 55.
2 The Cambridge edition of the novel has a comma after 'still', stressing immobility rather than persistence. Joseph Conrad, *The Secret Agent: A Simple Tale*, eds Bruce Harkness and S. W. Reid (Cambridge: Cambridge University Press, 1990), p. 193.
3 Stott notes that when Ossipon meets Winnie after the murder 'the prose is not simply describing the effects of a murderess upon the man who confronts her – it is also itself stimulating that effect. It builds up clichés, disrupts syntax, overloads the passage through repetition to the point of rupture' (Stott, *The Fabrication of the Late Victorian Femme Fatale*, p. 154).
4 Terence Cave, *Recognitions: A Study in Poetics* (Oxford: Clarendon Press, 1988), p. 472.
5 Cave, p. 472. Here, as elsewhere, my use of narrative terms is based on Genette's scheme in *Narrative Discourse*.
6 Cave, p. 469.
7 Cave, p. 473.
8 Cave, p. 473.
9 Cave, pp. 471–2.
10 Cave, p. 473.
11 Eve Kosofsky Sedgwick, 'A Poem is Being Written', *Representations*, 17 (Winter 1987), 110–43 (pp. 129–30).
12 For a critique of Girard's assumption of gender symmetry in the erotic triangle, see *BM*, 22.
13 See, for example, the description of the African men in a canoe (HOD, 61) and Marlow's reflections on the noises made by Africans on the river bank (96–7)
14 See 'Author's Note', *UWE*, x.
15 Ruppel, p. 32.
16 See Freud's discussion of automaton and gaze in E. T. A. Hoffmann's 'The Sand-Man', in 'The Uncanny', in *The Standard Edition of the Complete Psychological Works of Sigmund Freud*, XVII, pp. 217–56.
17 Letter of *c.* 7 April 1913 to J.B. Pinker, *CL*, V, 208.

18 Martin Ray notes that *Chance* sold 13 000 copies in the first two years, three times as many as *Under Western Eyes* in the corresponding period. Martin Ray, Introduction to *Chance* (Oxford: Oxford University Press, 1988), pp. vii–xix (p. vi).

19 On the question of the novel's putative appeal to women readers, see Laurence Davies, 'Conrad, *Chance* and Women Readers', in *CG*, 75–88.

20 Ray, p. x.

21 Roberts, 'Secret Agents and Secret Objects'.

22 This is a notable reversal of the attitude of the Marlow of 'Heart of Darkness', who notoriously claims that women's lack of involvement in worldly action renders them 'out of touch with truth' (59).

23 On the distinction between story time (the time in which events occur) and narrative time (the time of their telling), see Genette, p. 35.

24 This process clearly extends into the critical debate about feminist and gender issues in Conrad's work, in so far as male critics participate in this. Scott McCracken commented, as he and I were exchanging drafts and ideas on the subject, that 'all this traffic between us must surely amount to a textual configuration in itself: men writing to men about Conrad and women.' Thus Conrad's narrative strategy takes on a form of life outside his text, continuing to demand self-questioning by men.

25 Daphna Erdinast-Vulcan, 'Textuality and Surrogacy in Conrad's *Chance*', *L'Époque Conradienne* (1989), 51–65 (pp. 64, 54–5).

Chapter 7 Vision, Power and Homosocial Exchange

1 Critics who deal with aspects of the visual in Conrad's work include: David Simpson, *Fetishism & Imagination: Dickens, Melville, Conrad* (Baltimore, MD and London: Johns Hopkins University Press, 1982), p. 102ff.; Moser, pp. 111–30; Leo Gurko, *Joseph Conrad: Giant in Exile* (New York: Macmillan, 1962), pp. 197–223. Gurko makes the misogynist assumption, derived from Moser, that women who show determination are thereby exhibiting 'sexual aggressiveness' (Gurko, p. 202).

2 On Conrad's use of the romance genre, see Hampson, *Joseph Conrad; Betrayal and Identity*, p. 25 and Erdinast-Vulcan, *Joseph Conrad and the Modern Temper*, pp. 186–95, 197–200.

3 See Evelyn Fox Keller and Christine R. Grontkowski, 'The Mind's Eye', in *Discovering Reality: Feminist Perspectives on Epistemology, Metaphysics, Methodology, and Philosophy of Science*, eds Sandra Harding and Merril B. Hintikka (Dordrecht, Boston and London: D. Reidel, 1983), pp. 207–24.

4 Edward Said, *The World, the Text and the Critic*, pp. 93–4.

5 Watt, *Conrad in the Nineteenth Century*, p. 79.

6 Koestenbaum, p. 169.

7 Derrida argues that the white/black, light/dark oppositions are fundamental to Western metaphysics. See Jacques Derrida, 'The White Mythology: Metaphor in the Text of Philosophy', *Margins of Philosophy*, trans. Alan Bass (Brighton: Harvester, 1982), pp. 207–71.

8 Martin Jay, *Downcast Eyes: The Denigration of Vision in Twentieth-Century French Thought* (Berkeley, CA: University of California Press, 1993), p. 526.

9 Sigmund Freud, 'The Question of Lay Analysis', in *The Standard Edition of the Complete Psychological Works of Sigmund Freud*, XX, pp. 177–258 (p. 212). See Irigaray, *TS*, p. 48.

10 Watt, *Conrad in the Nineteenth Century*, pp. 169–80.

11 Watt, *Conrad in the Nineteenth Century*, p. 174.

12 Rosemary Betterton, 'Introduction: Feminism, Femininity and Representation', in *Looking On: Images of Femininity in the Visual Arts and Media*, ed. Rosemary Betterton (London and New York: Pandora Press, 1987), p. 11.

13 On the 'law of the self-same' in the work of Freud, see Irigaray, *S*, 32–4.

14 Toril Moi, *Sexual/Textual Politics: Feminist Literary Theory* (London and New York: Methuen, 1985), p. 180.

15 Luce Irigaray, 1978 interview in *Les femmes, la pornographie et l'érotisme*, eds M.- F. Hans and G. Lapouge (Paris), p. 50, quoted Griselda Pollock, *Vision and Difference*, p. 50.

16 Laura Mulvey, 'Visual Pleasure and Narrative Cinema', *Screen*, 16.4 (Winter 1975–76), 119–30, rpt. in *The Sexual Subject: A Screen Reader in Sexuality*, ed. Screen (London and New York: Routledge, 1992), pp. 22–34 (p. 27).

17 Mulvey, p. 26.

18 Mulvey, p. 29.

19 See de Lauretis; Edward Buscombe, Christine Gledhill, Alan Lovell and Christopher Williams, 'Psychoanalysis and Film', *The Sexual Subject*, pp. 35–46; Steve Neale, 'Masculinity As Spectacle', *Screen Reader*, pp. 277–87; Laura Marcus, 'Taking a Good Look' (review of Laura Mulvey, *Visual and Other Pleasures*), *New Formations*, 15 (Winter, 1991), 101–10. Marcus describes a number of critiques of Mulvey's articles, notably those in *The Female Gaze: Women as Viewers of Popular Culture*, eds Lorraine Gamman and Margaret Marshment (London: Women's Press, 1988).

20 Jacques Lacan, *The Four Fundamental Concepts of Psychoanalysis*, trans. Alan Sheridan (1977; London: Penguin, 1979), p. 106, quoted *MS*, 128.

21 See Whitford, 31–2, 104.

22 De Lauretis, pp. 23, 35.

23 Foucault, *Discipline and Punish*, p. 187.

24 Martin Jay, 'In the Empire of the Gaze: Foucault and the Denigration of Vision in Twentieth-century French Thought', in *Foucault: A Critical Reader*, ed. David Couzens Hoy (Oxford: Blackwell, 1986), pp. 175–204 (pp. 176, 195, 181, 195).

25 Jay, *Downcast Eyes*, p. 364.

26 On the Romantic element in Conrad's 'Preface' see Watt, *Conrad in the Nineteenth Century*, p. 78. On the constitution of Romantic conceptions of the artist in terms of 'male social roles and male power' see Christine Battersby, *Gender and Genius: Towards a Feminist Aesthetics* (London: Women's Press, 1989), pp. 13, 75–6, 103–4.

27 Keller and Grontkowski, p. 209.

28 William Faulkner, *Mosquitoes* (London: Chatto & Windus, 1964), p. 27. ·

29 De Lauretis defines 'woman' as 'a fictional construct, a distillate from diverse but congruent discourses dominant in Western cultures', whereas she defines 'women' as 'the real historical beings who cannot as yet be defined outside of those discursive formations' (de Lauretis, p. 5).

30 ﹒Hampson, *Betrayal and Identity*, p. 252.
31 Geddes, pp. 124, 127.
32 'Monsieur George, the young, arduous, and honest protagonist, is opposed by Captain Blunt, the "black knight" ... The other villain, Ortega, and Rita's sister, Thérèse, assume the roles of the "evil magician and the witch ... who seem to have a suggestion of erotic perversion about them" ... These two sinister figures are opposed by Dominic and Rose who are neatly fitted into the "moral antithesis" underlying the characterization in the romance' (Erdinast-Vulcan, *Joseph Conrad and the Modern Temper*, p. 187). The quotations in Erdinast-Vulcan's text are from Northop Frye, *Anatomy of Criticism* (Princeton, NJ: Princeton University Press, 1957), p. 196.
33 Robert Hampson notes that Ortega presents M. George 'with a distorted reflection of himself', but also helps him to 're-define himself', confident of his own sanity in contrast to Ortega's madness (Hampson, *Betrayal and Identity*, pp. 265–6).
34 Geddes, p. 134.
35 Conrad, letter of 1 August 1919 to Sidney Colvin, in G. Jean-Aubry, *Joseph Conrad: Life and Letters*, 2 vols (London: Heinemann, 1927), II, p. 224, quoted Geddes, p. 137.
36 Pamela Bickley and Robert Hampson, '"Lips That Have Been Kissed": Boccaccio, Verdi, Rossetti and *The Arrow of Gold*', *L'Époque Conradienne*, 1988, pp. 77–91 (p. 91).
37 Hampson, *Betrayal and Identity*, p. 251.
38 Hampson, *Betrayal and Identity*, pp. 266, 255, 257.
39 Hampson, *Betrayal and Identity*, p. 267, quoting Paul L. Wiley, *Conrad's Measure of Man* (Madison: University of Wisconsin Press, 1954), p. 166. For feminist readings of hysteria, see Chapter 3, notes 28 and 29 above.
40 Hampson, *Betrayal and Identity*, p. 257.
41 Robert Hampson, 'The Late Novels', in *The Cambridge Companion to Joseph Conrad*, ed. J. H. Stape (Cambridge: Cambridge University Press, 1996), pp. 140–59 (p. 150).

Chapter 8 Vision and the Economies of Empire and Masculinity

1 Elizabeth Bronfen, *Over Her Dead Body: Death, Femininity and the Body* (Manchester: Manchester University Press, 1992), p. 3.
2 Jeffrey Meyers describes the knife as 'an obvious symbol of his [Ricardo's] penis' (which is rather different from reading the knife as phallus, that is as a symbol of masculine power). This somewhat literal approach colours his whole reading of the episode, discussed below. Meyers, p. 86.
3 Robert Hampson notes that in *The Rover* the relationship of Arlette and Real is 'charted ocularly' ('The Late Novels', p. 153).
4 De Lauretis, pp. 68, 195.
5 Conrad makes extended ironic use of Edenic associations in *Victory*, as he does also in *Nostromo*.
6 Susan Gubar mistakenly writes that 'Heyst saves a girl called Lena (after the seductress Magdalena) from "murdering silence" in an all-female orchestra

by renaming her Alma (soul)'; in fact she is already known as Alma or Magdalen before Heyst meets her, while he renames her Lena. However, it is the similarity and associations of the names that are significant, along with Gubar's point that Lena is converted from being a performer to someone, in Heyst's eyes, who is 'like a script in an unknown language' (*V*, 222). Susan Gubar, '"The Blank Page" and the Issues of Female Creativity', in ed. Elaine Showalter, *The New Feminist Criticism: Essays of Women, Literature and Theory* (London: Virago, 1986), pp. 292–313 (p. 294).

7 'She was not so much unreadable as blank; and I did not know whether to admire her for it or dismiss her from my thoughts as a passive butt of ferocious misfortune' (*C*, 207)

8 Gubar, pp. 293–4.

9 Gubar, p. 294. The quotations are from *Victory*, p. 222. The phrase 'was unable to decipher' should read 'is unable to decipher'.

10 Mary Ann Doane, 'Film and the Masquerade: Theorizing the Female Spectator', in *The Sexual Subject*, pp. 227–43 (pp. 237–8).

11 Doane, p. 237, quoting Claire Johnston, 'Femininity and the Masquerade: Anne of the Indies', in *Jacques Tourneur*, eds Claire Johnston and Paul Willemen (Edinburgh: Edinburgh Film Festival, 1975), pp. 36–44 (p. 40).

12 Virginia Woolf makes a similar point, writing that 'women have served all these centuries as looking-glasses possessing the magic and delicious power of reflecting the figure of man at twice its natural size.' *A Room of One's Own* (London: Hogarth Press, 1929), p. 53.

13 See especially 'Women on the Market' and 'Commodities Among Themselves', *TS*, 170–91, 192–7.

14 'You mustn't look in my novel for the old stable ego of the character. There is another ego, according to whose action the individual is unrecognisable, and passes through, as it were, allotropic states which it needs a deeper sense than any we've been used to exercise, to discover are states of the same single radically unchanged element. (Like as diamond and coal are the same pure single element of carbon ...).' D .H. Lawrence, letter to Edward Garnett, 5 June 1914, in *D. H. Lawrence: Selected Literary Criticism*, ed. Anthony Beal (1956; London: Mercury Books, 1961), p. 18.

15 Koestenbaum, p. 169.

16 According to the OED, the earliest recorded use of 'queer' (as an adjective) meaning homosexual is 1922, in a United States government publication, while a 1937 article in the *Listener* magazine alludes to it as 'a word imported from America'. W. H. Auden is cited as using 'queer' as a noun, meaning a male homosexual, in 1932.

17 On the *flâneur*, see Chapter 5.

18 Robert Secor, *The Rhetoric of Shifting Perspectives in Conrad's 'Victory'* (University Park: Pennsylvania State University Press, 1971), p. 5.

19 The tendency of much of the philosophical tradition to negate the feminine is considered in Michèle Le Doeuff, *Hipparchia's Choice: An Essay Concerning Women, Philosophy, Etc*, trans. Trista Selous (Oxford and Cambridge, MA: Blackwell, 1991).

20 Jacqueline Rose, *Sexuality in the Field of Vision* (London: Verso, 1986), p. 227.

21 For other references to eyes and looking see pp. 93, 101, 103, 119, 130.

22 R. W. B. Lewis, 'The Current of Conrad's *Victory*', in *Joseph Conrad*, ed. Harold Bloom (New York and Philadelphia: Chelsea House, 1986), pp. 63–81 (p. 78).
23 Meyers, pp. 78, 83–4.
24 Meyers, p. 83.
25 Meyers, p. 85.
26 Lewis, pp. 63, 64.
27 Lewis, pp. 80, 81.
28 Lewis, p. 71.
29 For example, Cedric Watts considers Conrad in terms of the author's own phrase 'homo duplex': *Joseph Conrad* (Writers and Their Work) (Plymouth: Northcote House, 1994), p. 1; see also Watts, *The Deceptive Text: An Introduction to Covert Plots* (Brighton: Harvester Press, 1984), pp. 13–14, 21–4, on 'Heart of Darkness' as a 'Janiform' text (i.e. paradoxical or self-divided) and Kurtz as a divided character. Jacques Berthoud interprets Conrad's novels as making the tragic point that 'man seems capable of discovering the reality of his own values only through their defeat or contradiction': Berthoud, p. 189. See also Kenneth Graham, 'Conrad and Modernism', in *The Cambridge Companion to Joseph Conrad*, pp. 203–22 (pp. 215–19).
30 Stephen Heath, 'Difference', *Screen*, 19.3 (Autumn 1978), 51–112; rpt. in *The Sexual Subject*, pp. 47–106 (pp. 49–50, 60).
31 Heath, 'Difference', p. 50. De Lauretis quotes Lacan as follows: 'the interdiction against autoerotism bearing on *a particular organ*, which for that reason *acquires the value of an ultimate (or first) symbol of lack (manque)*, has the impact of pivotal experience', and comments that 'desire and signification are defined ultimately as a process inscribed in the male body, since they are dependent on the initial – and *pivotal* – experiencing of one's penis' (de Lauretis, p. 23).
32 Here using 'woman' in de Lauretis's sense (see Chapter 7, note 29 above).
33 Whitford, p. 19.
34 Whitford, p. 22.
35 On the first of these see the treatment of Don Juste and the Sulaco parliamentarians in *Nostromo*, 'putting all their trust into words of some sort, while murder and rapine stalked over the land' (N, 367–8), and of the supposed Russian love of words in *Under Western Eyes* and *The Secret Agent*. On Conrad's scepticism about, and commitment to, language, see Epstein, *passim* and Said, *The World, the Text and the Critic*, pp. 90–110. For Conrad's view of utopian visions, see the portrayal of the utopian hopes of the revolutionaries in *Under Western Eyes* and *The Secret Agent*.
36 See Mrs Gould's reflection: 'There was something inherent in the necessities of successful action which carried with it the moral degradation of the idea' (N, 521).

Bibliography

Works of Conrad

The Uniform Edition of the Works of Joseph Conrad (London: J. M. Dent & Sons, 1923–8).

The Collected Letters of Joseph Conrad, eds Fredrick R. Karl and Laurence Davies, 5 vols (Cambridge: Cambridge University Press, 1983–96).

Almayer's Folly: The Story of an Eastern River, eds Floyd Eugene Eddleman and David Leon Higdon, with an Introduction by Ian Watt (Cambridge: Cambridge University Press, 1994).

Heart of Darkness (Norton Critical Edition), ed. Robert Kimbrough, 2nd edn (New York and London: W. W. Norton, 1971).

An Outcast of the Islands, eds J. H. Stape and Hans van Marle (Oxford: Oxford University Press, 1992).

The Secret Agent: A Simple Tale, eds Bruce Harkness and S. W. Reid (Cambridge: Cambridge University Press, 1990).

Typhoon and Other Stories, ed. Paul Kirschner (London: Penguin, 1992).

Other works

Achebe, Chinua. 'An Image of Africa: Racism in Conrad's *Heart of Darkness*', In *Hopes and Impediments: Selected Essays 1965–1987* (London: Heinemann, 1988), pp. 1–13.

Althusser, Louis. *Lenin and Philosophy and Other Essays*, trans. Ben Brewster (London: New Left Books, 1971).

Appiah, Kwame Anthony. 'Race', in *Critical Terms for Literary Study*, eds Frank Lentricchia and Thomas McLaughlin (Chicago and London: University of Chicago Press, 1990), pp. 274–87.

Armstrong, Tim. *Modernism, Technology, and the Body: A Cultural Study* (Cambridge: Cambridge University Press, 1998).

Banting, Pamela. 'The Body as Pictogram: Rethinking Hélène Cixous's écriture féminine', *Textual Practice*, 6.2 (Summer 1992), 225–46.

Barthes, Roland. *Roland Barthes par roland barthes*, (Paris: Seuil, 1975).

Bartky, Sandra Lee. 'Foucault, Femininity, and the Modernization of Patriarchal Power', in *Feminism and Foucault*, eds Irene Diamond and Lee Quinby (Boston: Northeastern University Press, 1988), pp. 61–86.

Battersby, Christine. *Gender and Genius: Towards a Feminist Aesthetics* (London: Women's Press, 1989).

—— 'Her Body/Her Boundary: Gender and the Metaphysics of Containment', in *Journal of Philosophy and the Visual Arts: The Body*, ed. Andrew Benjamin (London: Academy Edition; Berlin: Ernst & Sohn, 1993), pp. 31–9.

Bennett, Andrew and Nicholas Royle. *An Introduction to Literature, Criticism and Theory: Key Critical Concepts* (Hemel Hempstead: Prentice Hall/Harvester

Wheatsheaf, 1995).

Bernheimer, Charles and Claire Kahane (eds). *In Dora's Case: Freud, Hysteria, Feminism* (London: Virago, 1985).

Betterton,   Rosemary.   'Introduction: Feminism,   Femininity   and Representation', in *Looking On: Images of Femininity in the Visual Arts and Media*, ed. Rosemary Betterton (London and New York: Pandora Press, 1987).

Bhabha, Homi. 'The Other Question', in *Contemporary Postcolonial Theory: A Reader*, ed. Padmini Mongia (London: Edward Arnold, 1996), pp. 37–54; reprinted from *Screen*, 24.6 (1983), 18–36.

—— *The Location of Culture* (London and New York: Routledge, 1994).

Bickley, Pamela and Robert Hampson. '"Lips That Have Been Kissed": Boccaccio, Verdi, Rossetti and *The Arrow of Gold*', *L'Époque Conradienne* (1988), pp. 77–91.

Bivona, Daniel. *Desire and Contradiction: Imperial Visions and Domestic Debates in Victorian Literature* (Manchester: Manchester University Press, 1990).

Bongie, Chris. *Exotic Memories: Literature, Colonialism and the Fin de Siècle* (Stanford, CA: Stanford University Press, 1991).

Bonney, William. 'Politics, Perception, and Gender in Conrad's *Lord Jim* and Greene's *The Quiet American*', *Conradiana*, 23.2 (Summer 1991), 99–122.

Braidotti, Rosi. *Patterns of Dissonance: A Study of Women in Contemporary Philosophy*, trans. Elizabeth Guild (Cambridge: Polity Press, 1991).

Bristow, Joseph. *Empire Boys* (London: HarperCollins, 1991).

Brodie, Susan Lundvall. 'Conrad's Feminine Perspective', *Conradiana*, 16 (1984), 141–54.

Bronfen, Elizabeth. *Over Her Dead Body: Death, Femininity and the Body* (Manchester: Manchester University Press, 1992).

Buci-Glucksmann, Christine. *La raison baroque de Baudelaire à Benjamin* (Paris: Édition Galilée, 1984).

Buscombe, Edward, Christine Gledhill, Alan Lovell and Christopher Williams. 'Psychoanalysis and Film', in *The Sexual Subject*, ed. Screen, pp. 35–46.

Cave, Terence. *Recognitions: A Study in Poetics* (Oxford: Clarendon Press, 1988).

Cixous, Hélène. 'The Laugh of the Medusa', trans. Keith Cohen and Paula Cohen, in *New French Feminisms*, eds Elaine Marks and Isabelle de Courtivron (Hemel Hempstead: Harvester Wheatsheaf, 1981).

—— 'Sorties: Out and Out: Attacks/Ways Out/Forays', in Hélène Cixous and Catherine Clément, *The Newly Born Woman*, trans. Betsy Wing (Manchester: Manchester University Press, 1986), pp. 63–132.

Connell, R. W. *Masculinities* (Cambridge: Polity Press, 1995).

Coward, Rosalind. *Female Desire: Women's Sexuality Today* (London: Paladin, 1984).

Cox, C. B. *Joseph Conrad: The Modern Imagination* (London: J. M. Dent & Sons, 1974).

Culler, Jonathan. *Structuralist Poetics: Structuralism, Linguistics and the Study of Literature* (London: Routledge & Kegan Paul, 1975).

Davies, Laurence. 'Conrad, Chance and Women Readers', in *Conrad and Gender*, ed. Roberts, pp. 75–88.

de Lauretis, Teresa. *Alice Doesn't: Feminism, Semiotics, Cinema* (London: Macmillan, 1984).

Derrida, Jacques. *Spurs: Nietzsche's Styles/Éperons: Les Styles de Nietzsche*, parallel

text with English translation by Barbara Harlow (Chicago and London: University of Chicago Press, 1978).
—— *Margins of Philosophy*, trans. Alan Bass (Brighton: Harvester, 1982).
Doane, Mary Ann. *Femmes Fatales: Feminism, Film Theory, Psychoanalysis* (London and New York: Routledge, 1991).
—— 'Film and the Masquerade: Theorizing the Female Spectator', in *The Sexual Subject*, ed. Screen, pp. 227–43.
Dollimore, Jonathan. 'Homophobia and Sexual Difference', *Oxford Literary Review* (special issue on *Sexual Difference*, ed. Robert Young), 8.1–8.2 (1986), 5–12.
—— *Sexual Dissidence: Augustine to Wilde, Freud to Foucault* (Oxford: Clarendon Press, 1991).
Dyer, Richard. 'Don't Look Now: The Male Pin-Up', in *The Sexual Subject*, ed. Screen, pp. 265–76
Eagleton, Terry. *Criticism and Ideology: A Study in Marxist Literary Theory* (London: Verso, 1976).
—— *Ideology: An Introduction* (London: Verso, 1991).
Elbert, Monika. 'The "Dialectic of Desire" in *'Twixt Land and Sea'*, in *Conrad and Gender*, ed. Roberts, pp. 123–46.
Epstein, Hugh. 'Trusting in Words of Some Sort: Aspects of the Use of Language in *Nostromo'*, *The Conradian*, 12.1 (May 1987), 17–31.
Erdinast-Vulcan, Daphna. 'Textuality and Surrogacy in Conrad's *Chance'*, *L'Époque Conradienne* (1989), 51–65.
—— *Joseph Conrad and the Modern Temper* (Oxford: Clarendon Press, 1991).
Faulkner, William. *Mosquitoes* (London: Chatto & Windus, 1964).
Featherstone, Mike, Mike Hepworth and Bryan S. Turner (eds). *The Body: Social Process and Cultural Theory* (London, Thousand Oaks, CA and New Delhi: Sage Publications, 1991).
Fletcher, John. 'Forster's Self-Erasure: *Maurice* and the Scene of Masculine Love', in *Sexual Sameness: Textual Differences in Lesbian and Gay Writing*, ed. Joseph Bristow (London and New York: Routledge, 1992), pp. 64–90.
Ford, Ford Madox. *Ford Madox Brown: A Record of his Life and Work* (London: Longmans, 1896).
—— (as Ford Madox Hueffer). *Ancient Lights and Certain New Reflections: Being the Memories of a Young Man* (London: Chapman & Hall, 1911).
Foucault, Michel. *Discipline and Punish: The Birth of the Prison*, trans. Alan Sheridan (Harmondsworth: Penguin, 1977).
—— *Power/Knowledge: Selected Interviews and Other Writings, 1972–1977*, ed. Colin Gordon, trans. Colin Gordon, Leo Marshall, John Mepham and Kate Soper (Brighton: Harvester Wheatsheaf, 1980).
—— 'The Order of Discourse', in *Untying the Text: A Post-Structuralist Reader*, ed. Robert Young (London: Routledge & Kegan Paul, 1981), pp. 48–78.
—— *The History of Sexuality: An Introduction*, trans. Robert Hurley (1978; Harmondsworth: Penguin, 1981).
Freud, Sigmund. 'The Uncanny', in *The Standard Edition of the Complete Psychological Works of Sigmund Freud*, trans. under the general editorship of James Strachey in collaboration with Anna Freud, assisted by Alix Strachey and Alan Tyson, 24 vols (London: Hogarth Press, 1953–74), vol. XVII, pp. 217–56.

—— *The Ego and the Id*, in *The Standard Edition of the Complete Psychological Works of Sigmund Freud*, vol. XIX, pp. 3–66.

—— 'The Question of Lay Analysis', in *The Standard Edition of the Complete Psychological Works of Sigmund Freud*, vol. XX, pp. 177–258.

Fussell, Paul. *The Great War and Modern Memory* (London: Oxford University Press, 1975).

Gallop, Jane. *Thinking Through the Body* (New York: Columbia University Press, 1988).

Gamman, Lorraine and Margaret Marshment (eds). *The Female Gaze: Women as Viewers of Popular Culture* (London: Women's Press, 1988).

Garnett, Edward (ed.). *Letters from Conrad 1895 to 1924* (London: Nonesuch, 1928).

Geddes, Gary. *Conrad's Later Novels* (Montreal: McGill-Queen's University Press, 1980).

Genette, Gérard. *Narrative Discourse*, trans. Jane E. Lewin (1980; Oxford: Blackwell, 1986).

Gilbert, Sandra M. and Susan Gubar. *The Madwoman in the Attic: the Woman Writer and the Nineteenth-Century Literary Imagination* (New Haven, CT and London: Yale University Press, 1979).

Gilman, Sander L. 'Black Bodies, White Bodies: Toward an Iconography of Female Sexuality in Late Nineteenth-Century Art, Medicine, and Literature', in *'Race', Writing and Difference*, ed. Henry Louis Gates, Jr (Chicago and London: University of Chicago Press, 1985), pp. 223–61.

Gilroy, Paul. 'White Man's Bonus' (review of Richard Dyer, *White*), *Times Literary Supplement*, 29 August 1997, p. 10.

Girard, René. *Deceit, Desire and the Novel: Self and Other in Literary Structure*, trans. Yvonne Freccero (Baltimore, MD and London: Johns Hopkins University Press, 1965).

Goodnow, Katherine Judith. *Kristeva in Focus: From Theory to Film Analysis* (PhD thesis, University of Bergen, 1994).

Graham, Kenneth. 'Conrad and Modernism', in *The Cambridge Companion to Joseph Conrad*, ed. J. H. Stape, pp. 203–22.

Griffin, Gabriele. *Difference in View: Woman and Modernism* (Basingstoke: Taylor & Francis, 1994).

Gubar, Susan. '"The Blank Page" and the Issues of Female Creativity', in *The New Feminist Criticism: Essays on Women, Literature and Theory*, ed. Elaine Showalter (London: Virago, 1986), pp. 292–313.

Guerard, A. J. *Conrad the Novelist* (Cambridge, MA: Harvard University Press, 1958).

Gurko, Leo. *Joseph Conrad: Giant in Exile* (New York: Macmillan, 1962).

Haggard, H. Rider. *King Solomon's Mines* (1885; London: Cassell, 1893).

—— *Allan Quartermain* (1887; London: George Harrap, 1931).

Hampson, Robert. *Joseph Conrad: Betrayal and Identity* (London: Macmillan, 1992).

—— '*Chance* and the Secret Life: Conrad, Thackeray, Stevenson', in *Conrad and Gender*, ed. Roberts, pp. 105–22.

—— 'The Late Novels', in *The Cambridge Companion to Joseph Conrad*, ed. J.H. Stape, pp. 140–59.

Hansford, James. 'Money, Language and the Body in "Typhoon"', *Conradiana*,

26.2/26.3 (Autumn 1994), 135–55.

Harpham, Geoffrey Galt. *One of Us: The Mastery of Joseph Conrad* (Chicago and London: University of Chicago Press, 1996).

Hartmann, Heidi. 'The Unhappy Marriage of Marxism and Feminism: Towards a More Progressive Union', in *Women and Revolution: A Discussion of the Unhappy Marriage of Marxism and Feminism*, ed. Lydia Sargent (Boston: South End Press, 1981), pp. 1–41.

Hawthorn, Jeremy. *Joseph Conrad: Language and Fictional Self-Consciousness*, (Lincoln: Nebraska University Press, 1979).

—— *Joseph Conrad: Narrative Technique and Ideological Commitment* (London: Edward Arnold, 1990).

—— *A Glossary of Contemporary Literary Theory*, 3rd edn (London: Arnold, 1998).

Heath, Stephen. 'Difference', *Screen*, 19.3 (Autumn 1978), 51–112; rpt. in *The Sexual Subject*, ed. Screen, pp. 47–106.

—— 'Male Feminism', in *Men in Feminism*, eds Alice Jardine and Paul Smith (1987; New York and London: Routledge, 1989), pp. 1–32.

Hodges, Robert R. 'Deep Fellowship: Homosexuality and Male Bonding in the Life and Fiction of Joseph Conrad', *Journal of Homosexuality*, 4 (Summer 1979), 379–93.

Humm, Maggie. *The Dictionary of Feminist Theory* (Hemel Hempstead: Harvester Wheatsheaf, 1989).

Hunter, Dianne. 'Hysteria, Psychoanalysis, and Feminism: The Case of Anna O.', *Feminist Studies*, 9 (1983), 465–88.

Hyam, Ronald. *Britain's Imperial Century 1815–1914: A Study of Empire and Expansion* (London: Batsford, 1976).

—— 'Empire and Sexual Opportunity', *Journal of Imperial and Commonwealth History*, 14.2 (1986), 34–89.

Irigaray, Luce, *This Sex Which is Not One*, trans. Catherine Porter (Ithaca, NY: Cornell University Press, 1985).

—— *Speculum of the Other Woman*, trans. Gillian C. Gill (Ithaca, NY: Cornell University Press, 1985).

Jagger, Alison M. and Susan R. Bordo (eds). *Gender/Body/Knowledge: Feminist Reconstructions of Being and Knowing* (New Brunswick, NJ and London: Rutgers University Press, 1989).

Jameson, Fredric. *The Political Unconscious: Narrative as a Socially Symbolic Act* (1981; London: Routledge, 1989).

JanMohamed, Abdul R. *Manichean Aesthetics: The Politics of Literature in Colonial Africa* (Amherst: University of Massachusetts Press, 1983).

Jardine, Alice A. *Gynesis: Configurations of Woman and Modernity* (Ithaca, NY: Cornell University Press, 1985).

Jay, Martin. 'In the Empire of the Gaze: Foucault and the Denigration of Vision in Twentieth-Century French Thought'. in *Foucault: A Critical Reader*, ed. David Couzens Hoy (Oxford: Blackwell, 1986), pp. 175–204.

—— *Downcast Eyes: The Denigration of Vision in Twentieth-Century French Thought* (Berkeley, CA: University of California Press, 1993).

Jean-Aubry, G. (ed.). *Twenty Letters to Joseph Conrad* (London: The First Edition Club, 1926).

—— (ed.). *Joseph Conrad: Life and Letters* (London: Heinemann, 1927).

Johnston, Claire. 'Femininity and the Masquerade: Anne of the Indies', in *Jacques Tourneur*, eds Claire Johnston and Paul Willemen (Edinburgh: Edinburgh Film Festival, 1975), pp. 36–44.

Jordan, Elaine. Introduction to *Joseph Conrad: Contemporary Critical Essays*, ed. Elaine Jordan (London: Macmillan, 1996), pp. 1–31.

Keller, Evelyn Fox and Christine R. Grontkowski. 'The Mind's Eye', in *Discovering Reality: Feminist Perspectives on Epistemology, Metaphysics, Methodology, and Philosophy of Science*, eds Sandra Harding and Merril B. Hintikka (Dordrecht, Boston and London: D. Reidel, 1983), pp. 207–24.

Kerr, Douglas. 'Crowds, Colonialism and *Lord Jim*', *The Conradian*, 18.2 (Autumn 1994), 49–64.

Klein, Karen. 'The Feminine Predicament in Conrad's *Nostromo*', in *Brandeis Essays in Literature*, ed. John Hazel Smith (Waltham, MA: Brandeis University, 1983), pp. 101–16.

Knowles, Owen. *A Conrad Chronology* (London: Macmillan, 1989).

Koestenbaum, Wayne. *Double Talk: The Erotics of Male Literary Collaboration* (New York and London: Routledge, 1989).

Krenn, Heliena. *Conrad's Lingard Trilogy: Empire, Race and Woman in the Malay Novels* (New York and London: Garland Publishing, 1990).

Kristeva, Julia. *Powers of Horror: An Essay on Abjection*, trans. Leon S. Roudiez (New York: Columbia University Press, 1982).

Kuhn, Annette. *Women's Pictures: Feminism and Cinema* (1982; London: Verso, 1983).

Lacan, Jacques. *The Four Fundamental Concepts of Psychoanalysis*, trans. Alan Sheridan (1977; London: Penguin, 1979).

Lane, Christopher. *The Ruling Passion: British Colonial Allegory and the Paradox of Homosexual Desire* (Durham, NC and London: Duke University Press, 1995).

Lange, Robert J. G. 'The Eyes Have It: Homoeroticism in *Lord Jim*', *West Virginia Philological Papers*, 38 (1992), 59–68.

Lawrence, D. H. *Selected Literary Criticism*, ed. Anthony Beal (1956; London: Mercury Books, 1961).

Leavis, F. R. *The Great Tradition* (1948; Harmondsworth: Penguin, 1972).

Le Doeuff, Michèle. *Hipparchia's Choice: An Essay Concerning Women, Philosophy, Etc*, trans. Trista Selous (Oxford and Cambridge, MA: Blackwell, 1991).

Lewis, R. W. B. 'The Current of Conrad's *Victory*', in *Joseph Conrad*, ed. Harold Bloom (New York and Philadelphia: Chelsea House, 1986), pp. 63–81.

Low, Gail Ching-Liang. *White Skins, Black Masks: Representation and Colonialism* (London and New York: Routledge, 1996).

MacCannell, Juliet Flower. *The Regime of the Brother: After the Patriarchy* (London: Routledge, 1991).

McCracken, Scott. '"A Hard and Absolute Condition of Existence": Reading Masculinity in *Lord Jim*', in *Conrad and Gender*, ed Roberts, pp. 17–38.

Marcus, Laura. 'Taking a Good Look' (review of Laura Mulvey, *Visual and Other Pleasures*), *New Formations*, 15 (Winter, 1991), 101–10.

Marx, Karl. *Marx-Engels Selected Works* (London: Lawrence & Wishart, 1951).

Meyer, Bernard C. *Joseph Conrad: A Psychoanalytic Biography* (Princeton, NJ: Princeton University Press, 1967).

Meyers, Jeffrey. *Homosexuality and Literature: 1890–1930* (London: Athlone Press, 1977).

Michelet, Jules. *La Femme*, in *Oeuvres completes*, vol. XVIII (Paris: Flammarion, 1985).

Miller, J. Hillis. *Poets of Reality: Six Twentieth-Century Writers* (London: Oxford University Press, 1966).

Mitchell, Juliet. *Psychoanalysis and Feminism* (London: Allen Lane, 1974).

Moffat, Wendy. 'Domestic Violence: The Simple Tale within *The Secret Agent*', *English Literature in Transition 1880–1920*, 37.4 (1994), 465–89.

Moi, Toril. *Sexual/Textual Politics: Feminist Literary Theory* (London and New York: Methuen, 1985).

Mongia, Padmini. 'Empire, Narrative and the Feminine in Conrad's *Lord Jim* and *Heart of Darkness*', in *Contexts for Conrad*, ed Keith Carabine, Owen Knowles and Wieslaw Krajka (East European Monographs; Boulder: University of Colorado Press, 1993), pp. 135–50; rpt. in *Under Postcolonial Eyes: Joseph Conrad after Empire*, eds Gail Fincham and Myrtle Hooper (Cape Town: University of Cape Town Press, 1996), pp. 120–32.

―― 'Ghosts of the Gothic: Spectral Women and Colonized Spaces in *Lord Jim*', in *Conrad and Gender*, ed. Roberts, pp. 1–16.

Moser, Thomas. *Joseph Conrad: Achievement and Decline* (Cambridge, MA: Harvard University Press, 1957).

Mulhern, Francis. 'English Reading', in *Nation and Narration*, ed. Homi Bhabha (London and New York: Routledge, 1990), pp. 256–7.

Mulvey, Laura. 'Visual Pleasure and Narrative Cinema', *Screen*, 16.4 (Winter 1975–6), 119–30; rpt. in *The Sexual Subject*, ed. Screen, pp. 22–34.

Nadelhaft, Ruth L. *Joseph Conrad* (Feminist Readings) (Hemel Hempstead: Harvester, 1991).

Neale, Steve. 'Sexual Difference in Cinema – Issues of Fantasy, Narrative and the Look', *Oxford Literary Review*, 8.1/8.2 (1986), 123–32.

―― 'Masculinity As Spectacle', in *The Sexual Subject*, ed. Screen, pp. 277–87.

Pajaczkowska, Claire. 'The Heterosexual Presumption: A Contribution to the Debate on Pornography', *Screen*, 22.1 (1981), 79–94.

Parry, Benita. 'Problems in Current Theories of Colonial Discourse', *Oxford Literary Review*, 9 (1987), 27–58.

Pollock, Griselda. *Vision and Difference: Femininity, Feminism and the Histories of Art* (London and New York: Routledge, 1988).

Raitt, Suzanne. *Virginia Woolf's To The Lighthouse* (Hemel Hempstead: Harvester Wheatsheaf, 1990).

Ray, Martin. Introduction to Joseph Conrad, *Chance* (Oxford: Oxford University Press, 1988), pp. vii–xix.

Reilly, Jim. *Shadowtime: History and Representation in Hardy, Conrad and Eliot* (London and New York: Routledge, 1993).

Rignall, John. 'Benjamin's *Flâneur* and the Problem of Realism', in *The Problems of Modernity: Adorno and Benjamin*, ed. Andrew Benjamin (London: Routledge, 1989), pp. 112–21.

Roberts, Andrew Michael. 'The Gaze and the Dummy: Sexual Politics in Conrad's *The Arrow of Gold*', in *Joseph Conrad: Critical Assessments*, ed. Keith Carabine, 4 vols (Robertsbridge, Sussex: Helm, 1992), III, 528–50.

―― '"What else could I tell him?": Confessing to Women and Lying to Men in Conrad's Fiction', *L'Époque Conradienne* (1993), 7–23.

—— (ed.). *Conrad and Gender* (Amsterdam and Atlanta, GA: Rodopi, 1993).

—— 'Secret Agents and Secret Objects: Action, Passivity and Gender in *Chance'*., in *Conrad and Gender*, ed. Roberts, pp. 89–104.

—— 'Economies of Empire and Masculinity in Conrad's *Victory'*, in *Imperialism and Gender: Constructions of Masculinity*, ed. C. E. Gittings (Hebden Bridge, West Yorkshire: Dangaroo Press, 1996), pp, 158–69.

—— (ed.). *Joseph Conrad* (Longman Critical Reader) (London and New York: Longman, 1998).

Rose, Jacqueline. *Sexuality in the Field of Vision* (London: Verso, 1986).

Rousseau, Jean-Jacques. *The Confessions*, trans. J. M. Cohen (Harmondsworth: Penguin, 1953).

Rubin, Gayle. 'The Traffic in Women: Notes on the "Political Economy" of Sex', in *Toward an Anthropology of Women*, ed. Rayna R. Reiter (New York and London: Monthly Review Press, 1975), pp. 157–210.

Ruppel, Richard. 'Joseph Conrad and the Ghost of Oscar Wilde', *The Conradian*, 23.1 (Spring 1998), 19–36.

Said, Edward. *The World, the Text and the Critic* (1983; London: Faber, 1984).

—— *Culture and Imperialism* (London: Chatto & Windus, 1993).

Scott, Bonnie Kime (ed.). *The Gender of Modernism: A Critical Anthology* (Bloomington and Indianapolis: Indiana University Press, 1990).

Screen (ed.). *The Sexual Subject: A Screen Reader in Sexuality* (London: Routledge, 1992).

Secor, Robert. *The Rhetoric of Shifting Perspectives in Conrad's 'Victory'* (University Park: Pennsylvania State University Press, 1971).

Sedgwick, Eve Kosofsky. *Between Men: English Literature and Male Homosocial Desire* (New York: Columbia University Press, 1985).

—— 'A Poem is Being Written', *Representations*, 17 (Winter 1987), 110–43.

—— *Epistemology of the Closet*. (1990; Hemel Hempstead: Harvester Wheatsheaf, 1991).

Shiach, Morag. 'Their "Symbolic" Exists, It Holds Power – We, the Sowers of Disorder, Know it Only Too Well', in *Between Feminism and Psychoanalysis*, ed. Teresa Brennan (London and New York: Routledge, 1989), pp. 153–67.

Showalter, Elaine. *The Female Malady: Women, Madness and English Culture, 1830–1980* (1985; London: Virago, 1987).

—— *Sexual Anarchy: Gender and Culture at the Fin de Siècle* (1990; London: Bloomsbury, 1991).

Silverman, Kaja. *The Acoustic Mirror: The Female Voice in Psychoanalysis and Cinema* (Bloomington and Indianapolis: Indiana University Press, 1988).

—— *Male Subjectivity at the Margins* (New York and London: Routledge, 1992).

Simpson, David. *Fetishism & Imagination: Dickens, Melville, Conrad* (Baltimore, MD and London: Johns Hopkins University Press, 1982).

Smith, Joanna M. '"Too Beautiful Altogether": Patriarchal Ideology in *Heart of Darkness'*, in *Joseph Conrad, Heart of Darkness: A Case Study in Contemporary Literature*, ed. Ross C. Murfin (New York: St. Martin's Press; Basingstoke: Macmillan, 1989), pp. 179–98

Stallybrass, Peter and Allon White. *The Politics and Poetics of Transgression* (London: Methuen, 1986).

Stape, J. H. Introduction to Joseph Conrad, *An Outcast of the Islands*, eds J. H.

Stape and Hans van Marle (Oxford and New York: Oxford University Press, 1992), pp. ix–xxv.

—— (ed.) *The Cambridge Companion to Joseph Conrad* (Cambridge: Cambridge University Press, 1996).

Stoler, Ann Laurer. 'Carnal Knowledge and Imperial Power: Gender, Race and Morality in Colonial Asia', in *Gender at the Crossroads of Knowledge: Feminist Anthropology in a Postmodern Era*, ed. Micaela di Leonardo (Berkely: University of California Press, 1991), pp. 51–101.

—— *Race and the Education of Desire: Foucault's* History of Sexuality *and the Colonial Order of Things* (Durham, NC and London: Duke University Press, 1995).

Stott, Rebecca. *The Fabrication of the Late Victorian Femme Fatale: The Kiss of Death* (London: Macmillan, 1992.

—— 'The Woman in Black: Race and Gender in *The Secret Agent*', in *Conrad and Gender*, ed. Roberts, pp. 39–58.

Straus, Nina Pelikan. 'The Exclusion of the Intended from Secret Sharing in Conrad's "Heart of Darkness"', *Novel*, 20 (1987), 123–37.

Sussman, Herbert. *Victorian Masculinities: Manhood and Masculine Poetics in Early Victorian Literature and Art* (Cambridge: Cambridge University Press, 1995).

Tanner, Tony. Introduction to *The Oxford Book of Sea Stories*, ed. Tony Tanner (Oxford and New York: Oxford University Press, 1995).

Thompson, Gordon. 'Conrad's Women', *Nineteenth-Century Fiction*, 32 (1978), 442–65.

Thorburn, David. *Conrad's Romanticism* (New Haven, CT: Yale University Press, 1974).

Tiger, Lionel. *Men in Groups* (New York: Random House, 1969).

Watt, Ian. *Conrad in the Nineteenth Century* (London: Chatto & Windus, 1980).

—— *Joseph Conrad: Nostromo* (Cambridge: Cambridge University Press, 1988).

Watts, Cedric. *The Deceptive Text: An Introduction to Covert Plots* (Brighton: Harvester Press, 1984).

—— 'Conrad and the Myth of the Monstrous Town', in *Conrad's Cities: Essays for Hans van Marle*, ed. Gene M. Moore (Amsterdam and Atlanta, GA: Rodopi, 1992) pp.17–30.

—— *Joseph Conrad* (Writers and Their Work) (Plymouth: Northcote House, 1994).

White, Andrea. *Joseph Conrad and the Adventure Tradition: Constructing and Deconstructing the Imperial Subject* (Cambridge: Cambridge University Press, 1993).

Whitford, Margaret. *Luce Irigaray: Philosophy in the Feminine* (London and New York: Routledge, 1991).

Wiley, Paul L. *Conrad's Measure of Man* (Madison: University of Wisconsin Press, 1954).

Williams, Linda Ruth. *Critical Desire: Psychoanalysis and the Literary Subject* (London: Edward Arnold, 1995).

Wolff, Janet. 'The Invisible *Flâneuse*: Women and the Literature of Modernity', in *The Problems of Modernity: Adorno and Benjamin*, ed. Andrew Benjamin (London: Routledge, 1989), pp. 141–56.

Wollaeger, Mark. *Joseph Conrad and the Fictions of Skepticism* (Stanford, CA:

242 *Bibliography*

Stanford University Press, 1990).
Woolf, Virginia. *A Room of One's Own* (London: Harcourt Brace Jovanovich, 1929).
Wright, Elizabeth (ed.). *Feminism and Psychoanalysis: A Critical Dictionary* (Oxford and Cambridge, MA: Blackwell, 1992).
Young, Robert. *White Mythologies: Writing History and the West* (London and New York: Routledge, 1990).

Index

abject(ion), 72–3, 79, 80, 82, 85, 92, 93, 116, 117
absence, 36, 172, 187, 196, 206, 207
Achebe, Chinua, 212n
action, 3, 97, 142, 146, 148, 155, 156, 157, 198, 200, 201, 210
adventure fiction, 2, 15–16, 18, 25, 45, 62, 163
Africa(ns), 125, 126, 133, 134, 146, 163, 167, 168, 213n, 218n
aggression, 29–30, 52, 56, 111
    see also violence
alienation, 3, 10, 70, 71, 108, 153, 183, 196
alterity, see other(ness)
Althusser, Louis, 6, 219
    Ideological State Apparatus, 61, 219n
    ideology, 109, 183
    interpellation, 183
ambivalence, 38, 124–5, 147, 161, 163
anthropology, 68
anti-heroism, 25, 27
aporia, 91, 102
Appiah, Kwame Anthony, 13–14
Armstrong, Tim, 71
Auden, W.H., 231n

Bakhtin, Mikhail, 73–4, 76, 83, 87, 114, 224n
Balzac, Honoré de, 48
Banting, Pamela, 69, 73, 91
Barthes, Roland, 74, 75
Bartky, Sandra Lee, 110–11, 223n
Battersby, Christine, 71, 72, 229n
Baudelaire, Charles, 48, 120
Bender, Todd K., 4
Benjamin, Walter, 120
Bennett, Andrew, 214n
Bennett, Arnold, 100
Berthoud, Jacques, 225n, 232n
Betterton, Rosemary, 229n

Bhabha, Homi, 15, 18, 19, 23–4, 35, 38
Bickley, Pamela, 180
binaries, 19, 20, 23, 32, 40, 44, 56, 61, 77, 168
Bivona, Daniel, 45, 64
Bloom, Harold, 212–13n
    see also Strong Poet, the
Bobrowski, Tadeusz, 45
Bodmer, Walter, 213n
body, the, 11, 31, 35, 53, 54, 65, 66–117, 144, 146, 169, 171, 172, 186, 187, 194, 198, 200
    classical and grotesque, 67, 72, 73–4, 76, 80–7, 92, 93, 117
    see also Foucault, Michel
Bogart, Humphrey, 52
Bongie, Chris, 17, 18, 21, 24, 35–6, 55, 62, 106, 107, 108
Booth, Wayne C., 225n
Braidotti, Rosi, 69, 91
Bristow, Joseph, 1, 16, 211n
British Empire, 2, 22
Brodie, Susan Lundvall, 211n
Bronfen, Elisabeth, 31, 187
Brown, Ford Madox, 46, 47
Buci-Glucksmann, Christine, 70, 71, 108
Buscombe, Edward, 229n

capitalism, 104, 115, 168–9, 199
caricature, 2–3, 150
Carlyle, Thomas, 47, 219n
carnival(esque), 74, 87, 180–1
Carpenter, Edward, 3
Cartesian, the, 174
Cave, Terence, 142–3, 152
certainty, 3, 25, 118, 200
Cervantes Saavedra, Miguel de
    Don Quixote, 61, 62
cinema, 56, 196
    see also film theory
city, the, 48–50, 55, 59, 61, 64, 82–3,

243

Printed in the United States
732800001B

9 780312 227821